imago

BOOK TWO

tales from the east

L. T. Suzuki

Book Cover, graphic design and layout:
Scott White
Shinobi Creative Services
email: shinobicreativeservices@shaw.ca

Imagine...

There is a secret place that exists; unknown to most, forgotten by many, and lives on only for the few who believe.

Though you cannot look to a map to find this magical realm, it is still very real. In this world, lost on a plane that hangs in the twilight where one enters a dream as sleep takes over the mind and body, Imago lives on.

Here, as in all places where man dwells, the eternal struggle between good and evil plays out. In this land, there are places fair and foul, heroes that are larger than life and villains that one hopes exists only in our nightmares.

In this mystical world, life is an extraordinary adventure where revenge and redemption, betrayal and salvation, and love; lost and found, are woven together to create this rich tapestry of life.

Where is this kingdom you ask? To find Imago all you must do is close your eyes, and believe...

*This book is dedicated to my muse
and inspiration, Nia Kioko and to Scott,
for his unwavering support and assistance.
Without his advice and attention to detail,
this book would not be possible...
With much love and gratitude.*

&

*To all the readers who imagined...
and believed.
Thank you for your support and interest.
Because of you,
the adventure continues.*

Contents

Synopsis

In Book I, Tales from the West, Prince Markus of Carcross leads an Order composed of three noble knights from the surrounding countries: Darius Calsair of Carcross; Faria Targott of Darross; and Lando Bayliss of Cedona. Accompanied by Prince Arerys of Wyndwood representing the kingdom of the Elves; Lindras Weatherstone, the Wizard of the West; and Prince Markus' faithful squire, Ewen Vatel, they combine forces to face an impending evil. These seven friends embark on a quest of monumental proportions that will determine the fate of the citizens of Imago.

Their perilous journey begins in the heart of western Imago, through to the enchanted forest of Wyndwood and westward to Mount Isa in a bid to claim the Stone of Salvation. A twist of fate forces the Order to venture far westward into Cedona where they first encounter the four dark emissaries, agents sent forth by Beyilzon, the Dark Lord. Pursued by these harbingers of evil, the Order seeks refuge in King Augustyn's white castle at Land's End. They are now forced to travel from the most extreme western point of Imago clear across to the Plains of Fire and beyond to Mount Hope.

Along the way they court disaster, are challenged to face their own fears and doubts, and they chance upon a most unlikely ally, a messenger from Orien: Nayla Treeborn, the daughter of a dark Elf. She reluctantly comes to their aid as they race to reach Mount Hope.

A journey fraught with many perils, they experience the loss of Darius, killed in battle when he is forced to take on the soldiers of the Dark Army with only Nayla by his side. The Order faces another devastating loss when they are outnumbered and pursued, fleeing into the Dragon's Lair in an attempt to escape capture. Instead, a long dormant creature comes to life. In a bid to spare the lives of his companions and to save the quest, Lindras is forced to face the dragon alone, but he mysteriously disappears during this frightening encounter.

Nayla too is forced to face her own personal tragedy when she is captured and tortured by a sadistic captain of the Dark Army. The Order also endures the loss of Faria; cut down during an attempt to redeem himself after betraying Markus and the others in a misguided bid to save the mission; and finally, the loss of Ewen; sacrificing his own life so Markus is able to defeat the Dark Lord.

In the midst of all this adversity, Lindras gains greater powers; Markus finds renewed hope for mankind; and Arerys and Nayla, as opposite as they are, share a kindred spirit that is destined to either unite a kingdom divided, or work to bring even greater division to the race of Elves.

After the defeat of the Dark Lord, the Sorcerer of Orien is seen riding off in the company of the last surviving dark horseman. Formerly known as Eldred Firestaff, the Wizard of the East, the surviving members of the Order are perplexed by the Sorcerer's presence during the events that will lead to the doom of man.

The Order divides. Nayla and Lando head east with her army in pursuit of the Sorcerer and Beyilzon's agent while Markus, Arerys and Lindras journey back to Mount Isa to deliver the Stone of Salvation to the Three Sisters for safekeeping.

Everything is not as it appears to be. Although the Dark Lord had been put to rest, now a new evil hounds the members of the Order as they go their separate ways.

Their adventure continues...

CHAPTER 1

INTO THE FIRE

Beware the wrath of the Sorcerer; his powers are now beyond this realm.

These words weighed heavily on his mind; repeating like the incessant drip... drip... dripping of the rain seeping through a hole in a roof that cannot be stopped. With twisted brows, clenched deep in thought, Lindras carefully considered these words of warning Tor Airshorn, the Wizard of the North, shared with him before parting company.

"Lindras!" called Markus again, turning his steed about to face the Wizard. "We shall spend the night here."

The Wizard's worrisome thoughts quickly dissipated. His blue-gray eyes sparkling from beneath his great hood as he gazed at the prince. "Yes, of course, Markus. We have traveled a good distance today."

Far off to the west, Arerys' keen hearing detected the sound of rushing water coursing down the slope of a mountain. *Perhaps it is the River of Souls,* thought the Elf. He involuntarily shivered as he recalled the night that Nayla had saved him from a death by drowning. Wedged between a boulder and submerged logs beneath the icy waters, he surely would have perished if Nayla had not taken matters into her own hands. To this day, he still found it remarkable that she had endangered her own life to spare his, especially since he had been less than congenial to her upon their first meeting.

The Elf's far-seeing eyes scanned the darkening landscape as the light of day quietly surrendered to the coming of the night. The first star of the evening shone low on the horizon as a half moon, veined and glowing softly like a milky piece of quartz, appeared behind a thin veil of clouds. *Nayla, sweet Nayla...* He wondered if she was gazing up at the same moon at this very same time.

Markus guided the others to the cover of a stand of fir trees where all dismounted from their steeds. He stretched before removing his horse's saddle. Valtar, who had remained silent during their trek arched his weary shoulders and stretched his back before proceeding to gather wood for a fire. He quietly went about his business. Without a word, Arerys proceeded to help with this task.

"This is not necessary, my lord," said Valtar.

"Yes it is. We all share in the chores."

"You are a prince; it is not for you or Prince Markus to worry about such mundane tasks."

"In the Order, we are all merely servants to a greater cause, our titles have little bearing in this group," assured Arerys, gathering dried grasses into a small heap to ignite beneath the pieces of kindling.

As the men gathered around the flames to share an evening meal, Lindras looked pensive as he chewed on the wooden mouthpiece of his old, worn earthenware pipe. Markus could sense that the Wizard was disturbed, thoroughly mired in his thoughts.

"What troubles you so, Wizard?" asked Markus, observing Lindras' long, weathered fingers absentmindedly twisting the bands of gold holding his silvery beard neatly in place.

Lindras shook his head in response. "After I broke the spell under which the Wizard of the North was placed by the evil Sorcerer, Tor warned me that Eldred was now endowed with much greater powers - powers beyond this realm. I have no doubt he had aligned himself with the Dark Lord, but his presence on Mount Hope leads me to believe his plan was far more nefarious."

"You seem so confident. Do you believe that his presence was purely self-serving?" queried Markus.

"I know Eldred Firestaff all too well; he wears his ambition on his sleeve. I hardly believe he would be content if he were to be relegated to the role of mere henchman or crony to Beyilzon."

"Do you believe he meant to steal away with the Stone of Salvation?"

"That is a question I continue to ponder. He is bold and cunning, brazen enough to risk all, even betraying the Dark Lord to secure greater power for himself."

"He was so close. Why did he not attempt it then?"

"Like the Dark Lord, he did not anticipate that Ewen would carry out his part. He too expected the boy to fail; it is likely that Ewen thwarted both their plans. With the Dark Army retreating into the Shadow Mountains and the show of force by the legions of soldiers loyal to the Alliance, not to mention the presence of Nayla's own army, the risk to abscond with the Stone was presumably far too great."

"Are you suggesting that the Sorcerer may still have his eyes set on claiming the Stone of Salvation?" asked Arerys.

"I would be a fool to lower my guard – to assume his interest was only a passing fancy."

"Does this quest not end?" groaned Markus, his hand brushing back his dark hair from his brows.

"Not until the Stone is returned safely to Mount Isa," answered Lindras. He looked upon the dark Elf as he stoked the flames of the campfire. "Valtar, what do you know of the Sorcerer of Orien?"

"Truth be told, there is not much that is known of this vile character. Where he resides, how he manages to come and go unnoticed is very much a mystery. Joval Stonecroft and Nayla Treeborn have ventured repeatedly into the Furai Mountains in a bid to seek him out. Other than encountering his snares, traps, and his followers, the Sorcerer is an elusive one."

"The Furai Mountains you say. Why there?" asked Lindras, his curiosity piqued.

"Rumor has it, the Sorcerer hides in the many caves and tunnels that riddle this mountainous terrain. From here, he can watch the goings-on of Lord Treeborn and the malcontents to the west while at the same time, keeping in close proximity with his ally, Tisai Darraku, the Regent of Orien. All the while, dabbling in his forbidden art."

"That is a strange pairing indeed. He despises man. Why would he align himself with a mortal?" questioned the Wizard.

"The regent gained control over the throne from Prince Tokusho, his young nephew after the Emperor and Empress of Orien met an untimely death. Those faithful to the royal family believe they were murdered," answered Valtar.

"Are you saying that the regent had his own family put to death?" asked Markus. "But why?"

"It is said that the regent was to ascend to the throne upon his brother's death. Emperor Shekata was twenty-two years his senior, and in failing health. The regent was sure that his moment was close at hand, and with no male heir to succeed him, it was only to be a matter of time. Until that is, Empress Metasu presented the emperor with a long-desired son. Upon Prince Tokusho's birth, Darraku's chance to be crowned as the new emperor was immediately dashed. It was a short time after that news had traveled across the land that the emperor and empress, as well as their entourage, were killed. It was said that all were lost when a road they traveled on through the mountain pass to the north was swept away in a freak storm. The prince, too young to ascend to the throne, was exiled to the north, to Shesake. Now, as the crown prince approaches his sixteenth birthday, the regent has gathered allies to secure his position just in case Prince Tokusho attempts to reclaim what is rightfully his: the throne and kingdom of Orien."

"But that still does not explain why Eldred would align himself with the regent," stated the Wizard.

"It is only hearsay, but those opposed to the regent claim that he has promised vast armies to aid the Sorcerer."

"For what purpose?" asked Markus.

"To mount an attack on western Imago," responded the dark Elf. "He means to breach the Iron Mountains - to bring war to these lands."

"And what does the regent have to gain through this strange alliance?" inquired Lindras.

"What he cherishes the most – to retain his tarnished crown and to maintain his hold on Orien. Ultimately, his desire is to cleanse it of those loyal to the prince and to purge it of the religious centers the prince has vowed to protect."

"Ha! That may explain why the Stone was so desired by Eldred. If he had been successful in absconding with the jewel, he would have no need for this evil partnership with the regent," said Lindras.

"Those loyal to Prince Tokusho and the elders of Orien pose a major threat to the regent. When Lord Dahlon Treeborn and our people joined forces with the mortals who fled eastern Orien to seek sanctuary beyond the Furai Mountains, the threat to the regent grew even more apparent. He is a godless soul; he rails against all religions for they place their gods above him. He wants absolute control – he wants his subjects to bow before him. He wants all to view him as *the God*."

"Surely the people can see that he is not a god? He is a mere mortal – a human, and at that, a rather poor excuse for one it would seem," responded the Wizard.

"The regent has brought much dissension to the lands. The people are now severely divided: the wealthy and the impoverished. He has surrounded himself with affluent landholders and powerful warlords. He is a sycophant of the worst kind; lavishing his cronies with high praise. And with this flattery comes the promise of wealth and power to those in his favor," attested Valtar, gazing at Markus as he spoke. "Man, whether he be from the west or the east of the Iron Mountains; can easily be swayed when tempted with promises of fortune or power."

Markus' eyes were unyielding as they met with the dark Elf's gaze. Acknowledging his words, the prince responded, "Yes, it is unfortunate how some men can be guided down the path to ruin."

"I mean no disrespect to you, my lord," replied Valtar, averting his eyes from the prince.

"I understand, but do not lose sight that there are many of us willing to die in the name of justice and peace."

"That is true, my lord," responded the dark Elf.

"Lindras, so you believe the Sorcerer may still attempt to steal away with the Stone of Salvation?" asked Arerys.

"As I said, it would be both foolish and naïve to assume that he would slink away like a beaten dog, with tail between his legs – skulking off to lick his wounds," reiterated Lindras. "Once the Stone is in the hands of the Watchers, Eldred shall never have access to it again. If he makes a bid to steal it, he must do so soon. He must make his attempt somewhere between here and Mount Isa."

"Well, it would be wise to remain ever vigilant to his presence," advised Arerys, slinging his bow and quiver onto his back. "I shall take the first watch."

Songbirds heralded the coming of the morning long before the sun peered over the mountains. Valtar, having taken the last watch, returned as the others were stirring from their sleep. He went about the business of replenishing everyone's water flask and gathering the horses for the journey ahead.

As they ate, Lindras determined it would be a good three leagues to the base of the mountain that would lead to Rock Ridge Pass. This journey would take them into the evening by the time they entered back into Darross.

The sun's warm rays preceded its golden orb, stretching its fingers of light beyond the peaks of the Iron Mountains to vanquish the darkness of the night. The Wizard led the way through the southwestern fringe of the Plains of Fire, guiding the others along this desolate, vast terrain until they arrived at the River of Souls. The riders dismounted to allow their horses a chance to drink and to rest before they began their ascent. Once they were ready to move on, Lindras turned southward, urging his steed up the mountain trail.

As the riders neared Rock Ridge Pass, Valtar's nose wrinkled in disgust – assaulted by the foul air. "What is that horrid stench?"

"Let us just say that some of the soldiers of the Dark Army had the misfortune of running afoul with the Order after Nayla lured them into an ambush," responded Markus, coaxing his steed to pick up the pace so they could be away from this place. Only a short distance away, Lindras had used his powers to bury the corpses, now lying in an advanced state of decay.

Arerys glanced at the rocky outcrop where the soldiers met their demise. He smiled as he recalled how Nayla's startling transformation, from fearsome warrior to wanton woman, enticed the soldiers of the Dark Army into following her, right into a deadly trap. In doing so, the Order had gained entry through the guarded pass. His smile quickly faded as he sighed; now only his memories of Nayla were to sustain him until they were reunited in Orien.

As the group reached the summit of the pass, the journey down promised to be easier. The precipitous terrain soon gave way to the gentler slopes that meandered down the mountainside. The group came to a stop. Arerys' sharp eyes scanned the landscape that rolled out before them, searching for unseen danger.

"What is this place, my lord?" asked Valtar. His hand shielded his brown eyes from the glare of the setting sun as he gazed upon the lush, green land caressed by spring's gentle hand. Everything on the horizon touched by the sun's rays was bathed in a warm, reddish-orange hue as the great orb hung low in the sky, precariously balanced on the pinnacles of the Cathedral Mountains far to the west.

"This is King Sebastian's domain: Darross. Below is the village of Heathrowen," answered Arerys, eyeing the dark Elf as he shifted uncomfortably on his horse. "Something is wrong?"

"No, not really, it is an injury that never healed as it should. Sometimes I think it had been better that Master Stonecroft had not spared my life." Valtar sat tall in his saddle, stretching his spine for some relief.

"You were injured in battle?"

"Yes, before I became Master Stonecroft's personal servant, I once served as a warrior in Captain Treeborn's battalion."

This bit of news surprised Arerys.

"If it had been anyone else who had spared my soul, I would be in the Twilight as we speak. Unfortunately, fate does not always cooperate. I now live my life in servitude to Master Stonecroft. Consider it a life debt. He is a close friend and I owe him much. As long as Joval remains in this realm, then I too shall remain."

"You are a full-blooded Elf, I do not understand why your injury persists," said Arerys.

"Had I been wounded by a weapon crafted by a mortal, then yes, I would be whole. As luck would have it, I fell to a weapon wielded by the Sorcerer."

Arerys took pity on him. Though Elves do not suffer from pestilence or sickness – the maladies that afflict humans, they can still be injured or killed. He had never known an injury of this nature, always healing with no ill effects.

"Well, we shall be in Heathrowen shortly, you can rest there," stated the fair Elf.

Valtar nodded in appreciation, urging his horse down the trail to catch up with Lindras and Markus.

Arerys' mount required no coaxing, the stallion followed close behind. As they journeyed downward, the fair Elf breathed in deeply. He filled his lungs with the evening air scented by the myriad of wild flowers growing in abundance along the slopes of the Aranak Mountains. Though the evil smells of war no longer hung heavy in the air, the Elf could not help but be cautious. Although the dark horseman and the Sorcerer of Orien were last seen fleeing towards the Iron Mountains after the Dark Lord's defeat, Arerys had a gnawing feeling in his heart that the two were in the midst of plotting something evil.

Under the dimming sky, the men rode into Heathrowen. Already alerted by King Sebastian's messenger of their coming, the citizens of the village greeted Prince Markus, Lindras, Arerys and Valtar with much jubilation. The innkeeper threw open the doors to his establishment, welcoming the heroes of Imago in for some well-deserved libation.

As they sat at the table, the young barmaid who had served them on a cold, rainy spring night when they were on their quest to Mount Hope approached their table. Her tray was laden with ale and wine as well as cheeses and bread. She smiled in recognition as she served them, but her smile quickly faded. She immediately realized that four members of the Order were no longer present. Faria Targott, Darius Calsair, Nayla Treeborn and Ewen Vatel, were conspicuously absent.

"My lord, whatever became of your companions? Do not tell me they have fallen in battle!"

"Sadly, yes," answered Markus. "Darius and Faria met an untimely end. The boy, Ewen has passed on too."

"No!" she gasped, upon hearing this news.

"Do not despair for their lives and deaths were not in vain," assured the prince.

The young woman shook her head in sadness, her gentle brown eyes glazed over as she fought back her tears. "Whatever became of the woman who came to my aid?"

"Fear not," answered Arerys, offering her a comforting smile. "She is well. She has returned to her home in Orien."

"Orien? Beyond the Iron Mountains?" She was stunned by this information.

"Yes, she is a great warrior – the captain of an army she now escorts back to her country."

"I never had a chance to thank her for helping me on that night," the woman said with a heavy sigh.

"I shall be seeing her in the near future, I shall thank her on your behalf."

"Please do, my lord," the barmaid responded, bowing in gratitude. "I am indebted to her."

Soon, a crowd gathered to hear Lindras' account of how the Dark Lord was brought down in defeat. Arerys studied the many war-weary faces of the men in the room. Though perhaps unfit to do battle, they nonetheless felt the ravages of war as it raged across Darross. Recognizing many of the intoxicated faces that hovered about them, the Elf wondered if these patrons did indeed have a home to go to.

As the night wore on, the Wizard continued to regale his mostly inebriated audience with tales of their great adventure. Lindras was typically animated as he retold his story; his voice rising and falling to bring his every word to life as his eyes flashed and his hands flew about as they spoke with great enthusiasm. Just watching Lindras Weatherstone exhausted Markus. Placing a hand on the Wizard's shoulder, he bade him a good night before retiring to a room upstairs. Lindras nodded in acknowledgement as he continued with his tale of adventure.

Markus turned to Arerys and Valtar. "Sleep calls and I shall not keep this mistress waiting."

"Very well. I shall keep an eye on the Wizard," responded Arerys, placing his hand over his empty goblet, motioning to the barmaid that he had sufficient.

Valtar rose up from the table, turning to Arerys. "I shall retire too, my lord. Is there anything you require before I take my leave?"

Arerys thought upon his words before answering, "Valtar, you may serve Joval Stonecroft, but you are not in my service. There is no need for such formality."

"I am sorry, my lord, but with all due respect, you are the Crown Prince of Wyndwood. It is my place to treat you accordingly; after all, I am merely a humble servant."

"Well, if you insist on doing what is asked of you, then consider this: I am asking you to treat me as you would anyone else. When I am not in Wyndwood, I prefer to travel the lands without the pomp and ceremony associated with being royalty. It is the best way to become acquainted with the people."

"As you wish, my lord,"

"Please address me as Arerys,"

"Very well," answered Valtar, stepping away from the table to retire for the night.

When the last patron was finally pushed out the door, Lindras and Arerys crept upstairs to catch some sleep before dawn arrived. As they quietly entered the room, Markus was embraced in a deep sleep. Valtar awoke briefly upon hearing the door open, but immediately fell back to sleep, seeing that it was only Arerys and the Wizard.

They took the two vacant beds opposite the ones Markus and Valtar occupied. Lindras, who was only a few minutes ago quite giddy with excitement, lapsed into a sudden sleep - snoring contentedly. Arerys removed his boots and threw his cloak, vest of chain mail and shirt onto the end of his bed. He lay back, closing his eyes. Sleep took over quickly, but as usual, his mind and ears remained attuned to the world.

As he slept, Arerys dreamt about Nayla. And in his dream, they were parting company on Mount Hope. He memorized her face as he leaned closer to steal away with one final kiss when his eyes suddenly flashed open. As he bolted up from his bed, Valtar too was awoken by a strange noise. There was a series of small explosions as well as the sounds of snapping and crackling!

"Do you hear that?" asked Valtar, rising from his bed.

"Yes! Markus! Lindras! Wake up!" shouted Arerys as he threw on his shirt and quickly forced his feet into his boots. "Quickly! Rouse yourselves!"

Markus and the Wizard rose from their slumber. "What is it, Arerys?" mumbled the prince, still half asleep.

The Elf proceeded to the door, but as his hand made contact with the warm door latch it became quickly apparent what the noise was.

"Fire!" shouted Arerys.

A black, acrid smoke began to seep under the door, rising into the room. Markus immediately leapt from his bed as the men hastily gathered their belongings as Arerys opened the door to peer down the darkened hallway.

"We cannot take the stairs! They are engulfed in flames!" Arerys' voice rose to be heard above the raging inferno.

"Quickly, Valtar, out the window. Help Lindras down!" ordered Markus, throwing their packs, weapons and the Wizard's staff to the ground below.

Valtar stepped out onto the overhang situated at the entrance to the inn, lowering himself down before landing lightly onto the ground. He reached up to assist Lindras as Markus too exited through the window. As Arerys stepped through to follow Markus, his keen ears heard the sound of a desperate cry for help echoing from down the hallway.

"Markus! There are others still inside!" shouted Arerys, disappearing back into the room.

"Arerys, it is too late! There are flames everywhere!" shouted Markus as he dropped to the ground. Somehow, he knew the Elf was not about to abandon those still trapped in the burning building. The prince stood back. *There must be another way in*, he thought as he watched the fire continue to grow and spread. He raced around to the back of the inn, but it was just as involved.

Upstairs, Arerys quickly dowsed his cloak in the large urn of water that sat upon the table between the beds. Throwing it over his body and head, he gulped down several breaths of fresh air before venturing into the dark, smoky hallway. He quickly checked each room until he finally came across the one closest to the burning stairwell. He could hear someone coughing and sobbing in the heat and darkness.

Arerys entered the room, quickly shutting the door behind him. Inside the barmaid was struggling to get her father, the innkeeper to the open window. Tears streamed down her face as she wrestled with the large man, who was now overcome by the smoke.

"Quickly! Out onto the window ledge!" ordered Arerys, peering down below. "There is a wagon filled with hay directly below, leap into it. I shall lower your father down. Make haste!"

The woman nodded to Arerys. As frightened as she was to jump, she was more frightened of being consumed by the voracious flames. She leapt from the window landing squarely into the wagon below. Arerys lifted the innkeeper off the floor, over his shoulder. He carefully lowered the man out the window. Leaning out, using both hands to deliver the man as close to his daughter's outstretched hands as possible, the Elf strained to lower him to safety.

By this time, Markus had already returned to the front of the inn. In desperation, he forced open the front door, ramming it with his shoulder. The rush of fresh, cold air fueled the intense blaze inside, creating an intense back draft, the force of which caused the windows and doors to suddenly explode.

The blast sent all hurling to the ground. Valtar rushed to aid Markus, pulling him away from the burning building and debris that showered down around them. This great explosion shook the very foundations of the building. The floor beneath Arerys' feet suddenly collapsed causing him to lose his grip. The innkeeper tumbled to the safety of his daughter's anxiously awaiting arms. She screamed as she watched in horror as the Elf instantly disappeared from the window as glass shattered and burning shards of wood spewed all around her with the violent explosion.

Arerys plunged straight down as the floor gave way, disintegrating beneath him. With the graceful agility of a cat, the Elf still managed to land lightly onto his feet, right into the midst of the flames. Throwing the still wet hood of his cloak over his head, Arerys' eyes squinted as they detected the entrance to the inn through the raging orange flames and quivering, hot air. Drawing his cloak around his body, he dashed for the open doorway. Through the inferno, he could see Markus, Lindras and Valtar frantically calling to alert the villagers, angered by their own helplessness. As Arerys raced for the doorway, he heard a loud, ominous *"creeaak"*! He glanced up just in time to see one of the flaming ceiling joists collapsing down towards him. Without even thinking, he immediately dove for the entrance. As he hit the ground, he rolled over his shoulder landing almost effortlessly back onto his feet. He rose up, to everyone's surprise, right into Markus' waiting arms!

"Thank goodness, Arerys!" said Markus with great relief. "Nayla would never forgive me if something had happened to you!"

"Well! This is a most unexpected! Are you hurt, Arerys?" asked Lindras, marveling at the Elf's luck and resilience.

"I am fine, Wizard," answered the Elf, wiping the grime and soot from his forehead.

The citizens of Heathrowen quickly converged around the inn, but all efforts to extinguish the flames were unsuccessful. The best they could do was to contain the fire, saving the surrounding buildings.

The innkeeper, overcome by smoke was safe, now in the care of the local healer. His daughter graciously thanked Arerys for rescuing them. She invited the men of the Order to spend the remainder of the night at her uncle's home. With the only inn situated in Heathrowen now in complete and utter ruin, Markus accepted her kind offer.

The following morning, the men returned to the inn. The villagers of Heathrowen had already gathered to pay sad homage to their cherished drinking establishment. Thin, gray smoke continued to drift high into the pale, morning sky; the charred building was reduced to an unrecognizable, smoldering heap of ashes and cinder. Markus approached the Wizard as his eyes studied the devastation.

"It is most fortuitous that we managed to escape an accident of this magnitude," stated the prince, surveying the damage.

"Fortuitous, yes… But was it really an accident, Markus?" queried the Wizard.

The prince watched as Arerys strolled through the rubble, searching through the cinder and charred remains. "Are you saying this fire was deliberately set?"

"Somehow, it would seem appropriate that if Eldred was to do away with us, he would use the method he is most familiar with… after all, his element is fire," responded Lindras.

Arerys approached Markus and the Wizard. "As far as I can determine, the blaze started from a candle left burning on the bar. The bottles of spirits fueled the flames, but whether this was a deliberate act, it is impossible to ascertain."

Valtar returned with Arerys' cloak. Freshly cleaned, it was now devoid of black soot and no longer reeked of smoke. The fair Elf thanked Valtar as he placed his cloak back over his shoulders.

The innkeeper pushed his way through the crowd that had gathered, wishing to thank Arerys for his heroic efforts. The fair Elf smiled modestly in response.

"I could not help but to overhear that you fear this may have been a malicious act," said the innkeeper, his voice sounding dry and raspy from the inhalation of smoke.

"Yes, it is a question we now ponder," answered Markus.

"I have no enemies, my lord," responded the innkeeper. "I know not one soul that would wish harm to my daughter or me."

"I am sure," acknowledged Markus. "However, we of the Order

most certainly do have enemies that would pay dearly to see us brought to an untimely end."

"Are you saying this fire was meant to do harm to you?" asked the innkeeper.

"That we cannot be certain of," answered the prince. "We shall depart immediately. If trouble dogs us, then we shall not allow it to remain here in Heathrowen any longer than necessary. Men, prepare to leave!"

Markus and the others retrieved their horses from the stable. They galloped out of the center of the village when a party of Heathrowen's citizens met them.

"Prince Markus, we cannot allow you to leave in this manner," said the innkeeper.

"Whatever do you mean?"

"My lord, if the Order is in peril, then the citizens of Imago must rise up to protect those who brought peace to our lands. Though many of our able-bodied men have yet to return from the Plains of Fire, at the very least, we who are loyal to King Sebastian can offer you safe passage through our lands. These men shall be honored to escort you to your next destination."

"That is most generous, kind sir," responded Markus with an appreciative nod. With still many leagues to travel, the prince graciously accepted the escort. Together, they charged off towards Wynfield.

In the back of Markus' mind, the mystery of the fire began to consume him with worry. *Could we indeed be facing the wrath of the Sorcerer? Could the last of Beyilzon's dark emissary be in pursuit once again? Or perhaps, two evils have joined forces and both are now hounding us?* Whatever the case, the prince could sense a shadow of foreboding; they were about to be caught in a rising tide of evil.

CHAPTER 2

DECEPTION PASS

"Dare we attempt a crossing this late in the day, Nayla?" asked Lando, his eyes taking in the vastness of the craggy, dark mountain looming before them.

Nayla's brown eyes scanned the inhospitable terrain. "We shall never reach the pass before nightfall. We shall venture on for as long as the daylight endures. It is far too dangerous to breach Deception Pass in the darkness of night."

"Deception Pass? That sounds rather ominous" replied Lando, intrigued by this sinister name.

"Yes, you shall discover why soon enough," said Nayla, coaxing her horse up the twisting path, her warriors now following her in single file.

In the dimming light, they trudged up the slope, the journey long and arduous as they ventured forward on the winding trail that traversed the mountain.

As darkness fell, Nayla and Joval had guided the men half way up the slope. "We shall stop for the night. Tomorrow we shall cross over into Orien," said Nayla as she dismounted from her steed.

"Nayla, I shall assign men to sentry duty. We cannot be too cautious," disclosed Joval, gathering some of the warriors for the first shift.

Nayla nodded in approval.

"Do you anticipate that the Sorcerer may attack?" asked Lando, drawing his Elven cloak tightly around his body as the cold mountain air embraced him in an unnatural chill.

"The last we saw, both he and the last of Beyilzon's dark emissary were both racing off in this direction. It is obvious they work in collaboration. When and where they shall strike is anyone's guess. Rest assured, Lando, we are well protected," responded Joval, gazing upon the army of warriors trailing behind them.

A dark shadow clung to the mountain as a thick blanket of clouds snagged and clung stubbornly onto its pinnacle. Under this cold, gray dawn the warriors were ready to march onward to Deception Pass. All on horseback dismounted, leading their steeds forward as the path narrowed and the incline grew steep. Joval and the warriors moved on with steady determination. He and the Elven warriors seemed to move tirelessly, undeterred by the high elevation however; the mortal warriors were beginning to feel the effects of the thinning air. Their breathing became deliberately slow and deep in an effort to stave off the effects of oxygen deprivation.

Nayla trailed at the rear of the procession, keeping Lando company. The knight was obviously struggling, his muscles were cramping painfully and his head throbbed as he drew in the thin, cold air into his aching lungs. Nayla too, suffered but nowhere near to the same extent as Lando. As he stopped for a moment to rub his bleary eyes, she rested next to him.

"Lando, your breaths are much too short and quick. You must slow down."

The knight leaned forward, clutching his throbbing head in his hands.

"Listen: You must take slower, deeper breaths," instructed Nayla. "Focus, Lando. Breathe in slow and deep through your nose, hold it, and then exhale slowly through your mouth."

Lando momentarily blinked at her, as though he did not hear a single word she had said.

"Do you understand, Lando?" asked Nayla, pulling him forward.

The knight nodded, he shook off his discomfort as Nayla faced him, trying to get him to emulate her controlled breathing cycle. After a long moment, Lando's lethargy seemed to diminish somewhat as he focused on his breathing. Nayla smiled as he found new energy once the throbbing in his head eased somewhat.

As they reached the pass that would deliver them into Orien, Nayla looked back at Lando. It was so cold their breath, like a frozen vapor, was suspended in the chilly air. She could see that the knight continued to control his breathing; he was no longer struggling. Joval brought the army to a halt; they would rest at the top before beginning their descent.

From high atop this lofty pass Nayla's eyes scanned the horizon far to the west. An uneasy chill braced her small body as she recalled the first time she set her sights on western Imago. Caught in a freak snowstorm, Nayla was alone - the last surviving warrior dispatched by the elders of Orien to breach the Iron Mountains in a bid to deliver word to the Elven King of Wyndwood for a call to arms. She thought she was doomed to die in the icy embrace of Deception Pass on that fateful day. She remembered how she looked to the east, back at her war-ravaged country and then westward. All around her, the bitter winds of war howled relentlessly. Where she found the strength to press on surprised her.

"Nayla!" shouted Joval.

She slowly turned to face the Elf.

"What troubles you? You seem lost in your thoughts," said Joval, his large hands rested on her shoulders as he gazed into her dark brown eyes.

"It is nothing. I was just remembering how I believed I would never look upon your face again when I first came to this forsaken place."

"Ah, it is *something* any time you think of me," replied Joval with a smile. "We shall rest and eat before we proceed."

"Very well."

Lando stood by Nayla's side, staring westward, across the infinite horizon. "Cedona is now but a memory," lamented the knight as his eyes took in the distant landscape, memorizing the landmarks that would lead him back to his country. "No doubt, I shall appreciate my home all the more, should I return."

"Of course, you shall return, Lando," said Nayla, offering him a reassuring smile. "Do not even doubt it. Do not lose faith, my friend."

"You are right," responded Lando with a nod. "I shall look upon this place when I return home."

As he turned away to join Joval, a heavy sigh escaped Naylà. Lando turned to face her. "Your thoughts turn to Arerys, do they not?"

"Yes," she answered in a small voice.

"You too must have faith, Nayla. You must believe that Arerys is fine – that you shall see him one day soon."

"I believe you are right, Lando," agreed Nayla, turning away from the western horizon.

No longer wishing to subject her army to the icy clutches of Deception Pass, Nayla ordered all to move out. As they filed through the mountain passage, the hairs on the back of Lando's neck stood up. All around this formidable terrain, corpses lay scattered about. This pass was not only the gateway to eastern Imago, it also served as an icy tomb atop of the world. Soldiers of the Dark Army, injured or too weak and cold, succumbed to the bitter elements of the Iron

Mountains. Their bodies, now craggy and frozen as hard as rock, blended in to form a permanent part of this most unforgiving mountain range.

Nayla noted the look of dismay on the knight's face. "It is quite the dreadful place, is it not? And to think, I myself almost became a casualty here. The weather has a tendency to change from bad to worse with little notice. It can be deceptively calm one moment, and then assaulted by a great storm the next."

"Now I understand why this place is called Deception Pass, the name is quite fitting," admitted Lando, his face screwed up in disgust as he stepped over a dead body blanketed by a thin, crisp layer of frost. The dead soldier's body lay on the ground, curled tightly into the fetal position. It was obvious he had expired trying to fend off the bitter cold.

As the group advanced through the pass, Joval led the way. Far to the east, the city of Nagana was awaiting their return. Joval's blue eyes gazed down at the trail before him; the mountain's landscape seemed strangely surreal, as though it floated above the earth as a heavy layer of cloud clung to the terrain below them. A cold, northerly wind kept the surrounding mountaintops shrouded in a constant mantle of snow for most of the year. In some areas, it was difficult to ascertain where snow ended and clouds began.

Lando and Nayla caught up to the Elf as his eyes attempted to penetrate the cloud-cover.

"What is it, Joval?" asked Nayla.

"An ill wind blows through these mountains, Nayla. I can sense it in the air - feel it in my bones," whispered Joval. "Something evil lurks here that I did not sense the first time we passed this way, now…"

"Now what? Is it the Sorcerer?" asked Lando, his dark, wavy hair catching in the sharp breeze.

"I cannot be sure," answered Joval. "I suggest we use utmost caution in negotiating this terrain. Whether the Sorcerer makes his presence known, or not, the slope on this side of the mountain, though not steep, may prove to be icy – treacherous, until we reach the lower grounds. In single file, men!"

Nayla abruptly turned to the east, her ears straining. "Did you hear that, Joval?"

"I hear nothing, only the wind."

"I heard someone's cry for help."

"You are mistaken, Nayla."

"No, Joval. Are all our men accounted for?" Her eyes quickly surveyed the group of warriors assembling before her.

"It is merely the wind, I tell you," insisted Joval as he frowned at her.

"No, I heard a voice call out my name, it was a plea for help! Quickly! Are all the men accounted for?"

Joval turned towards the warriors to conduct a head count, but Nayla was unable to wait any longer. Again, she heard a voice begging for her help. She slowly ventured to the edge of the snowy ledge, peering over the side, down into the dense massing of clouds suspended below. She could swear she heard a voice calling out to her. As she turned to regroup with her men, a terrible sense of foreboding seized her by her heart. The ground suddenly moaned as she felt it shift beneath her feet. She froze in her tracks.

Joval and Lando turned to see Nayla standing far out on the ledge; instantly, it became clear to the both of them she was standing on an unstable shelf of snow and ice that was ready to give away. Joval ran to her aid, but Nayla raised her arms, motioning him to stop.

"Come no closer, the entire ledge shall collapse," warned Nayla. "Throw a rope, but do not venture out!"

With no further prompting, one of the warriors immediately ran to remove the rope that was coiled in a pack on one of the horses as the others stared in horror as the ground beneath their captain continued to groan and began to buckle.

Nayla knew she had no other option. As the ice and snow beneath her shifted and crumbled away, she instinctively dove towards safety. She fell short, plunging downward.

Joval instantly leapt forward to catch her, the fingers of his right hand locked with those of her left, hooking together. As his body lurched dangerously over the ledge, Lando leapt onto Joval's legs, preventing him from going over with Nayla. He held the Elf steady as Joval strained to reach for her.

"Take my other hand, Nayla!" shouted Joval, stretching out to grab her right hand. He could feel her fingers trembling under her own weight, growing slick with sweat. "Try!" he pleaded. "You must try!"

Rarely had Joval ever seen Nayla look truly scared, not even in the heat of battle. Now, the fear in her eyes overwhelmed him. Death itself never frightened her, but could it be that for once in her life, she now had something she considered worth living for? Unable to reach Nayla's right hand, Joval made a desperate bid to better his grasp on her left hand. He could feel Nayla's fingernails sinking into his flesh as she tried desperately to better her hold. His heart was pounding wildly in his chest as his panic mounted. Joval could feel her straining fingers tiring, shaking uncontrollably and now, they slowly uncurled from his.

"Do not let go, Nayla! Do not even think on it!" demanded Joval as he strained to reach for her.

For a split-second, Nayla looked down at the emptiness below her, and then her glance shot upwards to the Elf. Fearful that she may take him over the cliff with her, she shook her head in silent defeat as her trembling fingers finally unleashed their grip from his.

Joval watched as Nayla slipped from his grasp. The only word he could manage echoed through the mountain range: "*NOOO!*"

His voice shattered the momentary silence, fading as quickly as Nayla had disappeared from his sight. The last image seared into his mind was her eyes wide open in fear: his own horrified expression reflected in her terrified eyes as she plummeted through the layer of clouds below, her cloak billowing out in the wind behind her.

Lando rolled onto his back, breathing hard; he stared up at the gray, bleak sky in shock and disbelief. Joval remained motionless, his hands still outstretched before him, as though reaching for a second chance.

"She is gone, Joval."

"No! Nayla is not dead. I would know if she were dead! I would feel it as surely as my own heart had stopped!"

The Elf defiantly rose to his feet. "Men! We must search for our captain! Lando, lead them down. I shall need two men and a horse to remain with me!"

The warriors quickly filed past Joval, following Lando down the treacherous path. The last two warriors, a mortal and an Elf, remained with a horse. A rope was already anchored around the steed. Joval quickly secured the other end of the rope around his waist. He was carefully lowered down the sheer face of the mountain. He kept his eyes cast down as snow and ice rained upon him from the crumbling ledge as his men continued to release more rope. Joval's eyes pierced through the dense cloud-cover searching for Nayla.

Twenty feet… Nothing.

Thirty feet… Still no sign of Nayla.

How far could she fall and still survive? What am I to do if she is still alive, but dying? He quickly dismissed these dark thoughts, choosing to focus on the task at hand. Nayla was alive. Somewhere down there, he felt in his heart that she was still alive.

At sixty feet, Joval was nearing the end of his tether. *Where is she? How far could she have fallen?* Joval was now lowered below the clouds that shrouded the mountain, his blue eyes searched about. At last, he spied her crumpled form, lying precariously on a ledge direct-ly below. She lay motionless; her head resting in a small puddle of blood - stark crimson against a blanket of icy, white snow.

Joval breathed an audible sigh of relief as he descended to her, but his descent came to an abrupt halt. There was no more rope. He had come to the end of his tether. The Elf looked down; he was still anoth-er twelve or so feet away from the ledge. He cursed beneath his breath. Joval carefully untied the rope from about his waist, taking it into both his hands; he proceeded to lower himself down until he dangled dan-gerously from the very end of his line. Kicking his legs out, he swung closer to the cliff wall, not wishing to land too close to the edge lest he bring it down, taking Nayla with him. With a final swing, he released the rope, landing lightly on the shelf projecting from the cliff. He knelt next to Nayla; she had the good fortune of landing on top of a layer of snow and ice. He could see immediately that she was still alive; her chest rose and fell at a slow but steady pace.

"Nayla," Joval whispered, his hand gently touched her face. Her lips were turning blue from the cold. Unresponsive to the sound of his voice, she remained motionless.

Joval called out to the warriors above. He instructed the mortal to lower the Elf down. Then, he was to drop the rope down to them and move on to advise Lando and the others that Nayla was alive, that they are to proceed to the path below them. From this point, he would lower Nayla down to safety.

While Joval waited for assistance, his hands quickly passed over Nayla's body; a disruption in the flow of her energy would indicate an injury. A break in the flow quickly revealed she had damaged her lower left ribcage, about four inches away from her spine. He leaned over her body, listening to the sounds of her breathing. To his relief, it was not labored, he did not detect the gurgling, bubbling sounds of blood fill-ing her lungs had splintering bones punctured this cavity. *Better her ribs than her backbone*, he thought as he continued to check for other injuries. Satisfied that her body had no other breaks or tears, he turned his attention to her wounded head.

Joval removed his great cloak, spreading it out flat. He carefully lifted Nayla onto the cloak, turning her over onto her right side. The cold surface she lay on served to staunch the flow of blood oozing from the cut on the back of her head, but Joval's concern grew as he noted the sharp chunk of ice Nayla had struck her head on. If her skull was fractured, if she was blooding inside her brain, he lacked the skills to save her. Then the thought crossed his mind: *A high Elf like Dahlon Treeborn could save her, but Nagana is too far away. Then again, would Dahlon even have the compassion to save his own daughter?*

Joval stifled his growing resentment; he turned his attention to getting her safely down from the ledge for soon night would be upon them. He gently placed the middle finger of his left hand along the length of Nayla's wound. Closing his eyes, he whispered a healing incantation.

After several minutes, the terrible gash was no more. The wound had miraculously sealed, leaving only a thin, red scar. The dark Elf clapped his hands over his head once. Closing his eyes, he briskly rubbed the palms of his hands together. Once they were sufficiently warmed, Joval placed them around Nayla's cold neck. He could feel her body heat dissipating quickly from this area. As his energy thawed her chilled form, she began to shiver; her body attempting to generate more heat on its own. In his bid to keep her alive, Nayla began to warm as Joval's energy ebbed like the receding tide.

When the Elven warrior finally reached the ledge, both worked swiftly to wrap their injured captain in Joval's cloak. It was to serve as a sling by which they would lower her down to safety. As he looked upon Nayla's still form, Joval now realized her fate was no longer in his hands. Whether she lived or died, either way, he prayed for the spirits to be merciful.

CHAPTER 3

FROM OUT OF THE DARKNESS

With eighteen of the villagers accompanying the men of the Order, all rode hard, traveling southwest towards Wynfield. Riding through fields and farmlands, they passed many signs of the Dark Army's assault on the lands south of the Aranak Mountains. The burnt out shells of barns and homes, discarded items the soldiers of the Dark Army had pillaged along their way, grave markers and other silent reminders of war lay scattered for all to witness. It was a stark contrast to the new life that now flourished with the coming of the spring.

Orchards with fruit trees in full blossom released sweet perfume and a bounty of nectar to lure the honey bees. Hidden safely in the leafy crowns of these trees; birds tended to their eggs and nestlings. Long-legged foals playfully frolicked about in the lush, green pastures as the attentive mares grazed and kept watch over their offspring.

The late morning sky slowly gave way to a massing of clouds. The sun peered in and out, one moment promising the warmth of its golden touch, the next, hiding its face behind a thin veil of gray. The men brought the horses to a stop, allowing their steeds to rest, graze and drink while they had a quick meal. As they ate, Markus could tell Lindras was still consumed in his thoughts.

Perhaps, the Wizard is right. Would I be a fool to believe that last night's fire was a mere coincidence – an unfortunate accident? The prince thought upon this as he looked to the south. He could see Arerys standing like a lone sentry atop a small hill, scanning the surrounding countryside. No doubt, the Elf shared the Wizard's concern.

Arerys' hand shaded his azure blue eyes against the glare of the sun whenever it chose to peek out from behind the clouds. As his gaze turned north to the Aranak Mountain Range, and then slowly eastward, his eyes scrutinized the horizon. In many ways, the Elf wished for the enemy to make themselves known, if they were to encounter the Sorcerer and his evil minions, he preferred a direct confrontation. Where before, a surprise attack was just part of the adventure, Arerys was now more concerned with avoiding such fiascos in order that he may live to see Nayla again. If those wishing to claim the Stone of

Salvation were indeed on their trail, they were very well hidden. His sharp eyes could not discern anything that he would consider a possible source of danger for the Order. He made his way back down to the others.

As he approached, he reported to Markus and Lindras that he could see no sign of impending evil.

"This is reassuring, Arerys," said Markus.

"Do not rest too easy, my friend. Just because I could not see them, it does not mean they are not out there," warned the Elf.

"It would be wise to remain vigilant," replied Lindras.

"I dare say; if trouble follows, we cannot endanger the citizens of Wynfield. We are best to give the village a wide berth," recommended Markus. "At this time, our only consolation is that the kings of the Alliance and the men in their service are a day, perhaps two, behind us. If danger approaches, it shall come from either the west or the east."

As the riders reached the outskirts of Wynfield, Markus thanked the men of Heathrowen. He bid them farewell before setting a course that would take he and the others on to Crow's Nest Pass. With King Sebastian's castle looming in the distance, surely the enemy would not be as bold or foolish as to attempt crossing the lands. Markus decided to ride on, they shall rest in the foothills of the pass for the night. In the morn, they would either proceed due west towards Castle Hill, straight through to the Fields of Shelon or journey south through the pass. From Crow's Nest Pass, they would venture through the forests of Wyndwood before turning west through the Fields of Shelon on to Mount Isa.

With the gray clouds continuing to build throughout the day, night fell with unsettling swiftness. Markus led the men to the cover of a stand of elm trees. Here, Valtar prepared a small fire. After all had eaten, Markus and Lindras brought out their pipes, the Elves deliberately sat upwind from the aromatic smoke drifting into the night air. How anyone could find pleasure in inhaling the fumes of burning plant matter was beyond them.

The men deliberated over tomorrow's route. To travel straight through to Castle Hill would shorten the excursion by perhaps six or seven hours, no more. Lindras reminded the men the chance they would meet up with the Sorcerer or his henchmen were highly unlikely if they were to take to the forest of Wyndwood.

"Lindras, do you truly believe that evil would dare lurk so close to

King Sebastian's castle? Knowing full well the king would leave an army to maintain control in his absence and to keep watch for incursions through the Gap?" asked Arerys.

The Wizard looked into the Elf's earnest eyes. He knew Arerys was willing to take his chances on a run to Castle Hill in a bid to get this quest over with once and for all so he may begin the journey east. Lindras carefully considered their options for he understood this decision must be tempered with the fact that the risks may outweigh the time saved.

As the night wore on, Arerys finally stood up from the fire. "I shall take the first watch, Markus."

"Very well," responded the prince, through a great yawn. "I shall keep you company."

"No, my lord. I shall take this watch with Arerys. Rest now," suggested Valtar.

"That is a thoughtful gesture, Valtar. Thank you."

Arerys led Valtar up the slope overlooking the camp. Below, he could see Markus and Lindras by the fire. They were quietly conversing. Arerys glanced up to the dark sky. High above, the wind blew the clouds about, allowing some of the stars to shine through the clear patches, only to snuff out their light again. The fair Elf noted that the moon had all but disappeared. His gaze came back to earth as he considered the dark Elf standing near to him. Aside from being Elves, the two had very little in common with the exception of Nayla Treeborn.

"So, do you know Nayla, well?" asked Arerys, wishing to end the awkward silence.

"Yes, as I said before, I was once a warrior. I served in her battalion," answered Valtar. His voice tightened as he felt obliged to engage in small talk. It was something he truly detested.

"Nayla seems to be well respected by her men."

"That she is," agreed the dark Elf.

"I take it; she has known Joval Stonecroft for a long while."

Valtar stared at him for a moment. "Yes, she has."

"I assume they are close."

"Yes." He kept his answers short and curt.

"How close?"

"I suggest you ask that of Master Stonecroft."

"It is a simple question," responded Arerys, perplexed by Valtar's response.

"Yes, but sometimes there are no simple answers."

"What are you insinuating?"

"If it sounds like I am, that is not my intention. Discretion has been the key to survivability in this business. I cannot speak of Master Stonecroft or Captain Treeborn."

"Upon whose orders? Stonecroft's?" asked Arerys, becoming more intrigued by the dark Elf's terse response.

Valtar stared at Arerys, their eyes locked for a moment. "No… It was Captain Treeborn who made this request."

Arerys grew quiet, his eyes turned away to face the ever-darkening horizon. He wondered why Nayla would forbid Valtar from disclosing any information about Joval. He knew Joval still cared deeply for Nayla and perhaps, at one time she may have felt the same, but Arerys knew in his heart that she was now in love with him. He had no doubts, yet he could not ignore his intuition that Valtar knew more than he was willing to divulge.

Arerys turned to face the dark Elf again. "I do not believe Nayla would make such a demand."

"That is your prerogative."

"Well, Valtar Briarwood, as a servant you seem so bent on doing what is right, to follow protocol. I tell you what; consider this to be a request from the Prince of Wyndwood: You shall answer my questions. Do you understand?"

"An inquisition…"

"Call it what you will. I ask – you answer."

"With all due respect, my lord, I hardly believe I have a choice. As you are so eager to point out, I am merely a humble servant, while you - you are born to a high house and one day shall sit upon the throne of Wyndwood. I have no choice in this matter."

"That is correct," answered Arerys, there was now a definite coolness to his tone.

"If I were to comply, do I have your word, on your honor, you shall not disclose that any of this came from me?"

"You have my word."

Valtar considered the fair Elf for a moment. *This could well be my opportunity to manipulate the situation to Joval's benefit,* he thought. Although he respected Nayla Treeborn as a warrior and a great captain, he was uncomfortable with her standing in life and the fact that his dear friend made the mistake of falling in love with her.

"Very well," the dark Elf finally answered.

"What is the nature of Joval's relationship to Nayla?"

"Over the years, he has been many things to Captain Treeborn. He fancies himself to be her self-appointed protector... her guardian."

"To protect her from whom? Dahlon Treeborn?"

"From anybody who would see fit to do her harm," he responded as he glared at Arerys. *You included*, thought the dark Elf as he leaned against his bow.

"What do you mean, 'he has been many things to her'?"

"He has been her friend, her mentor, and her..." He was reluctant to continue.

"And?" prompted Arerys.

"And her lover."

"I suspected that much," responded Arerys, attempting to sound nonchalant about this news. "Does he still love her?"

"I do believe the answer is quite obvious."

"What about Nayla? Does she love him?" asked Arerys.

Valtar observed the fair Elf's troubled face as he replied, "My lord, if you believe there is a need to ask such a question then perhaps you are the one having doubts about Captain Treeborn's integrity."

Arerys considered his words. In his heart, he knew Nayla was in love with him. Joval was nothing more than a ghost from her past that refused to be exorcised. Nayla had pledged her love to him and he, his undying love to her with a promise they would be together. He believed her. He was a fool to ask such a question of Valtar.

"I would never question Nayla's integrity. I am well aware of her troubled past. I understand she holds friendships more dearly than family loyalties. In her case, it stands to reason that if she and Joval share a long history; then sometimes the past is difficult to leave behind if one has no future to look forward to. This has changed now."

It was the only tactful way Arerys could think of to convey his true feelings. In his heart, it was not Nayla he questioned, it was Joval's own intentions that concerned him, and right now he was a little too close to what Arerys held dear to his heart.

"Just beware of that half-caste, my lord," warned Valtar. "She may be Lord Dahlon Treeborn's daughter, but she is neither mortal nor is she like us."

Half-caste? Arerys had never thought of her in such terms, but somehow, Valtar's use of this word made it apparent he viewed her as certainly less than an Elf and perhaps, something beneath a human.

"I am aware of what she is, Valtar."

"I beg to differ, my lord."

"How so?" asked Arerys, dissecting the dark Elf's thoughts.

"Have you not noticed her fighting skills? Do you not see how dangerous she is?"

"Yes, she is a skilled warrior."

"It is more than that. She bears that mark of the fearsome Kagai Warriors – she is a member of a secret sect of Shadow Warriors of the Furai Mountains. Some believe she is trained to assassinate, to infiltrate and spy. She is a greater danger than most men, mortal or Elf. I swear, she even possesses the ability to control great and powerful men such as Joval Stonecroft. Perhaps, she even controls you."

Arerys stared at Valtar for a moment as he recalled the strange tattoo, the dark symbols etched into Nayla's skin over her right shoulder blade. He had chanced upon it while she was recovering from her brutal assault during their trek to Mount Hope. He shook his head, as much to dispel the memory of that dreadful night, as to dissuade Valtar. He then laughed lightly at the dark Elf's suggestion. "I think not. As strong-willed as Nayla is, the only thing she has control over is my heart."

Valtar shrugged, and then smugly replied, "Yes, just as she holds control over Joval's."

"She does not love him."

"If that is so, then why can he not let go? Why can he not just forget about her, just turn away, even now?" snapped the dark Elf.

Arerys absorbed Valtar's words. *Perhaps*, he thought, *for the same reasons why I now know I cannot let go, nor forget.*

As a dreary dawn dissolved the darkness of night, the clouds continued to accumulate on the horizon, moving steadily westward. Arerys glanced up at the brooding pillars of threatening, gray storm clouds. They would herald a change in the weather; he could smell it in the air. It would only be a matter of time before the rains came down. He and the others made ready for their journey.

"The wind blows from the east, Markus. Why do we not ride with the wind against our backs? Take the direct course to Mount Isa," suggested Arerys, his wheat-colored hair fluttering in the stiff breeze as he felt the cool embrace of the wind beckoning him to follow.

Markus sympathized with him for he knew the Elf was motivated by his desire to return to Nayla as quickly as possible. He looked to Lindras. The Wizard's blue-gray eyes sparkled beneath the shadow of his great hood, even in the dull light of the morning. He shook his head in response to the Elf's question.

"It would be ill-advised to make the run to the Castle Hill. In all likelihood, if evil awaits us, I have my suspicions it would come to us from the west, through the Gap," warned the Wizard.

"Lindras is right, Arerys. We shall only be spared a few hours to take that route. If we take Crow's Nest Pass into Wyndwood, at least we know the borders are secure. Perhaps, we can even gather some of your men to secure a safe passage to Mount Isa," added Markus, tightening the cinch of his saddle.

"I side with the Wizard and Prince Markus, but my motivation is fueled by my desire to see this fabled forest with mine own eyes," said Valtar to Arerys. "In all honesty, I have always dreamed of seeing Wyndwood. Lest I never come by this way again, I wish to do so now."

With this consensus, Lindras, Valtar and Markus overruled the fair Elf. Arerys reluctantly conceded. Crestfallen, he mounted his steed without another word. He knew only more time would be wasted if he were to continue to argue his point: To Wyndwood it is.

As they made their way through the gentle, rolling hills of Crow's Nest Pass, Valtar rode ahead with Markus. Arerys deliberately hung back, wishing to speak to the Wizard in private.

"Lindras, you claim to know Joval Stonecroft. What do you know about Joval and Nayla – their history?"

For a long moment, Lindras was silent as he collected his thoughts. "Joval has known Nayla since she was a child. It is my understanding it was he who spirited her away from Nagana to live with the ascetic priests, the protectors of the religious centers in western Orien."

"With the so-called Shadow Warriors?"

"Yes, the legendary Kagai Warriors renowned for their fighting skills and fearless exploits when it comes to warfare," answered the Wizard.

"There is more, Lindras," stated Arerys, his eyes turning a deeper shade of blue as he contemplated his words.

"Well, is it safe to assume that Valtar has succeeded in sowing the seeds of doubt in your mind where Nayla and Joval are concerned?"

Arerys grew quiet; somehow, even hearing Nayla's name mentioned with Joval's in the same sentence made his nerves bristle with resentment and jealousy.

"Rest assured, Arerys, I have known Joval for almost as long as I have known you. Truth be told, in many ways, you two are very much alike."

The fair Elf stared at the Wizard in disbelief, unsure if he liked this comparison.

Lindras continued: "Joval is a warrior of great virtue. He has integrity. He is honest and loyal. Does he love Nayla? Yes. Would he die for her? Yes. Would he deliberately undermine you to destroy her chance for happiness? I do not believe so."

The Wizard could almost hear Arerys breathe a sigh of relief upon hearing his words.

"Besides, my friend, do not take Valtar's words to heart. Although I do not believe he would deliberately lie to you, you must remember, he is Joval's closest friend. Just as you would wish for Markus to acquire whatever his heart desires – to find happiness in his life, I am certain Valtar wishes the same for Joval. Nothing more."

"You are probably right, Lindras. I just cannot help but feel he was alluding to the fact that there was far more to their relationship than meets the eyes."

The Wizard abruptly brought his steed to a halt. "Truth be told Arerys, I know many years ago, Joval had great hopes of taking Nayla as his wife."

"They were betrothed? To wed?" asked Arerys, stunned by this revelation.

"I do not believe it ever went as far as that. Whatever happened, I do not know. Nayla departed, disappearing for many years. No doubt to wage war against the Sorcerer of Orien and those wishing to do harm to the very people she swore to protect."

"Why did she not tell me about this?"

"Perhaps for the same reason why you chose not to disclose to her about your prior dalliances with other women.".

"But that was in the past, Lindras," protested Arerys.

"Exactly." The Wizard urged his steed on, galloping off to catch up with Markus and Valtar.

As the men journeyed through the pass, a great show of light and the resonating echo of distant thunder from the dark clouds looming ever closer announced a change in the weather. The humidity increased with the rising temperature causing the air to become sticky and hot. As the day wore on, the bleak heavens finally opened up. The heavy clouds that brewed all day unleashed their rains, falling with a vengeance. The pounding raindrops splashed back up as it pummeled the ground. For the men of the Order, their only consolation was that the forest of Wyndwood was now less than half a league away.

With the coming of the storm, the skies grew unnaturally dark, as though the night was attempting to steal away with the light of day. The rains were unforgiving as they fell in a torrent, drenching all and chilling them to their bones. Arerys gazed up as a flash of lightning illuminated the steel gray clouds against a blackening sky. His eyes struggled to adapt to the sudden bright, flash of light, followed by immediate darkness. Something on the hillside before them caught his attention. Again, lightning danced across the heavens. Arerys, his fearful eyes already fixed on the hillside, immediately caught sight of a large, sinister shadow. It was the Dark Lord's emissary on his great black steed!

As Arerys drew his bow, Valtar too saw the awaiting evil. He immediately armed his bow and both Elves began launching arrows at the soldiers in the company of the dark horseman.

"Lindras! Go! Flee to Wyndwood!" ordered Markus, drawing his sword.

A small battalion of perhaps thirty soldiers armed with swords and halberds poured down from the surrounding hills onto the pass. Arerys' bid to take down the dark emissary was thwarted by the soldiers as they obscured his line of fire. He and Valtar quickly dispatched the insurgence, their arrows striking the soldiers down with deadly accuracy. As the remaining soldiers that successfully eluded the Elves' deadly projectiles closed in on Markus, both Arerys and Valtar charged to his side. Placing the prince in between them, they continued to release a torrent of arrows.

Arerys reached into his quiver, There was only one arrow left: one last chance to down the dark horseman. As seven of the remaining soldiers encircled the Order, Arerys looked up to the hillside to take aim at his evil adversary.

He was gone!

The Elf scanned the dark, sloping terrain, staring through the heavy curtain of rain, searching for his intended victim. The dark horseman was no longer there.

The sound of steel slamming against steel as Markus' sword deflected the blows of an enemy sword broke Arerys' concentration. He looked down in time to see a soldier sneaking up behind the prince, preparing to ram his blade through Markus' back. The Elf instinctively drew his bow, letting his last arrow fly. The soldier reeled from the impact, and with a final spin, collapsed behind Markus.

Arerys leapt down from his panicking steed, drawing his sword as he landed. He quickly turned his attention to Valtar; he could see the dark Elf was tiring as he fought off the soldiers that surrounded him from all sides. Arerys' blade quickly did away with two soldiers as they pressed in on Valtar. They did not even hear the fair Elf's silent approach until his deadly blade was upon them.

The dark Elf immediately turned his attention to one soldier while Arerys engaged in battle with the other. He confidently angled and pivoted away as he parried the soldier's wild slashes, and then in a flash turned on the man, countering with a vicious assault. As the soldier fell lifelessly to the earth, Arerys leapt over his body to aid Markus. Two soldiers were attempting to take the prince from opposite sides. Markus stepped backwards in a bid to keep both soldiers in his field of vision. As he did so, in the growing darkness he stumbled over a dead soldier that had fallen to Arerys' deadly aim.

"On your feet, Markus!" shouted Arerys, leaping over his fallen comrade to intercept the advancing soldiers. The Elf's blade came alive in the darkness as lightning flashed across the stormy sky. He veered towards the two soldiers, the tip of his sword pointed between them. In a blink of an eye, both soldiers lunged at Arerys. Instead of retreating, the Elf used a tactic he learned from Nayla. He quickly dropped to the ground, rolling between the two soldiers. He swiftly rose up to his feet behind them. Stunned by his sudden disappearance, they did not even see the Elf coming up from behind. As he pivoted around, his sword swept across in one broad stroke from right to left, slicing through the fabric, flesh and backbone of both hapless men. The soldiers, screaming in agony, fell onto their knees before collapsing forward into a large, murky puddle.

Leaping over the dead; Arerys pulled Markus up onto his feet. He flicked the blood off his sword before turning to help Valtar with the last soldier. From the corner of his eye he could make out a shadowy figure charging towards them from out of the darkness. The last of Beyilzon's agents swooped down upon them as though carried on the wind; Arerys sheathed his sword as he pushed Markus from his path. The dark emissary careened around the fallen soldiers as his steed raced towards Arerys. The dark horseman had set his sights on the fair Elf, singling him out from the others.

Arerys' hand reached behind him for an arrow; his quiver was still empty. Without a moment to lose, he dove towards a fallen soldier, lunging for the arrow protruding from the dead man's back as he went down. Slipping on the saturated battle ground, Arerys snapped the arrow as he broke his fall. Scrambling to his feet, he raced towards another arrow jutting out from a dead soldier's chest. His ears rang with the thundering hoof beats of the fast approaching steed. The dark emissary was descending upon him with great swiftness. Arerys yanked on the arrow with all his might. Stringing the nock of the arrow onto his bow as he rolled, he turned to face the darkness.

Before the Elf could draw his arrow, his bow was sent flying out of his hands. A searing pain sliced through his side causing him to crumple to his knees. In desperation, Arerys reached over with his right hand to draw his sword. He gasped - stunned to feel the heat of his own blood, to see it steaming in the cool night air, as it washed down his body. As the rain pounded down upon him, he could hear Markus cry out his name. His eyes gazed up to take in the sinister, black form looming above him. The deadly blade of an imposing sword glistened as lightning cracked, shattering an angry sky. Arerys screamed in pain as inch-by-inch, he struggled to draw his sword as his evil nemesis slowly raised his blade on high. The Elf's vision blurred as he stared upwards. He was going into shock. His eyes squinted, barely able to comprehend the intensity of the foe towering before him.

The dark horseman laughed in triumph; his sword now poised to decapitate Arerys. The Elf closed his eyes. Too weak to change his fate, he prepared for imminent death. Suddenly, he heard a familiar whine and felt the swift movement of air skim through his hair. It was immediately followed by a horrific scream that tore at his senses. Valtar's arrow flew straight and true, piercing the dark horseman through his black heart.

The last of Beyilzon's four agents was reduced to a mound of black ashes that was soon washed away by the rivulets of rainwater rolling down the pass. The Elf's sword slipped from his weakening grip. He clutched his side; feeling the gaping wound delivered by the dark horseman's sword. *How can this be?* Arerys wondered as he removed his hand. He gazed down at his wound, his chain mail cleanly sliced open. He cursed under his breath for now he realized that he was not downed by a mortal blade; only a weapon forged and blessed by the Dark Lord could have penetrated Elven mail in this manner.

For a brief moment, he stared at his stained, trembling hands. The rush of blood carried by the driving rain, spread in an ever-growing pool, rising like a crimson tide around him. His heart beat so wildly; it was pounding painfully in his head as his blood coursed out of his body. It was so unrelenting; it was all he could hear in his ears, distorting Markus' frantic voice as he called out his name. As he slowly tilted his head up, Arerys' eyes began to glaze over as they struggled to make out the blurred images of the prince and Valtar moving before him in slow motion.

Arerys fought to stave off the suffocating blackness he could feel was waiting to consume him. He struggled in vain to remain conscious, making a futile bid to stand on his own two feet, but everything around him began to swim, swirling into a deep, black abyss. His eyes rolled back as he finally collapsed into Markus' arms.

CHAPTER 4

A WARRIOR'S PLIGHT

Lando watched as Joval and another Elven warrior carried the sling on which Nayla now rested. Though there were many offers from the other warriors to take their captain down the slope, Joval steadfastly refused. With great care, making every attempt to keep the journey as smooth as possible, the men were almost half way down the mountain as darkness enveloped the slope.

"We shall rest here for the night," said Joval. They gently laid the sling onto the ground. Sheltered by steep walls on either side of this path, the army found some reprieve from the bitter winds blowing in from the north. The warriors worked together, setting up camp and building fires to warm themselves by.

Lando knelt next to Joval, watching as the Elf carefully dabbed the folded edge of a kerchief into a steaming bowl of water laced with the inner bark of the willow tree. He touched it to Nayla's dry lips.

"How does she fare?" asked Lando.

Joval shook his head. "I do not know. She is alive. She seems to be warming now, but it is her head injury that concerns me," whispered the Elf, carefully pouring just enough of the analgesic mixture into her mouth that her natural reflex was to swallow, not choke. "Had she been an Elf of full-blood, I would have a better chance of healing her. Only time will tell."

Lando rested against the cold, hard wall of rock, looking down at Nayla's still body. After all she had endured with the Order in their quest to save Imago from the Dark Lord, to succumb to an accident like this; it crushed his heart. Glancing up at Joval, he could see the Elf's eyes, dark with worry as he gently pulled the blanket up around Nayla's neck. It was at this moment Lando spied Joval's blue eyes flash in anger as they noticed for the first time, a long, thin, silvery scar running from under her chin, down the length of her neck.

"What is this? What happened to Nayla?" Joval demanded to know, his brows furrowing in anger.

"Nayla was captured by the enemy. She was beaten and tortured. She was ra…" Lando's words caught in his dry throat. He could not finish his sentence, averting his eyes from Joval's intense stare. Nayla had sacrificed herself so he and the boy could escape capture. He fought to erase the horrendous image from his mind when he discovered Nayla after her brutal assault.

Joval shook his head in anger. "I knew it. I knew something evil had befallen her. One night, I felt her soul cry out in anguish," sighed the Elf, the despair in his voice was evident. "I always know when she is in danger."

"How could you know?"

"Nayla is a part of my life. In some inexplicable way, our souls are so closely entwined; we know when the other is in grave danger. We can feel it in our hearts."

"I do not understand."

"I do not expect you to; most people never do understand this bond - this closeness we share."

"So, you have known Nayla for many years?"

"Yes, since she was a young child. In fact, on her mother's death bed, I swore to Lady Kareda Treeborn that I would keep her out of harm's way."

"Harm's way? Who would want to do her harm?"

Joval glanced into Lando's dark brown eyes. "If you only knew, you would truly be surprised." He gently pulled the blanket about Nayla's neck, attempting to keep her warm. "I swear there are times it would seem there are more who wished her dead, than alive."

"But who?" Lando asked again.

"The most obvious would be the Sorcerer and the Regent of Orien, Tisai Darraku. The regent himself would pay handsomely for her head."

"Why is she such a threat to them?"

"Lando, Nayla was raised by the ascetic priests of the Furai Mountains. The Kagai, or in the common speech, the Shadow Warriors are feared by those to the east. They excel in the art of war, are skilled in all forms of combat; they strike with unthinkable speed and ferocity, attacking usually at night. They fear not the darkness. Being of mixed blood, it was easy for Nayla to embrace and harness the elements – the energy that is all about us; it is the basis of their teachings. In some ways, she is more mortal because of her beliefs, in other ways; she has been able to hone her skills beyond any of the mortals. Her Elven blood does come to play when it comes to her senses. She is incredibly intuitive, more so than any Elf I have ever known."

"It is obvious she is more skilled than most warriors; yet, this fear seems unnatural; after all, she can be cut down."

"Do not underestimate her, my friend; you would not want to be on the wrong end of her sword. In her younger days, she would undertake dangerous missions that all other warriors failed to complete. What most would view as bravery, her ability to face incredible odds and take foolhardy risks, I myself know it is merely a reckless regard for her own life. More often than not, it is by sheer luck she survives to this day. Those living in eastern Orien truly fear her. She embraces the darkness, moving silently and swiftly; coming and going like a spirit. Many of her adversaries do not even know she has struck, until it is too late."

"Are you saying Nayla's powers are not of this world?"

"To the contrary, as I said, more mortal than Elf, she has embraced the teachings of the Kagai Warriors all too well. Combined with whatever Elven senses still course through her veins, she is a deadly force to contend with."

"Are there other Elves trained in the same manner?"

"Many of my men, me included, have trained in the fighting skills of the Kagai. That is why, though our combined forces are small, we have been able to hold the Sorcerer and the regent's great armies at bay. You may presume that we dark Elves have a slight edge over our fair counterparts in Wyndwood. Nayla however, was not only trained by these priests, she lived the life of the warrior, totally immersing herself in their teachings, their way of life. There lies the difference. She *is* a Shadow Warrior."

"So she is accepted by the mortals?"

"Most humans shun her, even my so-called wise and enlightened race of Elves deny her. The priests who raised her are fully aware of her abilities; they know she is the reason why the regent's armies rarely venture westward over the Furai Mountains. Is that the only reason why she continues her association with them? Who can say?"

"She does not live in Nagana? With Lord Treeborn?"

"Nayla comes and goes. When called upon by the elders to command an army or to infiltrate enemy camps; she comes. As for Dahlon Treeborn, she is bound by name and blood only. In Nayla's case, she holds friendships more closely than family ties."

"This, I fail to understand."

"One day, you might Lando. All I shall say for now is that her life has been far from easy. Although she is the daughter of a Treeborn, she has never been granted the privileges of one born to this high house."

"So she is alone in this world?"

"Not completely. There are some of us who are loyal to her. Those who befriend Nayla do so first and foremost because they are indebted to her. She is a friend to the weak and downtrodden, those whom the regent would see fit to do away with. Those who dare to come close enough to truly know her, given time, see through her armor. They discover that she is a just and compassionate soul, willing to die for a cause if need be. Those who come to know Nayla, come to love her. They too are willing to die for her."

"You included?" asked Lando, searching the dark Elf's eyes for the truth.

Joval's eyes did not stray from the knight's intense stare as he answered, "Yes… without question."

The morning sun's dull glow burned through a growing cloud-cover. Finally, Nayla stirred from her unnatural sleep. Even before sensing those around her, she was greeted by an agonizing pain stabbing through her back and coursing through her aching head. She slowly sat up, blinking hard as her eyes focused on her stark, desolate surroundings. Joval and Lando came to her side. Pain surfaced once more as she propped herself up onto her elbows.

"Either I died and took you both with me or you both foolishly risked your own lives to save mine," rasped Nayla, her throat parched from her long sleep.

"Now that is a strange way to say 'thank you', Nayla" smiled Joval, holding up a flask of water to her lips.

She took a small sip, but the cold water took its toll on her senses causing her head to throb all the more. Rubbing the back of her scalp with her hand, she winced in pain.

"You cracked your head pretty good there," pointed out Lando. "Joval managed to heal the wound, but we were unsure of the extent of your injury. Truth be told, you really had us worried. You have been unconscious for a good, long while."

"How long?"

"You slept all through the night and well into the morning, I would say a good fifteen or sixteen hours at least."

Nayla drew in a deep breath, flinching in obvious pain as her ribcage expanded, putting stress on the injury. She was unsure what caused her more grief, her cracked ribs or her aching head. She slowly sat up, her head braced between her two small hands as she wished for the pounding to cease.

"Do you remember anything?" questioned Joval, gazing into her eyes.

"I remember hearing a voice calling to me, and then falling. Plummeting through the layer of clouds…"

"You landed on a ledge, Nayla. How you managed that, I will never know. You should have fallen straight down into the crevasse below."

Nayla's cloudy eyes blinked hard as she tried to recall what had happened. "I remember thinking I was going to die. I remember trying to turn so when I hit the ground, I would at least break my neck or back, to end my life swiftly. It was strange. I was falling with incredible speed, and then I felt a powerful gust of wind rise up beneath me… Like a great hand slowing my fall. That was my last memory."

"Well, I would like to believe the Maker of All looked kindly upon you, Nayla," said Lando with a smile. "It may well be that it was by his good grace you are alive now."

"Perhaps, you are right, Lando. Why he would choose to spare my soul is beyond me, but I am grateful nevertheless." Nayla slowly drew her blanket off. Grasping Lando's broad shoulder to steady herself, she prepared to stand.

"I suggest you lie back down, Nayla. We shall carry you out," recommended Joval, motioning the warriors to begin their descent.

Nayla peered up at the dark Elf. "I think not, Joval. I shall not be carried out like an invalid."

"Captain, you are hardly in the position to decide on such matters. You cannot even stand on your own."

"Give me a moment."

"You do not have a moment. We are leaving now. For once, do as you are told, Nayla Treeborn."

She stared at Joval, her dark eyes smoldered with anger. She defiantly struggled to her feet, leaning heavily against the stony wall of the path. "Lando, get my horse."

"Nayla, I think you should listen to Joval."

"Not you too, Lando. Please… my horse."

Joval shook his head in anger. "You are too stubborn for your own good, woman!"

Turning away from the Elf, she muttered under her breath, "Yes, we are two of a kind. That is why we get along so well."

"I heard that!" snapped Joval.

Lando turned to the dark Elf. "So now what? What shall we do about her?"

"Do not talk as though I am not here," protested the warrior maiden.

"Do you know what, Lando? It was not by the Creator's good graces that she was spared, I do believe those in Hell had no room for the likes of her there. They probably tossed her onto the ledge to be rid of her!"

"I am not amused, Joval. For the last time, get my horse or I shall begin to walk."

"See, Lando! There is no room in Hell for someone as pig-headed and stubborn as she! In fact, she is the embodiment of Hell!"

"Joval! My horse, now!"

"Why do I put up with her?" Joval stomped off to retrieve their steeds.

"I love you too, Joval," whispered Nayla, as she winked at Lando.

"You deliberately antagonize him," observed Lando.

"It keeps him on his toes," she smiled through her pain.

"Are you sure you are well enough to ride down, Nayla?"

"We shall find out soon enough."

Joval returned on his steed, dismounting before her. "Get on," he ordered.

"Where is my horse?"

"You are riding with me."

"I think not."

"Well, think again."

She met Joval's fiery, blue eyes. His large frame towered above hers, dwarfing her diminutive stature as he glared down at her.

"Damn it, Nayla! I can be just as stubborn as you! Now get on the horse!" ordered the Elf.

"How dare you? I am your captain! You cannot speak to me in this tone!"

"Ha! You are wrong, my dear. You had appointed me as the Ambassador of Orien. Remember? Therefore, you follow my orders. Now, get on!"

"Then I shall revoke this appointment."

"You are impossible!" Joval threw his arms up in frustration.

"Well, you are-"

Before Nayla could finish her sentence, Lando unceremoniously threw her over his shoulder, lifting her onto the horse's back. The knight shook his head in disbelief; Joval and Nayla could go on forever with their war of words.

"Thank you, Lando," said Joval, taking his place behind Nayla.

As the army snaked their way down to the base of the mountain, Nayla glanced up at Joval. His icy stare remained fixed straight ahead even though he knew she was gazing up at him. She could sense his anger.

"I am sorry," said she, barely in a whisper.

Joval smiled inwardly. It was rare she would admit she was sorry for anything. "Apology accepted," the dark Elf replied. His voice carried in a gentle tone, betraying his true demeanor.

As they rode down a little farther, Joval confessed, "It concerns and angers me that you are so reluctant to accept help. You give it freely, yet you refuse it when you are most deserving. I swear Nayla, you had better learn to swallow your pride or it may be the death of you and it shall certainly be the end of your relationship with Arerys."

"I said I was sorry, Joval. You know how it is; the men expect more from me."

"Nayla, your pride shall lead to your ruin. If you die because you are too stubborn or proud to accept help, when help is warranted, then you shall die as a fool, not as a hero. Just keep in mind, accepting help is not a sign of weakness."

"You are right. Sometimes, old habits die hard."

"You know I worry about you, Nayla. That is all."

"You worry more than you should, Joval."

"Only because you give me good reason to worry," responded the Elf. "It would serve you well to take heed of my advice from time to time."

"I know."

"Enough talk for now, you should rest."

"I am fine, Joval."

"See! You do it again," Joval reminded her.

Nayla sighed in surrender. With his arms about her body, she leaned back against Joval's broad chest. She could hear the steady beat of his heart. The warm energy emanating from his body permeated into hers. She felt safe; the gentle, rocking motion of the horse as it traveled downwards lulled her into a dream-like state. Here, she found some reprieve from her throbbing head and her damaged body. She relaxed as she rested against Joval.

In this strange twilight, Nayla's thoughts brought her back to Arerys. She could see his kind blue eyes, his long, golden hair, and his sweet, disarming smile that stole her heart. He seemed so real. Her hand reached up to touch his face. He pressed it to his cheek, and then he placed her small hand into his to gently plant a kiss upon it.

In her mind's eye, she watched as she rode off to the east with her army only to have Arerys come charging back to steal away with one final kiss. Her heart found some comfort in his parting words as he promised to do everything in his power to return to her again. And then her heart sank as she watched him ride off to the west, disappearing in the distance with Markus and the Wizard.

How long Nayla lingered in this state, she was not sure, but when Joval woke her so they may dismount, the world was embraced in darkness once again. The Elf leapt down, helping Nayla ease herself to the ground. It was obvious to those in close proximity their captain was still in great pain.

"Sit, Nayla. Rest while the men set up camp for the night."

Nayla nodded. She knew better than with argue to Joval. She quietly slumped down to the ground, her aching head braced in her hands.

Eventually, Joval returned with a steaming cup of water. The analgesic properties of the willow gave the liquid a bitter flavor but Nayla needed no coaxing to swallow this medicine. In time, her injured head was reduced to a dull, throbbing pain although her cracked ribs continued to give her grief with each deep breath she inhaled. Without the benefit of a high Elf's powers, Joval's Elven touch managed to mend the shattered ribs, but her body, neither Elven nor mortal, had difficulty responding to such rapid healing after such extensive damage.

Lando knelt down next to Nayla. She looked up at the knight, offering him a weak smile. She tried to downplay the true extent of her pain, but he could see by the dullness of her eyes it was still very much there. Still, he admired her tenacity and her unwillingness to slow her men down.

"Joval and the others have erected your tent. You should lie down, Nayla. Sleep can only do you good," suggested Lando.

Nayla struggled to her feet as the knight helped to steady her as she made her way to her quarters. He noticed how she would stand a little taller and straighter as she walked past the men of her army, trying to minimize the intensity of her pain.

As they reached her tent, Joval stepped out. He raised the flap so

Nayla and Lando could pass through. Inside, he had already laid out her bedroll. A single candle burned gently, releasing a warm, welcoming glow.

Nayla thanked Lando for his assistance as he slipped out. Joval watched her as she stood in the center of the tent. She slowly lowered herself down onto the bedroll; he caught her by her shoulders as she fell forward with the stabbing pain that coursed through her. Her breathing was fast and shallow as Joval helped to ease her trembling form down. Nayla quietly knelt on her bedroll, her eyes staring at the soft glow of the candle as she attempted to slow her breathing – to think away her pain.

Joval tenderly placed a hand on her head, gently patting the crown of her raven hair almost as if he was patting the head of a small child. "Let me help you, Nayla. You cannot go on like this."

Nayla's eyes lacked their usual fire, they were glassy and vacant as they stared up at Joval; she simply nodded in agreement.

The Elf took his place behind Nayla, removing her cloak.

Nayla undid the clasps on her vest and the layer of chain mail, and with Joval's assistance; he carefully peeled it off her back. Her fingers struggled to untie the string holding the silk bodice closed. Finally undone, she slipped her blouse off her shoulders, down to her waist.

Joval held his hands over his head, clapping sharply once; he proceeded to briskly rub them together. Once the palms of his hands were sufficiently warmed, he gently placed them over Nayla's shattered ribcage. She flinched at the initial contact, and then he heard her release a gentle sigh as her chin dropped to her chest and her eyes slowly closed. Joval's touch eased the pain substantially. It was only during times like this, or when she was plagued by a malady that inflicts mortals, did Nayla wish she had the Elves' ability to heal rapidly from such injuries or to avoid sickness altogether.

Nayla could hear Joval's voice softly repeating a healing incantation in his people's tongue. His gentle voice and his Elvish words soothed her soul. Her eyes remained closed as she listened to him.

Joval could feel the tenseness and pain in her body slowly dissipating under his healing touch. He was pleased that he was able to offer her some relief, but as he worked on her battered body, it angered his heart as he looked upon her small back. Just beneath the tattoo she bore high on her right shoulder blade, the symbol of her allegiance to the brotherhood of the Kagai Warriors, he could make out the long silvery scars lining the length of her back.

How often he had wished he had come across her sooner; had he only had the foresight to remove her from Dahlon's custody before it had gotten this out of hand. Even to this day, over two centuries later, the memory of finding Nayla as a child of the mortal equivalent of a twelve-year-old, bound and gagged in the armory filled him with guilt. Her back was so severely caned her clothing was bloodied and tattered. It still troubled him to no end. It was not so much the nature of her beating; it was the memory of her eyes that continued to haunt him to this very day. Joval had seen grown men cry out, even faint during such a beating, but it was as though Nayla's soul had transmigrated from her body, no longer able to endure its physical existence. He could see it in her eyes; they were devoid of life – unable to show hate, sorrow, anger or happiness – only fear.

Just looking at Nayla caused Joval's heart to ache. She had endured so much in her life. He could sense how weary her soul and body had become since the last time they had ventured into war together. Where as his appearance had remained relatively unchanged since they first met when she was a child, her mortal blood accelerated her growth, speeding up the aging process, especially during her childhood and adolescent years. At eight-hundred-seventeen years of age, Joval looked the mortal equivalent of perhaps forty years. Nayla however, although she was five-hundred-twenty-seven years his junior, was probably the equivalent of a mortal woman of twenty-eight or twenty-nine. She was aging before his very eyes and it frightened him immensely. Unless the process slows down as she advanced in years, slowing as it does for Elves, in another one hundred years when she is three-hundred-ninety, she would be as old as he, perhaps even older.

When he thought upon this warrior's plight, Joval wished that Nayla was a full-blooded Elf or at least blessed with the eternal life of his people, but he knew only Lord Dahlon Treeborn could grant such a blessing. This would not be forthcoming.

Perhaps King Kal-lel of Wyndwood would grant this to Nayla if and when, she and Arerys wed. At least, this is one good thing that might result from this union, he thought.

As Nayla drew another long breath, Joval removed his hands from her back. The bruising had significantly faded. "Did that help?"

"Yes, Joval. Thank you," responded Nayla, her voice barely audible, as she drew her blouse back up around her shoulders. Her fingers clutched the bodice, closing it in front of her.

"You should get some sleep now, Nayla. I shall call on you in the morning. If your pain persists, we shall have another session before we depart."

"Thank you," she whispered again as she eased herself onto her bedroll. She lay face down, unable to lie on her back. She quickly slipped into a deep sleep.

Joval drew her cloak over her sleeping form, blowing out the candle as he departed from her tent. "Good night, Nayla," he softly whispered as he slipped out into the darkness.

The early morning call of songbirds announced the coming of the dawn. Gray clouds were beginning to gather high in the dull sky.

As Nayla allowed herself a quick drink of water to quench her thirst and a small piece of Elven bread to satisfy her hunger, Joval and Lando came around with their horses.

"Do not argue, Nayla. You shall be riding with me," ordered the dark Elf.

"That is fine," she responded in a small voice.

"I do not want to hear a single word from you."

"I said it is fine."

Joval was stunned, frowning at her suspiciously. He was braced for another war of words with the warrior maiden. Lando looked at him, shrugging his shoulders in dismay.

The Elf gave Nayla a leg up onto his steed's back, and then he took his place behind her. Normally, she was full of life and energy; today she was a shadow of her former self. Joval assessed that she was still not well. Somehow, he wished for more of her inane banter and opinionated thoughts, at least it was a sure sign she was fit.

Nayla rested quietly against Joval's chest. She felt her spirit being revitalized as she basked in her friend's life-force. As the day wore on, she conserved her energy, concentrating on recuperating rather than engaging in verbal jousts with her mentor. Although throughout their long history, they always shared a very tempestuous relationship, for now, Nayla took great comfort in Joval's presence.

By late afternoon, thick, gray clouds had continued to gather, looming high above them, but still, they gave no sign of releasing their liquid contents. As their horse plodded on at an easy pace, Nayla was once again lulled into a dream-like state. Her eyes closed as she leaned into Joval's body, her soul meandering back into the twilight.

In this place, she found her way back to Arerys. She gazed up to his face, staring intently, studying the dark motes that flecked the blue of his eyes. Nayla felt a warm energy fill a void inside her; she felt her soul being drawn deep into his heart. His fingertips softly traced her cheek, following the contour of her face where upon he lifted her chin so their mouths met. She felt her heart race as he gently pressed his lips to hers.

Suddenly, Arerys released an agonizing gasp. As their eyes locked, a look of excruciating pain was etched across his face. Nayla searched his eyes, searching for a sign of what was wrong. Slowly, he sank down to his knees, his hands desperately clutching at her as he crumpled to the ground. She knelt before him, with her arms around his body; she tried to pull him to his feet. His frightened eyes stared into hers; Nayla's hands moved to Arerys' shoulders, but she began to tremble in horror when she saw her hands covered in blood – his blood. Shocked, she caught him as he finally collapsed into her arms. There was blood everywhere. Nayla cried out in fear, but Arerys did not answer. He lay motionless. She screamed at him to wake up, but still, he did not answer. Nayla felt the panic rising in her, overwhelming her like a great tidal wave. She felt as though an invisible hand was squeezing her heart, stifling its beat, crushing the very life out of her. She sobbed as she held tightly onto Arerys. Soon the chilling embrace of a cold rain fell silently from the sky, mingling with her tears before washing them away. She looked down at the ground; all around her was a rising tide of crimson blood. Terrified for him, she screamed out his name.

"*ARERYS!*"

Nayla bolted up from Joval's embrace. The color instantly drained from her face. Her eyes were now wide open in absolute fear as they brimmed with tears.

"Nayla, what is wrong?" asked Joval, tightening his grip about her body.

"Arerys! Something evil has befallen him!" Her panicked breaths were short and fast. Joval could feel her heart racing wildly.

"Calm yourself, Nayla. You were only dreaming."

"No, Joval. It was not a dream. I know the difference. I could feel it in my heart. I could sense it in my soul. Something has happened to Arerys!"

"Nayla, you are weary – injured. You could be mistaken."

"Joval, I know what I feel. It is the same feeling I get when I know something dreadful has happened to you!"

The dark Elf shook his head. He knew exactly what Nayla was

speaking of. Even when they were hundreds of leagues apart, each time something happened - when one, or the other, walked a fine line between life and death, that split second when one's life flashes before one's eyes, they both knew in an instant, something terrible had happened.

"Nayla, please... for once you could be wrong."

"You know I have never been wrong about this feeling!"

"But your head, your mind may be playing tricks on you," insisted Joval. He glanced down upon her face. He could see great tears tumble from her eyes, rolling down her flushed cheeks. He could feel her body trembling with undeniable fear and anxiety. Her head tilted up, looking to the stars shining softly through the clear patches in the clouds on this moonless night. Nayla's dark eyes desperately searched the night sky for some sign of hope that may quell her fears as she prayed to an invisible god.

CHAPTER 5

A TIME FOR PRAYER

As the cold rain pelted down unmercifully upon him, Lindras felt the blood in his veins turn to ice. *Something is wrong, terribly wrong,* thought the Wizard. With the safety of Wyndwood just before him, he reeled his steed about, charging back through Crow's Nest Pass.

Through the driving rain and in the blackness of the night, the Wizard soon came upon Valtar and Markus. They were huddled over Arerys as he lay in a pool of his own blood. Lindras leapt down from his steed, his eyes dark with fear upon seeing the fair Elf's still body.

"What happened?" asked Lindras, his hand feeling Arerys' neck for a pulse.

"He was cut down by the blade of the dark emissary," cried Markus.

Lindras knelt closer; taking his staff in his hand he breathed life into the crystal. The orb glowed, driving back the darkness. He passed it over to the prince. "Hold it steady, Markus."

The Wizard quickly pulled at the chain mail and the blood-soaked shirt beneath it. To his horror, the blade had passed deep into Arerys' body just below his left ribcage, slicing through skin, flesh and deeper still.

"Please, Wizard, tell me he is not going to die!"

"It does not look good, Markus. Had he been a mortal, Arerys would have died immediately, this I know."

"We must stop the bleeding; he has already lost so much!"

Lindras leaned over Arerys' chest, listening for the sound of his heart. It was growing faint. "Valtar, are you trained to heal?"

"My training is minimal, Wizard. Cuts, aches and pains, but this… this is well beyond my capabilities!"

"We need to stop the bleeding, but how?" wondered Lindras aloud. He closed his eyes for a moment, concentrating on their dilemma. *What can we use? To build a fire to cauterize the wound is out of the question in this downpour, and time is of the essence. There must be something,* he thought. Suddenly, it dawned on him; he had the answer right on him all along. The Wizard's fingers fished out the cloth hidden behind his belt; he presented before Valtar and Markus the Stone of Salvation.

Markus knew immediately what Lindras was planning to do. He passed the Wizard's staff on to Valtar as he pulled up on Arerys' torn and bloodied clothing. With the wound now fully exposed, Markus used his hands and the falling rain to wipe away the blood so the wound was clearly exposed. Lindras carefully gripped the dazzling, red Stone in his hand, the cloth protecting his fingers, shielding them from its powers. The Wizard worked quickly, plunging the Stone deep into Arerys' wound. They could hear and smell the burning of flesh. Lindras asked Markus to hold the sides of the gaping wound closed as he lightly touched it with the Stone to sear the torn flesh together. The prince averted his eyes; he involuntarily retched as his senses were assaulted by the horrific sounds, smells and sight of Lindras' handiwork. As the Stone cauterized the wound, wisps of smoke curled into the air, only to be driven down by the torrential rainfall.

Lindras looked up at Valtar, "Skilled or not, Elf, you must do what you can to help Arerys."

The dark Elf nodded in response, handing the staff back to the Wizard. Placing his left hand over Arerys' wound; he closed his eyes and repeated an incantation several times. When he was done, he slowly removed his hand. To his astonishment, the wound was sealed, the burn marks made by the Stone – gone!

"Markus, I am afraid Arerys may already be too far gone. There is nothing more I can do. The nature of his wound is such that only a high Elf, Kal-lel and the elders of Wyndwood, may be able to save him now."

"You are right, Lindras. Where Kal-lel is at this point is anybody's guess, but Wyndwood is near. Make haste, Wizard! Ride like the wind! Gather the elders; have them meet us on route! Go!" instructed Markus.

As Lindras charged southward into the darkness and the heavy veil of cold, gray rain, Valtar helped Markus to raise Arerys onto his steed. Markus steadied the fair Elf against his body as they rode towards Wyndwood. The faster the horse's pace, the smoother the ride; the prince urged his horse on, galloping to the safety of Kal-lel's domain.

As the trio entered the deep forests of Wyndwood, to Markus' relief the rain finally ceased. The sound of residual raindrops falling from the leaves of the aspen and birch trees lining their path all but drowned out the sounds of the chorusing tree frogs.

Valtar glanced up to the heavens through the crowns of the trees; he could see the clouds had quickly dissolved, revealing a dark velveteen sky. The Elf's brown eyes gazed up to the many stars glowing gently against this ebony canvas, but the moon was strangely absent on this dreadful night.

The Wizard careened along a near invisible path around a stand of aspen trees. His eyes noted their size. They were much larger than those along the border of Wyndwood. He was nearing Aspenglow. In the distance, he could make out the soft glow of lights illuminating the boardwalks and homes of the Elf-folk. Although Lindras knew that Aspenglow was nearing, he could not help feel that it was shrinking away into the darkness, even as he approached ever closer. He could not get there soon enough.

Lindras' steed thundered through the wet forest. He could tell the stallion was exhausted. At this relentless pace, it was only a matter of time before the beast would slow considerably, perhaps even collapse from weariness. Up ahead, Aspenglow awaited his arrival; he had no choice but to urge his steed on.

As he charged onward, Elves hearing his approach lined the high walkways, stunned by the Wizard's unexpected arrival.

Lindras rode straight through into the center courtyard. He leapt off his horse, dashing to the bell that hung in the courtyard gazebo. Snatching the rope up into his hands, the Wizard desperately began yanking on the cord; the bell sounded its alarm, beckoning the elders of Wyndwood.

"It is the Wizard of the West," announced Tor-rin, leaning out the window for a better look.

"What brings Lindras Weatherstone to Aspenglow?" asked Sol-lel, rising from the table.

"Anytime the Wizard shows up unexpected and unannounced, it is never a good thing," muttered Ansat. "Let us not keep Lindras waiting."

The three elders, the high Elves that sat in council with King Kallel gathered their cloaks and hurried to the courtyard.

As the Elves poured forth from their homes in answer to Lindras' desperate call, the Wizard continued sounding the bell.

"Enough, Lindras Weatherstone! You shall wake up the dead with all this commotion!" shouted Ansat as he threw his lined and weathered hands over his pointed ears to protect them from the assault of the deafening clamor the Wizard was creating.

Lindras turned upon hearing the high Elf's voice. As soon as the elders gazed upon the Wizard's distressed face, they knew he was to be the bearer of bad tidings.

"What brings you here, my friend?" asked Tor-rin. "If you seek King Kal-lel, he has not yet returned from the crusade in Talibarr."

"I am aware of that Tor-rin. I am in urgent need of your presence. The elders must come with me, quickly!"

"Why the urgency, Wizard?" asked Sol-lel, his brows furrowing in concern.

"It is Prince Arerys! He is terribly hurt – cut down by the blade of the Dark Lord's making! You must come quickly," pleaded Lindras. "He is dying as we speak!"

"Where is he now?" asked Tor-rin, motioning the young squires to fetch their steeds.

"We were attacked just outside of Wyndwood – in Crow's Nest Pass. Prince Markus is with him. They journey into the forest, heading to Aspenglow. We are to meet them."

"This is not an exaggeration of the circumstances?" asked Ansat.

Lindras shook his head, "I am afraid not."

Ansat, the most senior of the high Elves turned to Tor-rin and Sol-lel. "Venture forth with the Wizard. I shall remain and make ready the healing altar."

"Ansat, can word be delivered to King Sebastian's castle in Darross? Kal-lel may very well stop there before continuing on. I beseech you; dispatch your swiftest falcon at the first light of dawn. We must get word to Kal-lel of Arerys' condition. You shall need the help of all your combined powers if he is to survive."

"Consider it done, Wizard," answered Ansat.

As Tor-rin instructed his apprentice to fetch his medicine bag, he heard the sounds of Lindras' exhausted steed gasping for its breath. Its body drenched in sweat, the stallion's nostrils flared as steaming blasts of spent air was exhaled through its nose and gaping, frothy mouth. Tor-rin motioned for a squire to deliver Ansat's mare to Lindras. As the Wizard proceeded to mount the horse, a familiar whinny caught his attention. He turned to see a great, gray steed cantering towards him. It was his stallion, Tempest.

The Wizard was pleasantly surprised to see his loyal steed had escaped when the Order was trapped in the gully in Talibarr. It pleased him to no end that Tempest followed his order, making his way back to the safety of Wyndwood. The stallion's head nodded in greeting as he trotted up to the Wizard. Lindras greeted his old friend, rubbing Tempest on his velvety muzzle.

"We must make haste, my friend. We have urgent business to tend to," he whispered into the horse's ears. Lindras leapt onto his stallion as Sol-lel and Tor-rin mounted their steeds.

The gray stallion reared up, and then charged northward, his ears twitching as he listened intently to the Wizard's voice. Lindras directed him on through the darkness, leading the way through the forest.

Over four hours had elapsed since Lindras left Arerys in the care of Markus and Valtar. If they were traveling at the same speed towards each other, it was only a matter a time before he and the elders should meet up with them. As the landscape passed by in a blur, whether Arerys was still alive was a question that plagued the Wizard with great worry.

Riding on, Lindras brought Tempest to an abrupt halt. The Wizard drew back his hood, his ears straining to hear the sounds of the night. "Up ahead! I hear the sounds of horses coming in our direction!" shouted Lindras. Taking the reins back in his weathered hands, he guided his steed on.

As Lindras and the elders approached, Markus leapt from his saddle. He caught Arerys as his limp form slipped off the steed. "Lindras! Thank goodness, it is you!" said Markus, holding the fair Elf in his arms.

Tor-rin leapt off his horse, racing to Arerys' side. "Place him down on the ground, Prince Markus. There is not a minute to lose."

Markus laid Arerys down onto the damp ground as Tor-rin rummaged through his medicine bag. From the blood-soaked clothing, he could immediately discern where the injury was. Sol-lel lifted the damaged mail and torn, stained shirt to reveal the wound He was momentarily taken aback when he realized the wound was closed – no longer bleeding.

"Is this your handiwork, Wizard?" asked Sol-lel.

"Yes, a combination of my efforts and Valtar Briarwood's."

Valtar nodded in acknowledgement. The elders briefly stopped to consider the stranger before resuming their efforts to save Arerys. There would be time enough later to speak to this dark Elf.

As Sol-lel gently placed his left hand over the Elf prince's damaged body, he closed his eyes. He called upon the powers of all the elders, past and present, and the grace of the Maker of All to heal. Tor-rin quietly went about the business of positioning nine abalone shells in a circle around Arerys, motioning Markus, Lindras and Valtar to remain outside this sacred area.

Tor-rin carefully placed nine candles, one in each shell, lighting them as he repeated an incantation. Lindras explained to Valtar and Markus that each candle and the light glowing from it symbolize the life-force of each elder, including the six previous high Elves who now reside in the Twilight. Markus observed the iridescent silvery-blue color of the mother-of-pearl lining the inside of each shell. It came alive as the light from the candle's flame gently danced against its luminescent backdrop. The soft glow emitted by each candle was strangely calming, bathing Arerys and the elders in its warm light. Markus suddenly felt his shoulders droop as he released a heavy sigh, both from relief and weariness. All he could do now was to wait and pray that Tor-rin and Sol-lel could work their Elven magic to save his dear friend.

Markus turned away, his eyes searching the heavens. Lindras quietly stood beside him, sensing his anxiety and grief.

"He must live, Lindras. If he does not, I dread the journey to Orien – to deliver this terrible news to Nayla. She will be devastated..."

"Be warned, Markus, if Arerys is mortally wounded, if he is beyond help, the elders shall deliver him to the Twilight otherwise, his soul shall be trapped in this realm."

"But Nayla cannot enter the Twilight. She cannot be united with Arerys upon his passing into this haven."

"I know," Lindras said, lowering his head in sadness.

As the elders tended to Arerys, Markus felt an unsettling chill envelope his body, tightening around his heavy heart. His worried eyes scanned the dark forest, and then gazed through the tree canopy into the velvety black skies. The clouds had all but disappeared; he could see the tiny stars shining brightly as they danced in and out between the leaves that swayed in the soft breeze, totally oblivious to the disastrous events of the evening. Though there were no clouds, droplets of water continued to fall upon them, like silver tears descending from heaven. Eventually, Markus came to realize the water that gently rained down upon them came from the trees. Water dripped off of the leaves, like rain falling from the sky. All around him, he could sense growing sorrow, as if the aspen, birch and willow trees, so prevalent in Wyndwood, were weeping for the fallen Elf.

Lindras, Valtar and Markus watched in silence as Tor-rin, kneeling over Arerys' still form, gently placed his hands on the Elf's forehead. Sol-lel carefully selected a mixture of dried herbs. Taking several desiccated, lacey, dark green leaves, he crushed them between his fingers before combining them with the other herbs, mixing them together before igniting them in a large abalone shell. He then stooped before a rain puddle, dowsing the small flame with a handful of water. Wisps of gray, aromatic smoke slowly rose and curled into the night air, dissolving into the darkness. Sol-lel slowly paced within the circle of the nine candles, the shell and its smoldering contents balanced in his right hand. In his left hand, a twig from an aspen tree was used to fan the smoke over Arerys' limp form. With broad, sweeping movements, the leaves of this twig drove the smoke into the middle of the circle.

Markus observed this healing ritual with reverent fascination. The scent of the medicinal herbs used by Sol-lel now hung heavy in the damp, night air. Oddly, as he breathed in the pungent fumes escaping from the circle of candles where Arerys lay, Markus felt his mind going fuzzy, his senses becoming dull as the sounds and smells lulled him into a dream-like state. He felt every fiber of his being relax as though every tense muscle and sinew were unwinding as the smoke entered his lungs, permeating his body. This strange sensation even seeped into his weary soul, lifting and embracing it. Although he was still soaked to his skin from the earlier rain, he no longer felt the clammy, cold dampness that clung to his body. His eyes half closed as a small smile crept across his face, his mind and body surrendering to the calming effectives of the healing smoke intended for Arerys.

Valtar glanced over at Markus. "What is it, my lord?"

"Nothing... Absolutely nothing," he whispered, his voice was slowed, slurring slightly, as he glanced over at the dark Elf through glazed eyes.

"It is the smoke, Valtar," noted Lindras. "Let us move off until the elders are done."

"That is not necessary, Wizard," smiled Markus. "I assure you, I am feeling quite fine."

"Yes, well... perhaps, a little too fine, Markus," answered Lindras, grasping the prince by his arm to lead him away.

When Lindras and Markus returned from their stroll, the elders had done what they could for the downed Elf. Arerys was now wrapped in a dry, warm blanket. He was seated on Valtar's steed, with the dark Elf supporting him.

"We must get Prince Arerys back to Aspenglow," said Tor-rin, throwing the strap of his medicine bag around his shoulder.

"Will he live?" asked Markus.

"I cannot say. He is weak. His heart barely beats. Truth be told, I do not know how he has survived up until now," replied Tor-rin, his blue eyes were overshadowed with worry. "By all accounts, he should be dead, and yet, something inside keeps him alive."

"You do understand that we may still have to release his soul to the Twilight?" asked Sol-lel, gazing upon Lindras' woeful face.

"As long as Arerys still lives, I beg of you, wait until King Kal-lel returns. Let his father decide his fate, if fate does not decide for him."

Sol-lel nodded in understanding, turning his steed southward, to the heart of Wyndwood. With the elders leading the way, Valtar with Arerys on his mount and the others following close behind, they raced through the early morning darkness to the safety of Aspenglow.

Songbirds failed to sing on this bleak morn. In the center courtyard and along the high walkways, the citizens of Wyndwood gathered. Though the able-bodied men had yet to return from war, those too old or too young to go into battle with their king joined the Elf maidens. The women wept openly as they looked with great sorrow upon their prince.

Squires quickly gathered all the horses and a stretcher was delivered to Tor-rin and Sol-lel so Arerys may be delivered to the sanctuary where Ansat had prepared the healing altar. Valtar assisted Markus to lay Arerys onto the stretcher. They carefully lifted the unconscious Elf. Carrying his still body, they followed Tor-rin and Sol-lel into the sanctuary. As Markus stepped into the room, the air was filled with the aromatic scent of smoldering herbs and the quiet was like that of a tomb. On the altar, nine candles burned, its light gently illuminating the interior of the building, a tenth candle, much larger than all the others, remained unlit.

Before Arerys was to be lifted onto the bed before the altar, the elders asked Markus and Valtar to help prepare their prince for ablution while they readied the medicines they required. Markus removed Arerys' mud and rain stained riding boots as Valtar unfastened the clasps of his cloak and vest, gently propping him against his shoulder as he slipped off his bloodied clothes and chain mail. Markus and

Valtar stepped aside to make way for the elders so they may sponge off the blood from the Elf's body, washing away the dirt, grime and sweat from his last battle. When they were done, Markus and Valtar lifted Arerys onto the healing bed. Tor-rin placed a warming blanket over his body.

Ansat turned to the altar, reciting an ancient incantation in Elvish as he lit the tenth candle.

"Is the candle to call upon a greater power to heal Arerys?" asked Markus.

"No," answered the Wizard in a solemn voice.

"No? What is its purpose?"

"When the candle burns no more, time has run out for our friend," whispered Lindras, resting heavily against his staff.

"What do you mean, 'time has run out'?"

"When the candle's wick ceases to burn, if Arerys still lives, but does not awaken, the elders shall release him."

"To the Twilight?" asked Markus.

"Yes, to the Twilight"

"How much time does he have?"

"Forty-eight hours," answered Lindras. "Whatever the case, King Kal-lel should be arriving no later than tomorrow eve. He, as Arerys' father, may decide upon his fate sooner."

"Whatever the outcome, I pray the Maker of All shall be merciful. may he look kindly upon Arerys' soul," sighed Markus, his heart was burdened with much sadness.

"The elders shall begin their vigil; they shall remain here by his side until the end."

"Do not say the end, Wizard. I cannot… I will not believe that after all Arerys had endured, to have run the gauntlet with the Order to save Imago, to have found the love of his life, that he will now succumb in such a manner," lamented Markus, his tears finally tumbling down his cheeks as he gazed upon his dear friend.

Lindras embraced Markus, comforting the weary prince. "I am sorry, Markus. You are right. Arerys is strong, had it been any other Elf, he would have passed on long ago."

As the three elders of Wyndwood took their place at the healing altar to begin their prayer vigil, Ansat urged Markus to find some rest, that he would be told if there was a change in Arerys' condition.

"Is there more I can do?" offered Markus.

"Yes," answered Ansat. "Pray for him."

As Lindras, Markus and Valtar emerged from the sanctuary, they squinted into a bright morning sun that bathed everything around them in a warm, golden hue. Lindras was quickly swallowed up in the clamor of all those who had gathered outside, awaiting news about the condition of their prince. The dark Elf's brown eyes studied the fair faces of the Elves of Wyndwood. They all stared back at him with great fascination, especially the young Elf maidens, for none had ever set eyes on the likes of him before. Amongst the many voices, Valtar's sensitive ears heard the subdued whisperings of a child asking her mother if he indeed was 'one of those dark Elves'. He simply smiled at the golden-haired child with expressive blue eyes. The last Elven child he had ever laid eyes on was Nayla Treeborn, but in his own mind, Nayla being half mortal, was not exactly his idea of an Elf.

Tor-rin's young apprentice made his way through the crowd. He gestured for Markus and Valtar to follow as he led them to King Kal-lel's residence. There, the royal household graciously welcomed both men into the king's home. They were offered a meal; however, it had been over twenty-four hours since they had slept. Whereas Markus was utterly exhausted, Valtar was merely tired. Although the dark Elf was willing to partake in a meal, he was ill at ease about being left-alone with these *fair* Elves. He too chose to retire for a few hours with the intention of joining Markus for a meal later. The head of Kal-lel's staff escorted them to their bed chambers, leaving the weary, unexpected guests to rest.

Markus fell into a deep sleep almost immediately upon resting his head down on a soft, perfumed pillow. Although he was not a citizen of Wyndwood, the prince always found peace in these tranquil forests. Valtar too slept, but like a cat of the wild, he was ever alert – his ears still hearing every sound.

Four hours passed. Valtar awoke fully rested. It was now late-morning. He rose from his bed, heading to a small table by the open window. Pouring some tepid water from an urn into a basin, he splashed the water onto his face and onto the back of his neck. It was as though the water refreshed and energized the Elf. As he gazed out the window, he felt the beating of his heart hasten. For the first time he realized he was now in the home of his father and forefathers; where all Elves once dwelled in Imago. Valtar drew in a deep breath, reveling in the beauty of the peaceful forest. In all his seven hundred and ninety one years of existence, he had often dreamed of this home he had never seen before. It was exactly as his father had described; lush, green, alive with life, its energy invigorating him to his very soul.

Valtar's eyes slowly closed and his heart sank, he finally understood why so many of his kind, the so-called *dark* Elves that once dwelled in this ancient forest departed into the Twilight. Although the mortals of Orien accepted them, the bamboo forests of eastern Imago were a far cry from the aspen, birch and willow forests of Wyndwood. Now he understood why his father and mother, like so many of Dahlon Treeborn's generation, left for the Elf haven. Valtar's eyes searched the forest and it was not so much the trees, but the energy surging through the forest, a life-giving pulse that made him feel more alive than he ever did before. This was the same energy that carried the steeds ridden by all who entered Wyndwood. It allowed the horses to run longer and faster before showing any signs of fatigue. He could feel the heart of the forest beating in time with his. For the first time in decades his damaged body did not feel the dull, gnawing pain that often made his life sheer misery.

So this is what is feels like to be home, thought Valtar. He felt his body and soul lulled into a state of absolute bliss, a feeling he had never experienced before. As his eyes pierced through the dense stand of deciduous trees, he could make out the pristine, emerald-green waters of the Lake in the Woods. His heart hungered for more. His eyes too longed to drink in the beauty of the forest around him and his lungs to breathe in the fresh, earthy smells of a forest after the spring rains. Even his skin felt alive, tingling as a cool breeze caressed him in its gentle embrace.

Slowly, Valtar's blood began to boil as he felt a rising tide of anger and resentment: *This is not fair. My people belong here too, we should never have left. We have just as much right to be in Wyndwood.*

Valtar thought upon King Kal-lel's decree made during the celebration marking the commencement of the Third Age of Peace. Perhaps, Kal-lel will remain true to his word that he would see their race united once again, living back here in Wyndwood. He supposed Arerys' union to Nayla may indeed be the one element to unite their people, but at what cost? For he knew if she wed Kal-lel's son, his dearest friend, Joval Stonecroft would retire into the Twilight without ever seeing this fabled forest.

Valtar had often wished Joval would do so, allowing him to find respite from his tortured body by ending his life-debt and allowing him to enter this haven too. Here, he would be free of pain - to be reunited with his family. Now his heart was torn for he realized with Kal-lel's new edict, allowing his people to return would result in a new life for him, but heartache for his friend. Joval would lose the love of his life to another.

As far as Valtar was concerned, Joval deserved better than the half-caste woman who was feared by most mortals and shunned by most Elves. He could never understand how Joval could be drawn to Nayla for she was strong-willed and stubborn, a wild spirit unwilling to be broken, let alone be tamed.

There must be a way that Joval can win back Nayla while allowing our people to still maintain diplomacy with King Kal-lel, pondered Valtar.

For a split second, the dark thought crossed his mind that Arerys' untimely demise may send Nayla rushing back to Joval's arms. Such an unfortunate turn of events, beyond anyone's control, surely would not jeopardize communications and damage a relationship in good standing with the King of Wyndwood. He shook his head, dismissing this disturbing idea, ashamed that he could even consider or wish for such a thing. *Perhaps there is another way I can drive a wedge between Arerys and his intended; a way to send Nayla back to Joval, but still force King Kal-lel's hand to allow the dark Elves to return to Wyndwood.*

"Valtar?" A familiar voice called through the door.

The dark Elf turned away from the window as a voice followed by a gentle rap on his door disrupted his troubled thoughts. He moved to open the door to find Markus standing before him.

"I knew you would be awake," said Markus. The prince was refreshed after his rest and was now dressed in fresh apparel. "I thought you might want to join me for a meal, and then perhaps a walk."

"Yes," said Valtar, eager to leave his room and venture forth into Wyndwood. He quickly threw on a clean shirt before following Markus to Kal-lel's dining hall.

Elf maidens delivered wine and food to their guests, smiling demurely at the men as they ate. Valtar smiled politely, thanking them as they quietly went about their business, moving gracefully around the table as though their steps were as light as air.

"Any word of Arerys' condition, my lord?" asked Valtar.

"He remains unchanged, the elders continue their watch. Lindras too remains by his side."

"And his father? Any word of King Kal-lel's return?"

"A falcon arrived from Darross Castle while we slept. King Sebastian sent forth one of his birds. The parchment read that Kal-lel and his army, at least those on horseback, shall be here by nightfall," answered Markus.

"Let us pray he is not too late," said Valtar.

"Yes, at this point, it is all we can do."

The dark Elf stared at Markus as his mind replayed the final moments before the fair Elf was brutally attacked. "Tell me, my lord, what was the creature that downed Prince Arerys?"

"That creature was one of the four dark horsemen that pursued us across the lands in search of the Stone of Salvation," answered Markus. "They were once in the service of Beyilzon, the Dark Lord, but it is now apparent there is an ungodly alliance with the Sorcerer of Orien."

"But who were they?"

"According to Lindras, they were once wealthy landowners and powerful warlords. It is said that centuries ago, before the Second Age of Peace, Beyilzon's promise of immortality and riches beyond their wildest dreams paved the way to their downfall."

"They were once mortal men?" asked Valtar.

"Yes. They were consumed by avarice and their lust for power. However, there was a price to be paid for what they desired. In this case, they sold their souls and the only promise the Dark Lord had delivered to them in return was eternal life."

"So they were damned to an eternal existence in this form?" asked Valtar, wishing to learn more.

"Indeed, they were bodies devoid of life; they had no soul, or at least a soul they could claim as their own. My concern now is what had the Sorcerer promised them for their allegiance? Obviously, whatever Eldred Firestaff offered was far more precious than eternal life or wealth for the Dark Lord's emissaries to turn against their master and face unspeakable retribution for their actions."

"I suppose the answer shall be revealed to us in due time," answered Valtar.

"Let us hope the answer is revealed before it is too late," responded Markus.

Valtar sat up straight and tall against the high back of his gilded chair. It was then he noticed an Elf maiden peering out from behind a large wooden pillar, quietly watching him. The dark Elf smiled at her, whereby the young maiden answered back with a shy smile of her own before withdrawing into the shadows.

Valtar was immediately drawn to her bright, blue eyes and her hair of spun-gold, cascading down well past her shoulders. Her pale skin, like carefully crafted porcelain was absolutely flawless. He had never seen a fair Elf maiden until he had set foot in Wyndwood and this one was a vision of fragile beauty. It was as though an exquisite creature of Elven lore had come to life.

"Who is she?" asked the dark Elf.

Markus glanced over his shoulder in time to see the Elf maiden retreat into the vestibule. "I believe she is Mar-ra, daughter of Tor-rin Greenshield, an elder. Why do you ask?"

"No reason, my lord. I was just curious."

Markus smiled at Valtar, noticing his eyes following her as she silently withdrew from their presence. "Would you care for an introduction?"

"Pardon me?"

"Would you care to meet her?"

"I think not, my lord. I am hardly suitable to meet a woman of such elegant beauty and refined breeding."

"Because you were not born into a high house or because you are not a *fair* Elf"

"Both," he simply stated, his brown eyes dropping away from the prince's gaze.

"In all honesty, Valtar, I hardly believe it matters in this day and age. Besides, do not all Elves who enter the Twilight go to the same haven? Or are the fair and dark Elves segregated there too?"

"That is an interesting point," answered Valtar as he reflected on Markus' words. No Elf has ever returned to this realm after entering the Twilight so there was really no sure way of knowing.

"I would like to believe your people, reputed to be one of the oldest and wisest races in Imago, have the good sense to live together in peace and harmony, if not in this world, at least in the Twilight."

"Let us hope," answered Valtar, rising up from the table to follow Markus.

Thanking their hostesses for the meal and the gracious hospitality; both men left the dining hall. Valtar glanced back to see the Elf maidens standing at the archway as they parted. The women smiled shyly, waving at the men as they made their way down the boardwalk. He noticed Mar-ra quietly watching their departure, retreating into the shadows as he smiled back at the ladies.

For Valtar, it was an odd experience to be admired by so many lovely Elf maidens. In Orien, the very few female Elves that did not retreat into the Twilight were already spoken for, so for this dark Elf, it was slightly unnerving to be surrounded by so many beautiful, young women. He supposed the abundance of eligible females had much to do with the fact that many of the men were either killed in battle, had retreated to the Twilight when severely injured, or had simply departed for this haven, having tired of the strife and turmoil in this realm. As he gazed at all the fair maidens that followed and watched him from a distance, Wyndwood's allure was gaining in appeal by leaps and bounds. His friends would undoubtedly appreciate the *scenery* in this enchanted forest.

Markus led Valtar to a footpath that gently meandered down, almost to the water's edge. This trail circled around the shores of the Lake in the Woods. The afternoon sun shone down on the placid water, its golden light dancing and shimmering like diamonds carried upon the ripples created by a gentle breeze.

Valtar drew in a deep breath, savoring the fresh scent of the forest after the rains. His brown eyes quickly grew accustomed to the dappled sunlight filtering through the tree canopy. They scanned the lush stands of large, graceful willow trees, its long, supple branches hanging down, swaying in the breeze. As far as the dark Elf could see, willow trees fringed the shores of the lake. He felt as though he had been here before but alas, he knew it was only in his dreams that he visited this fabled land.

"I find much comfort in the tranquil forests of Wyndwood," confided Markus, raising his hands to shield his eyes from the sun's glare off the emerald-green waters.

"Do you come to Wyndwood often?"

"Not often enough, my friend. This is where Arerys and I begin and end most of our adventures in western Imago; in many ways it feels like a second home," answered Markus. It then dawned on him that perhaps this was the last adventure they would share if the elders could not save Arerys. His heart began to sink with despair.

"What is bothering you, my lord? You look troubled."

"I feel a need to be by Arerys' side," said Markus.

"I understand," Valtar nodded.

"If you wish to remain here, you are free to do so."

"No, I shall return to the sanctuary with you. Besides, King Kal-
lel should be arriving soon if their travel was unimpeded."

"Very well," responded Markus.

As Markus and Valtar stepped into the sanctuary, the afternoon sun
streamed in through the high windows to fill the great room with light.
On the altar, nine candles continued to burn, being replaced as needed.
The tenth candle, the one measuring out Arerys' existence in this
realm, continued to burn, now almost to the halfway mark. Tor-rin,
Sol-lel and Ansat continued with their vigil, rotating every three hours
to continue a non-stop prayer session. Next to Arerys' side sat Lindras;
his head bowed low, his eyes closed as he leaned wearily against his
staff.

"Lindras," whispered Markus.

The Wizard slowly opened his eyes; he smiled upon seeing the
prince's face.

"Has there been any change to Arerys? Does he wake?" asked
Markus hopefully.

Lindras shook his head in disappointment. "He remains
unchanged. He has not even stirred from this sleep."

"Lindras, why do you not take a reprieve from this vigil? Show
Valtar around Aspenglow while I sit with Arerys."

"Very well, Markus. I can use some time to stretch my old, weary
legs," replied the Wizard. Although he was more than willing to
remain with Arerys, he could sense that Markus wished to be by his
friend's side.

Lindras took Valtar by his arm, leading the Elf back out of the
sanctuary towards the center courtyard.

Markus looked upon Arerys' ashen face; it troubled his heart to no
end knowing that he had not even stirred, lying in this state for over
twenty-four hours now. He glanced up at the glowing candle, its very
flame representing Arerys' life. The molten wax reluctantly trickled
down, gathering in a shapeless mass that solidified at the base of the
large candleholder.

He sat himself down in the chair by the Elf's side, taking his
friend's hand into his. Markus was startled by the coldness of Arerys'
touch; it was as though death had already made claim to his body. He
clasped the Elf's hand into his, praying for his recovery.

When he felt the light pressure of a hand gently resting upon his
shoulder, Markus opened his eyes. He glanced up and to his surprise it

was Kal-lel. Artel approached the bed, searching Markus' face for some sign of hope. The prince was silent. He averted his eyes, unable to bear the Elf's sadness. Artel dropped to his knees next to his brother's side. Overcome with grief, he began to weep for Arerys.

Though Kal-lel shed no tears, his sorrow was just as great. He gently stroked his son's golden hair, and then placed a kiss upon his forehead. Markus could see the king's overwhelming grief reflected in his eyes; and it was at this moment he realized Kal-lel intended to release Arerys' soul into the Twilight.

CHAPTER 6

BETWEEN HEAVEN AND HELL

As the sun quietly slipped behind the Iron Mountains, another day was coming to an end. Nayla had slept little since her frightening premonition. Although a full day had elapsed since she was overcome by this terrible feeling that something tragic, a terrible accident had laid claim to Arerys, she was still unable to shake the raw emotion. The intense feelings she experienced upon seeing this horrible vision still overwhelmed her. It was as though a fist had tightened around her heart, refusing to release its stranglehold. The physical pain from her injured head and damaged ribcage now paled in comparison to the pain she carried in her heart.

Joval could empathize with Nayla. He knew exactly what she was suffering through, for it was the same turbulent feelings of fear and anxiety they both endured when either was in dire trouble. It felt like a knife piercing through one's heart. He could sense the pain and fear Nayla experienced now, just as she could sense it when he was in trouble. She now shared this connection, this invisible bond with Arerys. And he was forced to accept this.

Joval and Lando tried in vain to comfort Nayla by attempting to convince her that the trauma to her head was the cause of her nightmarish vision. To their disappointment, their words fell on deaf ears as she continued to dwell on the haunting image that now tortured her mind.

As the warriors set up camp in preparation for the coming of the night, Nayla wandered off for a moment of solitude, to clear the muddled, worrisome thoughts of her troubled mind. She came upon a small clearing where she sat beneath the starry canopy of a moonless sky. With her back straight and her legs crossed, Nayla's fingers wove into the configuration used to summon the energy of the earth. It was within this element she felt most centered: focused and calm. Her breathing cycle was a long, deep breath in through her nose, followed by a long, deep breath out through her mouth. With each cleansing breath, Nayla pictured herself sinking deeper into the earth, becoming one with natural energy. As her mind cleared, her soul wandered on another plane.

In her mind's eye, she strolled through an unfamiliar forest where willow and aspen trees grew in abundance. She followed a trail where she came across a beautiful, emerald-green lake. The placid surface was only broken by the ripples created by a zephyr wind. As Nayla continued along the trail skirting the lake's shore, her eyes caught a glimpse of a lone figure standing silently amongst a stand of elegant willow trees. She hastened her steps for a better look and to her surprise; it was Arerys. Nayla called out his name upon which he slowly turned in her direction. She dashed towards him and as she neared, she saw in his familiar blue eyes a sadness about them that seemed to cry out to her heart. She reached out to touch Arerys' outstretched hand, but as she did so, he faded like the mist.

"No! Arerys, please come back. Please! I beg of you. Do not leave me," pleaded Nayla, as she fell down upon her knees in despair. Her heart raced as her eyes searched about for signs of his presence. There was nothing. He was gone.

Nayla's eyes slowly opened as great tears rolled down her cheeks. She released a heavy sigh as she was faced with the knowledge that Arerys was gone. Her heart was numb. For a moment, she felt, saw and heard nothing. There was only an overwhelming sense of emptiness, an absolute void.

"Nayla?"

Her eyes slowly came into focus as she heard Joval call her name. He knelt before her, his hand touching her face as his thumb wiped away her tears. As he gently lifted her chin, their eyes met. He could see into her soul and feel the very depth of her sorrow. Nayla threw her arms about Joval's neck. He held her close as she wept. He could feel her heart breaking as he wrapped his arms about her small, trembling body as she sobbed.

"He is gone, Joval. Arerys is gone," she whispered, her voice breaking under the weight of her despair.

"You do not know that, Nayla. For once you could be wrong."

"You know I have never been wrong about this feeling, Joval."

"As I said before Nayla, you must believe Arerys is fine. Do not be so quick to believe in the worst. At the very least, wait until the estimated date of his arrival in Nagana."

"But I can feel—"

"What you feel and what you know are two separate things at this moment. You received a great blow to your head; your judgment is obviously impaired."

"Then why does it feel so real? So final?" she sobbed.

Joval gazed into her deep brown eyes and gave her a reassuring smile. "I do recall that Arerys stated only death itself shall prevent him from returning to you. I believe he is a man of his word, give him this opportunity to prove you wrong, Nayla."

She slowly nodded her head in agreement; indeed, this was one time she desperately wanted to be proven wrong. Joval stood up, raising the warrior maiden to her feet.

"Rest assured, Nayla, Arerys shall return to you, perhaps even sooner than you believe," said Joval, his hands resting on her trembling shoulders. "I have no doubt, and neither should you."

Nayla gazed up into the Elf's lucid, blue eyes. She could sense he spoke with utter sincerity. She sighed wearily, "You are right, Joval. My imagination does get the best of me at times. Perhaps, I have taken one too many blows to my head in my lifetime."

Joval smiled down upon her and with a gentle laugh, he teased her. "Yes, little warrior, one can never tell what has rattled loose in that head of yours!" Together, they headed back to camp.

As darkness embraced the land, beneath a star-studded sky the warriors of Orien settled down for another night. Joval stationed a number of men along the perimeter of their camp for rotating sentry duty until the coming of dawn. Although there had been no sign of danger and the Sorcerer had yet to show his face, the feeling that some unseen threat followed them weighed heavily upon Joval. Nayla seemed to have forgotten what lured her dangerously close to the ledge at Deception Pass, but the dark Elf recalled feeling an evil presence carried in the thin mountain air just prior to Nayla's fall.

Joval's far-seeing eyes penetrated the dark landscape, piercing through the shadowy forms of the trees, searching for any telltale signs of the Sorcerer or his henchmen. All was quiet. As he approached Nayla's tent, he could hear her voice and that of Lando's.

"Nayla, it is I, Joval. May I enter?"

"Of course, you are welcome to join us," she called out in response.

In the soft glow of a candle, Lando sat across from Nayla as they conversed. He offered his folding stool to Joval, making himself comfortable on the bedroll next to the warrior maiden.

"Care for some wine, Joval?" asked Nayla, passing a flask over to him.

"What is the occasion?"

"Lando decided I needed some cheering up," she said with a smile. The Elf smiled back at her, taking a swig from the flask before handing it off to Lando.

"Is it working?" Joval asked with raised eyebrows.

"Not, really. My senses are about as sharp as a rusted spoon. I am sure I shall pay dearly for this in the morning," she answered with a laugh.

Lando took another sip from the flask. "Now where were we?"

"You were telling me about Arerys... Wyndwood... Remember?"

"Oh yes! Upon arriving in Wyndwood, King Kal-lel hosted a great banquet. All around us were beautiful Elf maidens. They were slender and tall, with flowing golden tresses and gentle blue eyes. Exquisite creatures they were."

Nayla's eyes gazed down upon her war-weary threads and her dark leather boots. She became painfully aware of her dark features and her stature, or lack thereof. Lando stopped speaking when he realized that his words hit a nerve with the little warrior maiden.

Her dark, soulful eyes stared up at Lando. For a moment he was not sure if Nayla was going to cry. Her eyes seemed liquid in the candle's light.

"What a pity! To be cursed with such beauty," she said with a plaintive sigh. "Thank goodness, I shall never know this problem."

Joval and Lando looked at each other, not knowing how to respond to her comment. They squirmed nervously until Nayla finally winked as she gave them an impish smile. With a lighthearted laugh, Nayla exclaimed, "Sorry! I was so rude to interrupt, Lando. Proceed."

"Yes, well... After we had finished our meal and were settling down for the night, once again the men spoke of the Elf maidens of Wyndwood. Faria had recalled King Kal-lel's comment that Arerys had not yet picked a maiden to be his intended. It was Artel, Arerys' brother, who made mention of the fact that Arerys was being difficult; that he was still looking for a woman full of spit and fire, one who would gladly exchange the safety of the forests of Wyndwood to share in adventures in lands far and away. He desired a woman who was beautiful like a flower yet as tough as thorns: a wild rose of sorts, I suppose."

"Hmm, I have always fancied myself to a thistle, never a rose," smiled Nayla wryly, contemplating Lando's words.

"Well, Arerys' choice of a mate was met with a degree of ridicule, especially from Faria," continued Lando.

"Somehow, it does not surprise me," responded Nayla. "Bless his soul."

Lando recalled with a laugh, "In fact, if I remember correctly, Faria said to Arerys that such a woman only exists in one's dream and if she did indeed appear, the dream would soon turn into a nightmare!"

Joval glanced over at Nayla. He suddenly burst out laughing so hard he fell off his stool onto the ground. The Elf's response caught her by surprise for Joval was normally very reserved, his emotions well under his control. "Your friend was accurate, Lando. Nayla can be quite the nightmare to deal with indeed. I hope Arerys is a glutton for punishment!"

Nayla glared at the Elf as he writhed about in laughter. Even for her, she was astonished as he was normally very composed, rarely displaying any type of emotional outbursts of this nature.

"Joval, your conduct is unbecoming of an Elf!" said the warrior maiden in reprisal. She abruptly rose up and before he knew it, she seized him by his left ear, unceremoniously hauling him back up onto his stool.

"Oww! Nayla, that was uncalled for!" growled Joval, rubbing the point of his Elven ear.

"It is nice to see that my closest friend can have such fun at my expense," she retorted, her eyes giving him a cool stare.

"I am sorry, Nayla. However, I believe I can attest to the fact that life with you can place any man somewhere between heaven and hell on any given day," said Joval with a chuckle. "I pray that Arerys knows what he has gotten himself into, Lando. Let us hope he can stand up to this little warrior."

Had she been a child, this would have been the most opportune moment to stick her tongue out at Joval. As tempted as she was, she refrained from using such childish tactics; it was not becoming or appropriate for the captain of an army, no matter how inebriated he or she may be.

"May I finish my story?" inquired Lando, passing the flask of wine back to Joval.

"Of course, Lando. I apologize for Joval's rudeness."

"My rudeness?" asked Joval, almost spewing a mouthful of wine in Nayla's direction.

"Just ignore him," ordered Nayla, dismissing the Elf by waving a hand in Joval's direction. "Continue, Lando."

"Even though Arerys had initial reservations about you, once he came to know you, he fell in love," said Lando.

Nayla blushed upon hearing his words. Although she was not statuesque or fair as the Elf maidens of Wyndwood, it was still *she* that Arerys chose above all others to be his intended.

"I believe I was the first person to whom Arerys disclosed his true feelings to. I know he was very reluctant to say anything to you for he thought your interests were in Darius, but I encouraged him to confess his feelings of love to you rather than speculate where your heart lay."

"I am grateful you spoke to him, Lando. I can only pray that he still feels as strongly as I do. I hope our love is strong enough to see him back to me."

"Fear not, Nayla. Arerys had waited all his life for a woman like you. He shall come," replied Lando, placing the cork seal back onto the flask. "And on this note, I shall take my leave."

The knight bade Nayla and Joval a good evening before parting from their company to find some sleep. As Joval too exited Nayla's tent, she asked, "Am I truly the nightmare you claim that I am, Joval?"

The dark Elf looked down into her eyes and smiled kindly at her. "You know I am only teasing, Nayla. I myself find your brash, wilful demeanor charming in its own way."

Nayla gazed up at Joval, uncertain of this backhanded compliment.

"You know I am careful of whom I call a friend. I am like you, Nayla, I choose my friends carefully and they are only welcome into my circle for good reason."

Although Joval had a quick wit and a sharp tongue, Nayla also knew he was a man of great integrity and honesty. She smiled upon hearing his words.

He gently kissed her upon her forehead, whispering, "Good night my dear friend." With those words said, he disappeared into the darkness.

As the last star withdrew its light from the early morning sky, Nayla and her army prepared to continue on their march eastward to Nagana. Joval determined that if they continued at this steady pace, they should reach their destination in another thirty-two days, thirty-five days at the very most. Although she was in no particular hurry to return, she knew that the men were eager to rebuild their lives and homes after the war. For Nayla, there was nothing that awaited her in Nagana, other than the opportunity to show her face to Dahlon Treeborn. *He shall certainly be surprised that I had lived through another mission,* she thought in amusement.

The journey east was marked by the gradual disappearance of the large fir and spruce trees that hugged the lower slopes of the Iron Mountains. In its place grew dense bamboo forests and ancient deciduous trees with small grayish-green, fan-shaped leaves. Lando marveled at the unusual vegetation, particularly the bamboo with its hollow, jointed stalks.

Traveling through the countryside, the ravages of war were apparent along the hills of Saijun. Nayla looked at the ghostly reminders of the homes and farms that were burnt to the ground by the soldiers of the Dark Army. They looked like terrible black scars blemishing the lush, green hillside. As villagers rushed down to greet the returning warriors, she took some comfort in seeing that many of the villagers managed to elude the enemy. They waved down at her army with great elation as she and her men marched on. The Taijins, the mortals of this land, were as resilient as the seasons. Just as the forces of evil could not halt the coming of the spring, the people too returned to reclaim their land and rebuild their homes.

Three young children rushed down to the roadside to greet the returning heroes. Nayla smiled down at their innocent faces smudged with soot from helping the men and women clean up the evidence of war. They stared with wide-eyed fascination at this female warrior. She was a small, yet imposing figure amongst all the larger mortals and towering Elves. She dismounted from her steed, passing her reins onto Lando. "Keep the men moving," she instructed him.

As Lando coaxed his steed to move forward to catch up with Joval's stallion, he glanced back. He watched as Nayla knelt down so she could be eye-level with the smallest child. He was moved to see this seasoned warrior delighting in the company of children. Hidden somewhere behind her deadly weaponry and her raiment of war there was still much compassion and humanity. This was obviously a side of Nayla's personality that both Arerys and Joval knew existed. She spoke in the language of the mortals, speaking to the children in a gentle tone. Her grasp of Taijina was impeccable, better than her understanding of Elvish. Reaching into the pouch that was slung over her shoulder, she distributed her Elven bread amongst the children. They eagerly accepted her offering, smiling broadly in gratitude.

Revitalized by her brief encounter with the children, Nayla's spirit was lifted, her soul felt energized again. As she watched her men march by, she shouted orders for the warriors to pick up their pace. She charged ahead to the front of the line and proceeded to run. The warriors fell in time, following their captain.

"Nayla, get on your horse," ordered Joval, as his steed trotted along next to her as she moved with grim determination.

"Not now, Joval."

"What about your injury?"

"My body shall tell me when to stop."

Like a long-distance runner setting her stride, Nayla continued at a steady pace for almost two leagues. As the sun burned high in the sky, she finally came to a stop. Instructing the men to fall out of line, they would drink, eat and rest for an hour before proceeding on until nightfall.

As her men dispersed, Nayla collapsed onto the ground, her arms wrapped around her aching ribs as she drew in long, deep breaths. She closed her eyes as she listened to the pounding of her heart and felt the intense glow of the sun warming her face.

Her eyes opened as a great shadow loomed over her, blocking out the sun's rays. It was Joval, next to him stood Lando. Both men greeted her with a severe look of consternation.

"What?" asked Nayla, her chest still heaving after her run.

"Why do you do this to yourself, Nayla?" asked Joval, frowning in disapproval at the warrior maiden.

Nayla slowly sat up, her injury still giving her grief.

"You are obviously still in pain," noted Lando, kneeling by her side.

Nayla smiled at the men. "If I were dead, I would feel no pain at all. That is the one good thing about pain, gentlemen, it lets you know that you are still alive. And right now, I am feeling very much alive." She flopped back onto the ground, clutching her side.

Lando stood up to fetch a flask of water for her. Joval sat by her side, shaking his head in dismay. "Nayla, you know you have nothing to prove to these men."

"I know, Joval. I felt a need to run, to feel my muscles burn... to feel my heart pound. I just wanted to stop thinking for awhile."

The Elf knew that Nayla wanted to totally immerse herself in a physical task. Running in her condition would require a great deal of concentration to block out the pain. He knew it was to give her worried mind a reprieve from thinking about Arerys.

"Besides, we are taking a little detour. I feel a need to see how my brothers have faired during our absence," said Nayla, between deep breaths.

"Still, Nayla, there is a reason why you have a horse," responded the Elf.

"Yes, Joval. I shall keep that in mind."

Nayla was always in a habit of dismounting and running with her men whenever she gave the orders to pick up their pace. She knew the Elven warriors seemed inexhaustible, capable of running tirelessly much longer and farther than the Taijin warriors. To her, in all fairness, how could she accurately gauge the condition of the mortal warriors; how quickly they were tiring, if she rode while they were made to run by their Elven brethens? She also learned early on that the men respected her more when she went out of her way to be one of them.

For three more days Nayla and the warriors moved at a relentless pace over hills and through valleys. As often as she could, she would march along with her men, but she found herself tiring sooner. Her decreasing stamina was evident as the warriors' pace slowed as they kept in time with their captain. By day's end, Nayla's legs felt as heavy as lead and she found herself sleeping for more than her usual five hours. She was quick to blame this need for sleep to the fact that her worrisome dreams of Arerys drained her body and soul each night.

As dusk settled quietly upon the land; the large orange sun retreated behind the Iron Mountains. The last of its waning light cast long shadows across the primeval landscape, bathing all it touched in a surreal, golden hue.

Following the sounds of a distant waterfall, Nayla led the men through a thick grove of bamboo. As they emerged from the forest, before them loomed a massive wall of stone. From atop of this cliff, water gushed downwards. The water rushed around a large rock formation that projected from the top center of the waterfall. Like a huge serpent rising out of its midst, this massive boulder of granite, carved and shaped by the forces of the turbulent waters, now protruded like an upturned head of a great dragon. It created two distinct waterfalls that became one as the water poured into a clear, deep pool. The icy waters splashed and boiled into this deep pocket, its inviting sounds beckoned Nayla like the sounds of nature's laughter.

As they stood at the edge of the pool, she pointed across to another towering grove of bamboo. "Here lies Reyu Falls. Beyond this waterfall is Anshen, my childhood home. We shall spend the night with my brothers," the warrior maiden shouted above the noise of the thundering waters.

"Must the men wade through this river? Or is there a bridge we may cross?" asked Lando, observing the wide, turbulent body of water that spilled over from the pool. Even the knight could see the water that churned and tumbled before them was deceptively deep and treacherous.

Nayla smiled at Lando. "Dismount and follow me," she said.

The warriors quickly fell into a single line, trailing behind her. She escorted Lando to the edge of the waterfall. Staying close to the cliff wall, she led her horse along a narrow path behind the sheer curtain of water. As Lando, Joval and the warriors followed the warrior maiden, the knight's eyes peered through the translucent veil that echoed and thundered as it cascaded into the pool, its sounds reverberating off the granite wall. He felt the coolness of the mist rising about them, the tiny droplets clinging to his skin and clothing. He felt his soul re-energized by the refreshing vapor as the mist swirled and enveloped all. The resonating splash of water as it tumbled into the pool stirred his soul.

As they stepped out from behind the waterfall and through the tall stands of bamboo, Lando's eyes opened wide in surprise. Before him lay a breathtaking landscape of forests and fields that surrounded a crystal blue lake. Just beyond in the distance, a backdrop of mountains, its peaks shrouded in a thin blanket of mist, sheltered this pristine haven. This northern most range of the Furai Mountains was a physical barrier that protected those living in western Orien from the incursions of the regent's armies. It was in these mountains that the mysterious Kagai Warriors built their fearsome reputation, protecting the religious centers that sprang up after many fled persecution from the governing body of Orien to the east.

Nayla looked upon Lando's surprised face. "It is as though a small peace of heaven had fallen to earth. Is it not?"

"Why, it is like a dream, as beautiful as some of the places in Cedona," gasped Lando, his eyes drinking in the sights of the land's abundant greenery and the sapphire blue waters of the serene lake.

"Listen," said Nayla, her hand cupping her ear.

"It is the call of the nightingale," responded Lando, his eyes scanning the forests for signs of the bird.

Nayla whistled softly in response, and then she listened again.

From across the lake, a gentle call answered hers.

"Let us be on our way," said Nayla, leading her horse to a near-invisible trail winding around to the other side of Lake Anzan. "They await our arrival."

As they forged on into the forest, subtle movements in the shadows caught Lando's attention, but each time he turned his head to observe, there was nothing to see but growing darkness.

"They are watching you," said Nayla. "There is no need for concern."

As they neared the small village, from out of the forest, a dozen or more warriors silently emerged. Dressed in garments of dark gray and charcoal, they were not unlike the mortal warriors in Nayla's battalion.

Nayla dropped down on her left knee and bowed her head in respect as an elderly man approached her. He eagerly hobbled forward towards the warrior maiden. As he came to a stop, the man leaned heavily on his staff. Speaking in Taijina, he addressed Nayla, calling her by the name given to her by her mother.

"Ah, Takaro! I am pleased you have returned. The world as we know it, still exists. Obviously, you have accomplished what you had set out to do."

"Yes, master. We journey on to Nagana, but I had to come by this way to see that you and my brothers were safe."

The old warrior priest smiled kindly at her, and then shook his head in disgust as he recalled the confrontations with the soldiers of the Dark Army. "The mortals that breached the Iron Mountains were a shameful excuse for an army! I do not believe I have ever witnessed a more undisciplined, unskilled show of force in my lifetime. If the battalions were led by captains, their presence was never really felt."

Nayla smiled at the elderly warrior. "Let us just say that the Dark Lord was preoccupied and unable to lead his followers into battle."

"Well, what they lacked in skill, they certainly made up for in sheer numbers. It became quickly obvious to all that these soldiers were seeking out your father's people. Word had spread quickly that the Elves had moved on to secure the fortress city of Nagana, the Dark Army followed in pursuit."

"The city still stands. Yes?"

He nodded his head in response. "The loss was great, but yes, Nagana stands."

Nayla rose up before the elderly warrior as Joval approached, bowing before him. The warrior reciprocated with a bow, pleased to see the Elf once again.

"Master Hunta Saibon, this is Sir Lando Bayliss. He serves a king from a country far to the west," said Joval, making the introduction in Taijina.

Upon hearing his name spoken of, the knight stepped forward and bowed before the ancient warrior.

"Welcome, sir," greeted Saibon, acknowledging his presence with a bow.

Lando was surprised that he was greeted in the common tongue. "Thank you," responded the knight, bowing again. "You know the common speech."

"Why yes, most of us do, just as we know Elvish. After all, just because we differ in appearance and speak in the language of our ancestors of Taija, it does not mean that we do not know or speak other languages," smiled the old warrior priest.

Nayla explained to Lando that the Elves had as much difficulty in mastering Taijina, as the mortals of Orien – the Taijins, had in speaking Elvish. The common speech used by the mortals in western Imago was an easier language to learn and master, and was now implemented as the common language used between most of the Elves and mortals in western Orien.

Master Saibon welcomed the warriors to set up camp for the night in a large field by the lake. He waved Nayla, Joval and Lando on to follow him to his home.

The Kagai Warrior priests of the Furai Mountains had little in the way of personal wealth; materialism was frowned upon. What little food and drink they had on hand, it was customary for them to share with their friends and guests before they partook themselves. In a small, barren room with only cushions to sit upon, they shared a simple meal. Saibon shared tales of the Kagai Warriors' bid to protect the surrounding villages from the attacks by the soldiers of the Dark Army. Although the Kagai Warriors were few in numbers, their method of fighting and their habit of attacking the enemy camp under the cover of night made them a fearsome, and in the eyes of their foes, a *supernatural* force to contend with.

Nayla shared tales of her adventures west of the Iron Mountains. She spoke mostly of her friends, the men of the Order, those she had found and lost during their bid to do away with the Dark Lord. When she was done, Joval shared his account of their battle on Mount Hope, of meeting with the kings of the Alliance, their journey home and of Nayla's accident at Deception Pass. He related to the warrior priest how she was almost lost when she tumbled down the mountain.

Saibon shook his head with concern. "Do not believe for a minute this was an unfortunate accident, Joval. You do not have to be reminded of how much the Regent of Orien despises Takaro. No doubt he conspires with the Sorcerer even as we speak. Has there been any other sign of that vile scoundrel?"

"No," responded Joval. "The lands have been quiet since that incident. The Sorcerer has yet to resurface."

After a moment of silence, Lando spoke up. "Forgive my ignorance, Master Saibon, why do you address Nayla as Takaro? Is its meaning significant?"

"It is the name my mother called me by," answered Nayla.

"In the language of my people, Takaro means *Noble Child*," added the elderly warrior, with a wry smile and a sparkle in his dark brown eyes. "However, *Stubborn Child* would be more appropriate at times. Nayla's willfulness often overshadows her ability to behave in a noble manner."

Lando laughed at Saibon's insight, after all, aside from Joval, this elderly warrior probably knew her better than anyone else.

"The hour grows late, master," said Nayla with a sigh. Her tired, aching body shifted restlessly upon her cushion. "I am in need of rest."

He could sense her pain; her eyes were dull as though the fire had been extinguished from them. "I have the medicine for what ails you, little warrior," he offered, standing up to brew a special cup of tea for his long-awaited guest.

"Well, I shall allow the two of you the opportunity to speak in private," offered Joval, rising up from the wooden floor. "I shall take my leave now."

Lando stood up to follow Joval, thanking Saibon for his kindness and hospitality. The warrior priest bade them both a good night as he carefully poured the hot tea into an earthenware bowl before passing it over to Nayla.

She nodded her thanks as she accepted the medicine. Swallowing the bland concoction, she quietly sipped the steaming brew. Saibon could sense that the medicine had little effect on what truly pained her.

He looked upon the warrior maiden with concern. "What troubles you, Takaro. And do not lie to me. You have lived long amongst my people, I know you too well. I know something consumes your thoughts and troubles your heart."

Nayla gazed at Saibon's twinkling dark eyes that were set into his deeply lined and weathered face. She thought upon his wisdom and the irony of the fact that although she was more than three times his age, he still possessed greater wisdom, worldly knowledge and infinitely more patience than she. Even in his advanced years, this eighty-two-year-old priest was a formidable warrior, still sharing his knowledge of the warrior arts with much younger disciples. Nayla reminisced how Hunta Saibon was so much like his father, grandfather, and great grandfather, all of whom Nayla had outlived.

Perhaps kindness, patience and wisdom are all qualities this mortal was born with, handed down from father to son, she thought, finding great comfort in his presence.

"Takaro, you know you can speak openly to me," encouraged Saibon, topping up her bowl.

Gazing into her eyes, he could see by the incipient tears that what ailed her could not be cured by his medicines. He could almost feel her heart shattering into a hundred pieces as she sat before him in silence.

Saibon smiled kindly at Nayla. "So, what is his name?"

As a single teardrop slowly trickled down her cheek, Nayla whispered, "Arerys, his name is Arerys Wingfield."

The warrior priest observed Nayla's little fingers subconsciously fondling a circlet of silver adorning the third finger of her left hand. "He pledged his love to you, did he not?"

Nayla nodded.

"Then what can be the problem, Takaro?"

"I am afraid he has met with a terrible fate, master. I saw him, I felt his despair… his pain."

"Takaro, I admit that you are far more sensitive to these feelings; premonitions if you will, than any mortal or Elf I know, but do not lose hope. Keep in mind that when your mother died, she appeared before you in her death to offer you comfort. That is how strong her love for you was; she found a way to reach you. You did not dream her, she came to you, as real as I sit before you now. I can sense your love for this fellow is strong, he too would find a way to reach out to you in the same manner if indeed he had met an untimely end."

Nayla absorbed his words, consoled by his wisdom.

Saibon closed his eyes. Although he could not foresee the future, he could feel the bond between Nayla and Arerys had not been broken. Though strained by distance, there was still a connection. "You must hold out for hope, my dear. Perhaps, he has fallen upon difficult times and what you saw and felt was his own despair in being separated from you."

"You are right, master," sighed Nayla. "I do not know why I worry as much as I do."

"Mothers tend to do that," said Saibon, a generous smile creasing his face.

"What would I know about being a mother," replied Nayla, casually brushing off his comment.

"You shall know soon enough."

Nayla frowned, unable to comprehend his words.

"Goodness, Takaro! Are you so busy battling the world that you ignore what your own body tells you? I thought I taught you better than that."

"My body tells me plenty," groaned Nayla. "It tells me that I am getting older, that I become more weary with each passing day. Soon I shall be too old to don weapons and armor to ride into battle."

"Takaro, that is not age wearing you down," he looked into her eyes. "You are with child."

"I beg your pardon," she gasped in an incredulous tone.

Saibon merely smiled at her.

Nayla was momentarily stunned by his words. "How could that be?"

"Well, if you do not know how this could have happened, then perhaps it was an act of divinity," said the warrior priest as he laughed, but not unkindly. "Otherwise, you would conceive like any other woman, mortal or Elf."

The warrior maiden studied Saibon's face, searching for signs that he may be teasing her. When his expression remained unchanged, her hand slowly passed down to her belly. She did not feel any different, just more lethargic than usual these past few days, but Nayla had accounted this to her injured head and body, and a mind plagued with worry.

"But master, how do you know this to be true?" asked Nayla.

"My dear, in my long life I have been around enough women to recognize the signs. You glow with life even though you feel drained at times. I can see it. I can sense this new life within you, its energy is strong."

"You can also be mistaken, old man," replied Nayla, with growing skepticism.

"Takaro, had you only taken the time to meditate, to purge yourself of all your worries and woes long enough to find your center again. You would have noticed all the telltale signs of impending motherhood."

"Master, I admit my mind has been burdened of late, but this?"

"Tell me, Takaro, do you still regard Joval as a trusted friend?"

"Of course."

"Remain here, I shall return," ordered Saibon, ambling out of the room, staff in hand.

He returned a short time later with Joval by his side. The dark Elf looked upon Nayla with concern for he knew she was prone to the same ailments that befell mortal man. "Are you ill, Nayla?"

"I think not," she replied.

"Nayla, rest here; lie on this mat," instructed Saibon.

"Why, master?"

"Do as I say, lay yourself down." His voice was growing impatient.

Nayla knew better than to question him further, she complied with his order.

"Close your eyes and relax. Breathe in slowly... calm your heart."

Nayla did as she was told; she focused on her breathing, regulating her heartbeat so it was slow and steady.

"Joval, place your ear here," Saibon pointed to the center of Nayla's chest. "Tell me what you hear."

Joval leaned over to listen. "I hear the beating of her heart. The air rushing through her lungs as she breathes..."

"Now, place your ear here," instructed Saibon, his hand pointed to her belly.

Joval did not question him. He promptly knelt down close and listened, even though he did not know what he was to be listening for.

Nayla glanced down to look upon Joval's face. His eyes were closed as he concentrated, listening intently. Suddenly, his blue eyes flashed open, he raised his head as he stared back at her.

"What is it, Joval?"

He did not answer, motioning her for silence. He moved up to listen to her heart again. It was beating a little faster, brought on by the anxiety of Joval's reaction, but the pounding of her heart was loud, beating at a steady pace. Joval moved back down to her belly and listened once again.

The race of Elves is blessed not only with eyes as sharp as those of a hawk, they also possess acute hearing. So sensitive it is; Elves could often hear danger approach long before it becomes visible. Joval's keen sense of hearing detected a faint, but distinct pulse: a tiny heart beating rapidly, deep inside her.

Joval knelt before Nayla, offering his hand to pull her up into a sitting position again.

"What is it?"

His eyes were wide with astonishment. "Nayla, you are with child."

"That is not possible, and even if it were true, you would not be able to hear anything. It is too soon!" responded the warrior maiden, her face blanched upon hearing his words.

"I can hear its heart beating within you," insisted the dark Elf.

"Is the child's father an Elf?" asked Saibon.

"Yes," she answered.

"You are half Elf yourself, Takaro. The child you carry is more Elf than mortal. It would stand to reason it shall grow much faster than if it were a mortal. In terms of my people, the child you have conceived is in its seventh, perhaps, eighth week in your womb. It shall only be after its third month, its development shall slow considerably if it follows the traits of an Elf," explained the warrior priest.

"Master Saibon is right, Nayla, but perhaps you shall not have to endure this condition for as long an Elf-woman does," said Joval. "After all, if I remember correctly, Lady Kareda carried you for merely twelve moons before giving birth."

Nayla's eyes were clouded with worry as she looked to Joval. She did not know whether she should laugh or cry upon his confirmation of this news. Although she felt great joy she now carried a part of Arerys within her, she was still without the man she loved, and now she feared that they might never be reunited. Her heart was torn. It was as though her life was now suspended somewhere between heaven and hell.

As though she was trying to protect the life she now carried inside, her arms wrapped around her small body. Her eyes were dark and liquid, fighting back her tears. "What if Arerys does not come? What if he is dead?" she asked, her soft voice breaking.

"Perish the thought, Nayla. We shall concern ourselves with this matter when the facts present itself, let us not hasten to believe in the worst," stated Joval. "For now, Lando and I shall both keep watch over you to ensure you do not engage in any asinine behavior or activities that shall only serve to jeopardize yourself and the child."

"Joval, do not tell Lando, not yet," pleaded Nayla.

The dark Elf frowned at her. His response was terse and to the point: "Only if I have your word that you shall do as I say. Do you understand? No more running, no fighting, no sword play, and so on"

"This is blackmail, Joval. Do you intend to kill me with boredom?"

"No, maybe kindness, but I intend to keep you safe."

Saibon stared at Nayla with raised eyebrows. "Takaro, you are as stubborn as the first day Joval brought you here. Put some trust in your friend, he means well."

"Of course, master," sighed Nayla

Joval smiled down at her in triumph. She stared up at him in surrender.

Nayla peered into the Elf's eyes, "Are you happy for me, Joval?"

"Of course, Nayla. If this brings you joy, then of course I am pleased for you." He embraced her in a gentle hug, always mindful of her injured ribcage.

Nayla was comforted by his kindness.

"When Arerys returns to you, he shall be doubly blessed," declared Joval, attempting to lift her spirits.

"It is time for you to rest, Takaro," recommended Saibon. He opened a wooden chest and removed a Taijinan warming blanket, offering it to her. "You are more than welcome to spend the night here."

"Thank you, master," said Nayla, accepting the blanket. "I have been away from home far too long. It would be nice to stay for even one night."

Joval bade them both a good evening before heading back to his tent. His silent form quickly dissolved into the velvet darkness of the night. He turned to see Nayla's lone figure standing in the doorway, her eyes gazing into the ebony sky.

Under a dreary overcast sky, the army broke camp after eating their morning meal. Nayla joined her men as they fell into rank in preparation for their march. Joval brought her steed about as she said her good-byes to her warrior brothers. She knelt, bowing before Saibon. The old warrior took Nayla by her hand, lifting her up onto her feet.

"Stay safe, Takaro. Remember, you can no longer think only of yourself. Understand?"

"Yes, master."

The warrior priest embraced his adopted daughter in a warm, reassuring hug. "Remember, you are always welcome here. Do not be a stranger."

With Joval leading the way, Saibon waved farewell to Nayla and the men in her company. "May the spirits look favorably upon you, may they keep you safe!"

And heaven help the fool who shall ever do harm to your child, thought Saibon. He knew that Nayla, trained in the art of war by he and his forefathers, would prove to be a deadly force to contend with if she was provoked in this manner. As surely as a tigress would instinctively kill anything or anyone that would do harm to her offspring, Saibon knew this little warrior would be no exception. As Nayla led her battalion away from Anshen, he watched them disappear westward from his diminishing sight.

CHAPTER 7

BY THE CANDLE'S LIGHT

Markus gazed up at Kal-lel, removing himself from the chair so the king may take his place by his son. Though he said not a word, the sadness in his eyes alone spoke volumes. Artel clutched his brother's cold hand. His tears streamed endlessly down his face as he wept for Arerys.

Kal-lel glanced up at the tenth candle; it burned slowly, measuring out his son's life. In another twenty-four hours, perhaps less, the candle's wick would burn no more. The elders approached the king, bowing in respect before giving word of Arerys' condition.

"He has remained unchanged for almost two days, my lord," stated Ansat. "We may continue our prayer vigil, but thus far, our prayers go unanswered."

"We have done what we can," added Tor-rin. "His soul now hangs in the balance, lingering between this earthly realm and that of the Twilight."

"Has he given any sign that he may rouse from this sleep?" whispered Kal-lel, stroking his son's long, golden hair.

"No, my lord," answered Sol-lel in a solemn voice. "He is as he was when he was first brought here."

Kal-lel's heart sank and his proud, erect stature appeared to collapse from the burden of his grief as he released a heavy sigh. "I wish for some time alone with Arerys."

"Very well, my lord," said Ansat. He gently lifted Artel to his feet, escorting him out of the sanctuary. Tor-rin and Sol-lel followed behind him. Markus remained.

"My lord, before I take my leave, I must speak my mind. I beg of you, do not act rashly. Do not hasten to send Arerys to the haven, not yet. I believe if he was meant to die, he would have succumbed long ago. He clings to life, to this realm, for a reason," pleaded the prince.

"I shall consider your words carefully, Markus," Kal-lel assured him, rising to his feet so he may gaze upon his son's still form.

"Thank you, my lord," responded Markus, bowing as he exited the sanctuary.

Kal-lel looked upon his son's ashen face. He appeared to be nothing more than in a deep sleep, but he knew it was much more than that. This sleep was most unnatural and now, he feared that Arerys might lose his soul to the ghost world of this realm if he did not take it upon himself to deliver his son to the Twilight. At least in this haven, he shall be reunited with his mother and when his time came, Kal-lel too would transmigrate to this haven.

Slowly drawing back the blanket covering Arerys' body, he studied the scar, a dreadful reminder of the wound inflicted by the dark emissary's sword. The wound itself had healed sufficiently and if Arerys survives, given time, it will all but disappear. Based on the size and depth of the treacherous wound, it was apparent to Kal-lel his son had lost a great volume of blood. He watched as Arerys' chest rose and fell with each long, slow breath he drew.

Kal-lel knew there was nothing more he could do to hasten the healing process. Taking his place at the healing bed, he placed his hands on either side of Arerys' head. He began repeating a series of incantations in a bid to stir his son's lost soul back; back so he may wake from this sleep. For over an hour, Kal-lel administered the ancient rites in an effort to revive Arerys. All attempts failed.

Kal-lel knelt by his son, taking his cold hand into his. Seeing him so unresponsive, untouched by his Elven magic destroyed him. Finally, his tears fell when he realized that not even he, the King of Wyndwood, a high Elf endowed with great powers, could do nothing to save his own son.

"Father?"

Kal-lel glanced up, standing before him was Artel. Lindras, Markus and Valtar were by his side.

"Father, does Arerys wake?" asked Artel, his eyes became a deeper shade of blue as the depth of his despair grew upon seeing his brother still lying motionless.

"No, Artel. I have done all I can. It is time to let him go," responded Kal-lel with great sadness.

"Please, my lord, not yet. Arerys' candle still burns. At least allow him that: Another day, just one more day!" pleaded Markus.

"Markus is right, my lord," added the Wizard. "Can you not allow him the time as allotted by this candle? The candle still burns and shall do so for another day."

Kal-lel took stock of the faces gathered around him. His cool, blue eyes gazed down upon his eldest son.

"Very well. We shall let fate decide. I shall wait for as long as the candle burns, but we shall keep a constant vigil; watch for any signs that he is to expire before the flame of the candle does. If he takes a turn for the worse, I shall have to move swiftly to deliver him to the Twilight," stated Kal-lel.

"This is fair," agreed Lindras, "and all that we shall ask for."

Kal-lel removed the silver chain and clasps holding his cape in place about his shoulders, spreading it gently over his son's still body. "He is much too cold," whispered the high Elf, drawing the essence of his body's own warmth still trapped in his cape up around Arerys' neck.

Valtar returned with Tor-rin's apprentice, bringing with them more chairs for those wishing to sit and wait, and to pray. Kal-lel and Artel took their place by Arerys' bed, clutching his hands into theirs. Ansat resumed his prayers at the healing altar as Tor-rin carefully administered a pale green liquid, lifting Arerys' head and carefully tipping just enough to wet his parched mouth. The tepid, bland concoction was painstakingly measured out. And each time, only enough was administered to allow the unconscious Elf to instinctively swallow the elixir.

As hour after torturous hour slowly dragged by, the citizens of Wyndwood gathered throughout the day, periodically checking with the elders as to the condition of their prince. Eventually, the day gave way to darkness, only to triumph again hours later as the light of the impending sun slowly dissolved the night sky, diminishing the gentle glow of the last stars clinging to the heavens. On this morning too, the songs of the wren and thrush could not be heard with the coming of the dawn. There was a growing melancholy filtering through the trees' canopy, blanketing the forest of Wyndwood in a disquieting hush.

Throughout the day, Kal-lel and Artel remained by Arerys' side. Markus, Lindras and even Valtar spent all of their waking hours in the sanctuary, always near to the fair Elf's side. Markus found himself staring at the tenth candle on the healing altar. Slowly it burned down, shrinking as the melting wax pooled and hardened around its base. He found himself wishing the candle to slow its progress for now only inches remained. By dusk, this flickering symbol of life would burn no more.

As time passed, Markus recalled his first introduction to Arerys. He was in his early teenage years when he first journeyed to Wyndwood with his father, King Bromwell. That was almost twenty-three years ago, a mere pittance in the lifetime of an Elf, but for

Markus, in his thirty-seventh year, it was significant. Although Arerys had remained unchanged, aging perhaps the equivalent of one mortal year during all this time, the Elf had the pleasure of watching the young Prince of Carcross grow and mature.

In many ways, the fair Elf was the brother Markus never had. Arerys had taught him much in his lifetime; from the basics of the Elvish language, to archery and even the uses of medicinal herbs. They had shared many adventures throughout western Imago, always returning to Wyndwood.

This is not the way this adventure was to end, thought Markus, staring at his friend as he lay in this unnatural sleep. It was disclosed by Enra, Watcher of the Present that this fair Elf's desire was to leave this earthly realm. Arerys wished to retire into the Twilight if he had the good fortune of surviving the perils of the quest in their bid to defeat the Dark Lord. Since then, his situation had changed drastically. The one thing that filled the void in his life, the one person he had only ever dreamed about had found her way into his heart, ultimately altering his plans. Whereby most Elf men were wed by the time he reached his five hundredth year of existence, Arerys was soon approaching his seven hundred and thirty-fourth year. He was unwilling to commit to an eternal pledge of love to any woman who was less than his idea of compatible.

Markus gazed up when he realized the sun had now set and the only light filling the sanctuary came from the candles burning upon the altar. Arerys' life candle continued to burn, but he was filled with bewilderment; the wick was basically unchanged since he last looked upon it. In fact, based on the lapse of time since dusk turned to night, the candle should, by all accounts, been extinguished some time ago.

Kal-lel rose up to his feet. "The time has come," he announced to all in his presence. "It is time to send Arerys on his way."

Markus slowly stood up to his feet, stunned to hear these words. "My lord, not yet! Look, the candle still burns for him. You cannot do this."

"I am afraid his time is at hand," responded Kal-lel, with great regret.

Markus stood between Kal-lel and Arerys' still form, blocking the king's access to his son. "My lord, I beg of you; wait. Wait until the candle burns no more. You promised you would."

Kal-lel glanced up at the candle, indeed, the flame continued to glow steadily. Its progress had advanced little, if any, since the sun had set low beyond the horizon. His brows furrowed with curiosity, unable to comprehend the nature of this mystery.

"Yes, my lord, you did promise," reminded the Wizard. "I know you are a man of your word, I know you shall at least give us this time."

Kal-lel sighed heavily as he considered the look of desperation etched clearly on the faces around him. He could tell by the look in Artel's eyes that he too wanted to wait until the very end, until the candle's flame ceased to be.

"Very well," whispered Kal-lel. "So be it. We shall wait."

The candle continued to burn late into the night. Its progress seemed to be slowed by the many eyes staring intently at its flame, as though their own will kept the wax from dripping away.

"This is most unusual," stated Ansat. "In all my life, I have never witnessed a phenomenon such as this. The candle should have died out hours ago."

"It is a sign, Ansat," smiled Lindras. "Arerys is meant to live."

"But he does not wake," lamented Kal-lel. "He cannot remain in this state for much longer."

"Until the candle's flame expires," reminded Markus. "Remember? You had promised."

After a prolonged silence, the tomb-like stillness of the sanctuary echoed with the reverberation of a hearty laugh. All eyes turned to Lindras as he made no attempt to stifle his jovial laughter.

"I find nothing humorous about this situation," said Kal-lel in a sharp tone.

"Forgive me, my lord," answered the Wizard with a chuckle. "I was just recalling the time you first taught Arerys how to use the Elven long bow. He almost laid an arrow into your foot the first time he let an arrow fly, and then he had the audacity to claim it was deliberate; to prove to you how close he can deliver it without actually hitting you."

"Yes," recalled Kal-lel. "When in reality, the nock of the arrow had slipped causing it to tumble up into the air before coming straight down." Kal-lel's stern look dissolved. He smiled as he remembered this particular moment, one of many spent with his son teaching him the finer points of using the bow.

"Yes, thank goodness his aim improved immensely since then," Lindras added.

"Especially when he started to use me for target practice," added

Artel in agreement.

"He did what?"

"When we were children," continued Artel, "Arerys would have me hold the target for him as we played hide and seek in the forest."

"Tell me you jest!"

"Oh, it was all done in good fun, father," laughed Artel. "Arerys would remove the dangerous tips, replacing them with a small leather pouch filled with sand. Besides, I was too young and naive at the time to realize what Arerys was really up to."

Artel grew silent as Kal-lel's cool blue eyes pierced through him. Eventually, his grave expression softened with a small smile, "That may explain how Arerys became so exceptional at hitting a moving target."

"Yes, and had I been mortal, no doubt I would still have the marks to prove it," laughed Artel, rubbing his backside as though erasing a phantom pain.

The sanctuary rang with the sound of laughter.

If Arerys is to leave our presence, at least it shall not be to the sounds of tears, thought Markus as he gazed down upon his dear friend. His eyes grew wide with surprise when he noticed Arerys stir from his slumber. Although his eyes remained closed, the fair Elf did finally move, even if it was ever so slightly.

Kal-lel too had noticed his son's head move in the midst of their conversation and laughter. He gently touched Arerys' face, searching for signs that he may finally awaken. He then realized the sounds of their voices and their laughter were what his son was responding to.

Perhaps, the reverent silence maintained in this sanctuary is not conducive to one in Arerys' state, wondered the Elf king. *Perhaps he needs familiar voices to guide his soul back to this realm.*

"Arerys! Can you hear me, my son?" asked Kal-lel, hopefully. He looked to those standing by his side. "Keep talking, the silence has done nothing but to prolong his sleep. I believe he can hear us. Continue to speak."

"Why, yes! Of course!" added Lindras in excitement. "This place is like a tomb! It is fit for the dead and the dying. Where are the sounds of life? Of laughter? Arerys' soul is following the sounds of our voices!"

"Artel, did you know the first two times your brother met Nayla Treeborn, he was going to do her in?" asked Markus, hoping against hope that hearing Nayla's name might rouse Arerys from this sleep.

"Kill her? His betrothed? No! Surely you jest?"

"Oh, I am quite serious," smiled Markus. "Mind you, it was with good reason. She was quite the pugilist - a feisty little warrior, so much so, we all believed that she, was a he."

"Thank goodness he had control, had he not, surely he would have perished in the River of Souls," added Lindras, recalling how Nayla spared Arerys a death by drowning. His bid to save Ewen from the clutches of the river had almost ended in tragedy.

Markus glanced back up at the flickering light of the ever-shrinking candle, and then he looked down upon his friend, "Come now, Arerys, wake from this sleep. We have a job to finish. Nayla awaits your arrival in Orien."

"I wish Nayla was here right now," lamented the Wizard. "Perhaps, hearing her voice would bring Arerys around."

"She would cajole and coerce, probably even threaten him with his own life that he would have no choice but to return to us," mused Markus.

Artel and the others chuckled at the prince's sentiment.

"I admit that Nayla Treeborn is quite the warrior, Markus, but do you truly believe Arerys would want to spend an eternity with Nayla?" asked Artel.

"I assure you, Artel, Arerys is quite fond of her," stated Markus.

"You stand corrected, Markus," a weak voice whispered. "I love Nayla."

All present stared down at Arerys. His eyelids fluttered open as he slowly returned to the land of the living. His eyes were dull: clouded, not their usual brilliant blue. "And yes, my brother, I do intend to spend an eternity with her," he added in a soft voice.

"Arerys!" shouted Artel with a broad smile. "Finally, you wake!"

Kal-lel stroked his son's head and with an audible sigh of relief, he added, "And not a moment too soon, my son."

Markus and Lindras smiled, slumping back wearily into their chairs. The prince was exhausted by their vigil, but the wait was definitely worthwhile. His eyes were cast upwards as he whispered a *thank you* to the Maker of All. As he did so, he noticed that the high ceiling of the sanctuary was no longer concealed in darkness. Through the tall windows, the pale light of dawn filtered through the trees. Throughout the forest, the melodious sound of songbirds ushered in the coming of a new morn. Markus smiled, recalling how, for the past two mornings, the sweet sounds of the birds could not be heard. His eyes gazed towards the altar, all the candles continued to burn, including the tenth one, the one that determined Arerys' existence in this realm. To Markus' astonishment, although the nub of a wick was floundering in the pool of molten wax, it continued to burn. In fact, it burned for well over twelve hours longer than it should have.

Markus smiled down at Arerys, giving his shoulder a firm, reassuring pat. "It is good to have you back, my friend. We shall talk later. I am well beyond being weary. I shall return after some rest."

As Markus, Lindras and Valtar left the sanctuary to allow Artel and Kal-lel time with Arerys, a crowd had gathered outside after hearing voices and laughter emanating from the building.

"Is there still hope, Wizard?" one voice called out.

"Yes, does Prince Arerys still live?" shouted another.

Lindras stood atop of the stairs, staff in one hand as the other motioned all for silence. The crowd grew quiet as they saw his eyes darken and face look deathly serious. As heads lowered in sadness, the Wizard's eyes twinkled beneath his great hood; slowly a smile crept across his face. He could no longer conceal his joy.

"Yes! Prince Arerys lives!" announced Lindras. "Your prince is very much alive!"

Within minutes, the cheers of the Elf-folk were joined by the bells that pealed throughout the forests of Wyndwood, chiming the good news for all, far and wide to hear: *'Prince Arerys lives! Prince Arerys lives!'* They poured forth from the forest to see first hand, that their prince did indeed survive his horrific ordeal.

Markus and Valtar left Lindras amongst the throng, where he took great pleasure in retelling the tale of Arerys' tragic mishap and his long awaited return. The two men headed to Kal-lel's residence where upon they were greeted by Mar-ra, Tor-rin Greenshield's daughter. She welcomed them, offering them drink and food.

"Though it is morning, my mind and body is in dire need of rest," said Markus. "Thank you. Perhaps later."

Mar-ra nodded in acknowledgement. "And what of you, sir?"

Valtar considered the Elf maiden for a moment, and then kindly smiled at her. "I do not wish to break fast alone. Perhaps you will join me?"

Mar-ra blushed; her clear, blue eyes shyly drew away. "I suppose I can join you until your hosts returns," she answered with a gentle smile.

"Very well then," said Valtar, surprised that this beautiful, fair maiden of Wyndwood was willing to partake in a meal with this humble *dark* Elf.

As Markus turned away to retire into his bed chamber, it pleased him to see that Valtar would have the opportunity to speak to this woman, to discover the lines that segregated the fair and dark Elves have blurred over the ages.

Markus closed the door to his bed chamber. He could hear the noise and commotion made by the jubilant Elves. Normally, these proud and dignified people were quite reserved and sedate by nature, always in control of their emotions, especially in public. But now, the news of Arerys' recovery brought overwhelming joy to the citizens of Wyndwood. For Markus, it was as though a heavy anvil was lifted from his weary shoulders.

He threw his cloak onto the foot of his bed. Absolutely exhausted, Markus collapsed on top of the counterpane for some much needed rest. Even though the noise from the outside world and the morning sun filled his room, the voices soon became a distant drone; the sun's golden light eventually dissolved into a velvet blanket of black as sleep quickly laid claim to his mind and body.

As the morning sun shone brightly upon the enchanted forest, Mar-ra Greenshield led Valtar Briarwood to a balcony overlooking the center courtyard. Seating the dark Elf on an elegantly carved, high-backed chair, she soon returned with fresh fruits and breads. Valtar rose from his seat, pulling a chair out for Mar-ra so she may sit across from him. The Elf maiden smiled, thanking him for his courteous gesture.

He could not help but notice how the sun's rays reflected like a dazzling yellow halo off of her light, golden tresses. And her eyes; they were of such a blue they looked the color of the morning sky. Mar-ra shifted uneasily in her chair, feeling Valtar's brown eyes staring intently at her.

He smiled at her, delighting in her shy, demure nature. He thought upon how different his captain, Nayla Treeborn was when compared to this fair maiden. They were as different as night and day! Where Nayla stood a mere five feet and two or three inches tall, this blonde beauty was almost as tall as he, Mar-ra was a statuesque five feet and ten inches tall. She was as slender as a willow sapling and delicate. Nayla on the other hand was as lean as Mar-ra, but with a single glance, one could tell she was no delicate flower. Her toned muscles were conditioned by her rigorous training and warrior lifestyle.

Valtar reveled in Mar-ra's gentle, reserved demeanor. He noticed how she would avert her eyes, like a shy deer, not wishing to make direct eye contact. Now, had this been Nayla, he would have been greeted with an icy stare that could stop one's blood and freeze it in one's veins. Had Nayla displayed even a modicum of modesty, perhaps he would find her easier to endure. He smiled at the exquisite, gentle beauty sitting before him, and then he shuddered to think what Joval and Arerys could find so appealing about the warrior maiden.

Although Nayla Treeborn was a great captain and skilled as a warrior, her brash, willful nature and her need to speak her mind severely grated on his nerves. He would never question Nayla's abilities on the field of battle, nor would he deliberately ignore her orders for her knowledge and experience in warfare far exceeded his own abilities. However, on a more personal level, as a woman, Valtar found her extremely difficult to accept. Even out of her battle raiment and stripped of her weapons, dressed as a woman should dress, she still had a hard edge to her. Perhaps, she had qualities that only men like Joval and Arerys could ever find appealing. Perhaps, there was more to her than meets the eyes, yet Valtar could never see this.

"Is there something wrong, sir?" asked Mar-ra. It was clear he was lost in his thoughts.

"No," he answered with a pleasant smile. "And please, call me Valtar."

"As you wish, Valtar," she responded with a lilting voice.

"You are one of the first fair Elves I have ever chanced to meet," revealed the Elf, gazing into her gentle blue eyes.

"Are you disappointed by what you see?"

"Oh no, to the contrary! Your people, the women-folk especially, they are just as I had imagined in my dreams."

Mar-ra watched as a breeze caught Valtar's long, dark hair, blowing it about like long, brown streamers caught in the gentle wind. "I, too had never seen the likes of a dark Elf until you came. I have always believed Lord Treeborn's people either retired into the Twilight or died out long ago, existing only in legends of old."

"Well, we do live and I do believe that most, if not all, of Treeborn's people dream of the day that we may return to the home of our forefathers."

"Is it a possibility?" she queried.

"I suppose anything is possible. I was at the Plains of Fire after the

Dark Lord's defeat when King Kal-lel issued an edict stating that he would take appropriate measures to see the rift between our people be mended."

"After all this time?"

"Apparently so. In fact, it is very much a reality for Prince Arerys is now betrothed to the daughter of Lord Dahlon Treeborn."

"No!" she gasped, stunned by this news. "You do not say!"

"I speak the truth, my lady."

"So he plans to wed a dark Elf?"

"To be more accurate, she is a half-caste. She is half Elf and half mortal. By appearance and demeanor, I would say that she is far more mortal than Elf."

"Goodness!" replied the Elf maiden. "This news shall not be taken well by the maidens of Wyndwood. Many desire his hand in marriage and have held other suitors at bay in the hope that the prince would eventually choose one of them."

"Yourself included, my lady?" asked Valtar.

Mar-ra's slender hand covered her mouth as she giggled at his suggestion. "It is common knowledge that Prince Arerys, though he be pleasing to the eyes and kind of heart; he is a restless spirit. He is an adventurer and a vagabond by nature, always on the move. He thrives on excitement and travel."

"And you do not desire a life of high adventure?"

"I belong in Wyndwood. I am a true sylvan Elf, a child of this kingdom, of this forest. For this reason, I am hardly what Prince Arerys would find desirable in a mate. I have no wish to leave the safety of this enchanted forest for adventures in faraway lands. Nor do I intend to take up arms. After all, if a man is gallant, then it is his duty to protect what he owns."

A woman after my own heart; smiled Valtar as he thought upon her words.

As Mar-ra bit into a ripe, red apple, its sweet juice slowly trickled down her chin. Valtar leaned across the table, gently dabbing it away with his napkin. She smiled sweetly at the dark Elf.

Dusk had settled upon Wyndwood when Markus stirred from his long slumber. As he stood upon his balcony, he could spy the sun through the trees, its large golden form sinking slowly behind the Cathedral Mountains to the west. A cool, evening breeze blew off the waters of the Lake in the Woods. He breathed in deeply, filling his lungs with the fresh earthy smells of the forest. Turning to step back into his room, Markus saw Valtar. He was in the company of an Elf maiden; they were wandering slowly along the trail leading from the lake.

Markus poured some water from an urn into a basin, splashing the tepid water onto his face and neck. He felt as though he had washed away all his woes and weariness. He smoothed back his dark hair with his damp hands before drying his hands and face upon a towel. Throwing his cloak over his shoulders, he slipped out of his room to make his way back to the sanctuary.

As he approached, all was strangely quiet. Markus hastened his pace, leaping up the stairway, three steps at a time to the heavy wooden door. His eyes quickly adjusted to the light of the dim room. Upon the altar, the candles burned no more. An eerie silence filled the great room as Markus approached the healing bed. Arerys was gone.

For a brief moment, panic rose in his heart. Perhaps he had only dreamed the fair Elf had roused from his unnatural sleep. *Suppose he had passed on*, thought the prince, his dark eyes darting about the room searching for signs of where Arerys now lay. Turning to exit, he almost stepped straight into Lindras. Markus gasped, startled by the Wizard's sudden appearance.

"Tell me I was not dreaming, Lindras. Tell me our friend lives," pleaded Markus.

The Wizard, leaning against his staff, looked upon the prince. He offered a comforting smile. "Fear not, Markus, Arerys is well. He demanded to be removed from this *tomb*. He now rests in the comfort of his own bed chamber."

Markus breathed a loud sigh of relief.

"He was asking for you," said Lindras.

"Let us not keep him waiting," replied Markus, holding the door open for Lindras to pass through.

Markus rapped lightly on the door upon which Artel greeted them, showing them in. Seated next to the bed was Kal-lel. He smiled at Markus and Lindras as they entered. Arerys was propped up against several pillows, a bed tray holding a bowl of now-cold broth and Elven bread still sat, barely touched.

Markus leaned over, embracing the Elf in a great hug. Words could not describe his relief and happiness that Arerys did not leave this realm. He looked into his eyes and he could see that the Elf was still in need of rest, still recovering from the severity of the wound inflicted upon him.

"It is a good thing Valtar's arrow met its mark," said Markus with a sigh. "It was he who saved your life."

"I shall thank him," Arerys smiled in gratitude, his eyes still lacked their usual luster.

Markus sat on the edge of the bed. "I was so sure we had lost you, my friend. These past few days have been long and trying. You had us most worried."

"It was never my intention to be wounded in such a manner, nor take such a long measure of time to heal. I fear we have lost valuable time and now Nayla..." his voice trailed.

"Yes, Nayla shall be awaiting your return, you best heal quickly so we may be on our way," said Markus.

"We shall now be at least a week overdue," lamented Arerys.

"Rest assured, Arerys, a week or a month, I hardly believe Nayla shall care as long as you return to her," replied Markus.

"Yes, Markus, you are right. Tomorrow we shall be on our way," said Arerys.

"I think not, my son," stated Kal-lel. "I know you have lost your heart to this woman, but do not tell me that you have lost your head, too. Common sense shall dictate: You shall not leave this bed until the elders determine you are fit enough to do so."

"But father!" protested the Elf.

"Not another word, Arerys. Your body and soul had received great trauma, allow yourself adequate time to heal lest you wish to return to Nayla as a ghost of your former self," cautioned Kal-lel in a stern voice.

"Your father is quite right," agreed Lindras. "Nayla is smart and strong, you shall require all your strength and wits about you if you wish to stand up to the likes of her."

Markus rested a hand on Arerys' shoulder. "For now, rest, eat and drink. Regain your health, and then we shall speak of completing our task."

Eight days had passed since Arerys had fallen under the sword of the dark horseman. His recovery was nothing less than miraculous, even by Elven standards. Since his waking, he continued to regain his health and strength with each passing day. Finally, on a bright spring morning, under a blue, cloudless sky, the men of the Order gathered in the central courtyard. Squires had readied their horses and to Arerys' delight, standing alongside the Wizard's great, gray steed was Markus' black stallion, Arrow and his trusty, dappled mare, RainDance.

RainDance trotted up to her master, gently nuzzling Arerys' neck with her soft, velvety muzzle in greeting. The Elf whispered words in Elvish, pleased to see his mare and the other horses had made their way from Talibarr back to the safety of Wyndwood.

Arerys stood before his father and brother, embracing them in a fond farewell.

"I do not know when we shall meet again, my son," said Kal-lel with great sadness. "I shall pray for your safety and that you meet with success in bringing the Sorcerer of Orien to justice. When you return with your betrothed, there shall be a grand celebration like none this kingdom has ever seen."

"Do not despair, father, I shall return," promised Arerys, his blue eyes sparkled with life. "I shall return with Nayla by my side and the wretched Sorcerer shall no longer be of concern. You shall see."

He gave his father and younger sibling a final hug, before leaping onto his steed's bare back. Markus, Lindras and Valtar bid farewell to Kal-lel, Artel and all those who came to see them off with great fanfare.

Although Arerys spent much of his life roaming the countries of western Imago, this time he did truly regret leaving the enchanted forests of Wyndwood. The Elf clucked his tongue on the roof of his mouth causing RainDance to turn westward, towards the trail that would take them around the shores of the Lake in the Woods. As the men prepared to follow Arerys, Mar-ra emerged from the crowd, approaching Valtar as he sat high on his steed.

The dark Elf leaned over to thank her for her kindness and warm hospitality.

"Do you intend to return to Wyndwood?" she asked in a whisper.

"Is that your desire?" he asked, his brown eyes searching her heart for an answer.

"Yes."

"So be it," Valtar responded with a warm smile. "I cannot say when, but I shall return." He stooped to discreetly plant a soft kiss upon the back of her delicate hand as she offered him a gentle smile.

"Let us be off!" shouted Arerys, coaxing RainDance on.

Aspenglow soon disappeared against the backdrop of the forest. The fair Elf led the men along the northeast shore of Lake in the

Woods. The morning sun's rays sparkled as it reflected upon the surface that rippled under the gentle touch of a westerly breeze. The variant shades of green of the trees and shrubs and the clear waters of the placid lake rushed by in a blur as the horses galloped westward to the Fields of Shelon.

All along the way, although unseen by Markus, both the Elves' far-seeing eyes detected the warriors of Wyndwood hidden along the hills and amongst the trees. Dressed in sylvan colors, they dissolved into the landscape, keeping watch for signs of danger as the men of the Order advanced through the forest. Each would raise his hand high in silent acknowledgement and farewell as the Elf prince galloped by.

Riding hard, by late morning, the men reached the edge of King Kal-lel's domain. As they emerged from the forest, before them lay the Fields of Shelon, but what awaited them as they faced the vast stretch of land surprised them all. For as far as their eyes could see, two lines of warriors from Wyndwood, as well as the knights and soldiers of Carcross, Darross and Cedona lined the way to Mount Isa. King Augustyn of Cedona approached on his horse, his hand held high in salutation.

"Well, this is an unexpected surprise," stated Markus as he brought his steed alongside the king's mount. He extended his right hand in greeting, grasping Augustyn's right wrist.

"King Sebastian had re-routed all of the soldiers of the Alliance returning from battle," announced Augustyn. "When he received word from Wyndwood that you had been ambushed on your way to return the Stone of Salvation, his falcons were dispatched immediately." Sebastian had mustered all of the able-bodied men on horseback to gather here in a bid to guarantee the Order a safe passage to the Temple of the Watchers.

"Well, this is truly a welcome sight," said Markus in appreciation. "It is apparent one can never tell where the Sorcerer, Eldred Firestaff may be lurking. Your presence is truly appreciated."

"King Sebastian's soldiers have been scouring the lands of Darross, between Castle Hill and Crow's Nest Pass, in search of that murderous fiend. They also guard the Gap, the passage between the Cathedral and Aranak Mountains," stated Augustyn. "So far, he either remains cleverly hidden or perhaps, he is so far away from here, his presence no longer poses a threat."

"On the eve of our attack I saw no sign of the Sorcerer," said Arerys, recalling the dark, stormy night in Crow's Nest Pass. "The dark horseman, with a small battalion of soldiers once loyal to the Dark Lord, acted alone. If the Sorcerer was present, I did not see, nor hear, any sign of him."

"It is better not to take any unnecessary risks," recommended Lindras, placing his right hand over his belt where he had safely tucked away the precious gem. "If he means to steal away with the Stone of Salvation, he shall have to do so before we reach the Temple. Once the Stone is in the hands of the Watchers, he shall be too close to the hands and eyes of the Maker of All. He shall never gain access to the Stone again."

It suddenly dawned on Arerys there might be a very good reason why the Sorcerer was not present on that fateful night. His throat became dry, involuntarily tightening as he tried to swallow the lump caught therein. He turned RainDance to face Markus and Lindras, a look of both distress and anger clouded his eyes. "He is not here for good reason, he is after Nayla!"

"You cannot be sure of that, Arerys," replied Markus.

"I can feel it. I can sense she is in danger."

"How can you be sure?" asked Markus. "Nayla is at least two hundred leagues away by now."

"The danger to her is very real and very possible," warned Valtar. "The Sorcerer has made many attempts on her life since she took up the cause for her people in Orien."

"Fear not, Prince Arerys, need I remind you, Lady Treeborn travels with one of my finest knights," said Augustyn in an attempt to quell the fair Elf's anxiety. "Lando Bayliss shall keep her safe, I promise you. He is a great warrior, he is wise in the ways of war."

"Yes, you are right, but my injury has delayed this mission. Time is of the essence," stated Arerys, with growing urgency. He turned RainDance westward to face the slate-blue peaks of the Cathedral Mountains. "Let us depart immediately."

Amid this great show of force, none who wished to live, dared to interfere with their journey to Mount Isa. With the Stone of Salvation in Lindras' safekeeping, and with row upon row of soldiers loyal to the Alliance lining an invisible trail, the men of the Order begin the final leg of their mission.

CHAPTER EIGHT

A HERO'S WELCOME

Moving with great speed and steady determination, Nayla and the warriors of Orien marched at a relentless pace. They stopped only long enough to eat and drink, coming to rest at dusk to set up camp for the night.

At dawn, she and the men were on the move once again. For thirty-four days since leaving Anshen, Nayla, with Lando and Joval by her side, journeyed south towards the fortress city of Nagana. The only solace they found on this grueling expedition was when they slept. It was the only respite from the monotony of their daily grind.

The trek had been long, but all were grateful that it had been uneventful. Both Joval and Nayla shared the same feeling that the malevolent Eldred Firestaff was in the midst of scheming an evil plot. It was much too peaceful as they ventured through the countryside. With Nagana only a half-day ride away, Nayla sent forth two warriors on horseback to deliver word of their impending arrival.

As they marched along the well-traveled road leading to their final destination, the reminders of a land ravaged by war were still evident. Deserted homes and farms, some burned, but all pillaged by the soldiers of the Dark Army dotted the landscape. In spite of the carnage, life still abound. Fruit trees were in full blossom; bees were hovering busily from flower to flower collecting nectar. Goats, sheep and other livestock that had escaped the enemies' dinner plate made their way back home with offspring. Here too, the survivors of the invasion returned to start anew, tearing down the remnants of their homes to start fresh and to salvage what they could of their former existence.

Amidst these signs of life, Nayla and the warriors would come across soldiers of the Dark Army. Long laid to rest, the corpses were scattered about. Riddled with maggots, they lay festering in various stages of decomposition. Though rancid with decay, the large, black ravens still found an easy meal, picking at the flesh that clung stubbornly to the bones. Nayla thought how barbaric the mortals of western Imago, at least of those in the Dark Lord's service, were to leave their comrades to be further desecrated by the elements and the beasts.

Had these been her soldiers, she would have seen fit to cremate, or at the very least bury, their bodies with honor.

With the walls of Nagana within sight, Nayla and the warriors marched at an easy pace. Spring came late to Orien and now, under the canopy of large cherry trees in full bloom lining the main road to the city, the triumphant warriors returned home. She peered up at the late afternoon sun shining brightly through the broad crown of a cherry tree. Delicate, papery petals gently floated down, carried by an invisible breeze. The millions of cherry blossoms, their petals fluttering down upon the warriors like pink confetti, welcomed them back from war. Nayla's eyes closed as her lungs filled with the delicate fragrance of the cherry blossoms. The evil stench of war was now but a memory.

As Nayla, Joval and Lando led the men through the gates of the city, they were greeted with great fanfare. The air was filled with the sounds of bells as they pealed, chiming loudly to the trumpeting of horns from the battlements of the high walls protecting Nagana. Nayla noticed the banners bearing the insignia of the fortress city once again flew high and proud from the spire of each watchtower.

Mortals and Elves alike, hurried to the center of the city to welcome the returning heroes. Under a crescendo of jubilant cheers and the sounds of many horns, Nayla, Joval and Lando dismounted in the courtyard before the palace. Nayla turned to her warriors, giving the order to fall out of line. Soon, the throngs of people wishing to welcome their loved ones rushed them.

Nayla was happy for her men, they had the good fortune of having friends and family who were eager to greet them. For her, strangers who knew of her and her fearsome reputation as a warrior and captain welcomed her. This was the only time she was readily accepted by both mortals and Elves, when she had done something that would warrant such a greeting. She sighed. Her heart was numb for she knew it was not love they felt for her; it was merely a show of gratitude. Otherwise, she was not even fit to be seen in the company of anyone's son who may show greater interest on a more intimate level.

The warrior maiden hastened her pace, silently withdrawing from the crowd. She raced up the stairs to the entrance of the palace, where guards lining the stairway, bowed low before her as she confidently strode by. With her swords in her hands and her cloak fluttering out behind her, Lando and Joval watched as the captain of the returning army disappeared through the gates of the palace, unnoticed by everyone else in the great crowd.

In the solitude of her room, Nayla carefully mounted her swords back onto the stand, turning the handle of each weapon so they were positioned to the left. During times of war, the handle of a sword was always placed so it may be grasped quickly with the right hand to facilitate a fast draw. Now, as the Third Age of Peace dawned upon their fair land, perhaps her weapons would be put to rest forever. Nayla shook her head; only in her dreams would this happen. Deep down, she knew it would only be a matter of time before she was to face her nemesis.

She gave the scabbard of her long sword a gentle pat, as though it was a trusted friend she was putting to rest. Once again, it had served her well in battle. As she removed her cloak, a gentle knock caught her attention.

"Lady Treeborn, it is I," a familiar voice called to her through the door.

Nayla smiled as she opened the door. In stepped a mortal woman who appeared to be in her mid-thirties. Her long, raven-black hair and deep brown eyes were typical of all Taijins. She, like Nayla, was diminutive in stature.

It was Nakoa, the woman who had the misfortune of being appointed by the elders of Orien to be her lady-in-waiting. Where all others had rejected this posting or fled the palace in defeat, unable to deal with the warrior maiden, Nakoa had taken on the challenge and had remained in her service for the past fifteen years. Inasmuch as she had been appointed to this position to teach Nayla how to behave like a lady born to a high house, Nayla had spent just as much time and effort in swaying Nakoa to accept a more rough and tumble existence, rather than constantly cowing to the whims of others.

Nakoa bowed before her. "I am pleased to see you have returned to our city," said Nakoa. Her voice was soft as she spoke in Taijina.

The warrior maiden greeted the woman with a warm hug, genuinely pleased to see her. She was one of the few mortals Nayla regarded as a trusted and loyal friend.

Nakoa smiled back, and then she frowned with an obvious look of disdain. "Goodness, my lady! You smell as bad as the horses and men in your company! I shall prepare your bath," she said, her nose wrinkling as she fanned the air with her hand.

"Well, I missed you too, Nakoa!" smiled Nayla, shedding her trappings of war. "Is it truly that bad?"

"Oh, yes. Can you not see that my eyes water?" answered Nakoa, with an profound look of distaste.

As Nakoa disappeared into the adjoining room, Nayla unlaced her high, leather riding boots, pulling them off of her little feet. Removing the thin leather strip holding her braided tresses in place, she ran her fingers through her long hair. It tumbled down, cascading around her small shoulders. She shed her protective chain mail and the remainder of her clothing. Sniffing her blouse, she promptly dropped it to the floor in a heap with the others. Her nose wrinkled in disgust at the repugnant odor emanating from her well-worn raiment.

Nakoa is right, she thought, *I do smell as bad as a horse, worse yet, a dead one.*

In the other room, she could hear water spilling into a large tub. As she entered, her senses were immediately seduced by the inviting scent of freshly picked gardenia blossoms and chrysanthemum petals that floated on the steaming water. She felt herself being lulled into a state of calm by the intoxicating perfume lingering in the air.

Nakoa used her hand to test the temperature before tipping in some more cold water. "It should be fine now, my lady."

"Thank you," sighed Nayla as she slipped into the tub. Soon, its warm, watery embrace engulfed her body and soul. She slowly sank beneath the surface, her long, dark tresses floated around her like seaweed in a tidal pool. Nayla could feel the grime and sweat from her many days on the road dissolve from her skin and wash away from her hair as she lay immersed.

When she finally surfaced for air, Nayla rested against the sloping back of the tub. For a lingering moment, her eyes studied the waxy, white petals of the gardenia. Each one a vision of perfection; so perfect, they did not look real. Her eyes closed as she inhaled the fragrant scent emanating from the water.

"My lady, what do you wish for me to do with your clothes?" asked Nakoa. Dare not handling the war-weary threads with her bare hands, she presented it before Nayla at the end of a staff.

"You may burn them for all I care," laughed the warrior maiden, watching Nakoa's face grimace in disgust.

"I have already considered doing just that. Suppose I see if the household staff dare tackle the job of washing your raiment before we resort to burning them?"

"That would be prudent, just do not leave with my vest of chain mail, please."

"As you wish, my lady. I shall return shortly."

Nayla leaned back, relaxing in the enchanting spell cast by the warmth and scent of the water when she heard a sharp rap on the door.

"Enter Nakoa!"

"It is I, Joval!"

"Come in!" shouted Nayla, refusing to leave the warm embrace of the water to greet her friend.

Joval and Lando entered her bed chamber.

"In here," she called, from the adjoining room.

The dark Elf casually strolled in with the knight following close behind.

Lando's eyes flew wide-open in shock; absolutely mortified that he had walked in on her in a state of total undress.

"What the…? Bloody hell, Nayla!" he stammered, throwing both his hands over his eyes. "Why did you not say you were naked?"

Joval laughed at the knight's startled response.

"I have never known anyone to bathe with clothes on, Lando." Her answer was matter-of-fact.

"Why did you not say you were bathing?" he countered, his back now turned to her.

"Why are you mortals such prudes? It is not as though you have never seen a naked woman before," Nayla responded, her bare shoulders shrugged in indifference.

Being a gentleman, Lando kept his eyes averted. He retorted, "A lady should show some sense of modesty, that is all."

"You are right, Lando. I agree," said Nayla with a wicked smile as she winked at Joval. "I shall pass your sentiments on to the first *lady* I see."

The dark Elf shook his head and smiled back at her, knowing full well she took certain pleasure in tormenting the knight in this manner.

"Well, I shall take my leave; wait for you in the other room," said Lando, removing himself from her presence.

"As you wish. I shall not be long."

"You know you are totally incorrigible," said the dark Elf as he sighed in resignation, watching Lando disappear from his sight.

"Whatever do you mean?" asked Nayla, peering up at Joval. Her deep brown eyes gave her an air of innocence, especially when she batted her long, dark lashes at him. It was as though she really did not know what he was speaking of. Her hand languidly stirred the water, sending pale yellow petals and gardenia blossoms swirling in a circle before her. She was not quite ready to leave yet.

After a moment, she broke the silence. "So what brings you here, Joval? Did you grow weary of the adoring crowds?" she asked, her words laced with sarcasm.

"The elders and your father were there to greet us had you only waited, Nayla. You should have stayed long enough to be honored with your men, to be recognized as the hero that you are."

"I do not wish to belittle your words, my friend, but as far as history shall go, your actions and those of the Elves and Taijins warriors shall be remembered. I shall be long forgotten for there is no room in the annals of history for this woman, and a half-caste at that," stated Nayla. There was no bitterness in her words; she was merely stating a fact.

"Tell me something, Joval. When Dahlon approached you and saw that I was not present, what was his expression when you told him that I still lived? That I had survived the suicide mission he had deployed me on?"

The dark Elf turned away from Nayla's intense stare, the fire in her eyes seemed to burn a hole straight through his very heart as she awaited an answer.

"He was pleased."

"You have never been good at lying to me. Do not lie to me now, Joval."

"Very well," he conceded with reluctance. "He was surprised."

"I thought as much," responded Nayla, rising up from the tub.

Joval held the towel open for her, as she stepped out, wrapping it about her body.

"The council wishes to meet with you," said Joval.

"Can it not wait?"

"You know you cannot avoid this; the elders insist."

"So be it, but you and Lando shall both accompany me to this meeting."

"Of course, Nayla."

He followed her into the room where Lando patiently waited. Upon hearing Nayla's voice as she approached, the knight averted his eyes, turning away. "Please tell me that you are decent, Nayla."

"Am I covered? Yes. Am I decent? That is a matter of opinion," laughed the warrior maiden.

As she stood in the center of the room, her nose wrinkled in disgust. "Before you attract the attention of hungry ravens and flies, I strongly recommend that you both bathe. You smell as bad as carrion."

Joval's eyes rolled in dismay at her candor as they exited the room. "Yes, yes. We are both quite aware of our condition. We shall freshen up before we meet with the council."

"Good! And have the servants burn your clothes while you are at it," suggested Nayla, closing the door behind them.

Nayla was in no hurry to meet with the council. She deliberately took her own sweet time while her lady-in-waiting anxiously coaxed and cajoled her to dress.

"With all due respect, my lady, you should wear a gown to this meeting," suggested Nakoa. "All eyes shall be on you, the warrior maiden of Orien."

Nayla glanced at the clothes in her wardrobe; here a supply of fine silk gowns awaited her whenever she returned to Nagana to conduct business. In her own home, she kept only three dresses when special occasions called for it, but those occasions had been few and far between. She took no pleasure in participating in social events. At times, it was easier to face the ravages of war on the field of battle than to endure the slings and arrows cast by those who were forced to treat her with respect for she was a daughter of a high Elf.

Nakoa was sedulous, holding forth one gown after another. Eventually, she settled on a beautiful gown of white with delicate pink blossoms embroidered throughout.

"This would look lovely on you," insisted her lady-in-waiting.

The little warrior frowned, realizing that Nakoa would persist until she had her dressed in what she deemed suitable for a gathering of this nature. Normally, whenever Nayla shed her chain mail, she relished donning a dress and doing her hair up in a feminine fashion. She took a certain amount of pride and pleasure knowing she could be both a warrior and a woman. For her, it was a matter of striking a balance, but today, her heart was not set on this.

"This one shall do," said Nayla, selecting a deep purple dress, devoid of any flowers or other patterns. "It is simple. Suitable for my execution," mused the warrior maiden.

"Pardon me, my lady?" Nakoa frowned at her words.

"Never you mind, Nakoa," smiled Nayla. "I was thinking out loud, that is all."

"Very well, my lady," replied Nakoa. She held the gown up as

Nayla removed her towel. As she slipped her arms through the sleeves, Nakoa winced in empathy as her eyes noted the silvery scars Nayla bore on her back. She could only guess how she had received these permanent reminders of old wounds for Nayla refused to disclose what had happened or who had inflicted her with such cruelty. Nakoa only knew that this warrior maiden carried these dreadful scars for as long as she had known her.

As Nayla held the dress closed, Nakoa worked diligently to wrap a wide sash high around her waist just below her breasts. Working the fabric around until it wound down low to her hips, Nakoa started to tie the sash into a bow.

Nayla felt it cinch low around her belly. "Not so tight, Nakoa, I wish to be able to breathe." She drew in a deep breath, absorbing the energy of the color purple; the color that heals. The silk fabric felt sensuous against her bare skin. *Perhaps it shall do me some good to be rid of my chain mail for the time being,* thought Nayla as her fingers caressed the luxuriant, satiny fabric.

Nakoa proceeded to use a wooden comb to smooth out and detangle her long hair. Nayla said not a word, closing her eyes as she remembered how, as a child, her mother used to comb out her hair each morning and each night. It was such a simple pleasure, and yet it was something Nayla never forgot, over two centuries later, she never forgot.

When she finally opened her eyes, Nakoa had transformed her from a deadly warrior to a beautiful maiden. Nayla blinked into the mirror as though she did not recognize the reflection staring back at her.

"Now this is more becoming," beamed Nakoa, smiling at Nayla's reflection. It was at this very moment Nakoa had noticed there was something different about Nayla. There was an energy; a radiance glowing from her being.

"What is it, Nakoa?"

"If I did not know better, I would say that you are in love."

"How so?" asked Nayla, her right hand discreetly concealed the silver ring Arerys had presented to her upon their betrothal.

"I cannot place it, but you seem radiant this evening. I do not recall ever seeing you like this in all our years together," said Nakoa, studying Nayla's reflection.

The warrior maiden simply smiled back at her long-time friend. Nakoa did not solicit for an explanation, nor did Nayla offer one. She decided to wait for a more appropriate moment before disclosing this surprising turn of events to her dear friend.

An abrupt knock on the door brought Nayla to her feet. Her lady-in-waiting answered the door, bowing as she greeted Joval, addressing him in Taijina. Her eyes widened in surprise as Lando passed through the door, bowing in response. His tall stature, his wavy, dark brown hair and the beard and moustache, peppered with gray made it very apparent that this mortal was not from eastern Imago. He had obviously ventured over from the other side of the Iron Mountains.

"Good evening!" said Lando quite loudly, enunciating each word in hopes that she would comprehend his question. "Do you understand the common speech?"

Nakoa considered the stranger towering before her. "It is not necessary to shout, sir. I assure you, I am not deaf," she responded in the common speech.

"Oh, my apologies," offered Lando, embarrassed by his own conduct.

Nayla approached the knight, taking him by his arm. "Nakoa, this is my friend, Lando Bayliss. He is a knight who serves a king from the distant country of Cedona, far to the west."

Nakoa bowed, and then smiled at the man.

"Nayla, it is time to go. The council await our presence," reminded Joval.

"Let us be done with this. Whether I face Dahlon's wrath now or later it makes no difference," said Nayla, with grim resolve.

Joval led the way through the courtyard, up the stairs to the meeting hall. As they neared, the dark Elf stopped in the vestibule. "Nayla, I assume the elders wish to extol the virtues of your skills as a warrior and your heroic feat on Mount Hope. I can only guess this is what your father intends to do too."

"Who can say what Dahlon's intentions are?" responded Nayla with a weary sigh.

"Do you intend to tell him of Prince Arerys?"

Nayla searched Joval's eyes for his support. "You are my friend, Joval. What do you advise? After all, you know my father better than I do."

"Nayla, it inevitable that Lord Treeborn shall find out. Something of this importance and magnitude cannot be concealed for long. It shall only be a matter of time. And given your present situation, it is far better he hear it now from you, than later from another party."

Nayla nodded her head in agreement. "I shall tell you this; to be flogged or caned would be a more pleasant experience than dealing with that man."

"Fear not, Nayla, we are your friends, we shall stand by you," assured Lando, patting the little warrior on her small shoulder.

"I know your father; he will not take this news well. I may be able to help him understand the benefits of such a union."

"Very well, Joval."

"Fortunately, I can understand the political benefits to your father and for our people if the door is opened for us to return to Wyndwood. I know many dream of going home to this place of our forefathers. And for commerce too, trade between the two countries shall be good for the people of both western and eastern Imago."

"At least Dahlon had the wisdom and good sense to appoint you as the Stewart of Nagana," smiled Nayla.

"We should make the announcement of your betrothal to Prince Arerys in the presence of the elders," recommended the Elf. "I believe their attendance when we deliver this news shall serve to temper your father's reaction."

"You think of everything, my friend," responded Nayla.

As they entered the room, Nayla, Joval and Lando approached the council together. They knelt down and bowed to those in their presence before seating themselves at the great table.

"Well, this is a sight that pleases me; Nayla and Joval together again," smiled Dahlon in approval, "returning from battle to preserve justice and peace throughout our lands."

Nayla and Joval exchanged uneasy glances at each other.

The elders thanked the three warriors for their efforts in sparing Imago from a reign of terror had Beyilzon laid claim to the lands. With his defeat, the Dark Army was vanquished from Orien. In all their infinite wisdom, somehow the elders knew Nayla would succeed where everyone else had failed. They knew she would be instrumental in bringing peace to their country. She was most deserving of this hero's welcome.

"She has done more than merely spare us the wrath of the Dark Lord. Nayla has opened the door for our people to return to Wyndwood," announced Joval.

Dahlon stared in utter disbelief. The elders looked at each in other in surprise.

"How so?" questioned Dahlon.

"King Kal-lel's son, Prince Arerys has requested Lady Treeborn's hand in marriage," responded Joval, on Nayla's behalf.

The elders were delighted by this news. Dahlon on the other hand, was dumbfounded by this announcement.

Sensing Dahlon's response, Joval was quick to add: "Think on it, my lord! After all these years, the marriage of Prince Arerys to Lady Treeborn shall be a union that shall unite a race that has been too long divided."

"And King Kal-lel approves of this union?" asked Dahlon, his words were tainted with skepticism as he deliberated on Joval's statement. "I find it impossible to believe he would allow his son to wed a woman such as her."

Nayla, who had remained silent until now, glared at Dahlon. "Why? Because I am neither Elf, nor mortal? Because my blood is not pure?"

Joval reached over, squeezing Nayla's hand. Though no words were exchanged, she knew the Elf wished for her to remain calm, to be silent.

"It is true, my lord. I was there when King Kal-lel announced to the kings of the Alliance, and all those in their presence, that the marriage would heal the rift and unite our people once again. Prince Arerys wished to marry immediately; it was King Kal-lel who maintained that he receive your blessing first.

"I wish to have a moment alone with my daughter," said Dahlon.

"Very well, my lord," replied Joval. He gave Nayla's hand a reassuring squeeze as he stood up. Taking a step back, both he and Lando bowed before turning to leave the room.

The elders smiled at Nayla as they, too departed their company.

At least they were elated by this news, thought Nayla, bowing to them in respect as they left.

Once they were alone, Dahlon slowly rose up from the table. He quietly paced the length of the room. Finally, he came to a stop, staring down at Nayla. He considered the diminutive form sitting before him. He breathed a weary sigh, his contempt for her weighed heavily on him like an anchor chained around his neck, dragging him down.

Nayla locked eyes with her father, refusing to be intimated by his icy stare or his great stature. She waited patiently for him to speak.

He shook his head as he searched for the words to express his growing rage, waiting for the elders to be well out of earshot.

"How dare you, Nayla!"

"Dare I what? Survive the quest or accept a fair Elf's hand in marriage?"

"You do this to defy me!"

"I do this because I love Arerys. If you were wise, you would accept this union. Embrace the fact that your wayward daughter has found a way for you to save face amongst your people. They want to go home. This is the first step to rebuilding relationships. Do not let your pride stand in the way."

Dahlon's fists slammed down upon the table. "I do not believe Kal-lel Wingfield would accept you into his high house! You of all people!"

"I know what I am! Arerys knows what I am! And I am ashamed to admit that in my brief time spent with King Kal-lel, he has shown me more respect and love than you ever have in my entire life!"

Dahlon's blue eyes burned with undeniable hostility as he glared down at Nayla.

She stared back at him, unwilling to yield to his will. He did not intimidate her and it served to anger him all the more when she defiantly rose up onto her feet, refusing to back down.

"I forbid this union!"

"I shall wed Arerys. You cannot stop me."

"I shall disown you!"

"You cannot discard me so easily, you never owned me to begin with."

Dahlon stood before his daughter, staring down with unspeakable rage. *How can one so small cause me so much grief?*

Had it been anyone else, his overbearing presence would cause a weaker person to fold under the pressure. Instead, Nayla stood her ground, glaring up into his unyielding eyes.

"I shall put a stop to this!"

"Then what? Have your people speak of your bastard grandchild?" hissed the warrior maiden.

Dahlon was momentarily stunned by this news. He searched her face for signs that she may be lying to him. When her expression remained unchanged, he muttered beneath his breath, "You have conceived a child by a 'fair' Elf? By a Wingfield?"

"Yes."

For Nayla, his response was predictable. The senior Elf was trembling with absolute loathing for his daughter. His hand swept across the surface of the table sending drinking vessels hurling through the air. They smashed against the far wall. She was unmoved by his volatile behavior. It was nothing new to her.

"You are no better than a whore! You have been used by Kal-lel's son to bring disgrace to our house!"

"You are wrong. You do not know Arerys."

"Then where is your prince now? Why is he not here? You have been deceived! You do this to bring dishonor to the Treeborn name!"

"That is all you really care about. It has always been about you, and your name, and your honor."

No longer able to contain his boiling rage, Dahlon raised his hand to strike Nayla's face. As he closed in, she angled out of the way, her hand moved swiftly to intercept his. He pulled away from her grip. Once again he attempted to strike Nayla's face with the back of his fist, but once more she easily deflected his blow.

Suddenly, the door burst open and Joval stormed in, his cape billowing behind him as he came charging over to put an end to Nayla's torment. Dahlon was shocked by his abrupt appearance as the Elf took Nayla by her hand, pulling her away from his reach. Joval placed himself between father and daughter, physically barring Dahlon from approaching any closer.

"Do you want to strike someone?" shouted Joval, his blue eyes turned icy as they glared at the senior Elf. He stood toe-to-toe against Dahlon, his inflated chest thrust forward to create an imposing barrier to protect Nayla. His fists trembled in rage as he fought to control his own urge to lash out. "Do you want to feel powerful? Try hitting someone your own size for a change! If you ever lay a hand on Nayla again, by God I swear, I shall no longer protect your good name! I shall make sure our people know the true color of our great and wise leader!"

"You do not understand, Joval!" protested Dahlon in his own defense, shrinking back from the Elf's threatening posture. "Nayla has been used! She allowed herself to be used by a fair Elf to bring dishonor to our house."

"She has done no such thing. Prince Arerys is an honorable man, he has every intention of wedding Nayla."

Nayla shook her head in despair as she stepped out from behind her protector. She knew Joval's effort to palliate on her behalf would go unheeded. "If it is your honor you are so concerned about and you are so confident I have been used, then I shall leave. You shall never have to set eyes upon me again. All your high and powerful friends will never have to know. Your honor shall remain intact."

Joval looked upon Nayla, stunned by her response. "You cannot do this Nayla. I will not allow it."

"Yes, I can! And I shall!"

Joval motioned Nayla for silence. Turning to face Dahlon; he made a proposition that he knew could not be refused. "My lord, if you are correct, if Prince Arerys is not here by the last day of this month, then I shall take Nayla as my wife. I shall claim her unborn child as my own."

Nayla was equally shocked by Joval's offer.

Dahlon hastily considered the Elf's offer. "Very well, Joval Stonecroft, I wash my hands of her. Why you would want to even subject yourself to this life and to this woman, is well beyond my understanding. She is your problem to bear now." The high Elf turned away, leaving them alone in the room.

"Joval, why did you do that? You did not have to put yourself in such a position."

"Nayla, I will not have you live your life in exile. You are guilty of nothing. After all you have sacrificed, after all you have endured in the name of your father and this country; I shall not have you be treated as an outcast. You do not deserve such a fate."

Nayla shook her head in sadness for she understood the full ramifications of the dark Elf's decision. "Do you not see, Joval? I *am* an outcast. I have always been an outcast. This is nothing new to me. But for you? You shall be despised and scorned if it is revealed that this child is not your own. You shall be stripped of your rank and privilege as the Stewart of Nagana. You shall be ridiculed by all for your choices."

"Nayla, you are right. But it is a choice of my own making. Do you understand? It is *my* choice and I do so with my heart and both eyes open."

Nayla's small body was trembling; the fire that once burned in her eyes seemed to be extinguished, smothered by her overwhelming despair. Her only comfort was in knowing that Joval was still there by her side. It was always in his nature to be honorable, now she understood why their friendship had endured through the centuries.

Finally, unable to hold back any longer, bitter tears spilled from her eyes. Joval held her close to his chest. He knew she had deliberately waited for Dahlon to leave their presence before she permitted herself to feel in this manner. In her father's eyes, it was the ultimate sign of weakness, but Joval knew that not all tears were self-serving;

not all tears were shed in self-pity. He felt in his heart that Nayla's tears were not for herself, but for her unborn child.

Her own future as a half-caste was always in doubt. Her life had been wrought with great difficulties from the day she was born. Now this new life Nayla carried, already rejected by Dahlon Treeborn, was to be condemned to a similar fate. Being part mortal, part dark Elf and now, half fair Elf, unless things changed drastically, this child, too shall face difficult times in the days to come.

CHAPTER NINE

RETURN TO MOUNT ISA

As the men of the Order ventured out of the safety of the forest of Wyndwood onto the Fields of Shelon, they marveled at the sight before them. Over three thousands warriors, soldiers and knights of the Alliance waited to escort them. Arerys nervously scanned the vast expanse of land that lay between his father's domain and their final destination, Mount Isa. What his eyes could not see, his ears strained to detect. There was nothing. The wind carried no ill signs of evil on this day. The fair Elf quickly adjusted his new vest of chain mail hidden beneath his cloak. Removing his bow from over his shoulder, he held it in his left hand. Now he was ready. He coaxed RainDance forward.

Markus brought Arrow alongside his mare. He leaned over to his friend to reassure him, "Arerys, I do believe we shall be quite safe as we venture forth."

"I prefer to side with caution, Markus. Just as we believed we would be safer taking the road into Wyndwood; we were wrong. I cannot afford another mishap. I have already lost precious time I shall never regain. I cannot endure another mistake of that magnitude again."

"I can understand," sympathized Lindras. "Arerys is right, Markus. One can never be too careful where Eldred Firestaff is concerned."

"Fear not, Prince Arerys, even as we speak, King Sebastian and a battalion of his men guard the Gap. King Bromwell and his soldiers secure Rock Ridge Pass and shall remain there to escort the Order on through Talibarr to the Iron Mountains," promised Augustyn. "You shall not be hindered in your travels, not this time."

Markus took great comfort in knowing he would be crossing paths with his father and the knights of Carcross as they leave Darross to enter the dreaded land of Talibarr. Although the Dark Lord was no longer a threat and the last of his dark emissaries was also laid to rest, the Sorcerer of Orien was still a very real danger.

"The warriors of Darross, Wyndwood and those of Carcross shall accompany us to Mount Isa before turning back. For myself and the men in my service, we shall provide you with safe passage to the Temple of the Watchers. Once the Stone of Salvation is safely delivered to the Three Sisters, I shall continue on my journey westward to Cedona, homeward to Land's End," said Augustyn, turning his steed to face the slate-blue mountains on the horizon. "Let us be on our way!"

As the men of the Order forged ahead, Markus felt confident that if the Sorcerer and his followers were indeed watching, they would reconsider before mounting an attack on such a formidable show of force. If they were near, their numbers had to be small to go unnoticed by the soldiers of the Alliance guarding key entry points leading from Talibarr into Darross.

They dare not stand in our way, thought Markus, glancing at the great army now escorting the men of the Order.

Riding hard through the hills and vales of the sparsely treed land, the men stopped only long enough to allow the steeds sufficient time to rest and a brief opportunity to drink and graze. At all times, the soldiers of the Alliance stood guard, scanning the horizon for signs of approaching enemy forces.

The journey through the Fields of Shelon was thankfully uneventful. By day's end, the Order had reached the base of Mount Isa. Here, in the shadow of the mountain, the soldiers prepared for the coming of the night. They deliberately set up tents for Markus, Lindras, Arerys and Valtar in the middle of the encampment.

The warriors of Wyndwood were posted to rotating sentry duty, allowing the others to acquire adequate rest for the next day's journey. With so many present, and requiring only several hours of sleep to sustain them, the Elves kept vigil. Their far-seeing eyes penetrated the darkness, their ears filtering out the night sounds, separating those made by the nocturnal creatures from those that may represent danger.

With the first pale light of morning, the soldiers of the Alliance were ready to move out. Arerys thanked his warrior brothers, bidding them farewell as the Elves mounted their dappled gray steeds. They turned to the east, back to the forests of Wyndwood. As they galloped away across the Fields of Shelon, the captain of the army representing Carcross approached to wish Markus a safe journey. He would now take his men to meet with King Bromwell as they awaited their arrival on the outskirts of Heathrowen.

The soldiers and knights of Darross, now ready to take their leave planned to venture back, northward to escort the Order upon their return from the Temple on Mount Isa. They would rendezvous at Castle Hill, delivering them to the soldiers and knights in King Bromwell's service.

As Markus and the others watched the warriors of Darross, Wyndwood and Carcross depart, King Augustyn and the knights and soldiers of Cedona prepared for the difficult trek up the slopes of Mount Isa.

The men mounted their steeds as the men of the infantry fell into line. With Lindras in the lead on Tempest, his gray stallion showed the way up the slope. By daylight, the journey would not be as arduous as their first trek up this path when they had come to claim the Stone of Salvation. Under the cover of night with only the light of the stars and a waning crescent moon to show the way, the journey was far more treacherous and much more time consuming. Now, under a pale morning sky, unhampered by the suffocating darkness of night the horses were able to maintain better footing on the uneven, unstable terrain as they made the ascent.

As they approached a fork in the trail, Lindras dismounted. The Wizard was silent as he contemplated on the paths that lay before them.

"Well, Lindras, what do you recommend?" asked Markus, his eyes cautiously scanning the sloping terrain.

"I would hate to hazard a guess," he replied, his confidence already shaken. "I was wrong about Crow's Nest Pass; I would hate to be wrong again."

Arerys stood before them, examining the fork in the trail. After careful consideration, the fair Elf stated, "My intuition tells me that if indeed the Sorcerer wishes to make his intentions known, he shall do so on this path to the left."

"And how did you come to this conclusion?" asked Markus.

"I believe it is fair to assume the Sorcerer shall take the path we used the first time we came this way. He knows that we race against time to return the Stone to its rightful place. The path to the left is more treacherous, but it is more direct. There were areas that provided us with cover when we ventured forth, just as it would provide him with shelter to hide, from which to ambush us. The path to the right shall make for an easier but longer journey for it gradually winds up to the Temple. Although we shall not have the safety of cover when night comes, we now travel with the protection of King Augustyn and the brave knights and soldiers of Cedona."

"Very well! So be it, Arerys. We shall take the path to the right," said Markus, motioning for the army waiting behind them to proceed forward.

Soon, a long line of men and horses slowly snaked up the long trail meandering up the mountainside. Arerys' keen eyes were constantly studying the terrain, searching for hidden danger. His ears listened for any sign carried in the wind that would deceive the Sorcerer, alerting them to his presence.

As they ventured higher, all on horseback dismounted and led their charges up the path. The mortals and their steeds struggled with the high altitude, but Arerys, Lindras and Valtar were unaffected by the thinning air. Under normal situations, Arerys would be bounding up the path, scouting it out, and then returning with word to the others of what lay ahead. This time, he was not about to tempt fate. He remained close to the men serving to protect the Order.

By nightfall, both man and beast were made weary by the long, exhausting trek. With nowhere to go, the horses remained with their masters. Drinking from small pools of water springing from the rocks and nibbling on what meager grasses clung precariously to the loose substrate, the fatigued steeds remained still for the night. They conserved their energy for the journey that still lay ahead with the coming of the new day.

King Augustyn positioned some of his soldiers to move up to the front of the line so the members of the Order were protected from an attack, should it come from up ahead.

As a multitude of sparkling, white stars studded the deepening, cobalt blue sky, Markus settled down on the trail between Arerys and Lindras. Wrapping his Elven cloak tightly around his neck and shoulders, he shivered as his lungs drew in the cold, thin air, chilling his body from the inside out. He glanced down the mountain slope at the trail winding below them. In the darkness of the night he could see the red glow of pipes as the soldiers found some comfort and warmth from the smoke they shared with their comrades.

"We shall reach the summit by late morning if we are on the move by first light," said Lindras, chewing thoughtfully on the mouthpiece of his worn pipe.

"Tell me, Wizard, the Watchers - the Three Sisters, I have heard tales of these immortals," said Valtar, "They truly do exist?"

Lindras smiled at the dark Elf. "Indeed, they do."

"And you have seen them with your own eyes?"

"Of course, on a number of occasions over the ages."

"Are they like us?"

"Are they Elves? Is that what you are asking?"

"Yes," replied Valtar.

"They are not Elves. They came to being long before the race of Elves. In fact, we Wizards and the Elves, evolved from the likes of the Watchers," answered Lindras.

"Do they look like the fair Elves?" asked Valtar.

Lindras' brows furrowed as he thought upon this question. "No, they do not, neither do they look like the dark Elves. Like us, they are of fair complexion, but they possess flaming red hair and dazzling eyes of emerald green."

"I assure you, Valtar, they are quite the sight to behold. The Three Sisters are heavenly creatures of exquisite beauty," added Markus, his body stopped shivering as he recalled his first meeting with the Watchers when they began their quest for the Stone of Salvation.

"Are they goddesses?" asked Valtar.

"No, they are the oracles, the medium by which we may consult the Maker of All. The Three Sisters reveal to mankind and his kin of events that bear great significance to us when He sees fit to do so," answered Lindras.

"So they predict the future?"

"Each one is gifted in a different way," answered the Wizard, relighting his pipe. "Elora records the past, Enra watches as the present unfolds, while Eliya, the Watcher of the Future reveals the shadows of things to be."

"So the Watchers can steer the course of the future?"

"To the contrary, Eliya reveals to us the possibilities and our options, but it is our responsibility to choose the path of our fate. As Eliya once said, 'the future is not engraved in stone. Even a single grain of sand can tip the scales to set into motion a great many changes.' And her words are so very true," replied Lindras. "She merely shows us the possibilities, for ultimately, it is our own actions that determine the outcome of our destiny. Eliya holds no sway in how man or Elf conducts himself."

"Then I fail to see what purpose she can serve if she can see the future and yet, not advise us on what choices or actions to take to circumvent disaster," stated Valtar.

"Eliya's role is not to determine our fate, hers is to give us hope. When all else fails, she does exactly this; she gives us hope," said Lindras with a reassuring smile.

"Well, I can understand the need for the Watchers of the Present and the Future, but how important is Elora, the Watcher of the Past? After all, the past is the past, it holds no bearing with the here and now, or the future," commented the dark Elf.

Lindras stared at Valtar, obviously distressed by his comment. As a member of the Elven race, hailed as one of the oldest and wisest races in Imago, the Wizard was stunned by the dark Elf's ignorance. "My good man, Elora may possibly have the most important job for hers is to reveal our past successes and failures. She reminds us of our past triumphs and shortcomings for her job is to see that we have the wisdom to learn from our past mistakes."

Valtar mulled over the Wizard's words. "I suppose you have a point," he conceded.

"Truth be told, I have a prediction of my own," stated Lindras, his voice sounding deathly serious.

Arerys, Markus and Valtar leaned in closer to listen to the benevolent, old Wizard's words.

"I predict that within a very short time, I shall lapse into a state of unconsciousness and shall remain in this state until the first light of morning," said the Wizard as he leaned back against a rock, drawing the hood of his cloak over his eyes so he may sleep.

Arerys and Markus chuckled, not so much at Lindras' *prophetic* words, but at Valtar's own facial expression as he frowned in dismay at the Wizard's so-called prediction.

Soon, all with the exception of those on sentry duty were embraced in a deep sleep, exhausted by the day's journey. As his companions slept soundly in their less than comfortable surroundings, Arerys sat back peering up at the black, velveteen sky searching for a celestial sign that would promise a successful end to this mission. As his eyes penetrated the darkness, he wondered if Nayla too, at this very moment, was gazing upon the very same stars.

As the sun slowly crept over the Iron Mountains far to the east, the last star withdrew its light from the dawn sky. All along the winding trail, the warriors of Cedona woke from their slumber and prepared for another long, grueling trek to reach the summit.

After the morning fast was broken by a small meal, they were ready to move on. For Arerys, they could not move fast enough for today, once the Stone of Salvation was back in the hands of the Watchers, they could begin their journey eastward.

Although the trail was nowhere near as challenging as the other route taken by the Order during their first ascent of Mount Isa, the altitude continued to play havoc on the mortals as they trudged along the twisting path upwards with their steeds in tow. A cool, brisk breeze tugged at their clothing and ruffled their hair as it blew in from the north. Beads of perspiration evaporated from their foreheads under the wind's cooling touch. It was their only respite during this final leg of the journey. Markus trailed behind with King Augustyn and his men as Lindras forged ahead with Arerys and Valtar. The end was almost at hand.

A bright, warm sun sat high on a blue canvas where a gossamer veil of white clouds spread thinly across the horizon to the east. These feathery bands of soft clouds drifted lazily, pushed along by a high, invisible wind. As the Wizard and the Elves approached the summit, the cool breath of the north wind was no more; the air was warm and still. Up ahead the large granite pillars of the Temple of the Watchers came into view. Valtar stood in awe as his eyes took in the great stone structure and within, the Three Sisters.

Elora was busy recording the events of the past as Enra sat at the triangular, granite table gazing into her crystal orb to observe the great army advancing up the winding trail to the summit of Mount Isa. Eliya, Watcher of the Future stood at the entrance of the Temple, awaiting to receive the party for she knew of their impending arrival.

Valtar hastened towards the Temple.

"Valtar! Wait! Proceed no further!" shouted Lindras, too slow to grasp his shoulder to halt his advance.

The Wizard's words went unheeded as the dark Elf rushed ahead for a better look at the Temple and those inside.

"He shall find out the hard way, Lindras," said Arerys with a mischievous grin.

Just as the Wizard called out again for Valtar to halt, the dark Elf was abruptly thrown backwards by the explosive force of a wall of fire that suddenly erupted from the ground.

Arerys dashed over to Valtar's side, pulling him onto his feet. "The Wizard tried to warn you. You should have listened," admonished Arerys, brushing the dust off the dark Elf as he stood in a daze.

"Where did the fire come from?"

"It was always here," replied the fair Elf. "It does not become visible until those who are unwelcome into the Temple come too close."

As Markus arrived with King Augustyn by his side, he instructed the king and his men to remain, to keep watch for signs of evil as they returned the Stone to its rightful place. King Augustyn ordered his men to draw their weapons for if the Sorcerer were to make his claim, he shall be forced to do so now. With weapons at the ready, Markus approached the Wizard. Together, they joined Arerys in front of the wall of flames.

"Even the pure of heart shall not pass beyond these gates without the three keys," a disembodied voice declared.

"The three keys?" asked Valtar. "What keys?"

Arerys, Lindras and Markus glanced over at the dark Elf.

"We are the keys," answered Markus, as they turned to face the flames leaping high into the sky.

"What? What do you speak of?" Valtar failed to understand.

As the three proceeded to step towards the flames, the dark Elf moved to block their passage.

"Have you all taken leave of your senses?" asked Valtar. "Can you not feel these flames are real? That they burn?"

"Fear not, my friend," replied Lindras. "Have a little faith, we have come by this way before."

"This is madness! You shall perish in this fire!"

"We know what we do, Valtar," said Markus, giving him a knowing smile. "Please stand down."

Valtar shook his head in dismay, turning away from the three men. "I do not wish to bear witness to your demise if this is how you choose to end your life."

"We shall not be long, Valtar," promised the Wizard.

The dark Elf stood back with King Augustyn and his soldiers, watching as Markus, Lindras and Arerys faced the angry flames. All stared in disbelief as the trio advanced.

"Ready Markus?" asked the Wizard.

"Of course," replied the prince.

Lindras glanced over at the Elf. Arerys looked anxiously at the flames dancing high into the sky.

"Do you believe, Arerys?" asked Lindras, momentarily resting against his staff, its crystal orb coming alive as the light of the flames reflected against the polished globe.

Arerys' drew a deep breath whereupon he answered confidently, "Yes. Let us not keep the sisters waiting."

"Very well," agreed Lindras with a nod. With those words said, all three stepped into the flames and through the wall of fire. Untouched by the searing heat, Valtar and the others observed in amazement as the three men safely entered the Temple. The dark Elf's eyes focused on penetrating through the great, orange flames but the air, quivering with the intense heat, caused all that stood behind the curtain of fire to blur like a mirage on the desert.

As the men approached the Temple, Eliya stepped forward to greet them. "The time has come once again for us to meet, Wizard," said the Watcher of the Future as she bowed before him.

Lindras lowered his great hood, reciprocating with a bow. "Yes, and as you know, I come bearing the Stone of Salvation," said the Wizard. His long fingers carefully fished the precious gem out from its safe place, tucked behind his belt. He carefully unwrapped the Stone from a small square of cloth before presenting it back to Eliya.

The Watcher picked up the Stone, holding it forth for her sisters to see. She then placed it back onto the granite pedestal, concealing the gem beneath a black cloth.

"Let us hope we shall never have to call upon the Stone again," said Markus.

Eliya slowly turned to look upon the mortal, and then she gave him a knowing smile. "Yes, let us hope."

She stepped away from the pedestal, approaching the fair Elf. "I am Eliya, Watcher of the Future," she said. "This is Elora, Watcher of the Past and Enra, Watcher of the Present."

With her introduction, Enra and Elora stepped forward and bowed. Arerys bowed in respect, his silence spoke volumes of his reverence for the Three Sisters. Although he knew of them and his father had spoken of them from his past visits to the Temple during the war that resulted in the Second Age of Peace, nothing prepared him for this encounter. Kal-lel's description, as accurate as it was, did them no justice. The Watchers were more beautiful than he had ever imagined: Their flowing mane of red tresses, their startling green eyes set against skin as translucent and white as alabaster stole his breath away. They wore flowing, shimmering white gowns that sparkled as though it was covered with dew kissed by the first light of the morning sun. This heavenly attire only served to enhance their beauty and accentuate their statuesque height.

Eliya smiled kindly at the Elf. "Prince Arerys, as your father did before you, now you stand before us. Where your father struggled day by day, dealing with the here and now to deliver salvation to Imago, now you must work to secure its future."

"I do not understand, my lady. We have accomplished the mission. Beyilzon is dead; delivered back to Hell by Prince Markus himself."

"Yes. It is true the Dark Lord is gone, but now other evil forces are at work and their intentions are just as cruel and devious as what Beyilzon had in mind, had he succeeded in his bid to claim Imago."

"The Sorcerer of Orien?" inquired Arerys.

Eliya merely nodded her head once in acknowledgment.

"So Beyilzon's defeat on Mount Hope was a hollow victory?" asked Markus, his shoulders slumping from the burden of this news.

"That is far from the truth, Prince Markus. Your victory, no matter how fleeting you believe it to be, is a symbol of hope; that truth, justice and peace, all you hold so dear is truly attainable no matter how insurmountable the obstacles may seem that lie before you. In times of war, hope may be the one element that sustains mankind when there is nothing else. Hope is the one thing that allows you to persevere."

"Why did you not warn us of Eldred Firestaff when we were here last?" asked Markus.

"You were already faced with the monumental task of defeating the Dark Lord, do you truly believe I would further burden you with this additional knowledge?" asked Eliya, Watcher of the Future.

"The Wizard of the North warned me that Eldred is now gifted with greater powers. Is it true?" asked Lindras.

"Tor Airshorn is right, but I would hardly call the Sorcerer's power a gift. He duped the Dark Lord into bestowing him with greater powers, and then he showed his gratitude by turning Beyilzon's emissaries, the four dark horsemen against him. He controlled them in a bid to abscond with the Stone for his own evil purposes."

"I fail to understand how he accomplished this," stated the Wizard. "What did Eldred promise to Beyilzon's agents to sway them to turn against their master?"

"Think, Wizard, what is the one thing they do not possess and yet they crave more than riches or power?" asked Elora, holding forth her crystal orb to reveal a moment in the past.

Lindras stared at the crystal, watching as Eldred Firestaff rallied the dark emissaries to do his bidding early in their race to Mount Hope.

"A soul!" declared the Wizard. "He promised to return their souls back to them."

Elora nodded in acknowledgement. "Yes. Although their physical form that is trapped on this earth can be destroyed, unless they die a mortal's death, Beyilzon still maintains control over their tormented souls. The Sorcerer offered to make them human again so they may die a mortal's death. In doing so, they can break their allegiance to the Dark Lord once and for all. Condemned to this life of servitude, living in Beyilzon's shadow proved too much for them, knowing that he had no intention of fulfilling his promise other than to provide an immortal life of which they have no control or say."

"An eternal life of damnation, a soulless life with no meaning other than to serve the Dark Lord is the ultimate price to pay for their greed and pride," admitted Arerys.

"Eldred Firestaff is truly devious! He is more cunning and evil than I thought possible," averred Lindras.

"Is our job now to find him and kill him?" asked Markus, looking to Eliya for possible answers.

"You shall not act as the judge and executioner, Prince Markus," replied Eliya. "He is to be judged by his peers and his fate determined by his Father."

"He eluded capture once before, avoiding judgment by the Maker of All. Just as Eldred Firestaff believes mankind should be punished for their shortcomings, that they should be held accountable for their actions, he too must be held accountable for his own deeds," stated Elora, Watcher of the Past.

"Then why does the Maker of All not deal with him here and now? Why must we be made to deliver him to justice?" asked Markus.

Elora studied Markus for a moment before answering, her green eyes shone like dazzling stones of emerald as she considered his question. "Because Prince Markus, Eldred Firestaff, the one we once knew as the Wizard of the East, is the product of man's own follies. His contempt for man is born out man's own contempt. Though there are many good souls, there are also men who willingly seek to destroy what is good and just in this world. His soul has been twisted and his heart rages in anger because of this. He is not unlike your many religious zealots. Blinded to the truth and now hiding behind the veil of righteousness, they believe their actions can be justified because they think it serves a greater good. Eldred is no different."

Enra, Watcher of the Present held forth her crystal orb. "See, even as we speak, the Sorcerer delves into his black art."

Markus, Lindras and Arerys peered into her orb; it glowed as though it were on fire. Somewhere deep in the bowels of the earth, they witnessed Eldred at work. Hidden in a gloomy, subterranean lair surrounded by the energy of his element, fire, the Sorcerer toiled in his forbidden art. Suddenly, he froze, turning slowly as if he knew full well that eyes were upon him; observing his every move. An evil smile crept across his face, his dark, recessed eyes glowed red as they reflected the flames belching from the molten lava pooling around him.

"He knows we are watching!" stated Lindras.

As the three continued to gaze into Enra's crystal orb, Eldred threw back his head as he released a maniacal laugh. Raising his staff on high, he called upon the powers he had been vested with. Great orange flames leapt up high around him, obscuring their view.

"This is not good. The Wizard of the North warned me that Eldred was more powerful than any of us could ever imagine," said Lindras, exhaling a weary sigh. "I did not want to believe it was possible."

"Your brother, Tor was here, Lindras. He told me how his last encounter with Eldred many years ago resulted in his transformation into a dragon and how you had broken the spell to release him," said Enra.

"And where is Tor now?" asked the Wizard.

"At this very moment, he seeks out Tylon Riverdon, the Wizard of the South. He seeks his counsel after his latest altercation with the Sorcerer. He had followed Eldred to the east, to the other side of the Iron Mountains. It was at Deception Pass that Eldred used his powers in an attempt to destroy Nayla Treeborn," revealed Elora.

"Nayla is hurt?" asked Arerys, his blue eyes darkened with worry, startled by this revelation.

"Fear not, Elf. The Wizard of the North intervened in time to spare her life. Nayla recovers from her injuries," answered Enra.

"You were right, Arerys. That explains Eldred's absence on the night that we were ambushed in Crow's Nest Pass. He *is* after Nayla," admitted Markus.

"You say she recovers from her injuries. How does Nayla fare, how badly was she hurt?" asked the fair Elf, the panic rising in his voice.

Elora's green eyes stared into Arerys', calming his worried soul. "She shall recover, Prince Arerys, but it is her heart that is greatly troubled."

"Her heart? She knows I love her. I shall be returning to her," declared Arerys.

"Oh, she has no doubts that you love her. What consumes her now is that she fears for your life. Whether you know it or not, you have a bond with Nayla that is strong, you share a common energy; a life-force if you will. Though time and distance may separate you, she knows and feels your pain and anguish."

"Are you telling me Nayla knows that I was hurt?" asked Arerys, stunned by her claim.

"Let us say she knows something evil befell you," responded Enra.

"I fail to understand how," responded the perplexed Elf. "And if the Stone was so crucial to him, why did the Sorcerer not pursue us himself than to spend his time tormenting Nayla?"

"Though he may be able to see the here and now, he does not yet possess the power to foresee the future. When he sent forth the dark horseman do his bidding in an attempt to steal away with the Stone, he did so in order that he may put his plans into motion to do away with Lady Treeborn. He did not anticipate his servant would fail him. Had he known, he would have launched his own personal assault to claim the Stone of Salvation."

"Perhaps he shall give up this endeavor, now that he has failed to acquire the Stone," suggested Arerys, his voice sounding hopeful.

"That will not be the case. He is now hell-bent on destroying Lady Treeborn. Without the power of the Stone, he shall take whatever measures he feels necessary to do her harm. Even now, he gathers his forces in preparation for war."

"But why her? Why Nayla?" asked Arerys.

"Because he knows it is the love you two share that may herald the beginning of the end for him."

"Well, his powers do not scare me. He shall have to answer to me if Nayla is harmed."

"That is all well and good, Prince Arerys, your intentions are noble indeed, but be warned: there may be those working against you, driving a wedge between you and your true love. You must sum up the courage and conviction to determine what is fact, and what is false. Do not be betrayed by what you may see or hear. Matters of the heart shall require that you not hear with your ears but instead, that you listen with your heart. Above all else, your heart will not betray you; trust in what you feel. Whether your union to Nayla Treeborn works to unite or further divide the race of Elves; it is still to be determined. Just keep in mind you have much to gain if you succeed and even more to lose, if you fail."

"And if I fail to unite our people?"

"If you fail, then it shall mark the beginning of great calamities. The Sorcerer shall gain greater strength. He seeks to divide and conquer, but a race already divided shall fall easily as its foundations are already unstable. If your nation fails to rise up as one to meet this challenge, it is destined to fall as a nation divided. The Sorcerer knows you and Nayla Treeborn are like two rivers flowing from different directions. Once two rivers merge and become one, he knows it shall be one of such force and power, he may not be able to contain it."

"I fail to understand, my lady," said Arerys. "If he despises the human race, then why does he mean to destroy Nayla and our people?"

"It is simple, Prince Arerys, from the beginning of time, your people, the Elves, were placed here as the healers and guardians of Imago. Your people have stood by the mortals, attempting to guide and counsel mankind, much as the four Wizards did. Eldred despises the Elves for it is this alliance, this brotherhood that stands in his way."

Eliya looked upon Markus. "Though your future as the savior of Imago was sanctioned long ago before you came to being, your own future now depends on your ability to let go; to be free of your past. There are some ghosts better left behind, Prince Markus. What you have longed for in the past may now come back to haunt you, impeding your future and leading to your ruin if you are seduced by the powers of long forgotten feelings. Where Prince Arerys must learn to trust in his heart; yours may betray you. Love is a very powerful emotion, Prince Markus, it has led to the ruin of even the greatest of men. The high Elf, Dahlon Treeborn can attest to this, and you are no exception."

"I do not understand," stated Markus.

"In time you shall."

She then turned to Lindras. "Wizard, though you mean well, your confrontation with the Sorcerer of Orien shall lead to your own demise if you do not possess the power to face him. Tor Airshorn had warned you that Eldred Firestaff now possesses powers beyond this realm. You cannot face this adversary alone; he shall attempt to claim all those you hold dear to your heart one by one. You shall require the powers to move heaven and earth if you wish to see his reign of terror come to an end, but ultimately, it shall be your own capacity to show compassion that shall determine his fate and the fate of mankind and Elves."

"If I understand correctly, it is as it was before. You are telling me that we are to contain him, not to dispense punishment," stated Lindras, his fingers absentmindedly fondled the bands of gold holding his beard in place as he cogitated on her words.

"That is correct," acknowledged Eliya.

"And if we should fail again?"

"If you are unsuccessful in your bid, the Third Age of Peace shall be short-lived. Imago shall be immersed in war once again. First, he shall strike down the race of Elves, then he shall come after the race of man," warned the Watcher of the Future.

With these final words said, the wall of fire abruptly disappeared. It was time for the men to part company; they bowed in respect before the Three Sisters. As the men walked away, Arerys turned about for one final look at the Watchers. They bowed in a gesture of farewell.

As Lindras led the way from the Temple, the wall of flames erupted from the ground once more to protect the hallowed sanctuary from the uninvited. King Augustyn's soldiers and knights that had gathered on the summit would not be permitted entry into the Temple of the Watchers, and even now, the flames and the air quivering and rippling with the intense heat obscured their view of the Three Sisters.

Lindras turned to King Augustyn. "This is where we shall part company, my lord. The Stone of Salvation is now in its rightful place. It shall be well-guarded by the Watchers."

"I pray you have a safe journey to Orien; that you meet with success," said Augustyn, clasping the Wizard's wrist in farewell.

"Thank you for your escort, my lord," said Markus, "I wish you a swift and safe journey through Cedona. Let us hope our next meeting will be under much happier circumstances."

"When you see Lando Bayliss, wish him well. Tell him I anxiously await his safe return," said Augustyn.

"I shall do that," responded Markus with a bow.

Valtar and the men of the Order watched as the knights and soldiers of Cedona marched in single file past them. Each man glanced at the wall of fire surrounding the Temple of the Watchers as they made their way down the summit, forging on, loyally following their king westward into Cedona, onward to Land's End.

Lindras, Markus, Arerys and Valtar now stood alone on the summit of Mount Hope. Their eyes scanned the eastern horizon, taking in the vastness of the great land. Far in the distance stood the peaks of the Iron Mountains, beyond awaited their next destination: Orien.

CHAPTER 10

EAST TO ORIEN

The journey down Mount Isa was swift in comparison to the long, arduous trek up the slope. The men stopped only long enough to eat and drink; and to allow the horses sufficient time to rest and gain some sustenance on the scant vegetation as they reached the lower elevations.

Coming to a halt at the foot of Mount Isa, darkness fell rapidly upon the countryside, enveloping everyone and everything in a velvety cloak of blackness. The men of the Order settled for the evening. Arerys removed the bridles from all the horses and the saddle from Markus' steed so they may graze and rest unfettered through the night.

Valtar began to gather wood for a fire, but Markus put an abrupt end to the task. "Tonight, we are on our own. Let us not bring unwanted attention to ourselves," recommended the prince.

"But the Stone has been returned to the Watchers, has it not?" asked the dark Elf, bewildered by Markus' wariness.

"Indeed it has, but the danger is still very real."

"Yes, Valtar," warned the Wizard. "Markus is right. Let us side with caution. The Sorcerer may have eyes searching for us."

"Very well," said Valtar, discarding his armload of wood. He settled down next to the Wizard, watching as Lindras lit his pipe. His blue-gray eyes sparkled within the shadow of his hood as they reflected the orange embers glowing in the bowl of his pipe.

Arerys returned with the riding gear as well as food, tossing a pack to Valtar. It was filled with Elven bread, fruit and for Markus, cured venison. The dark Elf handed out the provisions as the men of the Order sat with nothing more than a sliver of a moon to provide them with light.

For Lindras and the Elves, the moon provided more than sufficient light, whereas Markus struggled to focus his diminishing sight in the growing darkness. He found some comfort in the warm glow of his pipe as he settled back to join Lindras for a communal smoke.

"So tell me, Arerys," said Valtar, "the Watchers, were they as beautiful as Markus had described?"

"Yes," answered the fair Elf. "And no."

"I fail to understand this."

"They were as Markus described, yet to have seen them with mine own eyes..." replied Arerys. "I lack the words that would do them justice."

"They must truly be heavenly creatures then," decided the dark Elf.

"That they are," admitted Arerys with a weary sigh.

"And did they have any sage words of advice to share with you?"

"In fact, they did," answered Arerys, staring the Elf directly into his dark eyes. "Eliya had warned me there may be those working to destroy what I have with Nayla Treeborn."

"Interesting," responded Valtar, turning away from the fair Elf's steely gaze.

Arerys considered Valtar for a moment, studying this Elf sitting before him. He wondered if his good friend, Joval Stonecroft, was indeed working to drive a wedge between he and Nayla. Certainly, from where he stood, there was little he could do other than to return to her as expediently as possible. *I must put my trust in Nayla,* thought Arerys, thinking upon Eliya's words of wisdom. *I must hear with my ears, but listen with my heart.*

And what of you, Prince Markus?" asked Valtar. "What grand plans or secrets did the Watchers reveal to you?"

"Truth be told, I have yet to understand Eliya's words of warning," admitted Markus. "Whereas Arerys was advised to follow his heart, I was warned that mine might betray me."

"Hmm, that sounds rather dark and ominous," said Valtar.

"I am most perplexed by her words: 'love has led to the ruin of even the greatest of men'. She stated Lord Dahlon Treeborn could attest to this."

"Perhaps, Eliya was warning that you might fall in love with the wrong woman," suggested Valtar. "That may be why she made mention of Lord Treeborn. He had the misfortune of becoming embroiled with a mortal, a Taijin woman who bore him a daughter."

Arerys glared at the dark Elf. He knew exactly what Valtar was insinuating.

"That is a preposterous notion, Valtar," laughed Markus. His laugh quickly faded as he thought upon his wife, Elana. "There was only one woman whom I ever loved. She died long ago. There shall be no other."

"My apologies, my lord. I did not mean to be crass," said Valtar, bowing in humility.

Markus glanced over to Lindras. He was stooped over, quietly chewing on the mouthpiece of his pipe as his fingers continually fondled the bands of gold adorning his long, silvery beard. The prince knew immediately the Wizard was reflecting upon the words of the Watchers.

"So Lindras, I can see that the Sorcerer of Orien is a growing concern for you," noted Markus.

The Wizard nodded in agreement, "Yes, he is definitely more than a mere pebble in my shoe. To minimize the potential danger he poses would be foolish indeed."

"Fear not, Wizard," smiled Arerys. "As of tomorrow, we shall begin our trek to Orien. We shall bring Eldred Firestaff to justice."

"Perhaps I should send the three of you ahead," said Lindras, releasing a thin, gray wisp of smoke into the night air. "Ride on without me."

"What do you speak of Lindras," asked Markus. Both he and Arerys suddenly sat upright upon hearing his words.

"Think on it, men," responded Lindras after careful deliberation. "Eliya warned that I lack the power to face Eldred alone. He already had an altercation with Tor Airshorn long ago, one which need I remind you, the Wizard of the North was unable to escape."

"Are you saying you wish us to proceed to Orien without you?" questioned Arerys.

"I am considering all of the possibilities, Arerys. Perhaps, it would serve us better if I were to venture south."

"South?" asked Markus. "Eldred is in Orien. That is to the east."

"Yes, I am fully aware of that," answered Lindras. "Whom I seek dwells in the southern peaks of the Cathedral Mountains."

"You wish to seek out Tylon Riverdon?" asked Arerys.

"Yes," replied the Wizard. "Eliya stated I shall require the powers to move heaven and earth to bring Eldred down onto his knees. I believe she was attempting to tell me that I shall need the help of my brothers, both Tor and Tylon if we are to meet with any degree of success in our bid to capture the Sorcerer."

The men were silent as they reflected on Lindras' words.

Finally, Arerys spoke: "Lindras, whether you choose to seek out the Wizard of the South or continue the journey to Orien with us, I must speak my mind. I cannot postpone this trek. I must get to Nagana, to Nayla before it is too late. You know the Sorcerer is after her. I cannot stand by knowing that he plots against her. Come tomorrow, I must be on my way. With, or without you, I must go."

Lindras nodded his head in understanding.

Markus turned to the Wizard. "Lindras, Eliya disclosed that Tor was already in search of Tylon. Obviously, he is trying to enlist his aid. Why else would he seek his counsel?"

Lindras' weathered fingers twirled the long strands of his moustache as he considered Markus' words. "Perhaps you are correct. After all, Tor Airshorn promised to assist me after I had lifted the curse Eldred had subjected him to. I do not believe he relished being turned into a dragon. In fact, he was most grateful I had reversed the spell. Perhaps he is prepared to return the favor, so to speak. "

"Let me ask this of you, Lindras. Do you have faith that Tor Airshorn would do what is right? That he would do what is honorable?" asked Markus.

"Of course he would," Lindras answered, agitated that the prince would question Tor's character.

"Then you have no need to seek out the Wizard of the South," replied Markus. "Tor is doing so even as we speak."

"Markus is right," said Arerys in agreement. "If the great Tor Airshorn is a wise and benevolent Wizard, if he is anything at all like you, Lindras, he shall come to our aid."

Lindras drew back his great hood as he took stock of the faces before him. After another contemplative puff on his pipe, he finally responded, "So be it. Tomorrow, we shall venture on to Orien."

With the coming of dawn, Arerys and Valtar readied the horses and replenished the water flasks. Markus stirred from his sleep as Arrow's velvety black muzzle pressed against his head. His steed began nibbling at his head of hair. With his eyes still closed, the prince used one hand to blindly wave off the stallion. Arrow continued to accost him, this time snorting loudly into his master's ear. Markus countered by pulling his blanket high over his head, shielding himself from the steed's hot, grassy breath. Suddenly, the prince's blanket was yanked clear off of his dozing form.

"Arrow!" shouted Markus, annoyed by the beast's persistence.

"It is I, Arerys," responded the Elf, tossing the blanket back at the prince. "Dawn is breaking, rouse yourself, Markus."

He gazed up at the fair Elf through half-closed eyes, still bleary with sleep. Upon realizing it was no longer his horse coaxing him to wake, Markus slowly sat up and stretched. He watched as the Elf moved on to Lindras, gently prodding the Wizard until he received the appropriate response. Lindras, having fallen asleep in a sitting position, stretched and slowly rose to his feet. It was apparent to all that Arerys wished to be on his way.

After a morning meal was quickly consumed, Markus escorted the men eastward through the Fields of Shelon. As the morning wore on and the sun continued its steady ascent, the day became unseasonably warm. The heat and humidity felt stifling as they rode on under the glaring midday sun. There was no shade to provide the men with a reprieve from the sun's intense glow as they ventured on through the near treeless land, over gentle, rolling hills and vales. They stopped to allow the horses a chance to drink from a creek before pressing on towards Castle Hill.

In the distance, Arerys' far-seeing eyes could make out the soldiers of Darross as they surveyed the land from atop the great hill. They kept watch for possible danger, ready to intercept the enemy if they were to make their presence known. Although the Elf could clearly make them out, it was safe to assume that these mortals had yet to discern their movement across the vast field.

A large, golden sun seemed precariously balanced on one of the smaller peaks of the Cathedral Mountain Range. Its light shone down like a thin, transparent leaf of gold, bathing everything it touched in a yellow haze. The shadows it cast were like long, dark fingers creeping slowly across the landscape; pursuing the men of the Order as it stretched eastward to Castle Hill. Here, King Sebastian and his knights and soldiers awaited their arrival, having already set up camp in anticipation of their meeting.

The men dismounted as Sebastian's squires gathered the horses to ready them for the night. The king welcomed them, delivering them to the fireside where wine and food were already set out for their enjoyment.

"So, Prince Arerys, you look none the worse for wear," stated Sebastian, pleased that Kal-lel's son had made it through his ordeal. "Word had spread rapidly of your condition after the ambush in Crow's Nest Pass."

"Yes, well I have fully recovered and I am more than ready to do battle with the Sorcerer," assured the fair Elf.

"My lord, how is it that Beyilzon's agent and a battalion of his soldiers made it through Darross undetected by your men?" asked Markus, settling down next to Lindras.

"I can only assume they ventured through the Gap, two or three at a time so as not to draw attention to themselves," suggested Sebastian. "Most assuredly, under the cover of night they had traveled." The king sighed in resignation, "I have only so many men to spare, Prince Markus. Even before the war on the Plains of Fire, my losses had been great. Many of my men died here in Darross fighting back the incursions that swelled over the Aranak Mountains leading up to the final confrontation."

"I understand," said Markus, sensing the burden of guilt the king felt in failing to circumvent the disaster at Crow's Nest Pass. "It is not my intention to lay blame. I merely wish to ascertain whether the Sorcerer used some kind of devilry to slip by unnoticed for I know your men to be noble and honorable; diligent in their duties. Under normal conditions, I know your knights and soldiers would have put a stop to any enemy encroachment."

"The few men left to secure the castle and guard the entry into Darross via the Gap were posted to sentry duty both day and night," explained the king.

"So, nothing untoward occurred on your lands prior to our ambush?" inquired Lindras.

"No," responded Sebastian, shrugging his shoulders. "However, there was one eve when all hands were called upon to extinguish a great fire in the stables."

The men of the Order found themselves staring at each other, knowing instantly what had transpired.

"It is clear now," stated Lindras, leaning heavily against his staff. "That fire was no accident, my lord. Eldred had set a diversion to draw attention away from the Gap. That is how they entered Darross. The Sorcerer of Orien, or more likely, one of his henchmen deliberately set fire to your stables."

"Is that not rather obvious?" asked Arerys. "To use fire, his own element? That would certainly draw attention to him."

"Eldred is an egotistical fool!" denounced Lindras; his tanned, weathered hand flew through the air, waving off the Sorcerer's unseen presence. "It is his way. He wants all to know he is at work here."

"Well, I assure you, Wizard," said Sebastian with great confidence. "Your travel through Darross shall be unimpeded. My men shall grant you safe passage to Rock Ridge Pass."

"I have no doubt," smiled the Wizard, slowly standing to his feet. "And on that note, I shall lay my weary bones down to rest. I shall see all of you in the morn."

A gray dawn marked the beginning of a new day. As usual, Arerys was the first to rise. As he waited patiently for the others to wake from their sleep, he went about the business of gathering their horses to prepare them for another long journey. The Elf's eyes scanned the northeast horizon where dark, billowing cumulus clouds snagged onto the peaks of the Aranak Mountain Range.

The weather holds little promise. The sun shall not be showing its face today, thought Arerys as his gaze traveled eastwards, looking to the faint yellow globe barely able to penetrate the ever-thickening cloud-cover over the mountains. Nonetheless, he was ready to venture forth come what may.

Though his steps were light, Arerys made little effort to stifle the noises of his movement as he saddled Arrow, allowing the stirrups to clatter loudly against each other as he tossed the saddle onto the steed's back.

Markus slowly sat up, stretching and yawning. He watched the Elf adjust the saddle and then tighten the cinch. He was not surprised in the least that Arerys would be up at the crack of dawn, eager to move out.

After joining King Sebastian for a morning meal, the Order was ready to begin their journey to Beckham.

"There has been no news of enemy advancement from the west or the north. You shall have an easy ride ahead of you. You shall have thirty of my most trusted men on the fastest steeds to escort you," promised the king, pointing to his knights as they mounted their horses. "Alas, it is with much regret that my greatest knight is not here to guide the way."

"Sir Faria Targott shall ride with us in spirit, my lord," replied Markus. "I feel he is still with us, still a part of this Order."

"Yes," responded Sebastian with a nod of agreement. "You are quite right. There are times when I stand high on the battlement of my castle to look out over this fair land. I swear I feel his presence in the wind as it blows over the hills and through the valleys of this country he lived and died for."

Markus placed his hand on the king's shoulder. "He is near to us, my lord."

"Indeed he is. Perhaps Faria shall watch over you."

Arerys breathed a bit easier, taking note of the knights assigned to accompany the Order. It pleased him to no end that together, they shall be an imposing force to reckon with if evil should come their way. He hoisted himself onto RainDance's back, turning the mare about to face King Sebastian.

"Again, thank you my lord," said Arerys. "One day I shall return your kindness."

"No need for that," stated Sebastian. "We of Darross have been the recipients of kindness extended by your father and his people many times over. Remember, if it had not been for you and the men of the Order, we would all be enslaved by the Dark Lord by now."

Markus, Lindras and Valtar all thanked the king for his generosity before turning to join the knights of Darross. In a cloud of dust that melted into the gray morning sky, the men were on their way, galloping off northeast towards the village of Beckham.

With Tempest in the lead, the horse kept to a straight course that would take them to their destination. Unencumbered, the horses ridden by those in the Order traveled with relative ease, unlike the steeds bearing the weight of knights clad in suits of steel. Their horses became winded much sooner, requiring more frequent rest stops. As grateful as Arerys was for their escort, he also felt compelled to leave them behind in the wake of his dust in his eagerness to keep moving. However, he knew better than to tempt fate.

As the day wore on under a bleak, heavy sky, the darkness of night swallowed up the land with unsettling swiftness. There were still two leagues to go before they reached Beckham, but the men knew they had traveled as far as they were able to do so on this dreary day.

"The winds of change; I can feel it," said Arerys, his blue eyes piercing the growing darkness as he breathed in the cool, damp air. "The rains are coming. We best make camp now."

All were in agreement. The knights worked at a feverish rate to pitch the tents and gather dry firewood before they were consumed by the absolute blackness of night. Slowly the ground began to drown with moisture as heavy raindrops fell from the heavens. Soon, the men all disappeared into the tents with the exception of those posted to sentry duty.

Markus and Arerys joined Lindras and Valtar in their tent. Inside, the soft glow of a coal oil lamp illuminated the quarters. The men of the Order gathered for an evening meal. Arerys ate little as he thought upon Nayla. He felt a great void in his heart.

Markus pressed some food into the Elf's hand. "Eat, my friend. Though you have recovered from your injury; you must still keep your strength up. Need I remind you, we still have far to go."

Arerys merely nodded in agreement as he accepted the food but still, he did not eat.

Lindras pushed back his great hood. His eyes twinkled and his silver hair shimmered with the light cast by the lantern. He gave Arerys a knowing smile. "Your thoughts are with Nayla, yes?"

"Yes," responded Arerys, staring vacantly at the food in his hand.

"Rest assured Arerys, Lando and Joval shall keep her safe."

"I know," sighed Arerys. "I just cannot help but worry for her well-being."

"If I know Captain Treeborn, it is *she* who is keeping Joval and Lando safe," said Valtar, his response was matter-of-fact. "She is a most capable warrior, Arerys. She has eluded the Sorcerer's many attempts to do away with her in the past; it shall be no different this time."

Arerys was quietly surprised by the dark Elf's comment. He knew Valtar was not fond of Nayla, so he was taken aback by his words of confidence, that she would rise above whatever obstacles or snares may lie in wait for her.

Wishing to relieve Arerys' worried mind, Lindras changed the subject. He smiled as he addressed Valtar, "So is it true what Markus tells me? You have taken a liking to one of the fair maidens of Wyndwood?"

Arerys looked upon the dark Elf, sitting up straight and tall upon hearing the Wizard's words.

Seeing the fair Elf's reaction, Valtar's eyes lowered, he was in no mood for a lecture from the Prince of Wyndwood. He did not wish to hear of an unspoken decree that would forbid him from seeing Mar-ra Greenshield. His answer was direct and succinct: "Yes."

"Her name? What is her name?" queried the Wizard, with great interest.

"It matters not," replied Valtar. "I have my doubts that I shall ever return to Wyndwood."

"It does matter," declared Arerys. "If you are a man of honor, you shall hold true to your words. You shall return to see Mar-ra."

"How did you know?" asked Valtar, momentarily startled by his declaration.

Arerys smiled at the dark Elf, "Let us just say, an Elf maiden in love is not one to keep a secret. Besides, I heard you make a promise to her on the morn of our departure."

"Oh my," stammered Valtar. "Her father…"

"What of Tor-rin Greenshield?" shrugged Arerys.

"He is an elder, a high Elf. He shall never approve of this."

"Do not be so sure, Valtar. If Tor-rin disapproved he would never have allowed you to spend time with his precious daughter," stated the fair Elf.

"Besides, Arerys already spoke highly of you to Tor-rin," added Markus. "He told Tor-rin that it was you who had saved his life in Crow's Nest Pass."

"It makes no difference. After all, I am a dark Elf."

"Perhaps Tor-rin is blind to color," mused the Wizard. "I hardly think it matters to him. What does matter is King Kal-lel and the elders view you as a hero; the Elf that saved the life of the Prince of Wyndwood. It is apparent to all concerned, when you let your arrow fly, it did not occur to you whether the Elf you spared was *dark* or *fair*, you did what was right."

"You spoke of me to Tor-rin?" asked Valtar, stunned by this revelation.

"Is that a problem?" responded Arerys.

"No," answered the dark Elf. "I just assumed that…"

"That I would object?"

"Yes."

"Why would I? None of us, Elf or mortal, can help falling in love. Sometimes, it happens at the most unexpected time to the most unsuspecting person. It is merely a wonderful happenstance," said Arerys with a smile, reflecting upon his own love for Nayla.

"As I stated before, I am a dark Elf."

"So? And she is fair, yet it has not stopped Mar-ra from seeing that there is more to you than your dark hair and your brown eyes. Just as I am sure, you can see there is more to Mar-ra than her beauty."

Valtar considered the fair Elf for a moment. "Do you find her to be beautiful?"

"Most certainly," acknowledged Arerys. "If you have not noticed, the Elf maidens are of exceptional beauty."

"That is interesting," replied Valtar, thinking on his words.

"How so?"

"You claim that the maidens of Wyndwood are of exceptional beauty and yet, you have chosen a woman that is neither true Elf, nor human. I fail to understand this attraction."

"As I said, one cannot help who one falls in love with. Yes, the Elf maidens are all fair; it is like looking upon one beautiful rose after another. Each one is a vision of perfection, and then one day you happen upon a rare and unusual flower growing alone amidst a multitude of roses. You are drawn to its color, its shape, its perfume. Although it is not a rose, it does not mean that it is less beautiful."

"Point well taken," said Valtar, absorbing Arerys' words with great interest.

There was more Arerys could have said, but he held his tongue. It was only after he had lowered his defenses, seeing Nayla for who she really was, that he fell in love. Initially drawn to the beauty of her dark, exotic looks, a combination of her Taijin and Elven blood, as well as her spirited nature and fighting skills, he was very pleasantly surprised by her attitude to the act of procreation.

Where the Elf maidens are of refined, delicate beauty, their shy, demure nature also made them rather passive bedmates. He often had the impression that their ever so reserved demeanor curbed their sexual appetite. Conjugal pairings were viewed as merely an expected part of their womanly duties; passively lying there for the man to fulfill his own pleasures.

Nayla on the other hand not only gave him a tremendous amount of gratification, she readily sought it for herself. She was extremely responsive to his every touch, to his every move and it only served to heighten his own desire and feelings of pleasure. Their lovemaking was fueled by a boundless passion he never knew was possible. There was nothing at all passive about their intimate encounters.

Arerys' thoughts of Nayla quickly dissipated as Markus rose up to his feet. With a great yawn, he bade the others a good night, "I shall go to seek some sleep for tomorrow shall be another long day. Good evening, gentlemen."

As he lifted the flap of the tent to exit, Markus glanced up at the knights guarding the camp. They stood steadfast in the chilling downpour, their eyes fixed on the dark surroundings. They did not move, speak or utter one word of complaint as they stood guard in the bitterly cold rain. Somehow, Markus could picture Faria Targott, their departed captain, standing stoically amongst his men, undaunted by the miserable conditions, doing what he was appointed to do; to serve his king and protect those assigned to his care, no matter what. *Perhaps Faria's spirit lives on through his men,* thought Markus. *May they draw strength from his soul for tonight we shall sleep and be safe.*

The darkness of night quietly dissolved under the warming touch of the sun's golden light. Arerys woke to the chorus of finches skimming low over the tall grasses that rippled like waves under the invisible hand of an early morning breeze. He leapt up from his bedroll, noticing that Markus was already stirring from his sleep and would probably require little, if any, prompting to wake.

He hastily threw his cloak about his shoulders as he exited the tent, heading to a nearby creek. RainDance raised her head, water dribbling from her mouth as she whinnied in recognition of the Elf. Arerys gave the mare a firm pat on her withers as he knelt down to splash the cold, clear water onto his face. He reveled in its cool, invigorating brace. He felt wide-awake; alert to everything around him. He glanced up in time to see Markus emerge from the tent, rotating his right shoulder that had been dislocated some time ago. Although he was able to wield his sword again, stiffness would creep in as he slept, especially when the nights were cool. Last night's rain did little to help his condition.

After sharing a morning meal with the knights of Darross, the men were ready to move on.

"It is only another league to Beckham, and then a day's ride to Heathrowen, captain. There is no need for you and the men in your service to journey on. You are free to head back to the castle," said Markus. "I am sure King Sebastian is anxiously awaiting the return of all his men so he can begin the business of rebuilding his country."

"It is kind of you to make the offer, my lord," nodded the captain in thanks. "However, I swore to my liege that I shall safely deliver the men of the Order to King Bromwell. That is what I intend to do. I shall not fall short of performing my duties."

"Very well," smiled Markus, he knew the knight could not be swayed. "Then let us not disappoint your king."

Immediately after the tents were disassembled and packed onto the horses, the knights of Darross and the men of the Order were on the move. They rode hard, again with Lindras riding high on Tempest, leading the way.

In the light of day, their eyes took in the devastation. Beckham was one of the first places in Darross to be ravaged by the cruel hands of war. Many of the homes in the abandoned village, as well as the out-lying farms, were reduced to ashes. Those left standing were now just empty shells; devoid of life, ransacked by the soldiers of the Dark Army as they made their way westward in their bid to hunt down the members of the Order.

Although the lands looked decimated, blackened by fires, a pletho-ra of bright magenta flower spikes flourished. The tall fireweeds swayed in the gentle breeze, brightening the harsh landscape. They grew in great profusion from the burned ground. The rosy-pink flow-ers secreted sweet nectar, attracting bees, butterflies and humming-birds. The men took comfort in knowing that nature was reclaiming the land acre by acre, healing the scars made by the enemy soldiers.

Arerys brought RainDance to an abrupt halt. Approaching from the south, the Elf could make out distant forms trudging towards the deserted village. His hand shielded his clear blue eyes from the glare of the morning sun as he stared out, trying to ascertain the identity of those moving in their direction. He sat straight and tall, straining to see. Markus brought Arrow along next to Arerys' mare. He could see the look of distress on the Elf's face as he studied the dark forms on the horizon.

A sigh of relief escaped him, the Elf relaxed as he turned his horse about.

"What is it?" asked Lindras, bringing his steed next to RainDance.

"It is the villagers. They return," stated the Elf, pointing to the steady procession. "I can make out the people and their possessions, what little they have left."

"Life is returning once more. That is a good omen," said Markus. "Let us make haste."

The prince was eager to be on his way; his father should be await-ing their arrival outside of Heathrowen. Stopping only long enough to allow the horses adequate time to rest, the men also took the time to take in sustenance.

Valtar used the opportunity to replenish their flasks from a water pump at an abandoned farmhouse, as he worked the hand pump, cold, clean water gushed forth from the spout. The Elf cupped a handful of water, sniffing it first before tasting it. To his surprise the water was fresh and clear, no doubt springing from an artesian well deep within the ground.

As the men and knights of Darross neared the large hill overlook-ing the valley where the village of Heathrowen was nestled, Arerys' sharp eyes caught sight of a lone horseman. The rider watched their approach before suddenly turning his horse about. He disappeared from view and his abrupt disappearance coincided with the sound of a distant horn that could be heard by all.

"Let us hope he was one of your countrymen, Markus," said Lindras, urging his steed on.

"We shall find out soon enough, Wizard," replied the prince, following close behind.

"He disappeared before I could make him out," said Arerys with disappointment. "Perhaps we should change our approach, just in case."

The captain brought his steed up next to Markus' stallion. "Remain here, my lord. I shall take my men ahead; see what awaits us in the valley."

"Very well, but I want you to retreat upon the first sign of danger," warned Markus.

The captain nodded in understanding, waving his men on to follow him. They charged up the incline, coming to a stop as they crested the hill. Arerys and Valtar both watched, waiting for a sign from the captain that they may advance.

After a long moment, the captain raised his hand, motioning for the men of the Order to move ahead.

Markus and the others charged up the hill, coming to an abrupt halt when they reached the top. Looking down into the deepening shadows of the valley below, they saw many small figures falling into line, creating row upon row of soldiers. A huge encampment stretching through the bowel of the valley all the way to the outskirts of Heathrowen lay before them. "That cannot be!" gasped Markus, surprised by what his eyes beheld.

"It is your people," confirmed Arerys, his sharp eyes recognizing King Bromwell as he assembled his men.

"There must be thousands of them," stated the prince.

"You cannot say your father came unprepared," smiled Arerys.

Markus turned to the captain, "Night shall soon be upon us; you and your men have come this far. Please stay amongst the soldiers of Carcross for this one night."

"As you wish, my lord," responded the captain, signaling his men to follow him down into the valley.

The sun slipped behind the distant mountains, its waning light turned the sky a deep violet blue. As the first stars of the evening twinkled on high in the heavens, the men approached the awaiting army. They were greeted by Markus' father, King Bromwell. The prince gazed upon the rows of knights and soldiers, recognizing many of the faces lined up before him. He smiled and nodded in acknowledgement, grateful that they had shown up in such force.

Markus dismounted from Arrow, bowing first before giving his father a warm hug. "I knew you would be here. I just never believed you would be here with all the men of Carcross!"

"That is a slight exaggeration, my son," smiled Bromwell, releasing his embrace. "Besides, King Kal-lel's request that those loyal to the Alliance should come together once again was not about to be ignored. I will not jeopardize the lives of those in the Order, especially that of my son's."

"But the men, there are so many!"

"Let us just say that we were in the general vicinity," responded the king, directing Markus and the others to follow him to the campfire. With a single wave of his hand, Bromwell dismissed the men in his service. The knights and soldiers quickly fell out of line, returning to the business of readying for the coming of the night.

With another wave, food and wine were delivered immediately to the men of the Order as well as the knights of Darross as they retired only a short distance from the light of the fire.

"In times like this, word does travel swiftly," stated Bromwell. "We were returning southward when King Sebastian's messenger caught up with us between Hansford and the Broken Hills. I immediately sent those on horseback to meet you in the Fields of Shelon. As for the infantry, they merely turned around and marched back, waiting for your arrival here near Heathrowen."

"I am grateful that you would do us this service," thanked the fair Elf, bowing his head in obvious gratitude.

"Of course I would do this, Arerys," Bromwell stated emphatically. "Not only are you a friend to my son, you are also like a son to me; how could I not?"

"Have the lands been quiet?" asked Lindras, resting against his staff. "Has there been any sign of evil?"

"There has been nothing," noted Bromwell. "Not even stragglers - deserters of the Dark Army, to speak of. It may well be that our sheer numbers was enough to drive them off for we have made our presence known from here, straight through Rock Ridge Pass into Talibarr."

"That is a good sign indeed," nodded the Wizard, searching his pack for his pipe. "Let us hope that your show of force was enough to drive Eldred's cronies cowering back over the Iron Mountains."

"It may be advisable to take some of the men on through to Orien," recommended the king.

"I do not believe it will be necessary, my lord" said Valtar.

"How so?" asked Bromwell, looking upon the dark Elf.

"If Eldred is indeed back in Orien, I know for a fact his energies shall be focused on those who mean to flush him out from his lair. Joval Stonecroft and Captain Treeborn will most certainly be countering his efforts. They shall stymie his every move in a bid to capture him," Valtar answered with the greatest confidence.

"I cannot help but fear for Nayla's life," admitted Arerys.

"Your energy is better spent on how you plan to confront and capture that foul villain," suggested Valtar.

"I cannot ignore the fact the Watcher had warned me that Nayla was somehow wounded by the Sorcerer. She may still be injured," said Arerys.

"She may be injured, but she is not dead. Joval shall die first before he allows Nayla to succumb to Firestaff," stated Valtar. His dark eyes burned as they glared at the fair Elf, as though he would hold Nayla personally accountable for Joval's demise if that was to be his fate.

As Valtar stated his case, Arerys also knew he meant to make it perfectly clear it was to be Joval's undying devotion for Nayla that would cause him to sacrifice his own life to spare hers. Again, Eliya's words of warning, that forces may be at work to tear him and Nayla apart gnawed at his heart.

"Valtar is right," agreed Lindras. "Once the Sorcerer is forced back over the Iron Mountain, he shall be spending all his waking hours attempting to avoid capture."

"Can you be sure of this?" asked Markus.

"Who can ever be absolutely sure of anything?" responded the Wizard, his shoulders arched in a shrug. "If he remains true to his nature, he shall do what he did the last time I sought him out. He shall lay low, attempting to quietly disappear until I return to western Imago. However, this time I shall not be returning alone."

Under a star-studded ebony sky, the men of the Order slept well. With the soldiers of Carcross keeping watch through the night into the wee hours of the morning, there was not one sign of danger. All was quiet. It was only after the gray dawn was made warm by the rising sun did the men finally stir from their slumber.

After a morning meal, the knights of Darross bade farewell to the men of the Order. Markus thanked them for their service, watching as they disappeared westward over the hill, heading back to King Sebastian's castle.

"We shall be on our way too, Arerys," stated the prince, observing as a young squire readied their horses.

These words pleased the Elf. He was eager to be on his way, but he did not want to rush Markus for he knew it would be an undisclosed length of time before he would be seeing his father again.

"The army shall be ready to move in a few hours," stated King Bromwell.

Arerys was momentarily startled by his announcement. "What do you mean, *'a few hours'*?"

"It shall take some time to break this camp down; to be ready to begin our journey," advised the king.

"Father, surely you do not mean for the entire army to accompany us to the Iron Mountains?" asked Markus.

"Why, of course I do," answered Bromwell.

Markus looked to Arerys; he could see that the Elf was distressed. To travel in the company of an infantry of this size would only slow their progress.

"My lord, though I know it is your intention to keep us safe, I assure you, an army of this size is… is…" stammered the Elf, searching for the appropriate words so as not to offend the king.

"Is far more than what we shall need," finished Markus. "Before us stand the finest knights of western Imago. Their skill and valor alone make them a formidable force, even in small numbers. If we move with an army, we shall only take those on horseback."

Arerys nodded to Markus in agreement.

Bromwell considered his son's words carefully, and then he responded, "Very well, Markus, so be it. I shall gather the rest of my men and head back to Carcross."

"Thank you, my lord," said Arerys, with much gratitude. "And the rest of your fine warriors shall be set on a course back to your fair land once we have reached the Iron Mountains."

"We shall be off as soon as the knights are ready to move out," stated Markus.

With the sun still low over the Iron Mountains, the knights of Carcross mounted their steeds in preparation to escort the men of the Order into Talibarr. Ten men across and twenty men deep, they patiently waited for word from Prince Markus to begin their trek across enemy territory.

Lindras, Arerys and Valtar thanked King Bromwell for his hospitality and for offering the men in his service for this task. They mounted their steeds and watched as Markus knelt and bowed before his father. Rising up onto his feet, Markus embraced his father in a farewell hug.

"I suspect that I shall not see you again until Eldred Firestaff has been brought to justice," said Bromwell, searching Markus' eyes.

"After all we have endured, and lost to keep Imago safe from the Dark Lord, I shall not allow that heathen the opportunity to dash our hopes for a lasting peace," answered Markus. "Nor will I allow him to steal away with Arerys' chance for eternal bliss. The Sorcerer means to do away with Nayla Treeborn and I have a feeling that if he is successful in doing so, it shall mark the beginning of the end."

Bromwell sighed with a heavy heart, "You make it sound so dire, my son."

"It is," whispered Markus, his eyes saddened as he felt the despair in his father's voice.

"But Markus," responded Bromwell, in a hushed tone so not all would hear, "you have already fought and won for peace in western Imago. This menace that you seek has not declared war against us. There is peace in our lands once again; this battle is not for you to undertake. It is for Lord Dahlon Treeborn and those to the east to bear."

"For an eternity, Arerys' people have stood beside mankind through the best and worst of times. Now, as the shadow of this dark cloud looms before us, I cannot help but feel that the race of Elves is in need of help - our help, if they are to endure," stated Markus, hoping for some semblance of understanding from his father.

"And what shall you do if your words and actions hold no sway in what becomes of the Elves? What if your efforts are all in vain?" asked the king.

"I must try, father," replied the prince. "If we fail in our quest, not only shall it lead to the ruin of Elves, mankind shall fall in their shadow."

The king embraced his son one final time. "In all the years I have spent teaching you, I never suspected that my efforts to groom you into a kind, compassionate and just ruler ever truly sank in, until now," said Bromwell, offering his son an understanding smile. "It gives me great comfort in knowing that my words did not go unheeded. Be off now. I shall see you when your task is done."

King Bromwell stood amongst the soldiers of his infantry, watching in silence as Markus led the men of the Order and the knights of Carcross northward to Talibarr.

The journey over the Aranak Mountains by way of Rock Ridge Pass onto the Plains of Fire took an entire day. As dusk settled on the desolate land of the Dark Lord's former stronghold, the men of the Order and the knights in their service prepared to settle for the evening. They spent a quiet and uneventful night in this forsaken land, waking at dawn's first light.

As they journeyed eastward towards the Iron Mountains, the men observed the evidence of war all around them. Across the Plains of Fire, for as far as they could see, broken swords and halberds, spent and shattered arrows, and abandoned shields lay scattered about.

The wounded men of the Alliance, left in the care of the Elves of Wyndwood, had long departed. They had headed back after they were well enough to make the trek to their respective countries. Those who were not as fortunate were left behind. Along the way, stacks of rocks served as grave markers for the fallen soldiers.

Venturing up the slope of Mount Hope, the men looked upon the grim landscape. The decaying corpses of the soldiers loyal to the Dark Lord lay scattered about where Joval Stonecroft and the warriors of Orien had taken up arms. They had quickly and efficiently annihilated the enemy soldiers so that Nayla and the men of the Order might complete their quest. As they breached the ridge where Nayla's army had joined forces with the Alliance, the sun was sinking low in the late afternoon sky.

They ventured as far as the base of the Iron Mountains. Here in the shadow of this formidable mountain range, the knights of Carcross set up camp for the evening. A rotating shift of men conducted sentry duty throughout the long, dark night, keeping watch over the Order.

With the rising of the sun, Markus and the others awoke from their sleep. The prince emerged from his tent to find Arerys had already bridled all the horses and was in the midst of tightening the cinch on his steed's saddle. Arrow snorted at Markus, tossing his head about in restlessness. He had no doubt that Arerys had whispered some Elvish words to his stallion, perhaps promising Arrow an endless supply of oats if he could persuade his master to get a move on.

Lindras emerged from his tent, propping himself against his staff. His eyes sparkled in anticipation as he gazed up at the mountain slope. With his hand, he shielded his eyes as the sun peered over the craggy pinnacle. "If we press on hard all day, I believe we can reach Deception Pass by day's end."

Valtar's glance traveled from the Wizard to Markus. "*We* may be able to, but a mortal cannot. The air shall be thin as we near the summit. I think it would be wise to venture only as far as Prince Markus can humanly do so," suggested the Elf.

Markus studied the dark mountain looming before them. It was much larger than Mount Isa, its jagged peak snagging errant clouds that drifted too close. The trail traversing the face of the mountain was only wide enough to allow a single man and horse to move upwards at a time. The zigzagging path would lessen the steepness of the ascent, but it shall prove to be a long, difficult trek nonetheless.

"I shall try to keep up as best I can," sighed Markus, his dark eyes taking in the vastness of the towering, bleak land mass. He already anticipated the ill effects of the thin mountain air as it takes its toll on his body as they make their way up the slope.

As the knights of Carcross prepared to leave the men of the Order, Markus glanced through the row upon row of men, seeking out their captain. It suddenly dawned on him that the one man he sought was no longer in their company. Darius Calsair was long laid to rest at the Citadel where he and Nayla fought off an attack in a bid to protect Ewen Vatel. His heart sank as he thought upon his departed friend. It was times like this, when he ventured into regions unknown, that he took comfort in Darius' presence. The bold and daring knight relished adventure and though he had never journeyed east of the Iron Mountains, Darius would certainly have risen to the challenge, taking up his sword and bow to protect the prince from harm.

Markus realized it was not so much Darius' ability and skill with his weapons that he desired, but rather his company; the camaraderie they once shared. It was his courage and good-humor he missed the most. The knight had a habit of facing danger with fire in his eyes and a smile upon his face, charging headlong into battle, doing what he was sworn to do, to uphold justice and to protect the innocent. He was a knight through and through, living and ultimately dying by the edge of his sword as he honored his pledge to serve king and country.

The prince could still remember how Darius oozed with charisma. With his imposing stature and dashing good-looks, he was notorious for his ability to charm the ladies of Carcross, enchanting them with his disarming smile, bright blue eyes and his heart of gold. *What I would give to have Darius by our side now,* thought Markus, gazing upon the new captain of his father's army.

The captain bowed before Markus. "If we are no longer required, we shall be on our way, my lord."

"Yes," responded the prince. "Thank you for the escort. You best be off now. With any luck you shall catch up to my father and his men well before they reach the borders of Carcross."

"Keep safe, my lord," said the captain, mounting his steed. "I shall report to King Bromwell that we have delivered you to the Iron Mountains; that you begin your journey into Orien."

The men of the Order watched as the captain turned his stallion about, leading his men westward to Rock Ridge Pass and then southward to Carcross.

It was only when the distant cry of an eagle flying high in the morning sky caught their attention did their thoughts return to the task at hand.

Markus gazed up at the massive barrier that divided Imago. The daunting chore of climbing up to Deception Pass awaited them.

"Shall we be on our way?" asked Valtar, taking his horse by the reins.

Arerys looked to Markus and Lindras, as formidable as this mountain appeared before him, the Elf knew that what awaited him on the other side was worth dying for.

"I am ready," replied Arerys with confidence, eager to be on his way.

Lindras nodded as he turned to Markus, watching as the prince's eyes followed the long, winding path up the mountainside. "How do we even begin such a monumental task?" he asked; trepidation filled his voice.

The Wizard smiled kindly at Markus and answered, "It is simple, my friend. Place one foot in front and the other shall follow, and so on, and so forth... our journey begins."

CHAPTER 11

A PROMISE BROKEN

"I do not believe I can take one more step," gasped Markus, struggling for his breath as he leaned against Arrow's withers. His eyes were squeezed shut in response to his aching head that pounded unmercifully as his lungs fought to suck in the thin air.

"Darkness shall be upon us soon," announced Lindras. "We shall rest for the night." His eyes gazed to the western horizon, watching as the sun sank behind the distant mountains, its waning light fading from the sky.

"It is best we stop here; proceed at first light," agreed Valtar. "Believe me; you do not want to spend the night in Deception Pass." The dark Elf left his steed to make his way to Markus.

"My lord, I can see that the air is causing you much grief. Your breathing is much too fast and shallow. You must take slower, deeper breaths if you wish to stave off the effects of this mountain air," stated Valtar, taking Markus by his arm to seat him upon a large rock. He looked the prince in his eyes as he spoke, "Listen to me. Take a deep; slow breath in through your nose, hold it for the count of three, and then release your breath slowly through you mouth."

Markus did as Valtar instructed. As he exhaled, the Elf urged him to repeat the process again and then once more. As the pounding in his head eased somewhat, he slowly sank to the ground in exhaustion. Arerys removed the bedroll that was secured to his steed's saddle, delivering it to Markus.

"Do you wish to eat before you rest?" asked the Elf.

"My need for sleep far exceeds my desire to eat," replied Markus, between deep breaths. "Truth be told, I do not believe I have the fortitude to keep anything down at this moment. Sleep is the better option for I have a feeling the last stretch to the pass shall require all of my strength."

"Very well," said Arerys. "We shall keep watch through the night. Rest while you can."

A gray dawn ushered in the beginning of another day. The sun had yet to show its face over the mountains when Markus finally stirred from his sleep. He slowly opened his eyes, blinking hard as they focused on a dark form silhouetted against a bleak sky. It was Arerys. The Elf was balanced on a jagged boulder jutting out from the mountainside. His sharp eyes studied the trail leading up to Deception Pass. It was obvious to Markus that Arerys was searching for signs of danger, for possible snares set by the Sorcerer.

As he struggled to sit up, he turned his gaze up the path where the sounds of Lindras' loud snoring broke the solitude. The Wizard was sound asleep, as usual, sitting upright. His hands firmly gripping his staff as he leaned upon it. Further up the path, Markus could see Valtar. The Elf was replenishing the water flasks at a small waterfall that cascaded down past the trail.

Markus stretched and rubbed his eyes as he rose to his feet. He drew in a long, slow breath of air, pleasantly surprised that his head was no longer throbbing with pain. Arerys leapt down from the outcropping boulder upon seeing that the prince was awake. He grabbed the pack containing food to deliver to him.

As Markus ate, the fair Elf strolled over to where Lindras was still braced in a deep asleep. "Wizard! Morning is upon us. Rouse yourself!"

Lindras responded by snorting loudly, still soundly embraced in a dream of no doubt, epic proportions.

The Elf gently prodded the Wizard. Still, there was no response.

Arerys finally pried the staff from the Wizard's hands, upon which Lindras bolted up from his slumber just as he was about to tip forward; no longer propped up by his magical staff. He appeared momentarily disheveled by the Elf's antic, grunting his displeasure as he righted himself.

"It would serve you well to treat an old Wizard with a little more respect!" grumbled Lindras.

Arerys laughed, handing the staff back to him.

"Do not believe for a moment that I would not turn you into a pillar of stone," threatened the Wizard. A shrewd smile crept across his face as he pointed the crystal embedded atop of his staff towards the Elf.

"Forgive me, my friend," said Arerys with a broad grin. "I did not mean to offend you. Today we enter Orien and my heart feels as though it is no longer bound by shackles."

"Oh, to be in love," groaned Lindras in feigned disgust. "That in itself can be a curse!"

"Now be kind, Lindras," reprimanded Markus. "It may very well be Arerys' love for Nayla that shall see us through this trek."

By late morning, the Elves and the Wizard moved up at a steady pace, stopping frequently to allow Markus to catch up as he trudged along the path. As they neared the summit, Valtar led them through a narrow pass. For a lingering moment, all stopped to take in the breath-taking view from atop of the world. To the west, Talibarr and Darross stretched out before them for as far as they could see. To the east the rugged, ancient lands of Orien lay in wait.

A cold wind suddenly howled through the pass, its chilling embrace took them by surprise. Though the sun shone brightly, caus-ing the frost and snow to sparkle a blinding white, the air was still bit-terly cold. Markus drew in another long, slow breath. As he exhaled, his warmed breath was momentarily suspended in the frosty air before being swept away by an invisible wind.

Valtar motioned for all to keep moving. "We best be on our way. We must travel as far down this mountain as possible before the com-ing of the night," recommended the Elf, coaxing his steed to follow him through the pass.

"Valtar is right," agreed Lindras. "We are now entering the Sorcerer's domain. There is no telling what that wicked soul may be planning for us. Let us be off."

As Markus and Arerys followed, the frozen corpses of soldiers lay scattered about; a testament to the will of the elements. Markus drew his Elven cloak about his body as a cold wind whispered around him. He shuddered as its chilling breath touched him to his very soul.

Standing next to Valtar, both Markus and Arerys looked across to the unfamiliar eastern horizon. The Elves studied the winding trail leading down the treacherous slope. Ice and snow continued to cling stubbornly to this face of the mountain. There was no sign of the Sorcerer or his minions; the only threat that loomed was the perilous trek down. Arerys stepped gingerly to the edge of a snow-encrusted ledge. He peered down, his eyes piercing through the layer of clouds clinging to the mountainside below him. Suddenly he gasped, jolted by an alarming vision. "Something evil happened here! Something hap-pened to Nayla!"

"Come away from there, Arerys!" called out Lindras. "It is not safe to stand so close to the edge."

Markus cautiously made his way closer, but Arerys raised his hand, warning him not to advance. He stepped lightly away from the ledge.

"What makes you believe something happened here?" quizzed Markus.

"I saw it," whispered Arerys. His heart was pounding loudly, still overwhelmed by the image that flashed in his mind. "I do not know how it can be, but I saw her falling. Falling through those clouds below."

"Perhaps the thin air affects Elves after all," suggested Markus, in an attempt to quell his fears. "Your imagination gets the best of you."

"No, Markus, I know what I saw. I could sense her fear; it was so real I could taste it," answered Arerys.

"You could be mistaken, Arerys," said Lindras.

"Or perhaps he is right," declared Valtar. All three turned to look upon him.

Valtar pointed to the icy ledge, "Look, over there. I see signs of a rope cutting into the ice and snow."

Arerys stared at the indentations made by a rope that was obviously lowered over the edge. Instantly, the Elf knew what had happened, a momentary look of panic clouded his blue eyes.

Markus rested a reassuring hand on Arerys' shoulder. "Fear not, my friend. Remember, Elora stated that Nayla did indeed fall victim to one of Eldred's plots but keep in mind, she did not die. Nayla recovers from her injuries."

Arerys nodded his head in silent agreement. He quickly attempted to vanquish the terrifying image now seared into his memory. "You are right, Nayla is fine. Let us leave this place immediately."

Valtar escorted the others down the trail while all the time, Arerys' watchful eyes scanned the terrain searching for signs that might indicate what had happened to Nayla when she and her army passed through on their return trip to Orien.

The descent from Deception Pass was much faster than the long, difficult hike up the western face of the mountain. Traveling down the slope, long shadows stretched across the lands as the sun sank ever lower behind the jagged pinnacles of the Iron Mountains. The pale blue sky was beginning to assume its evening hue as the light of day quietly surrendered to the coming of the night.

As the four riders reached the foot of the mountain, the scraggly pine and fir trees gradually gave way to an ancient deciduous forest.

All about them, tall stands of towering bamboo reached skyward. Arerys glanced up to the lacy, green canopy, watching as small, sparrow-sized birds fluttered between the leaves. The bright yellow markings on the wings flashed as the birds darted in and out of the branches in aerial pursuit, their shrill song carried far through the forest. In shady locations along streams and small waterfalls, feathery fronds of dark green ferns created lush, elegant crowns of vegetation. In the distance, Arerys could make out the form of several deer, silently retreating into the safety of a nearby thicket as the men neared.

With the land soon engulfed by an ink black sky, with nothing more than the light emitted by millions of twinkling stars and a thin sliver of a crescent moon, the men settled down for the night. Like a lone sentry, silhouetted against the sky, Arerys took the first watch while the others slept. Leaning against his bow, his eyes searched the dark horizon. Though they still had far to travel, his only comfort came from the knowledge that he was now one day closer to reaching his final destination. He was one day closer to seeing Nayla again.

Arerys wasted little time in the morning. Each day he was the first to rise, even before Valtar returned from the final shift of sentry duty. He would ready the horses, sort out their meals, and collect fresh water, all in an effort to save time. And each night, Arerys took the first watch, trading off with Valtar in the wee hours of the morning. For five days and nights they continued this routine as they made their way through the strange lands; its rugged terrain punctuated by deep valleys, steep ravines and great bamboo forests.

Emerging from the depth of a valley, Valtar brought his steed to a halt. His dark brown eyes strained as they searched the terrain that spread out before him. The fading colors of the evening landscape, subdued by the twilight made it all the more difficult, even for an Elf, to detect fine details. A hush fell upon the land as the world prepared for the transition from dusk to darkness. The animals settling down to sleep would soon be replaced by those that embrace the night. Soon, these nocturnal creatures will stir from their daytime slumber, coming alive as a cloak of blackness shrouds the countryside.

Arerys brought RainDance alongside Valtar's stallion. Squinting into the dimming sky, he gazed upon the valley below, and then east towards a mountain range.

"This is our route," stated Valtar. "Tonight, we shall rest in Hebeku Valley. Tomorrow, we shall skirt the great bamboo forests as we venture towards the Furai Mountains, and then we shall set a course southward on Esshu Road. It shall deliver us to Nagana."

Lindras and Markus followed behind Arerys as Valtar led the way down to the floor of the small, narrow valley. As they journeyed on into the growing darkness, Arerys listened, sitting tall on RainDance as he strained to hear.

"Valtar, surely there are creatures of the night that would make their presence known by now?" asked the fair Elf.

"Of course, there are crickets, cicadas, frogs, even birds such as owls and nightingales that come alive with the impending darkness," responded Valtar.

"If that is the case, where are they now? I hear nothing."

Valtar brought his steed to a stop as he listened. Lindras and Markus brought their horses about, noting the look of concern on the fair Elf's face.

"Arerys is quite right," whispered Lindras. "The night is deathly quiet. The animals hide in fear."

"This is not good," responded Markus, his eyes nervously darting from side to side in a desperate bid to pick up some sign of life.

Arerys' head tilted ever so slightly as he strained to hear, attempting to listen through the eerie silence. "There is an evil that lurks in this valley. I can feel it in my soul," said the Elf, in a hushed tone.

Valtar was now visibly alarmed by a presence he could not see, but now, he too could sense. "We must leave! We cannot stay here!"

"But where do we go?" asked Markus.

"There is a safe haven on the other side of this valley. If we get to the Reyu River, if we can cross it, then Anshen is less than two leagues to the east. If we can get there, we shall be safe," stated Valtar.

"What is in Anshen?" asked Markus.

"The Shadow Warriors of the Furai Mountains: Nayla's people, the Kagai Warriors," answered the Elf, his heels digging into his steed's flanks. His horse reared up before bolting through the valley. The others followed close behind as darkness continued to engulf the forest.

Arerys was acutely aware that the void created by the absence of night creatures was soon replaced by an unearthly sound. He could hear the fast approaching thunder of hoof beats and the clamor of weapons rattling against armor.

Valtar too could hear this ungodly sound, glancing back at the fair Elf, he shouted. "Make haste, men! We have not a moment to spare!"

Though Markus could not yet hear the impending danger, he knew from the urgency in Valtar's voice that something evil was fast approaching in their direction. Urging Arrow on, the darkening landscape was a blur as they raced eastward.

With still another league to go before reaching the river, Valtar and Arerys could not only hear the danger, they could feel it pressing down hard upon them. They could smell a malodorous scent rife with the sweat and the blood of others. It hung heavy in the air, growing stronger with each passing minute. They knew it was only a matter of time before the enemy would descend upon them.

Their pounding hearts, only eclipsed by the frantic pace of their steeds' hoof beats, continued to race in anticipation of the looming danger. But now, these noises were drowned out by the sounds of soldiers on horseback approaching from the north, south and west. They were being surrounded!

"Imperial Soldiers!" yelled Valtar.

Arerys snatched the bow that was slung over his back. Dropping his reins, he urged RainDance onward as he reached for an arrow. His eyes quickly made out the form of soldiers, swords raised high, charging towards them. He took aim and began launching his arrows with deadly accuracy, downing the soldiers on the front line of attack. Valtar too took up his bow to begin his own barrage, instructing Lindras and Markus to ride on ahead.

Suddenly, Arrow and Tempest reared up, snorting and whinnying in fear, almost pitching Markus and Lindras to the ground. A dozen soldiers cut off their path, there was nowhere left to run.

All four dismounted, releasing their frightened steeds to escape. The men stood with their backs towards each other so they faced the encroaching enemy. Markus drew his sword while Lindras held forth his staff, steadying it in both hands, as Arerys and Valtar, arrows now depleted, unsheathed their swords.

"Come no closer!" warned Lindras, lowering the tip of his staff to the ground. The crystal glowed, its light intensifying with his growing rage. "One more step and the ground shall swallow you up!"

Immediately, the soldiers recognized Lindras to be some form of Wizard, but his hesitance in acting upon this threat caused doubt over his supposed powers. They chose to ignore his warning, veering ever closer.

Lindras instinctively closed his eyes, uttering a spell as he pointed his staff to the ground. The tortured earth groaned and buckled around them, tearing as it split open, creating a chasm between the men of the Order and the army that now surrounded them.

"Now what, Lindras? How do you intend to finish them off?" asked Markus, his sword still pointed to the enemy.

Lindras raised his staff high over his head. "By my will, the ground shall quake and fall beneath their feet! They shall be consumed by the earth!" he declared, driving the end of his staff downward.

A loud tremor echoed in their ears as the earth rumbled beneath their feet as all fought to steady themselves.

"Haaah!" exclaimed Lindras in triumph.

As the quake passed, to their dismay the soldiers still stood before them. All present were momentarily baffled by the Wizard's strange magic. The soldiers soon realized that Lindras was rather ineffective in harnessing his own powers. Suddenly, the ground collapsed beneath the Wizard and his companions, dropping them unceremoniously into a sink-hole twelve feet into the earth.

A stunned silence was abruptly replaced by a burst of laughter as the soldiers peered down into the pit at the men of the Order.

Markus shook his head in disbelief as Arerys and Valtar helped the flustered Wizard onto his feet.

"Do you intend to use your powers to bury us now? Perhaps, spare the enemy the task of filling our graves?" scowled the prince, frustrated by Lindras' efforts.

As the men glanced upwards, soldiers rimming the edge of the pit jeered and laughed at their plight and impending demise.

"My! What a sorry excuse you are for an all-powerful Wizard!" taunted a voice from above, speaking in Taijina. Another round of laughter followed the comment.

"What are they saying?" asked Markus.

"I do believe they are praising the Wizard's skills," replied Valtar in a sarcastic tone.

Silence befell them as the soldiers looking down into the pit backed away to allow others to fill their ranks on the edge. To none of their surprise, they stared up to face the points of numerous spears turned upon them.

The leader of this new division smiled a knowing smile, revealing his intentions by spitting in disgust upon the group as he spoke in Taijina. "You might call yourselves warriors in your own country, but here—"

Without warning, the soldiers hovering above them screamed as they tumbled into the pit. The others were simply mowed down as two dark horses harnessed to a log careened through the hapless crowd. The log was stripped of its branches and mounted onto a set of wheels. As the wheels turned carrying the log forward, it set into motion a number of deadly, spinning blades embedded into the log.

More unsuspecting soldiers were knocked backwards as an unseen force swung down from the trees, striking all in its path. They panicked, their eyes struggling to see in the consuming darkness as an invisible enemy ambushed them. More terrified screams ensued as log after log continued to swing down from above, some slamming together, crushing the soldiers caught in between.

"What is happening up there?" asked Markus, removing his blade from a soldier's back.

"We shall find out soon enough," stated Arerys, bracing himself against the side of the pit, his knees and arms bent as Nayla had once shown them. "Up you go, Markus."

The prince used Arerys' knees and arms like the rungs of a ladder, climbing up onto the Elf's shoulders. As he stood upright on top of Arerys, freedom was still out of his reach. The Elf straightened up, raising Markus higher against the wall. It was still not enough. Arerys strained as he pushed himself up onto his toes. The weight was now becoming unbearable. He grimaced as the prince finally hoisted himself up and over.

All around him was absolute pandemonium. The soldiers were fleeing in sheer terror as an invisible foe dispensed arrows, launched airborne logs, and snared the soldiers in traps that catapulted them high into the treetops.

Remaining low to the ground, Markus peered into the pit. He could see that Arerys was already in the midst of delivering Valtar. He reached down to grab hold of the Elf, lifting him over the edge to safety. As Arerys raised Lindras up, Valtar and Markus took hold of the Wizard, pulling him out.

Man and Elf leaned forward, taking hold of Arerys' wrists as he leapt up to reach their outstretched hands. Together, they pulled the fair Elf out of the pit. As they rose to their feet, swords drawn to engage in battle, they were met with frightened soldiers dispersing into the forest. They were stumbling and falling over each other and the bodies of their fallen comrades as they cowered and fled the hail of arrows showering down upon them. In the mayhem, some of the fleeing soldiers ran directly towards the men of the Order. With swords at the ready, Markus and the others made short work of them, striking the enemy down swiftly with their cold steel.

Markus quickly ducked beneath the blade of a soldier. Rising up, he cut diagonally, striking the soldier from his left hip upwards across to his right shoulder. A stifled scream of agony mixed with disbelief gurgled out of the soldier's mouth as his entrails protruded from his midriff, eviscerated by Markus' deadly weapon. The prince calmly stepped over his writhing body in search of his next unfortunate foe. To his left, Arerys and Valtar were both engaged in their own duel, to his right, Lindras made do with his staff, swinging and pummeling his adversary with an unorthodox, but effective swinging action.

Markus collided headlong into the next soldier. Slamming their swords together, the prince countered each strike, deftly angling and deflecting the soldier's blows. Retaliating with a vengeance, the Imperial Soldier sliced at Markus horizontally, aiming to separate his head from his shoulders. Dropping below the blade, Markus rose up slamming the soldier across his chest with his right shoulder. As he tumbled to the ground, Markus stood up to drive his blade through the soldier's heart. He rammed it through with such force he could feel the earth with the tip of the sword. Giving it a final, defiant twist, he retracted his blade.

Turning to assist Lindras, he noticed a second soldier rapidly closing in from behind on the Wizard as he awkwardly used his staff to trounce another soldier. Raising his weapon high overhead, Lindras' staff was drawn up and over, swinging down behind him so he may gather greater momentum to deliver a debilitating strike upon the soldier standing before him. However, the backwards swing unintentionally clobbered the approaching foe, knocking him unconscious to the ground.

Lindras looked down at the soldier. "I believe I am getting good at this now, Markus," he said with great confidence. He started to spin the staff over his head, as if to strike fear in the soldiers of his obvious skills. "Now let us see what you can do against this!"

With no need to assist Lindras now, Markus spun around to aid Arerys. As the prince turned about, the Wizard stepped back and tripped on a rock, sending the spinning staff on a direct course to Markus, striking him hard on his head. The prince instantly dropped down upon his knees. His sword tumbling from his grasp as he keeled forward, collapsing onto the ground in a heap.

An eerie silence enveloped the unfamiliar forest. Arerys' keen eyes penetrated the darkness, watching as the last surviving soldiers fled in absolute terror, heading northward. He knelt beside the unconscious Markus while Valtar, sword still drawn, gazed up to the treetops. He watched as ghostly forms silently made their way down from the trees with incredible agility. Soon, Arerys, with Markus propped up in his arms, glanced up to see many dark forms silhouetted against the night sky, they moved like shadows, approaching swiftly and soundlessly. The Elf quickly lay Markus back down so he may draw his sword once again.

Valtar's hand stopped the fair Elf's movement, while he used the other hand to sheath his own weapon. Fifteen mortals, Taijins to be exact, stood before them. Their swords and bows were turned on them, ready to unleash their wrath.

"Who are they?" whispered Arerys, his eyes darting from one warrior to the next.

"They are the Shadow Warriors," warned Valtar, raising his hands up so they could see that he was unarmed. "Do not make any sudden movements or you shall be dead before you know it."

"Kagai Warriors, I mean you no harm," announced the dark Elf. "I am Valtar Briarwood, a loyal servant to Joval Stonecroft, sent forth by the elders of Orien."

"Hmm, a servant to Master Stonecroft you say?" asked a voice from the darkness. "Then I shall consider you too to be a friend. I am Hunta Saibon"

Lindras passed his hand over the crystal orb of his staff, shedding some light on those who surrounded them. Much to their surprise, an aged and weathered warrior, stooped from many years, shuffled closer towards them. His tanned, wrinkled face illuminated by the glow of the Wizard's staff, revealed a kindly, welcoming smile.

"I am Lindras Weatherstone, the Wizard of the West," said Lindras with a bow. "This fellow lying before you is Prince Markus of Carcross."

Turning to look upon the fair Elf, Saibon announced, "And you are Arerys Wingfield, the Prince of Wyndwood."

A soft blur of light slowly came into focus. It was a candle's flickering flame burning in the corner of the room. Markus raised himself onto his elbows, blinking hard into the light as he fought to recognize his unfamiliar surroundings. In the center of the room he could make out Arerys, Valtar and Lindras speaking in hushed voices to a stranger.

Arerys stood up, moving to where Markus lay upon hearing him stir from his unnatural sleep. Delivering a bowl of water to the prince, the Elf helped to prop him up so he could drink.

"Where are we?" asked Markus, soothing his parched throat with a gulp of water. "And who is he?"

"Fear not, Markus. We are in a safe haven. We are in Anshen. And that man is Nayla's father," stated Arerys.

"Dahlon Treeborn?"

"No, his name is Hunta Saibon. I suppose it is more accurate to say that Nayla regards him and his predecessors with the same consideration and respect had they been her real father. Master Saibon and his forefathers raised and trained Nayla when she was brought here as a child by Joval Stonecroft."

Saibon waved Markus over to the table, speaking in the common tongue; "Are you well enough to join us Prince Markus?"

Arerys helped his friend onto his unsteady feet, leading him to a low table in the center of the room. Lowering the prince down so he may seat himself on a cushion upon the floor, Arerys took his place next to him.

Markus rubbed the top of his aching head, wincing in pain as his fingers gingerly probed the tender, protruding bump swelling from the crown of his head.

"My apologies, Markus. I suppose I was somewhat zealous in wielding my staff," said Lindras. "I shall be more mindful of those in my proximity the next time."

"The next time?" remarked Markus, glaring at the Wizard through pained eyes. "I think not! We shall all stand well away from you the next time you brandish that staff. And I would also recommend that you refrain from using your new powers until you have mastered your craft."

Lindras rolled his eyes in dismay. "Forgive this old Wizard for trying to be of service," he lamented. "The powers I have been blessed with are not to be trifled with or treated lightly, that is true. It is like any art that must be practiced and honed to perfection however, unlike my brothers Tor Airshorn, Tylon Riverdon and even Eldred Firestaff, I have deliberately chosen not to practice my art. Where the other Wizards dabble in their magic and deliberately distance themselves from man, I chose to live amongst mankind, even if it means to forsake my own powers."

"Why do you not perfect your skills so you may do good?"

groaned Markus.

"When you are endowed with such potent powers, it is easy to control men by a mere wave of a magical staff and some simple incantations. I choose to live amongst man and to deal with them using logic and reason than to resort to powers that intimidate and frighten people, bending them to my will using trickery and magic. Your father is no fool, Markus. How readily do you believe King Bromwell would embrace me into his council if I had relied on my powers to sway others?"

"But your powers can take down the likes of the Sorcerer if only you learn to control them. Surely even you can see that?" argued the prince.

"Believe me, it is much more difficult to use reason than magic to survive in a mortal's world. I myself know first hand that power, absolute power, can also lead to absolute corruption. Look at what has become of the Wizard of the East. Had Eldred only had the wisdom to deal with man on man's own terms; with greater compassion and humanity, than to coerce men by using threats and the powers of the black arts, he may not have fallen to the wayside as he has," stated Lindras, his blue-gray eyes simmered as they stared back at Markus. He searched the prince's dark eyes, looking for signs of understanding.

Saibon raised his hand in gesture for calm to prevail. "The Wizard is quite right. Treachery only begets treachery. Even with the fighting arts, it is so very easy to kill. It is far more difficult to steady the hand and not take a life when one is trained in such a manner. It is wise to keep in mind that with great powers come even greater responsibilities."

Lindras smiled in thanks to the elderly warrior, relieved that at least there was one who understood his predicament.

Markus silently considered the words of the stranger before them. Watching him as he fetched a boiling pot of tea, the prince knew the old man was correct in his thinking.

Saibon pushed an earthenware bowl of the steaming concoction before Markus. "Drink this, you will feel better for it."

Markus carefully picked up the bowl in his hand. Holding it close to his nose, he took a sniff before sampling the brew. A thin, gray miasma floated over the surface of the liquid, like the noxious vapors that rise from the swamps. His head instantly recoiled from the pungent, earthy smell emanating from the dark liquid.

"Smelling it shall only make your head feel worse," cautioned

Saibon. "I recommend drinking it instead."

"What is this?" asked Markus, studying the strange contents floating up to the surface.

Saibon answered with a laugh, "It is better you do not know."

"Trust in him, my lord," advised Valtar. "Master Saibon is renown in these parts for his knowledge of medicinal plants and cures for whatever ails mortal man."

Markus held his breath as he gulped down a mouthful of the liquid. To his relief, it actually smelled much worse than it tasted. "Thank you, Master Saibon," he said as he placed the bowl onto the table. "So, may I assume you are of healer status?"

"Amongst other things," he answered, giving his shoulders a modest shrug. "I am what you refer to in the common speech, an ascetic priest."

"A holy man that deals in war?" asked Arerys, startled by this revelation.

"I prefer to think of myself as a mortal man placed here to protect what is holy," responded Saibon. "Yes, I am a warrior and I train others so they, too may protect what is sacred and precious to all who fled from the east to avoid religious persecution and a life of poverty."

Markus studied the wizened form sitting before him. Saibon was a true paradox: elderly, unassuming and slight in build, yet there was an energy about him that made the prince feel he still wielded incredible powers within his aging body.

"It was most fortunate we had chanced upon you on this night," said Markus, grateful for the assistance.

"Chance had nothing to do with it. We had been following the Imperial Soldiers, preparing to deploy decoys to lure them into our trap. Your appearance was merely timely, I withheld my men and the four of you did the job for us!" announced Saibon.

"So you knew of their coming?" asked Arerys.

"Of course," smiled Saibon, his dark eyes twinkling in the candlelight. "It is my business to know of everything and everyone that sets foot onto our lands west of the Furai Mountains and east of the Iron Mountains. Besides, it can hardly be said that the four of you move like the silent shadows of the forest."

"How did you know of my identity?" asked Arerys, perplexed by Saibon's awareness. "How did you know who I was?"

"It was a matter of simple deduction, my friend," stated the warrior priest. "There were only two Elves present. Valtar made his identity immediately known, that could only mean that you are Arerys Wingfield. Besides a lady warrior spoke in great detail of the golden-haired Prince of Wyndwood."

"Nayla! She was here?" The excitement in Arerys' voice was obvious.

"Nayla?" Saibon was momentarily puzzled. "Oh yes, but in these parts she goes by the name of Takaro."

"The Taijin name her mother gave her," stated the fair Elf.

"Indeed," said Saibon, with a nod. "Takaro and her army passed through Anshen on their journey to Nagana."

"Is she well?" asked the Elf.

"As well as can be expected for one who chooses to lead such a difficult life," answered the elderly warrior.

"I was warned that she had been hurt. Tell me it is not so," said Arerys.

"She mends. In due time, she will recover. As for her condition, I shall let you be the judge when you see her in Nagana," said Saibon. "That reminds me. Are you not overdue for your arrival in the fortress city?"

"I am afraid we are long overdue," admitted Arerys with much regret.

"Have you recovered sufficiently?"

The Elf frowned at Saibon. "Recovered?"

"Yes. Nayla claimed that something evil befell you. Am I a fool to assume this was the reason for your delay?"

"I do not understand. How did she know?"

"Ah, let us just say that those close to her have a strong bond, joined by forces unseen to her mind and to her heart. Even when separated by great distance, Nayla is able to sense their fears and anguish. Obviously you are dear to her. She felt your pain, witnessed your plight… She is gifted with the sight. Her ability to see premonitions is strong; even more so than in any Elf gifted with this sense."

"This sense you speak of may have existed many thousands of years ago, well before my father's and his father's time, but now it is merely hearsay," stated Arerys, skeptical of this mortal's claims.

"For an enlightened race, you have a closed mind," Saibon responded rather tersely.

"To the contrary, Arerys," added Valtar, looking intently at the fair Elf. "What Master Saibon states, we dark Elves know this to be true. This ability is within all of us, even mortal man. It is an ability that must be honed, and most all of believed, for it to be developed to its utmost power. Some of us have this ability, but none to the same extent as Nayla."

Arerys was stunned by Valtar's admission.

"To predict an event prior to its occurrence or to sense such things as it happens is a gift bestowed only to the Three Sisters," responded Arerys, unwilling to be swayed by Valtar or the old warrior's comments.

"Prince Arerys, do not deny that there has been times when you have come across familiar places you have never seen before. Or perhaps, you have chanced upon a familiar face that you cannot place, and yet you know you have seen this person in another place, another time."

The fair Elf gave his words more consideration. "I mean you no disrespect Master Saibon; perhaps my kind through the ages have become somewhat jaded, preferring to believe in those things that are more tangible."

"That is sad to hear. Of all the races in Imago, the Elves are a magical and enchanting people, capable of many incredible things. To hear that you have lost the will to believe in such abilities is truly disheartening," said Saibon with a disappointed sigh. "Your travels in this ancient land shall present many new and incredible possibilities. Perhaps, given time you shall have a change of heart."

"This sage is right, Arerys," said Lindras. "The world is full of wondrous possibilities as long as one's eyes are open to them."

"Perhaps you are right, Wizard," acknowledged the Elf. "My apologies again, Master Saibon, it was not my intention to insult you or your beliefs."

The elderly warrior smiled back in understanding at Arerys.

Markus, already feeling the healing effects of the herbal tea prepared by the warrior priest, no longer felt the throbbing in his head. He was feeling well enough to join in conversation again.

"Thank you for coming to our aid, Master Saibon. We would not have survived had an army of your formidable size come to our assistance."

"Formidable size?" repeated Saibon with a chuckle. "There was but fifteen of my men present to bear witness to your plight. In fact, they all returned to the village with us. Of course, you would have no knowledge or recollection of this."

"That is impossible! There were at least one hundred Imperial

Soldiers. How can it be so?"

"In my thinking, any more warriors and I would deem it to be rather excessive," answered Saibon.

"Excessive?" asked Markus, puzzled by his words.

"As you can see, we managed. There were other warriors, but I chose to place them where they may ambush the surviving soldiers as they fled northward. Think of it as a safety precaution so none may return to the regent with word of our whereabouts. It is better he believes that his soldiers had mysteriously disappeared in our *haunted* forests. It only serves to heighten their fear of us."

"Still, you must have a vast army to take on such a formidable foe! How many warriors are in your company?"

"Of my people, the Kagai sect, we are thirty-seven strong; that is including Takaro."

"How do your people manage to survive such attacks when your numbers are so few?" asked Markus, astounded by the warrior priest's claim.

"What we lack in numbers we have sufficiently made up for with ingenuity and our will to survive," answered Saibon, modestly.

"I fail to understand how," replied Markus.

"It is simple. We move by the cover of night and we constantly change our strategy so the enemy is taken totally unaware. The element of surprise works in our favor. The Imperial Soldiers believe we number in the thousands for we are able to anticipate their movements and stymie their every attempt to destroy our people. Needless to say, in the darkness, it is difficult for them to ascertain exactly how many we are and from which direction we mount our attack."

"So you must have spies?" asked Arerys, intrigued by his words.

"Call them what you will. There are those skilled in infiltrating the enemy camps to extract valuable information."

"The Kagai Warriors are legendary in Orien," stated Valtar. "They are greatly feared by the enemy. It is only because we have an alliance that Treeborn's people, we dark Elves, and the Taijins, those loyal to the prince and the elders of Orien, have endured thus far."

"Speaking of Lord Treeborn, when were you to arrive in Nagana?" asked Saibon.

Arerys shook his head in regret, speaking in sadness, "We have journeyed long and hard, barely with time enough to allow our steeds rest and sustenance. Alas, we are now a good fortnight behind schedule."

"Hmm, that is not good," responded the warrior priest, thoughtfully rubbing his chin with his tanned and weathered fingers as he absorbed Arerys' words."

"I fear Nayla shall give up hope of my ever returning to her," lamented the Elf.

"Well, I have no doubt Takaro worries for you," agreed Saibon. "So it is true, you have taken Takaro as your betrothed."

"Most definitely," Arerys stated. "That is, if she is not so angry with me by now that she does not spurn me in bitterness."

"You do understand that Takaro is like a daughter to me?" asked the ancient warrior, his stare unyielding as it scrutinized the Elf. "I wish for her to find some happiness and truth be told, in all my years I would never had guessed it would be with an Elf of such noble standing that she would choose to bind herself to."

"Were you hoping that she would wed a mortal?" asked Arerys.

"My only desire was that she wed a man who would bring her peace of mind and give her a sense of belonging. Unfortunately, being neither Elf, nor mortal, she is doomed either way. Had you been a mortal man, you would die well before her time in this realm is over. Being an Elf, you understand she shall die well before you even reach your advanced years, do you not?"

"I am aware of that. Though I know she would refuse the gift of eternal life had Dahlon Treeborn offered it, I know in my heart she shall accept such a blessing from my father, the Lord of Wyndwood."

Saibon raised his eyebrows, contemplating Arerys' words. "Do not be so sure of yourself, Prince Arerys. Have you already asked her if she would accept the eternal life of your people?"

"No, but why would she not?"

"Takaro, Nayla if you prefer, has had a most difficult life. Although I know this so-called eternal life you speak of seems like a gift, are you sure that by granting her this *blessing* you may only be prolonging her suffering in this world. You know that she is denied by most Elves, even her own father fails to acknowledge her. And she is shunned by most mortals. Do you truly believe she shall be accepted when even amongst your own race there is dissension? Your people cannot even embrace their own differences. How do you believe they will embrace, even tolerate, the likes of her?"

"I am fully aware of what Nayla is. It makes no matter to me for I am blind to what makes us different; I can only see what binds our souls as one."

"But you *must* see that you two are different, do you not? Even your standing in life differs greatly. Though you are both children of high Elves, Nayla has never been given the privileges of one born to a high house. How do you feel she shall adapt to such a life?"

"If you strip away all that is earthly about us, you shall see that what we have in common, what we share, far outweighs all else. And I swear; my love for her is such that I shall do everything in my power to keep her safe and to make her happy. I assure you, Master Saibon, Nayla is loved. I would lay down my life for her, without question."

For a moment, Arerys contemplated whether to explain to Saibon that he, as an Elf, would not actually live for an eternity in this realm. If he chose to stay, although the aging process slows considerably with the advancing years, he too would eventually diminish and die of old age. By human standards, an Elf's longevity would, in comparison seem 'eternal'. Capable of existing in this physical form for thousands of years before succumbing to old-age, it is only when an Elf enters the Twilight that he would truly live for an eternity. It was cold comfort. If Nayla refuses the prolonged life of an Elf, she shall perish hundreds of years before he had even reached his senior years.

"I assure you, Master Saibon, my friend speaks the truth to you. I have witnessed the lengths he would go to just to be by her side again. I have seen the pain of his suffering at being separated from Nayla," testified Markus on Arerys' behalf.

"In the short span of time Nayla and Arerys have had together, they have endured much and their love continues to hold true," added Lindras. "I do not believe destiny would be so cruel as to allow these two lovers to find each other only to be torn asunder by those less tolerant and compassionate."

"Has your father already sanctioned this union? Does he truly accept Takaro for what she is?" asked Saibon with genuine concern. "Not only as one of mixed blood, but as the daughter of his old rival, Dahlon Treeborn?"

"Indeed he has," said Arerys.

Saibon's eyes turned to Valtar, searching for confirmation.

"He speaks the truth," said the dark Elf. "King Kal-lel proclaimed before the kings of the Alliance and all those in his presence including Joval Stonecroft and the warriors in his company that Prince Arerys shall wed Nayla."

"The winds of change blow," nodded Saibon in approval. "Perhaps, there is still hope then."

"I pray Nayla has not given up hope or all shall be lost. We have come so far and yet, there is still far to go," said Arerys.

"Fear not, Prince Arerys, tomorrow morn I shall send forth five of my best warriors. They shall ensure your safe passage to Nagana. Tonight, no harm shall come to you and your companions for all shall sleep in the safety of this village. Anshen is well guarded," promised the elderly warrior.

The darkness of night silently crept away with the coming of the morning light. Markus stood at the entrance of Saibon's small cottage, watching as the early morning mist that veiled the valley in a thin, ephemeral blanket of gray dissipated. As the warmth of the sun burned through, its light sparkled off the dew clinging to the grasses and the leaves of the trees and shrubs.

Markus took a moment to admire a large spider web shining in the sunlight. The tiny drops of dew, perfectly spaced and glistening like diamond beads, bejeweled the otherwise invisible silken strands spun by the large, black and yellow orb-weaving spiders.

Down by the sapphire-blue waters of Lake Anzan, its glass-like surface glimmering as it mirrored the rising sun; Markus could make out Valtar and Arerys. They were preparing the horses for the long journey that lay ahead.

"Did you sleep well, Markus?" asked Lindras, emerging from the cottage.

"Considering the knock on my head, yes, I slept well. Thank you for asking," responded Markus, his hand gingerly touching the crown of his head.

"My apologies again, Markus," said the Wizard, his eyes revealed sincere regret for his actions. "I promise I shall take greater care with my staff."

"Yes, I am sure you will," smiled Markus. Sensing Lindras' guilt, he no longer wished to prolong his torment.

"Master Saibon has been kind enough to prepare us a morning meal. Fetch Arerys and Valtar, let us not keep our kind host waiting," suggested the Wizard.

With their appetites sated, the men of the Order were now ready to continue their journey to the fortress city. In the company of five Taijins, the Kagai Warriors were to lead them to their final destination. Arerys was eager to be on his way.

He bowed in respect to Saibon. He now understood Nayla held this elderly warrior in the same reverence and respect as she would had he been her own father, but one that truly cherished her. The Elf wished to regard him in the same manner.

Saibon offered the fair Elf a warm smile and reciprocated with a bow of his own. "If you truly love Takaro, then you shall take heed of my words."

"Of course, Master Saibon," responded Arerys. "What do you wish to say?"

"I only ask that you treat Takaro with kindness and understanding; never with pity. And though she is a skilled warrior, she is still a woman. She is not immune to the angst and sorrow of heartbreak. Where you are concerned, remember to treat her as a woman first, not as a warrior."

Arerys was touched by his genuine love for this woman that Dahlon Treeborn had so willingly cast aside. "Of course, Master Saibon, I swear upon my life I shall do right by her. And I shall deliver glad tidings to Nayla on your behalf."

Markus, Lindras and Valtar wished the warrior priest well, thanking him for his assistance and warm hospitality. The Wizard turned to gesture in farewell one last time, watching the benevolent, old warrior resting upon his walking stick as he observed their departure. The warrior continued to wave, with his failing eyesight, he could no longer see that the men were well beyond any man's, save an Elf's, sight now.

The men followed the Kagai Warriors down past the lake, up the gentle slope leading out of the forest. They disappeared behind the curtain of water beneath Reyu Falls.

Markus was in awe, having been unconscious the first time they came by this way. He had no recollection of passing through the waters when he and the others were escorted to Anshen. As they walked along the narrow path in single file, the waters resonating roar as it thundered into the deep pool at the base of the fall echoed loudly in their ears. A cool mist rising from the churning, boiling pool shroud all in a damp blanket as tiny droplets clung to their clothes and skin.

It is no wonder the enemy fails to locate the Shadow Warriors, thought Markus as he marveled at this secret place, *protected by the Furai Mountains to the east and an impassable river to the west, lest the enemy discovers this passage under this waterfall, Anshen shall remain undiscovered and untouched.*

His body and soul was embraced by the invigorating energy emanating from the waters and the cool, refreshing vapor of mist that surrounded all. *Perhaps there is magic in the waters of this ancient land,* thought Markus as he stared through the translucent curtain cascading down from high above.

When the warriors determined it was safe to step out from behind the waterfall, they led the men of the Order southeast.

"It shall be a twenty-eight day ride, give or take a day or two, from these parts to Nagana," stated Valtar.

"I am ready. Let us be on our way," replied Arerys. Inwardly he rejoiced for now he felt there would be progress; Nagana no longer seemed like an impossible goal.

Through sun and driving rain, the men rode their steeds long and hard, coming to rest for the night when darkness prevented them from advancing any further. Upon their twentieth day of travel since departing Anshen, as the men settled to rest for another night, Arerys gazed up to the sky. It was the last night of spring. A bright full moon marked the coming of summer. The Elf slumped down next to Markus, sighing more in despair than weariness.

"The summer solstice is upon us," announced Arerys with disappointment. "Already the promise is broken."

"What promise do you speak of, Arerys?" asked Markus.

"I said to Nayla that I would return before the coming of the summer solstice. If all had gone well, we would have arrived one week ago, now the summer is upon us and Nagana is still another week away. I have failed miserably in holding true to this promise I made to her."

"Arerys, you had no control over what had happened to cause this delay," said Markus. "Nayla is level-headed, she shall understand."

"And what if she does not?"

"She loves you, my friend," reminded the prince, rising up to his feet to find rest beneath the shelter of an ancient tree with large, sprawling branches. "Need I say more?"

Alone in the darkness, Arerys gazed up to the infinite darkness of the ebony sky. The Elf's eyes stared up at the full moon suspended high in the sky. Its face, veined and pocked, produced a cold light that glowed down upon the unfamiliar landscape. It seem to mock him as he reflected on his promise now broken. As he studied the heavens, he chanced upon a shooting star blazing across the dark sky traveling southwest, its long tail of light diminishing into the blackness.

Arerys thought upon an Elven lore claiming that if two unattached Elves wishing for true love looked upon the same star as it travels across the night sky, destiny would bring them together: a true love preordained by an invisible god. The Elf smiled inwardly as he thought that perhaps at the very same moment, Nayla was looking upon the same brilliant star as it traveled across the heavens. He closed his eyes as he prayed that their paths would cross one day soon.

"Do not lose hope, Nayla. I shall be there. Whatever happens, do not lose hope," whispered Arerys, under his breath.

CHAPTER 12

A PROMISE MADE

From the still of her room, Nayla gazed out the window up to the heavens. It was a deep blue-black canvas from which a multitude of stars, like tiny diamonds shone brightly. Her eyes studied the celestial bodies adorning the evening sky. Gossamer wisps of clouds drifted lazily up high to create a thin veil that obscured the stars dotting the northerly horizon. A full moon, glowing like a round stone of milky-white quartz shone down upon her, bathing her in its pale light.

She turned her head to follow the path of a shooting star as it streaked across the blackness on the western horizon. According to the lore of the people of Taija, wishes are made on the first shooting star of the evening. If a wish is made and the star travels in the direction of the person making the wish, it is destined to come true. If the star journeys in the opposite direction, the wish will remain just that: a wish. In this case, Nayla was not sure what to make of it. The shooting star did neither; instead, it traveled southward, neither towards or away from her. Nonetheless, she felt compelled to make a desperate wish as the star disappeared, fading from her view.

Please Arerys, return to me, said Nayla in silent prayer. *Tomorrow shall mark the first day of summer. You had promised to be here.*

The sounds of cicadas filled the evening air that was heavily scented with night blooming jasmine. Nayla breathed in deeply, filling her lungs with the intoxicating perfume. A gentle rap on the door disrupted Nayla's worrisome thoughts.

Arerys! He has returned, she dared to believe. Her heart raced as she dashed across the room. As she threw the door wide open, her smile quickly faded. Joval stood before her.

"It is obvious you were expecting someone else," stated the Elf, sensing her disappointment.

Nayla was silent, turning away from him. She returned to her place by the open window to gaze out at the night sky.

Joval walked into the room, closing the door behind him. He could feel Nayla's overwhelming sadness for even he knew that Arerys should have been here by now. If he and the others were indeed two weeks behind them, Arerys should have arrived in Nagana days ago.

"Perhaps, Prince Arerys shall arrive tomorrow, Nayla," said Joval as he crossed the room. "After all, he is royalty. He means to be punctual. I have no doubt he shall make a grand entrance, right on time."

Nayla knew Joval was merely attempting to buoy her sagging spirits, but this he failed in miserably.

"He should have been here by now," she said in a whisper.

"What do you plan to do, Nayla? On the off-chance Prince Arerys does not come, what are your intentions?" asked the Elf, stooping to look into her sad, brown eyes.

"Joval, you know I do not hold you to your promise to wed," sighed Nayla, turning away from his gaze.

"You know I am a man of my word, Nayla. It was not an empty promise I had made to you and to Lord Treeborn. I intend to fulfill this promise if you will have me."

"If I truly cared for you, Joval, I would leave. I would not allow you to embroil yourself in my affairs nor would I subject you to the ridicule that shall follow if the truth be known."

"Nayla, if you truly cared, then you would bind yourself to me. And you know you must also consider the life you now carry. Your child has a right to a decent life. Where I know you are strong of will and spirit, that you can survive on your own, this child should not be forced to endure such a harsh life if it need not be this way."

Nayla's eyes were dark and liquid in the moonlight. Her small body trembled upon thinking of the prospect that Arerys might not return. The fleeting thought that he had a change of heart, that he had no intention of being reunited with her, pierced her very soul.

Joval's hand gently lifted her chin so their eyes met. "Nayla, though I made this promise to your father so he may save face, I care not whether it pleases him that we wed. I made this promise to you, and I stand by it. I intend to honor this promise. My question is: What do you intend to do?"

"Though it is not my intention to bring dishonor to your name, if I make this promise to you, then I too shall be honor-bound to see it through. As you said, I can no longer think only of myself. This child is deserving of a father and I know in my heart there is none better than you. It is far better that it bear the Stonecroft name than be cursed as a Treeborn," conceded Nayla, her voice breaking as the gravity of her decision bore down upon her.

Through the incipient tears, he could see her soul was crushed by

Arerys' long absence. Joval took her small hands into his, gently planting a kiss upon them.

"I know this is not easy for you, Nayla. I know in your heart you still pray for Arerys' return, but know this too; if the Prince of Wyndwood fails to show his face in due time, then I shall do right by you. And we shall have to move with haste, before we arouse suspicion."

Nayla nodded in agreement. "If this be our destiny, then all I ask is that you allow me time to grieve for Arerys."

"Of course, Nayla, that I shall do," said Joval in understanding. "The hour grows late. I shall see you in the morn. Perhaps your prince shall arrive tomorrow."

"I pray he does Joval, not only for me, but I wish to spare you a life of misery for you know how tongues wag. I wish to spare you the ridicule you shall be subjected to if -"

"Hush, Nayla," said Joval, placing a finger over her lips. "You should know by now I am not one to be affected by the barbed words cast by others. I am too strong for that, and so are you."

"If this were so, then why do I feel my strength has been sapped from me? Why do I feel that I am fading like a ghost?"

He gazed down upon her. She had always been a pillar of strength, but now her inner strength seemed to falter before his very eyes. He had witnessed her face devastating losses in the past. He had listened to her bear up to the weight of ridicule all of her life and he had administered to her wounds after the heat of a battle, never hearing her cry out in pain. It troubled Joval to no end for rarely had he ever seen her so vulnerable; the fire extinguished from her eyes.

"It is merely your troubled heart, Nayla. It is burdened with worry and grief, tormented by what it does not know."

"It is better to have never loved," whispered Nayla, fighting to hold back her tears.

"Do not say that," protested Joval. "Though true love is bittersweet at times, it is the one precious thing in this world that many fail to find in a lifetime and many others only pretend to have found. It is the energy that binds all living things and heals the hurts of this world. I pray you never close your mind and your heart to this truth."

Joval stooped to gently plant a kiss on Nayla's forehead. "Sleep now for tomorrow brings with it the promise of a new day. Just know this; come what may, I shall be by your side. Take heart in knowing that I shall not forsake you."

Nayla took great comfort in the Elf's words. She watched as Joval silently disappeared down the dim-lit corridor. Retreating back into the solitude of her room, Nayla looked upon the circlet of silver she wore upon the finger of her left hand; the ring Arerys had gifted to her. She removed it from her finger, placing it next to the tiny wooden fairy he had given to her on their parting.

"I shall not wear this ring again," whispered Nayla. "Unless Arerys returns to place it back upon my finger, here it shall remain."

Embraced in the cold light of the full moon flooding into her room, the quiet was broken only by Nayla's tears as she wept bitterly over a promise now broken and a new promise made.

Amid the boisterous cacophony of songs trilled by the many wrens, sparrows and finches residing in the courtyard, the city was coming to life as the light of the first summer sun ushered in the start of a new day and a new season.

Nayla woke with a start. She leapt from her bed and rushed to ready herself. Although at this stage of her pregnancy, she showed no outward signs of her condition, Nayla was very conscious of her state. She chose to don a long, flowing gown to conceal her form.

Before she slipped out of her room, Nayla listened for signs of her father in the area. Confident that Dahlon was not in the immediate vicinity, she silently made her way down the corridor and across the courtyard towards the stables.

"Nayla! Where do you go in such haste so early in the morn?" called out Lando.

She gestured for him to lower his voice. "I plan to ride to Sheya Ridge; from there I shall see Arerys' arrival," stated Nayla, turning to enter the stable where her mare awaited.

Lando knew the men of the Order, if all went well, should have arrived four or five days ago. "What makes you so sure he arrives today?"

"Because Arerys promised; he said that he would be here by the coming of the summer solstice. The day has arrived," said Nayla, motioning a squire to ready her horse.

"Now, Nayla, you know as well as I do that Arerys should have been here by now."

"Are you saying he shall not be coming?"

"No! What I am saying is that obviously Arerys and the others have been somehow delayed."

"They shall be here. I can feel it, Lando. I believe it to be true."

"I believe it too, Nayla, perhaps, just not today."

"Do not dash what little hope I have left. All of last night I spent trying to believe that Arerys would come. Do not take this away from me."

"Nayla, I just do not want to see your disappointment if Arerys fails to show today. I believe with all my heart he had the best intentions of arriving here on time, and I know he shall be here. All I am saying is that he is behind schedule, at this point in time, we can only hazard a guess as to when he shall arrive."

"I shall take heed of your words, my friend," said Nayla, leading her mare outside.

"I shall accompany you," said Lando, lifting the little warrior up onto her saddle. "Give me a moment to ready my steed and we shall be off."

"It is not necessary, Lando."

"Oh yes, it is," the knight replied. "Joval shall have my head if I allow you to venture forth on your own, unescorted. Heaven forbid if something happens to you. Besides, you know as well as I do that danger may lurk near to us."

"Very well, Lando," Nayla finally conceded.

From atop Sheya Ridge, Nayla and Lando took in the vast landscape sprawling before them beneath a near-cloudless, pale blue sky. To the west, the Iron Mountains loomed ominously on the horizon. To the north, curving towards the east before bending southward; lay the Furai Mountains. In between these two mountain ranges, ancient stands of bamboo forests grew in dense groves. A canopy of long, narrow leaves blanketed the valley below in a calming hue of jade green.

"So what have you and Joval been up to these past few days? I have seen little of you two."

"Let us just say we have been on a hunting expedition," replied Lando. "We have yet to flush out our quarry."

"The Sorcerer?" asked Nayla.

"Yes," replied the knight.

"He is an elusive one," admitted Nayla. "I can attest to that."

"It is like flushing a snake out from the tall grasses; difficult but not impossible," declared Lando, adding with confidence; "It shall only be a matter of time before we are on his trail."

"Is that where Joval is now? Does he continue his search?" asked

Nayla, her dark eyes scanning the road leading away from Nagana as she sought out any sign of Arerys and the others in his company.

"As we speak, he musters the warriors of Orien to hunt the scoundrel down. The lands have been far too quiet of late, and Joval senses that Eldred Firestaff is in the midst of sowing the seeds of destruction. He means to uproot his plans before they come to fruition."

"As powerful as the Sorcerer is, he is also a creature of habit," replied Nayla. "Joval is wise to take up arms with others for it is in Eldred's nature to lie low for a period of time before reappearing to vent his wrath with a vengeance. Perhaps, Joval shall catch him by surprise this time."

"All I can say is that your friend is certainly determined to bring Firestaff down upon his knees."

"Let us hope Joval does so quickly. If the Sorcerer is indeed hatching a plot with the regent I do not believe we have the manpower to face such a formidable enemy this time, not after losing so many of our warriors during our bid to drive the soldiers of the Dark Army back over the Iron Mountains."

"How many soldiers will he have control over if he does align himself with the regent?"

"The soldiers of the Imperial Army number in the thousands."

"And what of the warriors of Orien?" inquired the knight.

Nayla shook her head in regret as she answered, "We are only four or five hundred strong now."

"I am not asking of just the Taijin warriors, Nayla. How many exist counting the Elven warriors and the Kagai Warriors of Anshen?"

She turned away from Lando as she replied in a soft voice, "As I said, we are only four or five hundred strong."

As the morning sun continued its steady ascent into the sky, Nayla continued her vigil with Lando close by her side. It was already apparent that she was determined to remain on this lookout until Arerys arrived, or the sun disappeared over the west; whichever occurred first.

Lando knew her well enough to not even suggest that she retire for the day; to wait in the safety of the fortress city.

The sound of an approaching horse caught their attention. Nayla turned to see a messenger riding forth, dismounting as he brought his steed to an abrupt halt.

The young Taijin man bowed before Nayla, "My lady, I come with

word from the elders and Lord Treeborn that your presence is requested immediately."

"Why am I needed?"

"I am sorry, my lady, they did not reveal the nature of this meeting
to me, only that I was to fetch you and to return with haste."

"And if I choose not to go?"

"Then I shall have to return alone with word of your location, and
then they shall seek you out themselves," answered the messenger,
anxiously awaiting her response.

"I recommend you go, and do so now," advised Lando. "We shall
return here once you are done."

"So be it," conceded Nayla, mounting her steed.

"Thank you, my lady," responded the young man, greatly relieved
by her decision.

As all three riders turned their mounts back to Nagana, Lando
observed as Nayla took one last desperate glance towards the north,
her eyes scouring for signs that Arerys was on his way. Her search was
in vain.

It had been a number of days since Nayla had last met with her
father. She had taken great pains to avoid him since his tongue-lashing
when Joval had championed her, preventing her exile. This time, Joval
was nowhere to be seen. She steeled her nerves as she prepared to enter
the meeting room where the elders and Dahlon Treeborn awaited her
presence. She quickly bowed before seating herself before them.

Nayla waited as a woman delivered a steaming cup of tea to each
man. She had never seen this woman before, observing her as she collected her tray to leave. The woman barely acknowledged Nayla,
averting her eyes from the warrior maiden as she went about her business.

Perhaps she was brought into service during my absence, thought
Nayla as she watched the stranger depart the room. *No doubt, Nakoa
would know who this woman is. I shall ask her about this new help
when I see her.*

The elders greeted her with a bow while Dahlon looked on.

"Summer is now upon us, Nayla. Where is your prince?" queried
Dahlon, his tone meant to ridicule her. "What say you now?"

She glanced up to meet the icy stare of her father's cool, blue eyes.
"This is only the first day of summer, my lord," answered Nayla. "He
shall be here."

"And if he does not arrive by day's end?"

"He is coming."

"You pride yourself as a warrior, one who lives and dies by a code of honor. Tell me, Nayla, do you plan to abide by this so-called *warrior's code* now? Do you honor the promises you make? Or are your words, your promises easily broken?"

Nayla was silent.

"I have announced to the elders that Joval Stonecroft has requested your hand in marriage," stated Dahlon.

Nayla's eyes flashed as her gaze turned towards the elders. They nodded in acknowledgment upon hearing his words. The thought immediately crossed her mind that Dahlon had revealed her condition to them.

"Though the Prince of Wyndwood had already made such a request, he has failed to stake his claim," stated Dahlon.

"His claim? Do not speak of me as though I am merely chattel; property to be handed off to a man!" Nayla snapped.

Maiyo Sonkai, the eldest mortal on this council, raised his hand in a bid for calm. "Nayla, you must be sensible about this. Your father only wants what is best for you. Though the prospect of binding yourself to Elven aristocracy is a grand ideal indeed, you must consider the fact that perhaps Prince Arerys has had a change of heart."

Nayla fought to remain calm upon hearing Maiyo's words for in her heart she knew Dahlon's intentions were to merely protect his own interests, to ensure his standing amongst his peers.

"You are of an age that you should retire your sword and tend to more domestic duties. Surely to wed the Stewart of Nagana has some appeal to you? Though Joval Stonecroft may not be an Elf born to a high house, his accomplishments, his standing in the community – our country, must surely bear some weight with you?"

"His standing in life matters not," answered Nayla in a crisp tone. "If I am to wed Joval, it shall be because he is a man of honor and courage with a kind and compassionate soul, not because he bears a title that warrants respect."

"So do you plan to honor your promise to wed Joval if Prince Arerys fails to show his face?" asked Dahlon, his cruel eyes piercing her heart in an attempt to intimidate her into submission.

Nayla's tongue moistened her dry lips as her parched throat involuntarily tightened before she could answer.

"Well?" asked her father, "What shall it be? Was that a hollow promise you made to Joval, or do you intend to honor your words?"

"I... I shall," she answered in a voice that was barely audible.

"What did you say, Nayla?" asked Dahlon, his head cocked, pretending not to hear her words. "I did not hear you."

"I said, I shall," she repeated her words. This time she spoke louder, but her voice was trembling, breaking under the weight of her despair.

"Ah! Very good, Nayla," responded Dahlon. Though his voice sounded joyful to those sitting by him, the warrior maiden could sense the underlying mockery behind his pleasant smile.

"You have made a wise choice, Nayla," said Maiyo, with an approving smile to the elders seated next to him. "We are all very fond of Master Stonecroft so it pleases us to no end that he shall be taking a wife. Do you plan to follow Taijin tradition and wed under a harvest moon?"

Nayla's eyes were wide open in disbelief. "The day is not yet done! Arerys Wingfield may still come!"

"I am sorry, Nayla. Accept my humble apology. You are right. All I meant to do was to ask, if destiny is to unite Joval to you, when this event will take place," replied Maiyo, sincerely remorseful for his less than tactful approach.

"I do not wish to delay this until the coming of autumn," Nayla replied, now confident that these mortals were not aware of her condition. "If this is to be our destiny, then we wish to wed on the last day of this month."

The elders looked to each other in shock and dismay.

"It shall give us but only nine days to prepare for this celebration. How do we even attempt to organize an event of this grand scale, the marriage of Lord Dahlon Treeborn's daughter to the Stewart of Nagana, in such a short span of time?"

"With all due respect, Joval and I do not wish for pomp and ceremony, the money can be better spent elsewhere for the greater good of our people."

"But Nayla, our people expect it!" countered Maiyo. "After all the dark days that loomed over the country leading up to the expulsion of the Dark Army and the defeat of Beyilzon, our people need cause for celebration. *They*, mortals and Elves alike, are in need of this."

"I tell you what," negotiated Nayla, "you shall have your grand celebration, but only if you can do so by the last day of this month."

"Now be reasonable," argued the elder.

"Master Sonkai, fear not! You shall have all the pomp and ceremony befitting the marriage of the Stewart of Nagana, and it shall be so on the last day of this month as he had requested," promised Dahlon.

"I suppose it can be done," Maiyo sighed in defeat, "but it shall not be easy. We must begin preparations immediately."

"Then make it so," said Dahlon. "In fact, let us disband from this meeting now so the three of you can be off to put your plans into order."

The elders smiled upon the idea, hastening to their feet for it had been a long while since their people had reason to celebrate. They bowed before Nayla as they hurried out. She rose to her feet, bowing in return. The warrior maiden turned to leave the room, fully expecting to return to her vigil on Sheya Ridge.

"Where do you think you are going?" asked Dahlon. "I did not give you permission to leave. We are not done yet."

Nayla's nerves bristled at his tone; she had already endured enough of his cruel barbs. She drew in a long, slow breath before slowly turning to face her father. Beneath his unyielding stare, their eyes locked.

"Consider yourself lucky that a man of Joval's standing would even look twice at you, let alone bind himself to the likes of you," Dahlon uttered under his breath. "He has been like a son to me and it is with great regret and a heart filled with much despair that I shall be made to sanction this union. Though I have advised him against this, my words hold no sway. You shall be forever indebted to him for what you have done and what you shall subject him to."

Inside, Nayla raged for his harsh words cut with the same cruelty as had he taken a knife and slashed her very heart. "Are you done now?"

"No," answered Dahlon. "In fact, I am leaving this day for the Crown Prince of Orien has requested a meeting. He asked that I leave immediately."

"Will this meeting take place in Prince Tokusho's residence in exile?"

"He did not state where to meet. He asked only that I proceed to his estate in Shesake, but whether he plans to meet me there, or not, remains to be answered. I suspect Prince Tokusho has selected a secret place somewhere along the way."

"Did he divulge the nature of this meeting?"

"No, but this coincides with his impending birthday. I have my suspicions it has to do with his ascension to the throne. The air is rife with rumors that he plans to return to his place of birth to take away power from his uncle, even if it be by force," answered Dahlon.

"How does he plan to undertake such a feat? He does not have the soldiers to mount a successful attack on Keso; to reclaim the Imperial Palace."

"I am aware of that, but until we meet, I can only speculate what he has in mind. And it is on this note I shall take my leave," stated Dahlon. Turning to look upon Nayla one last time before he exited the room, he made his desires perfectly clear: "If Prince Arerys fails to show by sunset, Joval fully expects to be wed by the last day of this month. You shall honor him by keeping this promise. Do I make myself understood?"

"Understood," Nayla replied succinctly.

From high on Sheya Ridge, Nayla observed as Dahlon Treeborn and a small battalion of warriors rode off towards the Furai Mountains.

"The winds of war may soon howl across these lands once again, Lando," said Nayla. "It would seem that peace in Imago is always short-lived."

"Is that where Lord Treeborn goes?" asked the knight, his brown eyes followed the forms shrinking into the distance. "He has gone to do battle?"

"Oh no!" said Nayla with a cynical laugh. "Had this journey been to the battlefield, it would be me you would be seeing riding off, not Dahlon. He prefers to strategize and orchestrate the war from the safety of the fortress city."

Lando's broad hand brushed his dark brown hair back from his forehead before using it to shield his eyes from the glare of the late afternoon sun. The large, golden orb inched ever closer to the Iron Mountains, in another hour or so, it would sink from their view.

Nayla glanced over at the knight; though rugged in appearance, there was a gentleness about him. His hair and beard, peppered with gray strands, gave him a distinct air of dignity. A skilled and seasoned warrior, she could gaze into his eyes and tell that there was still much kindness and compassion in his soul. Somehow, she imagined that perhaps Darius Calsair would have been very much like Lando Bayliss in another ten years or so had he survived the attack at the Citadel. Darius was bold, daring and charismatic in a dashing way. Lando on the other hand was noble, bore a determined strength and had a quiet charm about him; a more mature, worldly version of Darius.

Lando turned to look at Nayla, sensing her eyes were fixed upon him. "What is it?"

She offered him a gentle smile and in a small voice answered, "I miss Darius."

"As I do too," acknowledged the knight. "I am sure Markus misses him dearly. Darius had taken a pledge to serve king and country, to protect the royal family and all they stand for. I know he respected Markus as a prince, but more importantly, Darius looked up to him as a brother. He did indeed protect him as if he were of his own blood."

"I am still astounded to this day that it was he who so willingly embraced me into the Order," recalled Nayla, smiling as she thought upon his gallantry. "It mattered not that I was neither mortal, nor Elf. Darius still accepted me."

Lando gave her a broad grin.

"Why do you smile so?"

"Your words hold true, my lady," said Lando as he laughed, but not unkindly. "He was never concerned about your race. What mattered most importantly to Darius was that you were a woman!"

Nayla scowled disapprovingly at the knight, but her scowl dissolved into a smile as she recalled Darius' many attempts to charm her. "He was a dear friend, Lando. I truly miss him."

"Yes, I believe he shall leave a great void in our lives for a long time to come," admitted Lando.

Nayla turned away from the knight, her gaze following the road leading to Nagana. There was still no sign of Arerys, Markus or Lindras. There were no telltale sounds of horses approaching from the distance, no birds nor beasts of the forests sounding their alarm calls to warn of intruders entering their domain. There were only the sounds of leaves rustling in the evening breeze, creatures settling down for the impending night and the growing chorus of cicadas desperately calling for a mate before their time to die.

A large, orange sun finally slipped from a fiery sky to sink behind the mountains. Its diminishing light quietly retreated with the coming of the night. Nayla blinked back her tears.

In the darkness of her room, she knew the time had come to pass: Arerys was not here. He did not arrive as he had promised. Now she was bound by her promise to Joval.

She took a deep breath and looked out into the night sky. *Where are you, Arerys? What has become of you?* Nayla's thoughts were in absolute turmoil as her eyes searched the darkness. Tears welled, leaving a trail of sadness upon her cheeks.

There was a gentle knock upon her door, but she remained unmoved. In her heart, she knew it was not Arerys.

Joval called her name once more as he stepped in, closing the door behind him.

"Have you come to stake your claim, Joval?" asked Nayla, her voice trembling in defeat.

His steps were light as he moved closer to her side. Sensing the bitterness in her words, he replied, "I cannot deny for my own personal gains, I am pleased that Arerys has failed to show his face, yet I am torn, for I can feel your despair and sorrow. One man's loss is another man's gain; somehow this is not how I had hoped to win you back."

"What kind of life will I condemn you to should I honor this promise?" asked Nayla in a whisper. "You are my dearest friend, Joval, and I pray you know that I would lay my life down for you, on or off the field of battle, but this… this is more than I can ask from you. I dread the thought of what you shall endure should the truth of our union be revealed."

"I care not for what others might say. You know that."

"Joval, we live in a cruel world, and these are cruel times. You have never been subjected to the ridicule and the indignities I have been forced to suffer. Though I was born to a high house, it never shielded me from the taunts and torment of those who shun me. I fear you shall face the people's wrath. This truly is a cruel twist of fate. Better for you had you left me as a child to die in the armory."

"Do not speak these words! I will not hear it!"

"Tell me, Joval, and speak the truth. You had once said that you make this choice of your own free will; with an open heart and open eyes. Does this still stand? For if it does not; I shall not hold you to this promise."

Joval stood behind her, his arms embraced her, holding her tenderly against his body. "You know I am not one to make promises lightly. I intend to honor my promise to you because, in case you have forgotten, my love for you had never diminished through the ages. I do this because I love you."

Nayla's chin dropped to her chest as fresh tears fell upon hearing his confession of undying love.

Joval released his embrace, turning her about to face him. "Nayla, I swear, I shall be a good husband to you and I shall love this child as if it were my own," he promised as he placed his hand over her belly.

"But it is not your child, Joval. It is not of your flesh and blood. Can you truly live with this knowledge?"

"You are the mother, how can I not love this child?"

Joval's hand caressed her face, lifting Nayla's chin so their eyes met. His fingertips wiped away the tears of sorrow from her cheeks. Her eyes closed at the softness of his touch. She recalled how Arerys would touch her in the same gentle way. The Elf drew Nayla close, he kissed her ever so tenderly upon her full, soft lips. A deep sigh escaped her as though her soul had finally surrendered to him. She slowly raised herself up onto her toes so she may answer his kiss.

As he kissed her throat, his hands slowly drew back her robe to expose the skin on her shoulders that glow a creamy white in the shafts of moonlight streaming in through the window. Joval's lips caressed her soft skin; he could hear Nayla sigh at his touch. He pulled at the sash that held her robe closed and as he did so, the silk fabric slipped away from her body, puddling softly around her feet. His hands caressed the soft skin on her back as he continued to kiss her passionately. Nayla pulled the ties and clasps that bound Joval's clothes, removing them with haste.

He lifted her into his arms and gently laid her upon the bed. He could not believe he was with Nayla again, after all the many years. The one woman he truly loved was back in his arms. He kissed her again, holding her close, her naked skin warm against his. He could feel Nayla's small body trembling against him as he kissed her mouth. His long, dark hair cascaded down around her face, shutting out the rest of the world. His fingers ran through her raven tresses, sweeping it back so he may kiss her along the tops of her shoulders. His hands caressed the length of her supine body. She moaned softly with pleasure as he kissed her throat and the nape of her neck.

With nothing more than the pale light of the moon shining down upon them, Nayla's eyes closed, attempting to block out everything else around her. The Elf's calming embrace allowed her mind to drift away into a velvety black fog as she surrendered her body and senses to Joval's tender touch.

"I love you," he whispered softly into her ears as he moved between her parted legs. "I have always loved you."

As she drew him closer down onto her body, she softly answered,

"I love you, Arerys."

Joval froze. He suddenly rolled off of her body, his passion instantly retreating in shock. Nayla's eyes flashed open upon realizing whose name had escaped her lips.

"I am sorry, Joval," cried Nayla. "Please forgive me."

"While I made love to you, you made love to Arerys' ghost! Is that how it shall be, Nayla?"

"Joval, please! I beg of you; if Arerys is dead, please give me time to grieve for him. Give me time to forget," she pleaded.

The Elf sat at the edge of the bed in silence. His broad hand swept his long, brown hair away from his sad eyes as he stared at Nayla in disbelief. He was absolutely devastated, unable to accept the name she had whispered into his ears.

"Can you truly forget, Nayla? I know first hand how hard it is to do. I know what it is like to love someone you can no longer have," confessed Joval. "In all these years, I never forgot about you. I still remember making love to you, wanting and yearning for you. And I have done the same as you; making love to another and pretending she was you."

"Forgive me, Joval. You deserve better than this," sobbed Nayla.

Joval's heart was crushed. As though a great dagger had ripped into his heart and tore at his very soul, he finally realized that Nayla's heart would always belong to the fair Elf, just as his would always belong to Nayla.

CHAPTER 13

THE TURNING OF THE TIDE

In his eagerness to be with Nayla, Joval was now confronted with the horrific backlash of his actions. He cursed at the thought that he should have given her the chance to grieve for Arerys. Perhaps, had he done so, had she been given the chance to come to terms with the fact the fair Elf was not to be returning, Nayla would have never uttered Arerys' name as she did. Though the fair Elf may well indeed be dead and vanquished to her memories, the harsh reality that she still loved him washed over Joval like an immense tidal wave. He left her room in haste, abandoning Nayla to weep, drowning in her own sorrow. His heart was absolutely mortified and his head still rang with the cruel, resonating sting of hearing the fair Elf's name she had whispered into his ears.

What a fool I am to have acted so rashly. How could I have ever believed that Nayla would forget Arerys so soon? Joval thought as he paced the deserted corridor. The early morning sun streamed in through the open windows, its shafts of light broken only by the Elf's form. Joval's brown hair was highlighted like burnished gold and his eyes were of a pale blue as the sun reflected upon him. He silently made his way towards Nayla's bed chamber.

As he arrived at her doorstep, Joval could hear movement inside her room. He knocked, but it went unanswered. Again, he rapped on her door, this time a little louder.

"I am busy, Nakoa!" shouted Nayla through the closed door. "Go away! Perhaps I shall see you later!"

"It is I, Joval. Please open the door, Nayla. I wish to speak to you."

For a lingering moment there was no answer or sounds of movement within the room. Finally, she opened the door.

"Nayla, I have come to apologize for my conduct last night," said the Elf.

"It should be I apologizing to you, Joval," responded Nayla, her downcast eyes were unable to look upon him.

"To the contrary, Nayla, it was never my intention to take advantage of you when you were in such a vulnerable state. It was crass and thoughtless of me to have allowed it to happen," Joval apologized, still appalled by his own actions.

"I allowed myself to be swept away by the passion of the moment," said the little warrior maiden.

"Well, whatever the case, I had promised to allow you time to grieve for Arerys," responded the Elf.

"I do grieve, Joval, and now I fear my grief shall be never ending," she replied, her voice barely audible.

"Take some comfort, Nayla, I believe Arerys had every intention of arriving here for he swore that only death itself would keep him away from you. I am afraid he shall be true to his words. I believe fate has conspired against him and now he has fallen into the darkness."

Nayla was crestfallen upon hearing Joval's words, but she knew he spoke the truth. Arerys was well overdue and there was no sign of his impending arrival. Perhaps her intuition was right after all; perhaps he had met with an untimely demise. For a fleeting moment, the memory of Arerys, cut down and dying in her arms, replayed in her mind. She involuntarily shuddered, fighting back the horrid memory.

"Do you forgive me?" asked the Elf, stooping down to look into her troubled eyes.

"There is nothing to forgive, Joval. Please understand I never meant to hurt you," said Nayla, with sincere regret. "I never meant to utter Arerys' name as I did."

"I know."

"I can fully understand if you wish to have nothing more to do with me. In light of what had happened, I do not expect you to carry through with your plans to wed. I shall be leaving today."

As devastated as he was by that single name she had whispered last night, Joval did not have the heart to spurn her.

"Nayla, had I only given you the time to grieve as I had promised, I may have well avoided the situation. I am as much to blame for our predicament."

"There shall be no such happenings again, I promise you. I shall be on my way."

"No, I will not hear of it. We shall wed if fate decrees it, but before we do, I must be certain of one thing," said Joval.

"What is that?"

"I need to know what has become of Arerys and the others. I cannot take you as my wife in good conscience knowing that Arerys may indeed be on his way or he lies injured, unable to proceed."

"Or he is dead," added Nayla stoically.

"Whatever the case, perhaps, you too shall find some peace of mind if we delve into Arerys' whereabouts."

"But where do we begin?"

"I shall head out this morn with Lando. While your father is away, I shall conduct a search. We shall ride as far and as long as we can with the intention of returning by the last day of this month. If we do not come across Arerys, at the very least, we shall meet up with Valtar and the others along the way. They shall tell us what has become of the Prince of Wyndwood."

"Would you truly do this for me, Joval?"

"Of course I would, Nayla."

"I am deeply indebted to you," stated the warrior maiden.

"All I ask is that you remain here, do not even consider leaving Nagana. If Lando and I do not return with Arerys, then we shall wed immediately, as planned," stated Joval.

"I shall wait for you," promised Nayla, embracing her dear friend in appreciation.

In the calm of the early morn, Nayla watched as Joval and Lando departed from the fortress city. Standing high on the battlement, she observed as they rode off to the north, a small cloud of dust rising up from behind their steeds as they charged off.

I need an answer, one way or another; I need to know what has become of you, Arerys, thought Nayla, her eyes following the two men as they embarked on their journey. The warrior maiden knew that Joval would hold true to his words. Come what may, he would return at the very latest on the last day of the month, if not sooner.

For three days, Joval and Lando journeyed north along Esshu road, retracing their steps from the Iron Mountains. And for three days, there was not one single sign of the men of the Order. Not even those they had encountered along the way had seen hide or hair of the odd ensemble Joval would describe. A Wizard, a mortal from the west and a fair Elf led by a dark Elf was an impossible combination to mistake for anyone. It was becoming clear to Joval these men were either inexplicably lost, or they never departed western Imago.

Dusk brought with it a change in the weather. There was a definite heaviness to the balmy air as the heat and humidity climbed, making the conditions hot and sticky. The air had become stifling to breathe. A storm was brewing over the Furai Mountains, heavy columns of cumulus clouds, laden with rain snagged against the jagged pinnacles. As though the great peaks were massive teeth tearing into the thick, billowing masses, rain began to fall. Joval could see the gray veil descending, moving steadily towards them.

"Let us head into the valley," suggested Joval. "We do not want to be caught in this storm on high grounds. I feel it in the air, lightning shall be following."

As they entered the valley, the boom of distant thunder echoed across the land sending frightened birds roosting in trees to take flight. In a panic, they winged westward, away from the approaching storm as lightning shattered the darkening sky to herald the impending downpour. Above the sound of the storm, Joval's sharp ears could hear the distant sound of terrified horses and the frantic voices of those speaking in Taijina.

"This way, Lando," ordered the Elf, steering his steed towards the commotion. "An evil tide washes through this valley. Something is afoot, there is trouble ahead."

As they neared a clearing in the forest, sounds of swords smashing against metal and flesh filled the air as screams of agony resonated through the valley. These horrifying sounds were drowned out by the crash of thunder and the relentless pounding of rain as a torrential downpour ensued.

Joval drew his sword, urging his steed onward. Lando followed close behind. Imperial Soldiers were in the midst of an attack; the Elf immediately recognized their intended victims: Markus, Lindras, Arerys and Valtar. Together, with five Kagai Warriors, they were fighting off a small battalion. Joval could see Valtar and Arerys had already unleashed the fury of their arrows by the number of fallen soldiers, but at least another fifteen soldiers remained standing.

Suddenly, the warriors turned on the Imperial Soldiers with unparalleled ferocity. An unearthly cry emanating from deep within the leader of the Kagai Warriors cut through the mayhem, stopping all in their tracks; all except his fellow warriors. They trained for this type of scenario over and over, using the confusion of the moment to gain the upper hand. Jolted into action, Joval and Lando joined the fray.

Markus instantly identified the two riders as they dismounted. He marveled at their unexpected arrival, calling out, "Your timing is impeccable!"

"And yours is not! You are tragically late!" stated Joval, his sword piercing the throat of an Imperial Soldier.

"We can explain!" shouted Lindras, clubbing a soldier into submission.

"There shall be time enough to explain later," answered the dark Elf, turning to face his next adversary. "My job is to see that you arrive in Nagana intact, and I shall do so."

Markus, Arerys and Lando fought the Imperial Soldiers with ferocious determination. They were startled by the fighting skill of their opponents. In all the battles against the Dark Lord's regimes, they had never encountered such skilled adversaries. Where the soldiers of the Dark Army were undisciplined and untrained, driven by sheer hate and adrenaline, these Imperial Soldiers were trained swordsmen, obviously well versed in the art of war. However, as skilled as they were, they were no match for the Kagai Warriors, who dispatched them, one by one, until all were no more.

Eventually, the only sound to be heard above the steady fall of rain was the pounding of their hearts and the labored breathing of exhausted warriors. Made weary by the intensity of the battle, Markus, Lando and Lindras slumped to the saturated ground.

Arerys turned to Joval. "I cannot tell you how pleased we are that you and Lando appeared when you did. We were greatly outnumbered and these soldiers were more skilled than we had ever anticipated."

"Fate would have it that you were to be found," stated Joval. "Lando and I departed from Nagana three days ago to search for you."

Arerys shook his head in sadness, "I am well overdue, this I know, by a good ten days or so by now."

"Truth to be told, I cannot tell you whether Nayla shall be more pleased that you are alive or more angry that you are so late," responded Joval, in all seriousness.

Markus spoke between gasps as he fought to catch his breath, "Do not be hard on Arerys. It was through no fault of his that we were delayed."

"Yes," added the Wizard, "We were ambushed by the dark horseman and his followers during our trek to return the Stone of Salvation to Mount Isa."

"A dark horseman?" asked Joval, his brows knitted into a frown as he listened to Lindras.

"Yes, the last surviving emissary to Beyilzon, the Dark Lord," responded the Wizard, leaning heavily upon his staff. "It was he that we spotted retreating with the Sorcerer on the day of Beyilzon's defeat on Mount Hope."

"Ah, yes! I recall that mysterious rider," remembered the dark Elf. "So, Eldred has a new alliance; another wretched fool to do his bidding."

Valtar smiled, "*Had*, is more like it."

"Yes, Valtar killed the dark horseman just as he was about to finish me off," stated Arerys.

"So you were wounded?" asked Joval.

"He was close to death!" exclaimed Lindras. "It took the combined powers of all the elders of Wyndwood and the grace of the Maker of All to see Arerys through this ordeal."

Joval laughed.

"I am quite serious, sir," Lindras replied curtly. "Arerys nearly did not survive the catastrophe."

"Oh, I am quite sure that you speak the truth, Wizard," answered the dark Elf. "I was merely thinking on how Arerys shall survive when Nayla vents her wrath upon the prince for his tardiness!"

"She is that angry?" asked Arerys.

Joval smiled, "In all fairness, I suppose she is more overcome with worry than anger."

Through the gray veil of rain, a look of relief washed over Arerys' face. "Is Nayla well?"

"In spite of all she had endured, she is well and she shall be all the better once she sees that you are safe."

Lando gave Arerys a reassuring smile as he added, "Joval is right, Nayla has been consumed with worry. She shall be most relieved her prince has returned."

Joval surveyed the dead soldiers that lay scattered about. "This is most unusual, Valtar. Never has the Imperial Army ventured this far south, so close to Nagana. I am surprised Master Saibon had not alerted us of this invasion. Though none had ever survived an incursion from the north, I am sure Master Saibon would have sent word if soldiers had slipped past his warriors through Hebeku Valley."

"We were attacked a few leagues outside of Anshen," stated Valtar. "It was there Master Saibon and his warriors first came to our aid, but they were already aware of the Imperial Army's presence. And believe me, none escaped alive. But you should know, Joval, these soldiers did not follow us from the north; they appeared riding from the southeast."

"That can only mean one thing," said Joval. "The secret pass through the Borai Mountain is secret no more. Somehow, the Imperial

Soldiers have discovered the route we have been using to enter eastern Orien."

"Is that possible?" asked Valtar.

"We have used spies in the past. There is nothing to say that the regent or his co-conspirator, the Sorcerer has somehow infiltrated the palace with a spy of their own. We must get word to Master Saibon to be on his guard. We must warn him that Imperial Soldiers have found another way to breach the Furai Mountains."

"Shall we send a messenger once we return to Nagana?" asked Valtar.

"No. Time is of the essence. Something evil is brewing in these lands. Master Saibon and his people must be warned immediately so they may keep a watch on Borai Mountain," said Joval.

The dark Elf turned to the leader of the Kagai Warriors, speaking to him in a mix of Taijina and the common speech. The leader immediately rallied his men and they quickly mounted their steeds. Two warriors headed through the valley northward back to Anshen, while the remaining three headed southeast to the mountain pass to guard this portal into western Orien. They would attempt to stem the tide of evil until help arrived.

Joval's first task on returning to Nagana would be to send forth a falcon with a warning to Hunta Saibon. The bird would be much faster and if the warriors should fail to return to Anshen, at least the falcon would deliver the message.

The thought that there were those who now breached the Furai Mountains from this point of entry greatly troubled Joval. It was previously thought to be known only to Master Saibon's people, the elders and those that used the pass for reconnaissance missions into eastern Orien. The chance that the enemy would stumble upon this passage was inconceivable. Obviously, there was a spy in their midst.

As they watched the warriors disappear into the driving rain and growing darkness, Markus and Lindras rose to their feet. The prince looked up to the heavens; it was clear the rains would not cease any time soon.

"Where to now, Joval?" asked Markus, sweeping his wet, almost black hair, from his forehead; "We are still a good distance away from Nagana, are we not?

"Indeed," admitted Joval, gathering his steed's reins. "It shall be a three-day ride to the fortress city, if we not meet with ill fortune on our way."

Arerys gave a sharp whistle, his eyes scanning the dark forest. He could hear RainDance snort in response. After a moment, the mare appeared through a grove of bamboo, followed by the other horses. Tempest took up the rear, preventing the others from straying from their intended path.

"I know of a cave close to here," said Joval, mounting his steed. "It is safe and dry. We shall seek shelter for the night."

Markus scrutinized the dark Elf for a moment before asking, "Perchance, there are no dragons in this cave, are there?"

Six days had passed since Joval and Lando had departed from the fortress city. The late afternoon sun shone a fiery red against the clouds latching onto the pinnacles of the distant mountains to the west. Invisible hands tugged upon the billowy masses, shredding them until the clouds were thinned; reduced to thin wisps spread high against the sky. The western horizon transformed from a blue to a pale mauve as dusk settled upon the lands.

Nayla stood alone, high on top of the battlement, waiting and watching. Her eyes searched in vain, adjusting to the dimming light as night predictably prepared to steal away with the day.

Her heart sank with the setting of the sun; another day done and still no sign of Arerys. Under the first stars to grace the heavens, in quiet surrender, Nayla silently retreated from the high walls protecting the city.

She made her way through the courtyard; her downcast eyes oblivious to the soldiers bowing to their captain as she walked by. The warrior maiden continued on through the gardens, coming to a stop at the entrance to the temple. She bowed her head in silent prayer, chiming a small brass bell to alert the spirits of her arrival and their requested presence before she entered.

Perhaps the spirits shall be merciful and hear my prayer this time, thought Nayla, stepping into the sanctuary.

Inside the empty room, its tall ceiling blackened by the accumulation of years of soot from the many candles that burned, Nayla knelt down.

She lit a single candle upon the altar, and then burned three sticks of incense used by her mother's people during times of mourning. A heady fragrance filled the air as the thin gray smoke swirled and dissipated high into the tall, dim-lit rafters. She stood in her solitude, and for a long moment, stared at the ring she held in the palm of her trembling hand. Her eyes closed as her fingers touched the band of silver. Her fingertip traced the delicate leaf pattern of the ring as she thought upon her last moment with Arerys before they went their separate ways.

Nayla's heart felt as though it would be crushed by the weight of not knowing: not knowing if Arerys would return; not knowing if he had changed his mind; not knowing if he was even alive.

"Where are you, Arerys? What has become of you?" whispered Nayla under her breath. "There is so little time. Please come back to me," she pleaded as she looked upon this symbol of his undying love.

In the distance, she heard the whisperings of soft voices and the resonating sound of footsteps approaching the sanctuary. Nayla's chin fell to her chest in disappointment; she recognized the heavy, steady footfalls of Lando and the barely noticeable, light steps of Joval. Among them were the footsteps belonging to both Elves and mortals; warriors they probably met up with on their journey home. No doubt they have returned with either no news of the fate of the Order, or with word that Arerys would not be coming.

As the footsteps neared, Nayla steeled her soul, bracing herself for the worst possible outcome. She took a deep breath and exhaled slowly, fighting desperately to hold back her tears. Finally, overcome by her grief and sadness, she began to sob.

"Why do you weep, Nayla? Did you think we would not return?" asked Joval in a gentle voice.

She was unable to meet his eyes, to face Joval to learn of Arerys' fate. She remained frozen at the altar. Suddenly, she felt a surge of warm energy that was once familiar to her. She raised her head and as she slowly turned, she saw standing at the entrance to the sanctuary, Lando and Valtar. They moved aside as Lindras, Markus and finally, Arerys appeared through the doorway.

Nayla's trembling hand covered her mouth as she gasped in surprise. She rose up, taking a faltering step towards the fair Elf, unsure if her eyes had deceived her. Arerys did not hesitate. He dashed towards Nayla, greeting her in a warm embrace that swept her clear off the floor as she threw her arms about his neck. He held her quaking body closely against his chest.

"Where were you, Arerys?" cried Nayla as she hugged him tightly. "I was so afraid for you."

"Hush, Nayla. I am here now," whispered Arerys as he kissed her upon her forehead, vanquishing her despair and sorrow. "I told you nothing short of death itself would keep me away from you."

"I missed you, Arerys," said Nayla as she gazed into his gentle, blue eyes. "I missed you more than you will ever know."

"I am glad," smiled the Elf as he searched Nayla's eyes. "For I have missed you dearly." He gently raised her chin, and then he tenderly kissed her, very slowly and with great passion, savoring her touch as a parched, desert-worn traveler would savor the last drops of water from his flask.

Nayla's eyes closed as tears spilled down her cheeks. Her heart, though weary from grief, was overflowing with joy that Arerys was indeed alive.

Lindras interrupted their moment of passion, clearing his throat to gain their attention. "Perhaps, we shall come back later," suggested the Wizard as he waved the others on towards the door.

"No, Lindras!" called Nayla as she and Arerys finally released their embrace. "Forgive me, for at this moment Arerys is very difficult to resist."

"You are forgiven, my child," smiled Lindras, wrapping his arms around her, enveloping her small frame in his great robe.

"Nayla, thank you for your patience, I would not have wanted to endure a trip back to Wyndwood if Arerys was to return without you," said Markus with a smile as he winked at the warrior maiden. "An Elf in love is not an easy thing to contend with!" He gave Nayla a warm hug, happy to see she was well.

Her attention returned to the Elf. "What happened to you, Arerys?" asked Nayla with genuine concern. "Something happened."

The Elf did not offer an answer, he merely held Nayla all the closer to him.

"I am sorry, my lady," apologized Markus. "We were delayed by an unforeseen peril. Let us say for now that the tides of fortune had turned against us, we were awash in a sea of despair and misery for a time."

"But you are here now," smiled Nayla.

"Yes," answered Markus. "Indeed we are."

The warrior maiden turned to face Valtar. Though she did not feel any love for this Elf, she felt compelled to praise him for his service for indeed, he did lead the men of the Order to the fortress city. "Thank you, Valtar. Thank you for delivering my friends safely to Nagana," said Nayla, with great appreciation.

Valtar bowed in acknowledgement, stepping back from the men of the Order.

"Nayla, I shall escort our guests to their quarters," said Joval. "They are weary for the journey has been long and mired with much difficulty. I am sure they are in need of rest. We shall talk more over a morning meal."

"Of course," said Nayla. "Yes, how rude of me. We shall all meet tomorrow morn."

Joval delivered each long-awaited guest to his bed chamber after which he and Lando both disappeared into their own quarters to change and purge themselves of the dirt and grime that accumulated during their trek to recover the men of the Order.

Alone in his bed chamber, Arerys removed his cloak and soiled riding clothes. In a small adjoining room, a bath was already drawn for him. He looked at his reflection in the tub of water. The scar left by the dark emissary's sword was still visible on his body where it sliced through his chain mail and cut deep through his flesh. Though fading with time, the scar would persist for at least another month, perhaps two.

The Elf closed his eyes as his body slipped beneath the warm, inviting water. He sank down, tipping his head back. His blonde hair darkened as he saturated the golden strands. He proceeded to rinse his face, and then taking the washcloth, he used it to wipe away the last traces of grime.

Ah, it feels wonderful to be clean again, thought Arerys. He sighed as he leaned back in the deep tub. His eyes opened as a light rapping on the door drew his attention.

"Yes?" responded Arerys.

He heard the door slowly open, and then quietly close - the latch being secured to lock the door.

"Arerys?"

"Over here, Nayla. I am afraid I am not decent," called the Elf from the tub.

Nayla slipped into the room. "That is fine by me," she smiled sublimely as she peered at the fair Elf. She knelt next to the tub. Taking the washcloth from his hand, she worked the slip of soap into a rich, fragrant lather. She proceeded to wash his shoulders and his chest, scrubbing in a gentle, circular motion. Enraptured by the touch of her hands on his body, he closed his eyes. He looked so at peace, as though his world was now as it should be.

"I was so worried for you, Arerys," whispered Nayla.

The Elf smiled at her, gently touching her face. His fingertip traced the faint, thin line of the scar she bore on her right cheek; a permanent reminder of their battle at Rock Ridge Pass. He drew her closer to kiss her as she leaned over the tub to meet his lips. He kissed her slowly and with great passion, listening to the sound of her heart beating loudly. Nayla answered his kiss, her lips parted as she drew his mouth onto hers. With a sudden *'splash'*, she toppled into the water on top of him. They continued their passionate, wet embrace.

Her ivory-colored silk robe became opaque as it clung to her wet body. He could see the pyramidal forms of her breasts, her dark nipples protruding against the slick fabric. He could feel them as they brushed up again his chest. Unable to control his desire any longer, Arerys rose up from the water, scooping her up into his arms.

He looked into her large, almond-shaped eyes. They were dark, yet a sparkle of light danced in them. Somewhere in there was his paradise. He could feel his soul being drawn deep inside.

His fingers hastened to untie the sash holding her robe closed. Peeling the wet silk away from her skin, it fell from her body, gathering in a damp heap around her little feet. He stroked her head, drawing back her long, dark tresses to expose her naked shoulders and neck. As his lips and tongue pressed against her supple flesh, her eyes slowly closed. He could hear a gentle sigh escape her lips as he plied her body with many kisses as his hands caressed the softness of her skin. As he rose up against her body to kiss her upon her lips, she stood up onto her toes to draw Arerys' mouth to hers. Her lips softly caressed his, and then she kissed him slowly and fully, savoring him as though he was a tantalizing morsel.

Arerys lifted her up into his arms and laid her upon the bed. Before he knew it, Nayla rolled over his body, pushing him down onto his back.

He gazed up to see her raven tresses tumbling down around her shoulders. Her silky hair brushed lightly against his chest as she stooped to kiss his mouth, his neck and down the length of his torso. He was beguiled by Nayla's gentle touch. The beating of his heart hastened as he released a slow, deep breath. As she kissed his chest and the hard, flat muscles across his stomach, she stopped as her fingers traced the silvery white scar on his side, just below his left ribcage. As she lay next to his body, she looked upon his face.

"What happened, Arerys?" she asked, a look of worry clouded her eyes. "This was not here before."

"That was the cause of our delay, Nayla," he answered, stroking her face with his fingertips. "Do not be concerned. I have recovered from my ordeal and you are certainly a great distraction for everything that ails me."

He pulled her towards him. She kissed him on his chest and then gently on the menacing scar. She looked up and smiled sweetly at Arerys. He kissed her upon her forehead and drew her closer to kiss her fully on her mouth. As he breathed in the soft perfume of her hair, Arerys whispered, "I love you, Nayla. I had missed you so much."

Nayla returned his kiss as she rose up to straddle his body. Arerys' hands stroked the silky smooth skin of her shoulders; his fingertips ever so lightly traveled down, tracing the round curves of her breasts. As his hands gently cupped the soft mounds of warm flesh, his thumbs began to teasingly caress the dark halos of skin in a slow, circular motion causing her nipples to harden under his touch. Nayla breathed in deeply, she could feel every nerve and muscle in her body unwinding; unraveling under his erotic manipulation.

She slowly lowered herself onto Arerys' hips, gasping as she felt the tip of his engorged manhood penetrate into her. His hands encircled her tiny waist as he raised her body over his, then as his hips arched upwards, he groaned with pleasure as he pulled her down on top of him. She was impaled upon his body as he raised himself until he was fully hilted, deep inside her.

Nayla's heart pounded hard inside her chest as she felt Arerys' every movement. She rose up and with the slow, corkscrew gyrations of her hips; she lowered her body down along his length. He grew harder in response to her torturous, sensuous movements. She bit her lower lip to stifle her cry as Arerys brought her to absolute rapture.

He gently rolled over Nayla's body so she was now beneath him. She met his thrusts, taking him in fully each time. He struggled to maintain control as her inner muscles rhythmically contracted, engulfing the turgid shaft of his erection in such an intense sensation of pleasure, it borderlined on pain. He throbbed in response each time the inner rings of muscles contracted in an undulating sensation, clasping and tightening around him.

His senses were heightened by the friction of their slippery connection. He forced his body against hers; grinding his hips against the soft, fleshy pad of her pubic mound. Nayla's eyes squeezed shut as her body and soul were carried away on another intense orgasmic wave.

Arerys' movements became more urgent, his energy boiling in his loins and spreading through his body as he felt himself on the verge of climaxing. He hungered for Nayla, needing to see, feel and taste her. He had to know that he was no longer dreaming; no longer trapped in an unnatural sleep where she was nothing more than a mirage, an image of hope as he walked a fine line between life and death. He needed to know that Nayla was real.

Withdrawing almost completely, he drove the entire length of his shaft back into her body; each stroke deliberate and paced until he was overwhelmed. He cried out as he delivered a final powerful thrust, plunging once more into her burning, wet core. His body shuddered, almost convulsing, as he dispersed his seed deep within Nayla.

He could feel her sharp fingernails sink into his shoulders as she climaxed in time with him. Arerys' breathing was sharp and jagged as his heart pounded hard in his chest, feeling the palpitations of Nayla's own heart beating against his. He felt as though all his senses overloaded with that last, deep thrust. He collapsed in her arms, feeling light-headed; all his energy sapped from his body. For a lingering moment, both said nothing. They lay in each other arms, enraptured by each other's warm embrace.

As night became morning, Nayla and Arerys slept peacefully as one. The first light of dawn filtered into the room as songbirds filled the courtyard below with their cheerful sounds. The Elf awoke, reaching over to gently kiss Nayla upon her cheek. She stirred from the first restful sleep she had in many long nights.

Her eyes slowly opened and she smiled as Arerys gazed upon her. He took up her left hand and gently kissed the band of silver she wore once more.

"Arerys, there is something I wish to tell you."

"What is it, Nayla?"

For a moment, she looked into his kind, familiar eyes, studying the dark motes that flecked his sapphire irises. "I do not know how to begin. How to tell you…"

Arerys' eyes darkened with worry as his words spilled out in haste, "Do not tell me you have changed your mind. Please tell me you still intend to take me as your husband."

"I do, if you are still willing to bind yourself to the likes of me," responded Nayla. "But that is not it."

Arerys breathed an audible sigh of relief, "Thank goodness!

Whatever it is, it matters not as long as I know you shall be by my side."

Suddenly, a sharp rap on the door disrupted their conversation.

"Yes?" answered Arerys, struggling to sit up as Nayla shrank down, quickly drawing the counterpane over her head to conceal herself.

"Arerys, you are expected in the dining hall," called Lindras, through the closed door.

"Very well," replied Arerys. "I shall be down momentarily."

"Good!" responded the Wizard. "Oh! By the way, Nayla, you are to join us as well."

Arerys could hear Lindras as he ambled off down the corridor.

"How did he know?" asked Nayla as she peered out from beneath the bedding.

CHAPTER 14

A TWIST OF THE KNIFE

"Enter!" shouted Joval through the closed door as he readied himself.

Valtar peered into the room. "I thought I would find you here," said the Elf, closing the door behind him.

"Valtar, come in! I never had the chance to welcome you as I should," stated Joval, greeting his friend with a brotherly hug. "It is good to see you home."

Valtar nodded and responded with a sigh, "I am glad we survived the trek."

"So, tell me, did you see the legendary forest of Wyndwood?"

"I did indeed; it is as we all dreamed it would be, and I now long to return. In fact, I have met a beautiful, enchanting maiden, the daughter of an elder."

"You do not say?" responded Joval with a smile denoting his pleasure.

"Oh yes, I promised that I would return to her when all is said and done here. And how about you? How did you fair in my absence? How goes it between you and Nayla?"

"The same."

"Does she still plan to wed the Prince of Wyndwood?"

"He is here now. Nothing shall stand between them, myself included. Yet, through a strange twist of fate, we were ready to wed."

"No!" said Valtar, startled by this news. "How so?"

"You shall not repeat a word of this: Nayla is with child."

"Heavens above!" responded Valtar with raised eyebrows. "Arerys' child I presume?"

"Yes, Dahlon was about to exile her, for he had grave doubts about Arerys' intentions. I offered to take her as my wife; to accept this child as my own. When Arerys failed to appear, I almost had her, Valtar. I was so close. I came to her room to console her and we ended up in each other's arms."

"So is there hope that she may fall in love with you again?"

Joval shook his head sadly, "No, her love for Arerys runs as deeply as my own love for her."

"If only Arerys had met an untimely demise, Nayla would be yours now."

"Do not speak in this manner, Valtar. For once, Nayla is truly happy."

"And what about you, Joval? You deserve happiness too."

Joval turned away from his friend as he responded with a heavy sigh, "Fate conspires against me yet again. Some things are just not meant to be."

"Unfortunately, my time spent with the Prince of Wyndwood proved fruitless. There was nothing I could say that would persuade him to abandon Nayla. He is honorable to a fault, may I add," stated Valtar with obvious contempt.

"You did nothing to undermine Nayla, did you Valtar?" queried Joval.

Valtar's gaze fell away from the Elf's unyielding stare.

Grasping him by his shoulders, Joval gave him a disconcerting shake as he asked, "Valtar? What did you do? You did not disclose to the prince, my past relationship with Nayla, did you?"

"Arerys asked some very pointed questions. He is a prince. I am a servant. How could I ignore his questions? Besides, the heir to the throne of Wyndwood should know exactly what he is getting if he wishes to carry out his plan to wed that half-caste," responded Valtar. His dislike for her was evident in his tone.

Joval's eyes glared coldly at the Elf. "Did you tell him about us?"

"I was not about to lie to the Prince of Wyndwood."

"Valtar, if Nayla catches wind of this, you shall be relieved of your duties, or worse!" stated Joval, his voice rising in anger.

"I admit Arerys was upset at first, but he realized that it was long ago. I suppose it did not help matters when I told him you still loved her."

"You said what?" Joval was astonished at Valtar's brashness.

"I told him you still loved Nayla. I thought he would change his mind about her, knowing that she was here with you. Instead, it made him even more determined to claim that woman."

"Valtar, I know you are my friend, I know you wish for me to be with Nayla again, but it shall not be. Her destiny is with Arerys. She is in good hands, she will be safe from Dahlon. She will no longer turn to me when she seeks a safe sanctuary. Perhaps it is my time to journey to the Twilight. At least in this haven Nayla shall no longer be a possibility."

"Do not say that Joval, not yet!" pleaded Valtar. "You must journey to Wyndwood. You must see our home with your own eyes."

"And watch Nayla from afar? With Arerys? I think not," responded Joval briskly, dismissing his friend with a wave of his hand. "Gather our guests and escort them to the dining hall. Tell them to begin without me. I shall join them shortly."

Valtar made his way through the guest house adjoining the palace. The Elf went from bed chamber to bed chamber. It quickly became apparent Lando or a servant had already gone about the business of gathering their newly arrived guests for a morning meal.

No doubt, Prince Arerys shall need not an escort to the dining hall. Nayla is probably with him at this very moment, thought Valtar as he silently moved through the long hallway. In the corridor leading to the dining hall he chanced upon Nayla and Joval in private conversation. He quickly withdrew from sight.

What do we have here? Valtar wondered, as he spied upon the pair. He watched discreetly as Joval took Nayla's hands into his. *I do believe fate is tempting me to take action.*

Valtar quietly retreated, swiftly heading off in the direction of Arerys' quarters.

Alone in the vestibule, Nayla greeted Joval.

"I never thanked you last night, Joval," apologized the warrior maiden. "Please forgive me if I minimized your role in returning Arerys to me. That was never my intention. If it had not been for you and Lando, heavens knows what would have happened."

"I understand, Nayla," said the Elf, smiling kindly at her. "There is no need for an apology. You were merely caught up in the excitement of the moment."

"Well, I know it was not easy for you to do this for me; to risk your life so that I may have a life. For this, I am eternally grateful to you."

Joval held her small hands in his as he responded, "I cannot lie that I had wished for a different outcome, but I would not be able to withstand seeing you suffer to be apart from the one you truly love."

"As you suffer now?" she asked, gazing into his sad eyes.

"Nayla, for over a century I have longed to be with you. Alas, fate conspires against me yet again. For one brief moment, I believed we would be united as one. There was a small glimmer of hope that you would take me as your husband. I know it shall never be."

"Joval, in time, you shall forget about me. If you only gave it chance, you shall find love with another," said Nayla, offering him words of comfort.

"Love is the cruelest of games to partake in, Nayla. So rarely is there a happy outcome," lamented the Elf. "I no longer wish to be a victim to love's follies."

As though her own words and actions had crushed the very life from his heart, Nayla could feel Joval's pain. She could see it in his eyes and feel it in his touch as she sadly whispered, "I wish I were not the reason for your suffering, Joval. It is times like this that I wished you never spared my life."

"I hate it when you speak in this manner," said the Elf, giving her hands a gentle squeeze. "Though my heart grows numb, I have learned to take this suffering in stride. But for you, for once the powers that be smile down upon you. You deserve happiness."

"But what of you, Joval? You are a kind and decent soul; it breaks my heart to see you like this."

"Do not feel pity for me, Nayla. I choose to walk this path." With that said, he embraced Nayla in a hug.

Just as Valtar's hand was about to knock upon the door, it suddenly flew open. Before him, the fair Elf stood, momentarily surprised by Valtar's unexpected arrival.

"Good morning, Valtar," greeted the Elf, with a smile. "What brings you to my door?"

"Joval asked that I gather and escort all to the dining hall," answered Valtar, leading the way. "I hope you found Lord Treeborn's accommodation suitable. Did you sleep well last night?"

Arerys smiled as he answered, "Oh yes, very well."

"So, you are happy to be reunited with Nayla?" asked Valtar.

"Most definitely," responded Arerys, walking alongside the dark Elf.

"Well, apparently Nayla is glad to have you back; any later and you would have lost her to Joval."

Arerys stopped in his tracks, grasping the Elf by his arm. "Whatever do you mean?"

"Had we arrived unexpectedly, you may have found Joval in Nayla's bed," responded Valtar, yanking his arm from Arerys' hold.

"What are you speaking of?" asked Arerys, his blue eyes piercing through Valtar.

"While we were on route, Nayla thought something terrible had become of you. She found solace in Joval's arms,"

"That is not so. You are a blatant liar. I know you and Joval plot against me, to prevent me from being with Nayla, but it shall take more than your lies to turn me against her."

"Perhaps you should ask her yourself. Even as we speak, she seeks time alone with her lover."

Arerys eyes burned as he glared at Valtar, scrutinizing him for signs that he was lying.

"Go forth. See for yourself, they are alone in the vestibule just outside the dining hall."

Arerys promptly marched away from Valtar. He entered the great room, storming passed Markus, Lando and Lindras as they bid him a good morning. Their words of greeting went unnoticed by Arerys as he peered into the corridor. His heart stopped when he saw Joval in an embrace with Nayla. Without a single word, Arerys dashed over to them, furiously wrenching her from Joval's arms.

"Arerys, what are you doing?" asked Nayla, startled by his sudden appearance and abrupt actions.

He said nothing. He glared at Joval as he led Nayla away by her arm.

"Arerys, you are hurting me! What is wrong? Have I done something?"

He hurriedly led her back to her room where upon he slammed the door behind them. Nayla was frightened at this sudden change in Arerys. She had never seen him look this angry before. He paced the length of her room, like a caged animal, fighting to calm himself so he may find the words to express his hurt and anger.

"Talk to me, Arerys! What has happened?"

"You tell me, Nayla!"

"I do not understand."

"Were you with Joval?"

"What do you speak of? Of course I was; you saw me. You were there."

"No, not now, while I was on my way to Orien!" retorted the Elf. "Did you bed him?"

Nayla was momentarily stunned; her eyes wide open in shock. She wanted to speak, but the words would not come.

"Tell me it is not so," pleaded the Elf.

"Arerys, it is not what you think."

"Was Joval in your bed?"

Panic set in as she watched Arerys' eyes darken in anger, his harsh tone rattled her nerves. "Let me explain, please!"

"You could not even wait for me!"

"Arerys, you were long overdue! I thought you to be dead!" declared Nayla in desperation.

"So you rush off to be with your lover!" admonished the Elf, reeling from the devastation of her betrayal.

"No, it was not like that!"

"Oh, I know all about you and Joval!" he spat as he seethed with jealousy.

"That was long ago, Arerys!"

"And yet, you were ready to be joined in wedlock to that Elf! Well, Nayla, you can go back to Joval! I am going back to Wyndwood!" Arerys stormed out of her room.

"Arerys, no! Do not leave!" she begged, seizing him by his arm to stop him. "Please let me explain!"

Arerys grabbed her by the shoulders and glared angrily into her eyes. "There is nothing to explain! We have nothing to talk about!" He stormed away from her, quickly disappearing down the corridor.

Nayla's heart raced. In a brief span of time she had climbed from the very pit of despair to the very pinnacle of happiness, only to have her hopes and dreams dashed in one fell swoop. She bolted to the dining hall where Joval, Markus, Lando and Lindras were engaged in conversation as they waited for Arerys and Nayla to join them.

Nayla rushed up to Joval, standing before him. Her small body was trembling as she fought to control her rage.

"What is it, Nayla?" asked Joval, sensing an overwhelming tide of anger emanating from her.

Without warning, Nayla slapped the Elf hard across his face. "How dare you, Joval? I thought you were my friend! I thought I could trust you!"

"What on earth do you speak of?" said Joval, his hand rubbing his smarting cheek.

"You told Arerys about us! You told him we were together!"

"I told him no such thing! I would never betray you like that!" He was stunned by Nayla's accusation. Then it dawned on him, *Valtar! It had to be Valtar!*

"He is leaving, Joval! Arerys is leaving! He would not even let me explain!" cried Nayla in anguish.

Joval suddenly turned away from her, heading out of the dining hall.

"Where do you go?" asked Nayla.

"I mean to speak to Arerys Wingfield!"

Her tears flowed endlessly as she turned away from Markus, Lando and Lindras. They stared in disbelief upon hearing this news.

"Nayla, please tell me this is not so! Arerys is my friend; please tell you have been faithful to him," pleaded Markus.

"Already you judge me Markus, yet you do not understand what has transpired."

"Then help me to understand! I know you love Arerys, so tell me what has happened?"

Nayla looked up into Markus' troubled eyes, and then she noticed a woman standing silently in the corner of the room, in the midst of delivering food to the table.

Markus gazed in her direction. He approached the woman, taking the tray from her hands. "We wish for a moment to speak in private," requested the prince.

"Of course, my lord," she responded, bowing as she exited the dining hall.

As soon as she disappeared from his sight, Markus turned to the trembling form before him. "Speak now, Nayla. You are amongst friends."

She hesitated for a moment, and then answered reluctantly, "I have conceived a child with Arerys. When Dahlon found out, I was condemned to a life in exile. He believes Arerys had used me to bring dishonor to his house. It was Joval who championed me, attempting to salvage my honor. He could not bear the thought of me being ostracized so he made a promise to Dahlon that he would bind to me and claim the child as his own if Arerys failed to show. When all of you were well overdue, when the day came and went and Arerys still did not come, I did turn to Joval. But nothing happened. I am in love with Arerys. Joval knows that, that is why he and Lando went to search for all of you. He could not marry me with a clear conscience knowing that Arerys may still be alive. So he went to look for you in hopes that even if Arerys was not in your presence, at least you would have word of his whereabouts and if indeed he had a change of heart."

"Does Arerys know you are with child?"

"No, he would not let me explain. Now it is too late. He is leaving," said Nayla through her tears.

Joval entered Arerys' bed chamber to find him hastily throwing his belongings into a pack. For a brief moment, he contemplated allowing the fair Elf to depart Nagana – never to return. Arerys deliberately chose to ignore his presence, continuing with his preparations.

Stopping Arerys in mid-stride, he caught him by his arm as he attempted to reason with the angry Elf. "Arerys, do not leave like this. If you truly love Nayla, you will not leave in this manner."

The fair Elf suddenly turned on Joval, yanking his arm from his grip. Grabbing him by his shoulders, Arerys slammed him up against the wall as he growled, "You can have her once more, Stonecroft!"

"Hear me out!" said Joval as he struggled against the younger Elf's powerful grip.

It was at this very moment Markus, Lando and Lindras stumbled into the room to see the two Elves grappling against each other.

Lando and Markus immediately seized them, pulling them apart. "Stop it, both of you! Arerys, calm down, listen to Joval!" ordered Markus.

"What is this? Have you turned against me too, Markus?" said Arerys, his eyes blazing with anger.

"Do not be a fool! If you love Nayla, then you shall hear Joval out!" shouted Markus.

"I am a fool! I have been played for a fool!" raged the fair Elf as he struggled against Markus' hold.

The Wizard stood between the two Elves, physically keeping them at bay. "Arerys! Please, listen to Joval!" pleaded Lindras.

"Why? So he can further twist the knife that Nayla has thrust into my back? I think not! I have been betrayed by that woman! I want nothing more to do with her! I am leaving!" Arerys turned to depart from the room, but Joval caught hold of his shoulder.

"Oh no, you are not!" insisted Joval, spinning Arerys about to face him. As he did so, Arerys' fist flew towards his face. The dark Elf swiftly pivoted away, allowing the fist to just skim past him.

Lindras took up his staff, herding Markus and Lando out of the room. As Arerys turned to follow, Lindras closed his eyes and with the power of his mind, brought the door slamming shut.

"Let me out, Lindras!" shouted Arerys as he angrily pulled at the latch, but to no avail – it was firmly locked into place.

"No! There you shall remain until you have come to your senses! It would serve you well to take heed of Joval's words," called the Wizard through the closed door.

"Lindras, what if they kill each other?" asked Markus.

"Then Nayla shall not have to concern herself with either one of them." answered Lindras, a smug look set upon his lined and weathered face.

"I am serious, Lindras! They shall do each other harm!"

"They may be angry, but they are not foolish," responded the Wizard.

"I beg to differ! Angry men have been known to do foolish things," protested the prince.

"No need for concern, Markus. Joval and Arerys are equally quick-tempered, but they will not do each other harm. They need to talk. They must resolve their differences or Nayla shall be forever torn between her love for Arerys and her loyalty to Joval."

Arerys turned to confront the dark Elf: "Nayla played me for a fool. She still loves you!"

Joval raised his hands in a sign of truce. "I wish it were true, but you are so wrong, Arerys. I admit that I wished for you never to have shown your face, for I stood to gain much. But it was not to be, and I admit I was in Nayla's bed, but through no fault of her own!" confessed Joval.

Upon hearing this admission, Arerys struck out to punch Joval, but again, the dark Elf easily angled away to avoid the blow.

"I do not wish to hear the sordid details of your tryst!" shouted Arerys. He seized the dark Elf by his shoulders, slamming Joval hard against the door. The force was such that Lindras, leaning against the other side, was jolted by the impact.

Joval retaliated. The knuckles of his fists struck down on Arerys' biceps, painfully breaking his hold. Grabbing the fair Elf, Joval quickly overpowered him. He threw Arerys hard against the opposite wall, his forearm pressing unmercifully against his throat.

"Oh, you shall hear me out!" snarled the dark Elf.

Arerys' struggled against Joval's hold as he gasped, "I would much rather die than to listen to any of your foul words."

"Truth be told, I would much rather pummel some sense into your thick skull than have to reason with the likes of you!" retorted Joval.

Arerys lashed out, striking Joval in his midriff. The blow sent the Elf flying backwards to the floor. "I have had enough of your insolence and lies!" he shouted as he turned away from Joval.

The dark Elf rolled easily over his back, swiftly rising up onto his feet. He charged towards Arerys, this time with his dagger drawn, "Oh you shall listen, if it is the last thing that you do!"

Just as Arerys turned to confront him, Joval tackled him, knocking the fair Elf to the ground. He straddled his body, pinning him down as he held the edge of his blade close to Arerys' throat.

"As I was saying before you so rudely interrupted: Dahlon knew you should have arrived on the fortnight hence. He had given Nayla until the last day of this month for you to return. When you failed to show by the summer solstice as *you* had promised her, Nayla was devastated."

"So she turned to you!" spat Arerys in disgust, his eyes burned with hate for this dark Elf.

"No! It was I who took advantage of her vulnerability; she agreed to marry me if you had failed to show."

"I am overdue by a fortnight and she rushes to marry? I can hardly say that it is a sign of devotion. She does not love me!"

"Unfortunately, she does love you, though you are not deserving of her! And yes, I admit I tried to make love to her on that night, but I was competing with your ghost for her affections. She loves you. Even if you had died, her heart would be forever imprisoned by your memory."

"I do not believe it. Valtar warned me about you!"

"Valtar Briarwood is loyal to me! He would do and say anything to see me back together with Nayla. He cannot accept this situation."

"Do you still love Nayla?"

Joval stared into Arerys' angry eyes as he answered, "Yes, I do not deny that I love her and I probably always shall." With that thought, he pulled the edge of his dagger away from Arerys' throat.

"Well, it is obvious she still loves you!" retorted Arerys, in growing rage.

The dark Elf shook his head in regret as he responded, "What she feels for me is not love. It was never love! It is nothing more than gratitude!"

"Gratitude? What do you mean by that?"

"What she feels for me is nothing more than gratitude. What she feels for you is true love!" said Joval, finally loosening his grip on Arerys, believing the fair Elf was now at least willing to listen.

"I do not understand this," said Arerys, scrambling to his feet.

"I do not expect you to understand our relationship. Yes, I admit we were lovers at one time, long ago," confided Joval, sheathing his weapon. "It took me a long time to accept that she did not love me - just as it took her a long time to understand that what she felt for me was not love."

"But there is a closeness you both share, I am not blind to it," stated Arerys.

"I have known Nayla since she was a child. You have no idea what indignities she had been forced to suffer. I was her sanctuary in the midst of all the treacheries she had been forced to endure. She knows nothing about family loyalty. She only knows the love and loyalty of her friends. I have seen her grow up fearful of people, not knowing who she can and cannot trust all because she suffered terribly in Dahlon's hands," said Joval with a heavy sigh.

"What does this have to do with anything?" snapped Arerys, still seething with anger.

"It has everything to do with Nayla and if you care half as much as you claim to, then you shall hear me out!" declared Joval, in mounting frustration.

"Proceed. You have my ears," replied Arerys curtly, his hands smoothing back his disheveled hair and clothes.

"It was I who spirited her away from here, to live with the ascetic priests. These mortals, the Kagai Warriors, taught her their ways. I never saw her again until almost sixty years later. By that time, she had matured into a young woman. She and her *brothers*, the Kagai Warriors, came to our aid during a great battle against the Imperial Soldiers. It was then, that I came to be her mentor, inducting her into the army stationed in Nagana where she trained my men. With her proven fighting skills she quickly moved up the military ranks. She was skilled as a warrior, but she was reckless, taking many chances with her life to accomplish missions and to win battles."

"To prove to Dahlon that she was competent?"

"Yes, but mostly because she had little regard for whether she herself, lived or died. Dahlon left her feeling that her life was of little value, that she was ugly and worthless, that she was undeserving of life or love. It was not long after she returned to Nagana that she tried to reclaim her place in the high house she was born to. Dahlon and she had a terrible row. I walked in to find Dahlon beating upon her, but Nayla refused to defend herself. Although, with her training and skills, it would have been easy for her to retaliate, even kill him. Nayla refused to fight back. I came to her defense. When all was said and done and we were alone, Nayla began to weep. I had never seen her cry before, not even when she had been wounded in battle. Dahlon ingrained in her that tears where a sign of weakness so she would never give him the satisfaction of seeing her cry. I shall tell you now, I was crushed to see her tears but to my dismay, her tears were not due to the humiliation or the beating she had endured. The tears she shed that day were for me," confided Joval.

Arerys frowned in response as he asked, "For you? But why? Were you, too injured during this confrontation?"

"No," answered Joval. "Apparently my actions touched Nayla beyond words. In all her life, from the time of her mother's death, nobody had ever come to her defense. I was the first and only person to ever come to her aid, to ever protect her from the one person who, by all rights, should have revered her, cherished and loved her."

The fair Elf knew that Joval was sincere in his words. And now he felt ashamed for he was no better than Dahlon Treeborn.

"So you see, Arerys, Nayla's love for me is founded on gratitude. I encouraged her to follow her heart, to be brave like her mother once was. I gave her a sense of self-worth; I taught her that she did have the capacity to love and to be loved. As I said before, it took a long time for Nayla to discern between love and gratitude."

Arerys stared into Joval's eyes, searching his soul for the truth and it was then he realized Eliya's warning that the *force* that would work against he and Nayla was never Joval, it had been Valtar all along.

"I can overlook her past relationship with you, but I cannot forgive her for this last indiscretion," stated Arerys.

"Well, if it is of any consolation, you should be pleased to know that she called out your name in the throes of passion, not mine. She chose to love and honor your memory."

"If she truly loved me, even if she believed I had died, she would have not turned to you in such haste. That is what I cannot accept, the fact that she was willing to marry you so soon."

"She had no choice," stated Joval, in Nayla's defense.

"Of course she had a choice!"

"It is obvious you never gave Nayla a chance to state her case. Did she not tell you of her condition?" asked the dark Elf.

"What do you speak of?"

Joval gave a disgruntled sigh as he shook his head in anger. "Nayla is with child, your child may I add. That is why we had planned to wed."

The length of silence was painful. Stunned by this news Arerys' mind reeled with the impact of Joval's words. He was momentarily rendered speechless. *My child!*

"Dahlon believed you had deliberately used Nayla to bring dishonor to his house. He planned to exile her so none would know of her condition or the father of the child. I could not allow her to live like that; I could not bear to see her suffer in this manner. She did not deserve a fate such as this so I offered to take her hand in marriage to allow Dahlon to save face and to allow Nayla a chance for a decent life. I was willing to accept this child as my own."

"I... I am going to be a father?" stammered Arerys, standing a little taller. It suddenly dawned on him how foolish he had been for not even allowing Nayla to explain. He had acted rashly, failing to take heed of Eliya's words of warning. Instead of listening to his heart, he was betrayed by Valtar's half truths. He now realized the depth of Joval's loyalty to this woman.

"Unfortunately, you and I are bound together by a common thread: *Nayla*. We both love her, but it is you, she loves. If you can find it in your heart to forgive her, I am sure she can find it hers to forgive an asinine fool such as yourself."

"We are going to have a baby..." said Arerys, the full meaning of the words were beginning to sink in.

"I recommend you speak to Nayla before it is too late," suggested Joval.

"Lindras! Open up! I must see Nayla!" shouted Arerys as he pounded on the door.

Lindras released the power of his mind, allowing Arerys to step out of the room. The Elf gave the Wizard, Markus, and then Lando an exuberant hug. "I am going to be a father!" he announced proudly. Arerys quickly disappeared down the corridor to find Nayla.

Lindras peered into the room to see Joval sitting on the corner of the bed. His aching head was lowered, braced in his hands.

"So, are you now friends?" asked the Wizard hopefully.

Joval's blue eyes peered up wearily at Lindras as he answered, "Let me just say we have come to an understanding."

CHAPTER 15

TO THE GATES OF HELL

Nayla angrily tore off her gown, quickly changing into her warrior raiment. Donning her chain mail, she concealed it beneath her vest. She threw what little belongings she had brought with her into a pack. Throwing her cape over her shoulders, she turned to leave. She looked briefly at her swords that lay mounted on the stand. Seizing the long sword, she fastened it to her belt over her left hip. Taking the short sword, she quickly thrust it into the knot of her belt.

The warrior maiden stopped long enough to consider the wooden figurine of a winged fairy Arerys had carefully crafted for her. It was a parting token of his love when they went on their separate ways from Mount Hope. She placed it back, next to the sword stand. *There is no need for such frivolous mementos now,* thought Nayla as she turned away.

Tossing the pack over her shoulder, the warrior maiden threw the door open to leave. She caught Nakoa at mid-knock. The woman's eyes were thrown wide open in surprise.

"My lady, where do you go in such haste?" asked Nakoa.

"I am leaving."

"But why?" she asked, bewildered by Nayla's behavior. "Prince Arerys has returned to you."

"I have not the time to explain to you, Nakoa. I must leave immediately," answered Nayla, attempting to push past the woman.

"Tell me what has happened, my lady!" pleaded Nakoa, continuing to block her exit.

"I have been betrayed by one man and discarded by the other. I have not the will, nor the strength to deal with either of them!"

She set her pack down, quickly removing the ring from her finger. Taking Nakoa's hand, she placed the circlet of silver into her palm.

"If you see Prince Arerys, please return this to him."

"What has happened, my lady? Please tell me!" pleaded Nakoa, grasping her by the arm to impede her departure.

"It is best not to concern yourself with this matter, Nakoa."

"When shall you return?"

"Never," she replied. "It is best that you forget about me. Consider me dead to this world. Do not even mention my name in passing to others."

Nakoa realized Nayla meant every word she said.

"If you feel the need to leave, then come with me. Stay with me, my lady," offered Nakoa.

"No, my friend. I do not wish to embroil you in my woes."

"But where will you go?"

"I shall go where none shall find me – where I shall be safe."

"But where?" Nakoa demanded to know.

Nayla turned to give her friend a final hug. "I wish not to be found, Nakoa. Perhaps our paths shall cross again at another place, in another time, but I have no intention of returning to this forsaken city."

"But what of your father?"

"He can go to hell," she responded, her voice devoid of emotion.

"And what of the elders, how shall they reach you if they are in need of your service?"

"They will have to do without me. Joval can cater to their whims. I am dead, Nakoa. I am dead to this world. Take what you may of my possessions. I have no need for them now."

With that said, Nayla slipped out through the doorway and silently disappeared down the corridor. Through her tears, Nakoa watched her friend head across the courtyard to the stables. She knew this warrior maiden was gone for good.

Arerys smiled as he dashed down the corridor to Nayla's bed chamber. Through the door, he could hear the soft sounds of a woman's cry.

"Nayla!" called the Elf as he stepped into the room. Instead, he found her lady-in-waiting, crumpled in a heap upon Nayla's bed. Her tears streaming down her rubicund cheeks as she sobbed.

Her eyes, moist with tears, burned as she glared at Arerys. "What did you do to her? What did you do to my lady to have her leave in this manner?

"Whatever do you mean?"

"She is gone! She is never coming back!" stated Nakoa in anger. "Here! She asked me to return this to you." She defiantly hurled the silver ring at Arerys. His quick reflexes allowed him to snatch the ring from mid-air. His hand opened so he may look upon his palm. He was stunned by what Nakoa presented him with.

"Where did she go?"

"I do not know."

"You do not know, or you will not say?"

"I told you! I do not know! She would not divulge her destination. She would only say that she wished not to be found."

"I must find her, Nakoa. She is not safe on her own!"

"Why does she feel she would be safer away from you?"

"You do not understand. I must get her back."

"You have already broken her heart. What more do you wish to do to her?"

"I swear, Nakoa, believe me, I love Nayla, more than you will ever know. I love her - and the child she carries," confessed Arerys.

Nakoa was stunned by his words, slumping down onto the bed. Realizing Nayla's dire situation, her tears fell fresh.

"Please, I beg of you, tell me, where did she go?"

As the great tears tumbled down her cheeks, Nakoa whispered, "Forgive me, Prince Arerys, I truly do not know."

"Think, Nakoa," begged Arerys. "She must have said something."

"She would only say that she was to go where she would be safe," she recalled. "She is going somewhere safe."

"But where?"

"That is all that she would disclose," Nakoa whispered through her tears.

Arerys raced across the courtyard where he came upon Joval and the others returning to the dining hall.

"She is gone, Joval!" declared Arerys, confronting the dark Elf.

"I cannot say I blame her," responded Joval. "She needs time to get over her anger; that is all."

"No, I mean to say that she has left Nagana!"

"What?" asked the dark Elf. He was reluctant to believe Arerys' words.

"She is alone out there?" gasped Lindras in disbelief.

"Yes! That is exactly what I mean," said Arerys. "Her lady-in-waiting stated that Nayla has left for good."

"She would not be so foolish to leave the safety of this city alone," said Lando. "Would she?"

"Think on it, she is a woman scorned," said Joval, turning to Arerys. "You have spurned her. She has been wounded by your callousness."

"There shall be time enough later to rake me over the coals, Joval. Tell me now! Where did she go?"

"Did Nakoa not say?" asked the dark Elf, his concern for Nayla escalated.

"No, she does not know. Nayla would not divulge this information to her."

"This is a vast country with many places to disappear in if one is determined to do so. She could be anywhere!" declared Joval.

"All Nakoa would say was that Nayla was going to where she would be safe," said Arerys.

The dark Elf contemplated these words for a moment. "There is only one place she truly feels safe," confided Joval.

"Anshen!" stated Arerys, a spark of hope ignited in his eyes.

Joval nodded. "Let us get our horses before she extends her lead by far!"

Nayla was well beyond her anger and hurt as she raced northward. Numbed by Joval's betrayal and Arerys' rejection, she had no more tears left to shed. Once she had put the situation in its proper perspective, all she had that truly mattered now was the life growing inside her.

I shall stay with my people in Anshen until the baby's birth, resolved Nayla in her mind. *We shall be safe there. Master Saibon shall disclose to no one that I am in this haven.*

The landscape passed by in a blur as the warrior maiden urged her mare on. She deliberately avoided the main road, choosing a near-invisible trail that ran almost parallel but on higher grounds. Here, she would go unnoticed by other travelers.

As her mare forged on through the forest trail, her steed's pace slowed considerably, as though alerted to an unseen evil.

"What is it, girl?" asked Nayla in a whisper, leaning towards her steed's twitching ears. Her eyes strained to pierce through the dense vegetation. Something, or someone, was heading in her direction. She could hear the steady plodding of hoof beats becoming louder. Nayla quickly coaxed her mare off the trail. She dismounted, drawing her sword in anticipation as she waited and watched in the shadows.

Nayla remained hidden behind a tree, peering out only when the horse on the trail below came to a faltering stop. She looked intently at the rider. The man could sense there was someone nearby. He was slumped against the horse's neck, groaning in obvious pain as he attempted to right himself. She gasped in surprise upon recognizing the rider as being one of her own: a Kagai Warrior. Nayla dashed down to the trail, her sudden appearance spooked the horse, causing it to rear up, displacing the warrior. Nayla caught the man as he slipped from the saddle. His dead weight sent the warrior maiden tumbling to the ground as she attempted to break his fall.

To her horror, the warrior was badly burned; his face, hands, and arms were raw, swollen and blistered, but Nayla knew he was a Kagai Warrior by the dark tattoo that was still visible, though distorted, through the blistering skin high on his right arm. It was identical to the one etched onto her shoulder blade.

"Takaro? Am I dreaming, or is it really you?" asked the warrior, speaking in Taijina. His eyes were swollen almost completely shut, yet he was able to make out the form kneeling by his side.

It was only upon hearing the warrior's voice that Nayla was able to identify the badly burned man. "Shenyu, what happened? Why are you so far from Anshen?" asked Nayla, holding her flask of water to his parched lips. He cried out as the cold water spilled onto the festering wounds of his once proud and handsome face.

"The secret pass on Borai Mountain has been discovered by the Sorcerer," answered Shenyu, "Four days ago, we were attacked by Imperial Soldiers as we escorted your friends from Anshen. Three of us headed east to guard the pass while two men returned to Anshen to deliver word to Master Saibon that the Furai Mountains have now been breached from the south."

"What of the others?"

"Megoto is dead. Baikasai had been captured. No doubt, he too is dead. And I shall be dead before I reach Nagana with this warning," said Shenyu in a weak voice.

"You shall not die. Neither will Baikasai. If he is still alive, I shall retrieve him from the Sorcerer's clutches."

"I tried, Takaro. Look at what has become of me. The same fate shall await you if you proceed alone."

Too weak to walk, Nayla dragged Shenyu beneath the cool shade of a tree, propping him up again the trunk.

"I have no medicines with me, my brother. Had I been an Elf, I would be able to relieve your pain instantly, but alas, I am not. I shall do for you what I can."

Nayla tore off her cape, shredding it into long, narrow strips. She quickly doused them into a cold, clear stream splashing down along the trail. With the greatest care, she gently wrapped the warrior's burns in the cold dressing. The man flinched at first, but sighed in relief as the icy chill of the wet bandages offered an instant, if but temporary, reprieve from his pain.

"I shall leave you with my flask of water. It is here by your hand," said Nayla, positioning the flask so it was within easy reach. "Between the shade and the breeze that blows, it shall keep the dressing cool."

"Are you going for help?"

"No. There shall be no time. If the Sorcerer has Baikasai, I must try to save him."

"Takaro, do not be foolish. Do not take unnecessary risks!" pleaded the wounded warrior.

"I cannot turn back knowing the Sorcerer has our brother! I shall not leave him to be tormented by that madman. I promise, I shall return soon," said Nayla, mounting her steed.

Shenyu's appeal for her to desist echoed behind her as the warrior maiden rode hard. She followed his trail to the base of Borai Mountain. At the mouth of the pass, concealed behind a grove of bamboo and a massive monolith of granite, Nayla found the scorched remains of Megoto. She wasted no time with his body, offering only a silent prayer as she passed by.

The trampled grasses, broken twigs and branches were obvious clues left by the surviving warrior. They led to a small entrance of a cave. She dismounted, leaving her mare behind. Nayla crouched down to peer inside the mouth of the cave. The entrance was deceiving for beyond, it led into a large chamber. She waited for her eyes to adjust to the dim light before immersing herself into the dank, dark cave.

At the far side of this chamber, a series of lit torches illuminated the way. It became clear she had stumbled upon one of the Sorcerer's underground lairs. Nayla drew her sword as she silently crept through the passage. Eventually, the single, gloomy corridor gave way to two tunnels. She studied the ground, looking for signs of which direction the warrior had been taken.

This fresh trail of blood must lead to Baikasai, thought Nayla, touching the damp, stained ground with her fingers.

The warrior maiden veered to the left, following the droplets of blood. Soon, Nayla was submerged in a labyrinth of deep tunnels and chambers. For over an hour she pressed onward. The air was stifling, becoming hotter as she ventured deeper into the bowels of the earth. Her eyes scanned a large chamber; before her, numerous stalagmites

towered above her own form. High above, large stalactites were suspended from the roof of the cave like the massive, treacherous fangs
of some long forgotten beast, ready to clamp down upon her.
Everywhere, molten pools of lava bubbled and belched from the
earth's core. It was as though she stood before the gates of Hell. The
foul stench of brimstone was all around her, assaulting her senses.
With grim determination, she trudged onward, searching for her warrior brother.

"Where are you taking us, Joval?" asked Markus. He brought
Arrow to an abrupt halt as the dark Elf led the search party off the main
road.

"Yes, Joval. We came from Anshen by way of Esshu Road," stated Arerys, bringing RainDance alongside Markus' steed. "Why are
you diverging from this route?"

"I am thinking as Nayla would; as a Kagai Warrior," responded
Joval. "She means not to be found so she will deliberately avoid all
well-traveled roads. As their name implies, Kagai in Taijina means
shadow. That is exactly what she will do, she will move in the shadows to go unnoticed."

Something inside him told Arerys to trust Joval. He questioned the
dark Elf no further, prompting RainDance to follow.

Charging northward, retracing Nayla's invisible trail as best they
could, the men rode with great urgency. They were acutely aware of
the fact that the once secret passage through the Furai Mountains was
secret no more. Having already survived one ambush by the Imperial
Soldiers, the men were at least aware of the possibility they may be
attacked once again. In Nayla's case, none had yet to warn her of this
new situation. If the Imperial Army gave pursuit, she would be outnumbered and taken by surprise.

Up ahead, Joval's far-seeing eyes came upon a lone figure resting
against a tree; his steed waiting patiently by his side. Arerys, too saw
the man swathed in bandages, by his manner of dress, he immediately
recognized him as one of the Kagai Warriors that had escorted the men
of the Order from Anshen.

Upon hearing the approach of horses, the warrior drew his sword
although now unable to see his prospective foes.

Joval approached him, speaking in Taijina, "Fear not, Kagai
Warrior. It is I, Joval Stonecroft."

The warrior struggled to sit upright as he lowered his sword.

"Master Stonecroft! It is I, Shenyu Menai. The Sorcerer – he has taken refuge somewhere on Borai Mountain!"

"We shall worry about him after we have tended to your wounds," stated Joval, carefully removing the dressing to assess his injury.

"You do not understand! Takaro is in pursuit. One of our brothers has been taken captive by the Sorcerer. Takaro has gone to rescue him. She is alone!"

Joval stood up; he cast his gaze towards a mountain, its summit shroud in a thick, ghostly mist – hidden away from prying eyes.

Unfamiliar with the Taijin language, Arerys still made out Nayla's name and the word 'Sorcerer'. Immediately, an unmistakable fear gripped his heart as he looked upon the dark Elf.

"This does not bode well," stated Arerys, searching Joval's eyes.

"What is it, Joval?" asked Markus.

"It is Nayla. She has gone after the Sorcerer!"

"She cannot stand up to that beast alone!" warned Lindras, leaping back onto Tempest.

Joval turned to Valtar, instructing him, "Use your powers to heal this warrior to the best of your abilities. When you are done, take him back to Nagana with you. Return with additional warriors. Do you understand?"

"Yes, I do. I shall return with the greatest expedience," promised Valtar, kneeling next to the warrior. He proceeded immediately to tend to the worst of the injury, his Elven touch soothing and healing the burned and blistered flesh.

Joval and the others followed the path made by Nayla as her steed charged towards Borai Mountain. In her haste, she was not discreet in her movements, crashing through young groves of bamboo and shrubs in her urgency to rescue Baikasai. It was only a matter of time before they came across a dead warrior. It was Megoto. Finally, they discovered Nayla's mare, anxiously snorting and pacing nervously outside the mouth of a cave.

The men quickly dismounted, abandoning their steeds as Joval led the way in. For a moment, all stood inside the vast, gloomy chamber, their eyes adjusting to the dim light within.

"Her footprints!" stated Arerys, pointing to the ground. Amongst those of the warrior that was obviously struggling against the Sorcerer, being half dragged and half pushed, Nayla's small impressions followed in pursuit.

The men followed the trail through gloomy chambers and meandering tunnels, poorly lit by the series of torches illuminating the way. Lindras passed his hand over the crystal orb set on his staff, shedding more light on their dreary surroundings. They journeyed on until the tunnel branched off into two separate passages.

The men stood before their choices, contemplating their next action.

"Look, there is blood!" said Lindras, pointing with his staff. The glow from the orb made the drying droplets of blood look black.

"Let us hope it is the blood of the Sorcerer," responded Joval.

"We shall follow," said Markus, pointing to the left entrance with his sword.

"It may be a trick," stated Joval. "The Sorcerer is a clever one; this may simply be a lure to draw us into his lair; right into a trap. There is also a chance Nayla had taken the tunnel to the right.

"Let us waste no more time," declared Arerys. "Markus, take Lando and Lindras. Take the passage to the right. Joval and I shall search the one to the left. Be careful everyone!"

Joval nodded in agreement. Once more, the Order divides. Markus led the way down the long, winding tunnel. In areas where the torches ceased to burn, Lindras called upon the light of his staff to guide them, taking them deeper into the bowels of the earth.

The Elves journeyed down the corridor, their eyes piercing the unnatural darkness. The only intermittent light illuminating their way now came from the bubbling pools of molten lava. The heat intensified as they ventured deeper still.

"How deep do these tunnels go?" asked Arerys.

"I could only hazard a guess," replied Joval. "If this is where the Sorcerer dwells, no doubt it shall take us straight to the gates of Hell itself."

"Well, we must be getting close," stated the fair Elf, drawing his cloak over his mouth and nose. "The air is foul. It reeks of brimstone."

"Perhaps, we shall meet your old friend, Beyilzon," said Joval.

"Do not even speak in jest about that, Joval," Arerys lashed back. "The Watchers had warned us that the Sorcerer had an alliance with the Dark Lord. However, Eldred Firestaff turned against Beyilzon in a bid for supremacy."

Suddenly, both Elves drew their swords, turning swiftly upon hearing footsteps echoing from behind them. Their eyes strained to pierce through the shadows. There was nothing. As they turned to resume their search, Joval and Arerys came face to face with the Sorcerer of Orien.

Before they could react, an invisible force emanating from his staff sent both Elves violently hurling across the chamber, striking hard against the far wall.

"My! My! What do we have here?" asked the Sorcerer, his staff still pointed towards the Elves, its invisible power pinning them against the cave wall like a giant hand of energy. "Prince Arerys of Wyndwood and Joval Stonecroft, the Stewart of Nagana, such esteemed guests! Welcome to our humble abode. Enjoy your stay for it shall be brief."

"We seek Nayla Treeborn! Where is she?" demanded Joval.

"Did you say 'we'? A dark Elf and a fair Elf; working in cooperation. Well, we shall not stand for it!" snapped Eldred. Suddenly, the Sorcerer's eyes darted to his left, just over his shoulder as he shouted, "Be quiet, I am talking to our guests!" The Elves looked confused. There was no one else there.

Arerys glared into Eldred's dark, recessed eyes. They were black and eerily lifeless except for the red light reflecting off the glowing lava bubbling around them. It was as though he was looking into the black soul of one already dead.

"Where is Nayla?" shouted Arerys, struggling against his invisible restraints.

"Ah, there is no need for concern," taunted the Sorcerer. "She is alive - for now."

"If you harm her, I swear I shall kill you slowly," snarled the fair Elf.

"Hmm, that shall be difficult for you to do if you are already dead. Besides, I do believe you have already done your fair share of harm to the warrior maiden."

"I would never harm Nayla. I love her!" declared Arerys.

"Well, it is a pity you did not take heed of the Watcher's warning," rebuked the Sorcerer. "Had you only listened to your heart than be swayed by the words of one who so intensely despises her, perhaps she would not be in the predicament she is in now."

"How... how did you know?" stammered Arerys.

"Call me ubiquitous! Call me omnipotent!" gloated Eldred with a cynical laugh. "I am many things and soon, all shall learn to scrape and bow to me! Yes, even you!" he turned to scream at his imaginary partner. It was obvious to the Elves that he was quite insane.

"Tell me where Nayla is! Tell me now!" demanded Joval.

The Sorcerer tossed his head back as he laughed, "You are in no position to make any demands. But if you need to know, she will be here soon enough."

For a brief instant, Joval and Arerys looked at each other. Suddenly, both Elves called out to the warrior maiden.

"Nayla, go back!" shouted Arerys.

"Run, Nayla! Get out of here!" called out Joval.

"Silence!" ordered Eldred, "Your squawking is becoming most tiresome!"

With a wave of his staff, Joval and Arerys were both hoisted by an invisible force, high to the ceiling of the chamber. The Sorcerer closed his eyes as he repeated an incantation. The ground began to quake as soil and rocks crumbled from the ceiling, splashing into the pools of lava below. Eldred laughed with delight as tree roots submerged deep into the earth came to life. Like great serpents slithering around their bodies, the massive roots coiled around the Elves, binding their arms, legs and even across their mouths so they were unable to call out to warn Nayla.

As the roots tightened around Joval and Arerys, they were raised higher into the ceiling, high above the floor of this subterranean chamber of horrors. They struggled and kicked, but to no avail. The more they fought, the tighter the roots bound them, dangling their bodies over a large pool of molten lava that boiled and churned like a cauldron of red-hot soup.

"Foolish Elves!" snorted Eldred with a demented laugh. "See what surprises I have in store for your little friend."

Nayla's ears picked up the desperate calls of Joval and Arerys. She ventured further into the recesses of the earth, but was abruptly thrown against the wall of the tunnel as the ground beneath her groaned and shuddered.

What are they doing here? Nayla wondered, as she righted herself. *No! That is the Sorcerer. He plays with my mind.* She moved with great stealth, silently creeping through the gloom. The heat was becoming almost unbearable as she journeyed ever closer to the source of evil.

As she neared the end of the tunnel, it emptied into a vast chamber. The floor was littered with broken stalactites and stalagmites, and pocked with churning pools of red lava.

"Nayla Treeborn," announced the Sorcerer. "Well, it is about time!" He stood before her, holding the Kagai Warrior by his neck, using his body as a shield. Baikasai's throat was cut and bleeding badly, forced to offer his blood as a lure to trap the warrior maiden. He leaned heavily against the Sorcerer, barely conscious and clinging to life.

"How noble and valiant of you to attempt rescuing your friend," sneered Eldred, "And what a complete and utter waste of time! This type of loyalty shall only get you killed!"

"Please! Do no more to harm him," pleaded Nayla.

"Or what? You shall *hurt* me?" mocked the Sorcerer. "I tell you this: If you can save him – you can have him!"

Without warning, in one swift movement, Eldred pitched the warrior into a large, bubbling pool of lava.

Nayla screamed out in horror as the warrior's own screams of agony echoed through the cave, resonating down the tunnel. Before she could even manage one step towards the warrior, a wave of lava had swallowed him up, churning and belching as it consumed its victim. She stared in shock and disbelief as Baikasai disappeared beneath the quivering, molten ooze.

"Pity, Nayla! Perhaps had you been a full-blooded Elf you would have been lighter on your feet!" taunted the Sorcerer.

The warrior maiden drew her sword, advancing towards her nemesis with every intention of killing him.

Eldred pointed his staff towards the ceiling as he cautioned, "I suggest you conserve your energies to handle more pressing issues."

"What can be more important than killing you!" snarled Nayla.

"Oh! Well, look up there," said Eldred, pointing with his staff. "Your friends have been waiting for you."

Nayla's eyes gazed up to the high ceiling of the chamber. To her horror, Joval and Arerys were suspended high above, side by side in a tangle of roots.

"I snap my fingers, and they both shall fall," smiled the Sorcerer. "So what shall it be? Would you rather waste your time trying to kill me? Or would you prefer to use you energies to save them?"

"You are totally insane!" snapped Nayla, staring up at the two Elves.

"Do not insult me! Call me an evil genius if you will! But do not doubt my ability for rational thought!" he hissed in contempt. "Insanity... who has the time for that?"

"Why do you do this?" cried out Nayla. "Why can you not follow in the path of your brother, Lindras."

"Lindras Weatherstone is a pathetic fool! He is altruistic to a fault. He cannot see mankind for what they really are. And the Elves! They are no better as they leave for the Twilight, passing this world on to the mortals so they may pillage and rape the lands, exploiting it for their own gains. Besides, I take no pleasure in fraternizing with lower life forms."

"You are a heartless soul prone to gross exaggeration!" stated Nayla.

"Well, think on this little warrior! Mankind has hidden far too long behind the cloaks of the Elves. Since Kal-lel and Dahlon wish to commiserate with the mortals, standing by and protecting these wanting, needful beings, I shall take them down in defeat."

"You shall never succeed! The Elves shall rise up against you and so shall the race of man!" declared Nayla.

"What do you care, Nayla Treeborn? Why do you feel so compelled to protect them both when neither race willingly accepts you into their fold? Why do you not join me instead? I shall make you my queen! Together, we can rule Imago. As my consort, the world shall be yours. I shall give you whatever your heart desires."

"It shall be a cold day in Hell when that happens, Sorcerer!" retorted Nayla, in disgust. "And what I desire most is to see you dead! Are you willing to die for me?"

"I am not amused by your rhetoric," spat Eldred, seething with rage. "However, what will amuse me is to watch you attempt to save your Elf friends." He pointed back up at Joval and Arerys.

"At the snap of my fingers, they shall both be hurled into that pit of lava. If you are lucky, you *may* be able to save one of them. So, who shall it be, Nayla? You must decide!" said Eldred, gleeful with anticipation.

Nayla stood before him, frozen in her tracks.

"Life is so full of drama, is it not?" Eldred mocked with great satisfaction. "You must choose between the love from your past or the path to your future. So who shall it be, Nayla? Are you going to choose the one that loves you, or the one that you love?"

"I beg of you! Do not do this!" pleaded Nayla.

"Oh well, it is too late. Perhaps you would like the Elves to plead their case? Perhaps they can tell you why you should pick one over the other. Or maybe not, they seem to be at a loss for words right about now!" laughed Eldred, as he directed Nayla's eyes to the roots that firmly wrapped around their faces, preventing them from uttering a single word.

"This is a cruel game!"

"Oh, this is no game, Nayla. Games can be started and stopped on a whim. Games offer hollow victories to the winner; of token prizes and inflated egos. The stakes are much higher where I am concerned."

"I will stop you! And if I fail, others shall come in my place!"

"Bring them on, warrior maiden," snarled Eldred, pointing his staff towards Joval and Arerys. "This is only the beginning! Wait until you see what *we* have in store for the Wizard of the West."

Nayla gazed up at the two Elves. Beads of sweat rolled from her forehead into her eyes, stinging them as she watched and waited.

"At the count of three, I shall let them fall!"

There was a deafening silence that braced the great chamber. The only sound she could hear was the resounding beat of her heart pounding wildly in her chest.

"THREE!" shouted the Sorcerer, snapping his fingers.

Nayla threw down her sword and raced towards the pool of lava, her eyes following the writhing forms descending from the ceiling. Suddenly, she leapt upon the broken tooth of a stalagmite, catapulting herself forwards with all her might. Launched into the air, she extended her arms out wide, catching both Joval and Arerys about their waists. Her body weight and momentum successfully knocked them backwards from the bubbling cauldron of lava.

"Curse you, Treeborn!" shouted the Sorcerer in anger, lowering his staff in her direction. As she hit the ground, Nayla rolled over her shoulder. With the greatest agility, she effortlessly rose up onto her feet. She glanced down to see that Joval and Arerys were both winded by the impact, but seemed unhurt. Without a word, she began her pursuit of the Sorcerer. Before Eldred could retaliate, the approaching voices drew his attention. Lindras was near! The Sorcerer immediately fled from the chamber.

Dashing through the cavern, Nayla dove for her sword, picking it up in her hand as she rolled back onto her feet. Without slowing her momentum, she gave chase.

Joval and Arerys struggled to their feet. Retrieving their weapons, they ran after Nayla. Entering the tunnel, the sounds of fast approaching footfalls alerted them. The Elves withdrew into the dark recesses of the tunnel, waiting. As the footsteps rounded a bend in the passage,

Joval and Arerys suddenly leapt out, swords drawn, ready to attack. Much to their surprise, they were met by the blades wielded by Markus and Lando.

"It is you!" said Markus in stunned surprise upon coming across Joval and Arerys.

"We thought we heard voices in here. We thought we heard Nayla!" stated Lindras, the glow of the crystal on his staff intensified as he stepped forward.

Joval and Arerys immediately lowered their swords. "She was here," stated Arerys. "She pursues the Sorcerer!"

"There is no time to lose! Come quickly!" ordered Joval, leading the way.

Through the intense heat and consuming darkness, Nayla forged on. Sword in one hand, the other feeling her way through the corridor illuminated only by the intermittent light of molten lava as it boiled to the surface. She persevered. Perspiration beaded her skin as the temperature continued to soar. Nayla endured the insufferable heat, knowing full well that had she not been part Elf, she would not be able to bear the suffocating heat for as long as she did.

Entering another sweltering subterranean chamber, her eyes instinctively closed with a blinding flash of light. Torches lining the walls of the chamber suddenly ignited, driving back the shadows of the interior of the large cavern.

"Ah! Alone at last, Nayla," sighed Eldred with a satisfied smirk as he sat upon his stony throne. His gnarled fingers beckoned her to approach. "Come hither, my dear."

The warrior maiden pointed the tip of her sword towards the Sorcerer as she advanced.

"Why do you waste my time? Do you believe that toy you wield is any match for me?" asked the Sorcerer, truly insulted by her bold, yet futile effort. With a wave of his staff, Nayla's sword was ripped from her hand, and sent hurling behind her.

Undaunted by his magic, she charged across the chamber, straight for the Sorcerer. Eldred lowered his staff at Nayla, sending a ball of fire blasting towards her. She deftly dodged the fiery projectile, but the impact as it exploded into the ground sent Nayla flying. Brilliant orange sparks rained down upon her as she struggled to her feet.

"You are a bigger fool than I ever suspected; selfish and self-serving to boot," cackled Eldred. "To bring peril upon yourself I can see, but to harm an innocent life? I am truly appalled!"

Nayla advanced towards the Sorcerer, her strides deliberate and confident, picking up in pace as she neared the stony throne that Eldred was so comfortably perched on.

Again, Eldred lowered his staff as he chortled, "You are willing to risk the life of your unborn child for the likes of me? I am truly flattered!"

Startled by his words, Nayla came to an abrupt halt, staring intently at her nemesis.

"Oh, I know, Nayla," sneered the Sorcerer, the knotted joints along his stick-like fingers thoughtfully rubbing against his pointed chin; the dark orbs of his recessed eyes glowed red. "Word has it that you are with child. And not just any child, you carry the heir to the throne of Wyndwood."

"You do not know what you speak of!" retorted Nayla, veering ever closer to the Sorcerer.

"I hardly think so. My source is highly reliable," said Eldred, as an evil smile curled across his face. "And believe me, one more Elf born to this world is one too many. Another Wingfield is unacceptable! But you seem intent on dying anyway!"

With her short sword drawn, a blood-curdling sound exploded from deep down inside Nayla as she charged towards the Sorcerer with deadly intention.

Eldred responded with a diabolical laugh that resonated throughout the cave, his staff poised at the warrior maiden. Another ball of orange-red flames shot towards her, but Nayla easily eluded the fiery mass.

The Sorcerer grunted in disgust as he pointed his staff once more. A massive ball of heat and flames blasted in her direction. Nayla reacted by diving to the ground but as the fireball struck; the percussion of the explosion picked her up, slamming her body violently into a pillar of stone.

The chamber swirled into a whirlpool of red and black before her eyes, as though she was caught in a maelstrom of fire and darkness. She slowly sank down the side of the pillar, collapsing to the ground as her world went black.

"You have been a thorn in my side for far too long," snarled Eldred, "but no more!" His alacrity to seize the moment made the Sorcerer incredibly agile as he leapt down from his throne, taking her sword up into his hand. He knelt by Nayla's prostrate body, lifting her by the crown of her hair. "Your head shall serve as adequate warning for Lindras and your friends!"

Yanking her head back so her throat was fully exposed, the Sorcerer bent closer, the blade of her short sword glistened, coming alive as it reflected the light of the torches that burned.

"Eldred Firestaff!" The Sorcerer's name boomed and resonated repeatedly through the great cavern.

The Sorcerer glanced up to see Lindras and his companions burst into the chamber.

Markus hurled his dagger towards Eldred, but the Sorcerer deflected the blade with a glancing blow from his staff. Turning the crystal orb onto the men of the Order, the Sorcerer released a ball of fire in their direction.

Lindras turned to face his adversary. The glow from his staff burst with resplendent white light, squelching the deadly flame into a harmless shower of golden sparks.

Eldred prepared to launch another assault as he backed into a tunnel. Just as he took aim, Lindras directed a blue bolt of energy from his crystal. It struck the roof of the cave directly above the mouth of the tunnel. A cloud of heavy dust followed an avalanche of rocks and boulders, sealing the entrance to the underground corridor.

Arerys did not wait for the dust to settle, sheathing his sword as he dashed to Nayla's crumpled form. He knelt by her side, for an instant gazing upon her, watching the slow rising and falling of her chest as she breathed.

"Oh, Nayla, what have I done?" lamented the fair Elf, gently lifting her head upon his lap.

Joval too knelt by her side. Resting his head low on her belly, he listened. As he raised his head, he looked upon Arerys and said with unmistakable sadness, "I cannot hear the baby's heart. It beats no more."

"No! That cannot be! You are mistaken!" cried out Arerys. "We must get Nayla back to Nagana! We must get help!"

"It is too late," said Joval with a heavy sigh.

"No!" groaned Arerys, clutching Nayla against his chest. "No! This cannot be happening! Lindras, do something! Anything! I beg of you!"

The Wizard looked upon the fair Elf, shaking his head. "This is well beyond me, Arerys. You know I do not possess the power to give life where none is to be had. I am sorry."

Markus knelt before his friend, his hands resting on Arerys' trembling shoulders. "Let us leave now, before the Sorcerer returns to vent his wrath."

"Then let him come!" snapped Arerys through his tears.

"Not like this, my friend," said Markus. "I assure you, this is far from over. Eldred Firestaff shall pay dearly for what he has done. He shall receive his comeuppance in due time."

Lando knelt by the fair Elf, Nayla's sword in his hand, "I swear upon my life, Arerys, we shall bring the Sorcerer to justice. For now, let us leave this hell-hole before we cook from the heat. Let us get Nayla to a safe place."

Arerys lifted her limp body into his arms, tears spilling from his eyes. "I am sorry, Nayla," he whispered, his voice breaking under the overwhelming weight of his despair. "I am so sorry."

CHAPTER 16

THE CHARM OF A VIPER

"Nayla, can you hear me?" whispered Arerys. "Please wake up."

He stroked her long, dark tresses, kissing her gently upon her forehead as she stirred from her unnatural sleep.

Nayla's eyes slowly fluttered open, the gray fog clearing from her mind as those before her came into focus.

"You are safe, my lady," said Nakoa with a welcoming smile. "You are home."

"Anshen?" asked Nayla, struggling to sit up.

Arerys laid his hands upon her shoulders, persuading her to lie back down. "No, we are in Nagana."

"What happened?" asked Nayla, fighting to recall the events leading up to her return to the fortress city.

"The Sorcerer…" answered Arerys, clutching her hands into his.

"Drink this, my lady," said a woman, holding forth a steaming bowl of tea.

Nayla's eyes fixed onto the stranger. She was the same woman she had seen in the meeting hall delivering drinks to the elders and her father on the day of Dahlon's departure from the city. She was the very same one who was in the dining hall when she had confided to Markus that she carried Arerys' child.

"Who are you?" asked Nayla, staring at the woman. The warrior maiden scrutinized her face and the hands holding the bowl of herbal tea. She looked perhaps four or five mortal years younger than Nakoa. It was obvious to Nayla this woman was fairly new to manual labor for her hands showed no signs of the usual wear and stresses bore by most relegated to domestic duties in and around the palace grounds.

"This is Taiko Saikyu, my lady. She has been hired on by Lord Treeborn as domestic help," said Nakoa.

"I am also a midwife, my lady," added the stranger. "I am here to help you."

"Help me? I am in no need of help," stated Nayla, backing away from the woman. "What is the meaning of this, Arerys?"

"Nayla, try to remain calm," persuaded the Elf, in a gentle voice.

"What is happening?"

"My lady, drink this," coaxed Nakoa, taking the bowl from Taiko's hands. "It shall help."

"Whatever do you mean? What is it?"

Taiko poured boiling water into a large basin. "It is a tea to help a woman in your condition," she answered, turning to hold forth the ingredients: the leaves of a red berry plant and a pale yellow root that grew in the shape of a man. "Trust me, you shall feel better once you are done."

Nayla turned to Arerys and immediately she knew something was terribly wrong. Tears began to well and trickle down his cheeks. Her trembling hand reached up to touch his face. He pressed her hand against his cheek as he whispered, "I am so sorry, Nayla."

"What... what do you mean? You are scaring me, Arerys."

"There was an accident, Nayla. The Sorcerer... the baby, our baby..." stammered the Elf in a whisper.

"What of our baby?" cried Nayla; her whole body began to tremble.

"Our baby is dead," answered Arerys though his tears.

"No! That cannot be!"

"I am sorry, Nayla. Please forgive me," pleaded the Elf.

"Nakoa, this is a mistake," whispered Nayla. "Tell Arerys he is mistaken."

Nakoa looked upon her mistress; she blinked back her tears as she listened to Nayla's desperate plea. She said nothing, shaking her head in response.

"Quickly, my lady, drink this. The life you carry is no more; you cannot keep it inside much longer. You shall be poisoned. Now please, drink!" insisted Taiko, snatching the bowl from Nakoa's grasp.

"No!" wailed Nayla. Just as she struck out to knock the bowl from Taiko's hand, she was seized by a stabbing pain. Her hands dropped down to her belly as she doubled over.

"It has begun," said Taiko. "She has brought on labor herself."

Nayla's eyes were large and liquid; a look of sheer panic filled her. Arerys threw his arms about her trembling body, holding her close as she cried out.

"Prince Arerys, you must leave now," urged Taiko.

"No! I shall not leave Nayla!"

"This is no place for a man! There is nothing you can do to help her! Now leave!" demanded Taiko.

"Please, my lord," begged Nakoa, pulling on Arerys' arm.

"No!" Arerys shouted in defiance, tightening his embrace around Nayla.

Taiko threw the door open, motioning for Markus and Lando to enter. "Get him out of here!" ordered the midwife. "Now!"

"Come, Arerys," coaxed Markus, his hand resting of the Elf's shoulder. "It is time to go."

"I shall not leave, Nayla. Not this time! Not ever!" shouted Arerys, shrugging his shoulder to escape his touch.

"Do not make us do this, Arerys," pleaded Markus, seizing him by his arm.

"Leave us be!" demanded the fair Elf, loosening his hold on Nayla as she groaned in pain as another contraction racked her body.

Lando and Markus simultaneously grabbed a hold of Arerys' struggling form, prying him away from Nayla. Half dragging, half pushing him across the room, Nakoa wept as she held Nayla down, watching as her mistress desperately reached for Arerys' outstretched hand.

"No!" sobbed Nayla. "Arerys!"

Taiko promptly slammed the door shut, securing the latch so none may enter.

"Now, let us get this over with," said Taiko, drawing back the counterpane.

In the corridor outside of Nayla's bed chamber, the men of the Order gathered and waited. All knew the outcome was not to be good. Arerys anxiously paced, his hands nervously running through his flowing, golden hair as his frustration and anger mounted.

"Why is this happening?" groaned Arerys. "That was my child!"

"It was not meant to be," said Lindras in a gentle voice.

"It *was* meant to be, but it has been snatched away from me! Why?" asked Arerys as he railed against his growing rage.

"God only knows," responded the Wizard.

"Why did the Maker of All allow this to happen?"

"It was not His fault," claimed Lando. "If you want someone to blame then blame the Sorcerer. He is the one who did this to Nayla!"

"If the Maker of All is all powerful, all mighty, then where was He when Nayla needed him? Answer me that!" demanded Arerys as he shook Lando by his shoulders.

"He spared Nayla, did he not?" responded the knight.

"Arerys, we all feel your loss, but none as greatly as you do at this very moment," Markus sympathized, his hands prying the Elf's grip off of Lando. "I know the pain of such a loss, but count your blessings, my friend. I lost Elana as well as my son in childbirth. For you, Nayla is still alive. She will endure."

As time crawled by, through the closed door, the men could hear Nayla's heart rendering cry followed by the sounds of Nakoa's hysterical sobbing. Markus could see the fear in Arerys' eyes as he listened. Joval turned away from the men as silent tears rolled down his cheeks. He could feel Nayla's anguish. As sure as a knife had been driven into his own heart, the dark Elf was overwhelmed with grief and sadness.

Suddenly, the door opened as Taiko Saikyu stepped out, a bundle of crimson stained towels discreetly tucked under her arm.

"It is done, my lord," stated Taiko, turning to head down the corridor. As she stepped away, Arerys caught her by her shoulder, stopping her departure. The woman turned to face the Elf. She could see that he was looking at the bloodied bundle she held. The midwife looked into his eyes for a moment, and then disclosed, "It was a boy child, my lord."

Arerys' eyes slowly closed as her words crushed his heart. He collapsed to his knees as he wept bitterly, his body shuddering as he sobbed. Markus knelt by his friend's side, consoling him.

Lando's heart sank as he watched helplessly, tears welling in his eyes. He noticed Joval silently disappear down the corridor as Lindras turned to him.

"I have some business to tend to, Lando," confided the Wizard. "I shall leave immediately."

"What shall I tell Markus?" asked the knight.

"Tell him I shall return in due time," whispered Lindras, turning to the courtyard. "Tell him that help is imminent."

Joval seethed with undeniable rage as he stormed down the corridor to Valtar's quarters. As he neared, his acute hearing could make out the noise of movement within his room. Without so much as a knock on the door, the Elf barged straight in. Valtar was in the midst of pouring a glass of wine, spilling some as he was startled by Joval's sudden appearance.

"What is this?" asked Joval. "Are you celebrating perchance?"

Valtar frowned at his friend, and then smiled as he answered, "Yes in fact, to the successful rescue of Nayla Treeborn from the clutches of that foul beast. Care to join me?"

He raised a goblet of red wine to Joval, offering it to him.

The senior Elf glared at his servant. His hand lashed out, knocking it from his grasp.

"You are in a foul mood. What was that for?" asked Valtar, stunned by his abruptness.

"Are you an imbecilic dolt? Or do you take me for some kind of fool?" snarled Joval.

"I plead ignorance," sniffed Valtar, picking up another goblet.

Outraged by Valtar's cavalier attitude, Joval seized him by the lapels of his vest, thrusting him hard against the wall. "What you did to Nayla is truly despicable. I always knew your dislike for her was intense, I just never believed you would stoop so low as to do something this vile to bring her to her ruin."

"I merely told the Prince of Wyndwood the truth," stated Valtar.

"Oh, you did more than that! Do not trivialize what you have done!"

"What I did, I do for you, because you are my friend," explained Valtar.

"A *friend* you say? This is a complete and utter travesty! You do not know the meaning of the word. A friend would not stab a friend in the back!"

"Now see here, Joval, as a *friend*, I shall excuse your harsh words. You are letting your temper get the best of you!"

"If you truly were my friend you would never have done this knowing full well what Nayla means to me."

"But Joval…"

"I am ashamed to have counted you as a friend!"

"Do not say that, Joval. Surely you jest?"

"I suppose you shall gain some satisfaction in knowing that Nayla has lost her child. She has suffered a miscarriage thanks to you!"

"Of course I take no satisfaction in this knowledge! But to blame me; you go too far! I had nothing to do with her departure from Nagana or her run-in with the Sorcerer!" protested Valtar.

Joval's response was immediate. He slammed Valtar against the wall, raising him off the floor in rage.

"Do not even deny your part in all of this! I see you for what you truly are now! At this moment, you disgust me! Even to gaze upon you makes me ill!"

"Your words are tainted by your anger, Joval. Calm yourself or speak to me no more!"

"Calm myself? How dare you? You arrogant bastard!" raged the Elf, pinning Valtar against the wall. "You fail to comprehend the severity of the situation! You have no idea what events you have set into motion!"

"Then I shall fix things! What can I do to make things right?" pleaded Valtar, prying at Joval's fingers to loosen his hold.

"The seeds of your treachery grow deep. We are about to enter a war like none this country has ever seen. Our ranks grow thin and now, any hope of King Kal-lel and Lord Treeborn uniting our people has been dashed by your selfish act. The Alliance shall *not* be coming to our aid. Our people shall be crushed by the might of the Imperial Army and blackness shall descend upon this land. And it is all because you hate Nayla!"

"What I did to her, I do for you," reiterated Valtar, attempting to pacify his master. "I truly believed she would turn to you once Arerys spurned her in jealousy."

"I am no fool, Valtar. You labor under false pretenses. Do not use me as an excuse for your reckless and malicious conduct."

"If that is how you truly feel, then I shall fix things, Joval. I shall do whatever you ask! Whatever it takes to make things right!" pleaded Valtar.

"If I were not already burdened by the proprieties of being the Stewart of Nagana, I would see fit to kill you myself!" snarled Joval, his blue eyes turning icy as he glared at Valtar with true contempt.

"Do not speak in this manner, Joval. You do not mean this! You are merely incensed," said Valtar. His attempts to palliate only served to enrage Joval all the more.

"Incensed?" growled Joval. "You have no idea just how truly incensed I am! The mere sight of you repulses me! I want you out of here! You are dead to me! Do you understand?"

"You cannot be serious!" cried Valtar, recoiling from the harshness of his tone.

"If I should see you again within this lifetime, it shall be too soon. You have destroyed Nayla, you have wreaked havoc in the lives of those who care for her, and now, we shall all pay dearly for your cruel and hateful act. Be gone!" demanded Joval, releasing his grip on the Elf. "You have until dusk!"

Valtar began to tremble after their harsh exchange of words. Joval's parting order began to sink in. Never in all the centuries they

had shared a friendship - a brotherhood, had he ever seen Joval so outraged. But more so, for the very first time, he fully comprehended the
catastrophic ramification of his actions.

"Collect yourself, Arerys," whispered Markus, raising the Elf onto
his feet. "Though I know your loss is most devastating, it shall do no
good for Nayla to see you like this."

"What do I say to her?" asked Arerys, looking forlorn.

"Tell her how much you love her," answered the prince.

"How can I face her?"

"She shall need your strength more so than ever before," said
Markus, rapping lightly on the door of the bed chamber. "Your presence shall be most welcomed. Do not keep her waiting."

The door opened as Nakoa peered through. Her eyes were blood-
shot from tears shed as she tried to console and ease her mistress' pain.
She motioned for Arerys to enter as she whispered, "She rests now, my
lord. Taiko Saikyu, the mid-wife has given her medicine to induce
sleep."

Arerys crept into the room, silently taking his place at her bedside.
He did not even notice when Nakoa left the room as Markus closed the
door behind her. The Elf breathed a weary sigh as he looked upon
Nayla's sleeping face. He leaned over and tenderly kissed her upon her
forehead, taking her hand into his.

Here, Arerys remained. The minutes passed like hours as he
patiently waited for Nayla to wake. She tossed and turned in restlessness, as though she was reliving her torment in the Sorcerer's subterranean lair. The Elf watched helplessly, stroking her hair and speaking
to Nayla in a gentle tone in an effort to comfort her as she lay trapped
in her tortured dreams.

Throughout the night Nakoa peered into her mistress' chamber,
asking Arerys if there was anything he required or if Nayla's condition
had changed. Each time, his answer was the same as he continued his
lone vigil by her bedside.

"My lord, the day shall break soon, why do you not sleep? I shall
stay by Lady Treeborn's side," suggested Nakoa in a whisper.

"Thank you, but I wish to remain here should Nayla wake,"
replied Arerys in a soft tone.

"But you must be exhausted."

"I shall be fine," answered Arerys. "You however, have been up
for many long hours, Nakoa. I suggest that you seek some rest. I shall

alert you when Nayla comes awake."

"I am weary," admitted Nakoa with a sigh as she looked upon her mistress. "Promise you shall call on me when she wakes?"

"Most certainly," answered Arerys.

Nakoa quietly closed the door behind her, leaving the Elf to resume his vigil. Arerys gently kissed Nayla upon her hand as he sat in his chair, leaning forward upon the bed, waiting for her to rise.

The gentle light of the early morning sun filtered in through the window, bathing the room in a warm, golden glow. Some time during the wee hours of the morning, the Elf had succumbed to his own weariness. He had fallen asleep in his chair, slumped forward across the edge of the bed still clutching Nayla's hand. His eyes slowly opened, waking to the touch of her hand upon his head, softly caressing his golden strands with her fingers.

He gazed over to her, smiling in relief to see she had now risen from her slumber. "Nayla, how long have you been awake?"

"Long enough to recall what had transpired," she answered as she looked at him thoughtfully. After a reflective pause, she gazed into Arerys' tired eyes and whispered, "You came for me. You had followed me to the very gates of Hell."

"And I would do it again, Nayla," responded the Elf, caressing her face with his hand. "How do you fare this morn?"

"Numb... I feel numb... and empty inside," she answered in a soft voice. "It is as though the life that had been extinguished from within now creates a terrible void in my heart."

"Nayla, this loss... our child... I am so sorry," stammered the Elf. Overwhelmed by grief, he was unable to express his true sorrow.

"As I am too," she said in complete understanding.

"It is my fault, Nayla."

"Arerys, you had no way of knowing," she said as she gazed into his sad, blue eyes.

"Had I listened to you, had I allowed you to speak than to be consumed by my own jealousy this never would have happened," lamented Arerys.

"Truth be told, Arerys, had I been you, had I been the one to see you with another woman, one you share a history with, I undoubtedly would have responded in a like manner," admitted Nayla.

"Why did I allow my emotions to be swayed by the likes of Valtar?" groaned the Elf, his head lowered in shame.

"Valtar is devious," said Nayla. "I always knew his contempt for me ran deep and I feared from the start when we departed from Mount Hope that he would prattle on to you about the past where Joval and I were concerned, but now, he has gone too far."

"Do not worry about that scoundrel, Nayla," responded Arerys. "I shall deal with him in due time."

"No, Arerys, he is my concern. Valtar and I are long overdue for a confrontation. There shall be no vindication for him this time. Not even Joval will dare stand between us when I get my hands on him. And the Sorcerer too, he shall pay dearly for what he has done."

"Enough talk of retribution, Nayla. You are in need of rest; to recover from your ordeal," stated Arerys in a firm voice as he drew the counterpane around her neck.

"Why are my times of bliss so few and so fleeting," wondered Nayla, seeking solace in Arerys' arms.

"Your time shall come, Nayla, I promise you," answered the Elf, holding her close to his chest.

"It was to be a boy child, Arerys. Did you know?" asked Nayla, her voice trembling as she spoke.

"Yes, I know," answered the Elf.

"My loss is great and yet, I have no more tears to weep. It is as though I have nothing left inside of me," whispered Nayla, her eyes were dark with sorrow as though the light in them were now smothered by the burden of her grief.

"I understand, Nayla," replied Arerys. "I feel the same however my love for you goes on. Though our loss has been great and I too feel this void, my love for you has not diminished. I pray you feel the same for me."

"Do you truly feel this way? You still love me in spite of everything Valtar has said and done to turn you against me?" asked Nayla.

"Most definitely!" declared Arerys. "My love for you has only grown in the face of all this adversity. It is immeasurable; it is as deep as the deepest ocean and it shall be enduring as the enchanted forest of Wyndwood, if you will take me as your husband."

"Will you love me until the day I die?" asked Nayla in a gentle voice.

"Longer Nayla, for much longer than that," promised Arerys, kissing the circlet of silver she wore on her finger.

"Joval! Where is Joval Stonecroft?" raged Dahlon Treeborn as he stormed towards the meeting hall.

"My lord, I shall fetch him," answered his servant, flustered by the Elf's foul mood.

"Do so, and make haste! I do not like the rumors that have been set adrift in my absence!" shouted Dahlon as he waved the man away.

As the small Taijin servant scurried down the corridor and rounded the corner, he nearly collided with Joval. The Elf had quickly side-stepped upon hearing the mortal's heavy footfalls as he neared.

"Master Stonecroft! Make haste to the meeting hall, Lord Treeborn has returned. He demands to see you, immediately!"

"Can it not wait?" asked the Elf as he fastened the clasp of his cape.

"I beseech you, my lord, please, to the meeting hall!" pleaded the servant, bowing before his towering form.

"Very well," conceded the Elf. "Run along. I shall be but a moment."

Dahlon Treeborn paced the length of the meeting hall, anxiously awaiting the arrival of Joval. He stopped long enough to consider Taiko as she delivered his steaming cup of tea.

"So Taiko, are the rumors true? The Prince of Wyndwood is in our fair city?"

"Indeed, my lord," answered the servant. "In fact, he is with Lady Treeborn as we speak. He stays by her side as she recovers."

"Recovers? Ha! I always knew she was of weak, mortal blood. So she has she taken ill?" asked Dahlon.

"Well, my lord, I...I..." she stammered, her eyes lowered under his steady gaze.

"Either she is ill, or she is not. So, what is it?" queried the Elf, his impatience growing. "Speak, woman!"

"I do not know of a delicate way to broach this subject, my lord," answered Taiko.

"Do not waste my time, just say what needs to be said and be done with it," ordered Dahlon.

"I must regretfully say that Lady Treeborn had suffered a miscarriage," informed Taiko with some reluctance.

"Are you positive?" asked the Elf.

"Yes, my lord. I was the one who tended to her," responded Taiko.

"Hmm, that is a fortunate turn of events," muttered Dahlon.

"Pardon me, my lord?"

"Never you mind, woman," replied Dahlon, "You better be off now. I am expecting others."

"Very well, my lord," said Taiko, bowing as she exited the room. As she turned to leave, Joval appeared at the doorway.

"Enter Joval!" ordered Dahlon, motioning the Elf to join him at the table.

"It is my understanding I had rushed back for your nuptials all for naught."

"Bad news travels quickly, my lord. No, I shall not be wed to Nayla."

"How can that be bad news, Joval. Think on it. You shall not be encumbered with a child that is not your own, nor shall you have to bind yourself to Nayla. Now you can find yourself a nice girl to wed!"

"A *nice* girl? There is absolutely nothing wrong with your daughter. I would have been privileged to have had her as my wife," retorted Joval.

"You know what I mean, my friend," stated Dahlon.

"No, I do not," countered Joval, his nerves bristling from the senior Elf's candor.

"It is my understanding the Prince of Wyndwood has graced our city with his presence," said Dahlon.

"Yes, Prince Arerys has arrived in the company of Lindras Weatherstone and Prince Markus of Carcross."

"As the Stewart of Nagana, have you shown them around our fair city?"

"There has been no time for such leisurely pursuits. There are more pressing issues to concern ourselves with," grunted Joval.

"What can be more pressing than to woo those of the Alliance?" asked Joval. "Believe me, as Prince Tokusho sows the seeds of rebellion, we shall need the help of those in western Imago if we are to survive."

"There is the matter of a spy. There appears to be a traitor amongst us," stated Joval. "Someone has disclosed to the Sorcerer the passage on Borai Mountain."

"I think not, Joval. My warriors are loyal to me. They dare not breathe a word of this secret passage. They are sworn to a code."

"Believe what you will, but the secret passage is secret no more. Imperial Soldiers breached the Furai Mountains to mount an attack on Prince Arerys and his party only two days outside of Nagana."

Dahlon gasped in disbelief. "That cannot be! We passed by that way on our return trip. All was quiet. We saw no one."

"I speak the truth, my lord. I ventured to Borai Mountain with those of the Order to search for Nayla. We had come across a wounded Kagai Warrior. He directed us on our way for Nayla had set forth to rescue a warrior held captive by the Sorcerer."

"And you saw the Sorcerer?"

"With mine own eyes I did. In fact, he was ready to slit Nayla's throat when we came upon him."

"Where is he now?"

"He fled deep into a tunnel, perhaps straight to Hell for all I know. Lindras used his powers to seal off the cave in hopes that it prevents his escape."

"Damn it all! This does not bode well for our people, Joval. If it is true, the Imperial Army shall no longer have to run the gauntlet from the north past the Kagai Warriors. Master Saibon and his people have always served as a buffer for us, sparing us the trouble of confronting these soldiers here in Nagana."

"I shall tell you now, if they attack, they shall use the passage and there will be nothing we can do to stop their advance," warned Joval.

"We must gather our men, and the Kagai Warriors; all who are able-bodied to go to war."

"So we may all be slaughtered? There must be another way to avoid this calamity! What did Prince Tokusho have to say?"

"He is intent on claiming his title and throne."

"You must get word to him, to cease or postpone his plans until we can gather our forces and devise a strategy that we may put into place to allow us even half a chance at victory!"

"It is too late. Even as we speak, events that shall lead to a war of catastrophic proportions have begun to unfold in the east."

"Then we must destroy the enemy before they set foot on our lands. We must dismantle them from their very foundations," suggested Joval.

"Yes, of course," agreed Dahlon. "Let us instigate their demise by bringing instability within."

"I shall send word to Master Saibon we shall be in need of his best spies and assassins," offered Joval.

"There shall be no time for that, nor is there any need, Joval. His best warrior is already amongst us."

"Nayla? You cannot send her! She is not up for such a task!" protested Joval.

"Oh, she will be," retorted Dahlon. "Believe me; the stakes are as such that she will not be able to refuse this assignment. In the meantime, fetch the Prince of Wyndwood. I wish to meet this Elf."

Arerys greeted Nakoa at the door. She knew by his smile that Nayla was awake. She set a bed tray down with food and drinks for both of them.

"I thought you would prefer to stay here with my lady," said Nakoa, pleased to see the fair Elf and her mistress were as one again.

"Thank you, Nakoa," smiled Nayla.

"How do you feel this morn?" she asked as she poured some fresh, hot tea into the cups.

"I have seen better days," said Nayla with a sigh. "I shall recover."

"Yes, and I shall see to it that you remain in your bed for the next few days," ordered Nakoa, eyeing the warrior maiden for her understanding and cooperation.

"Do not worry, Nakoa. I shall make sure she remains here," promised Arerys.

Nakoa moved away from the bedside to answer a loud knock upon the door. Arerys rose up from his chair when he saw it was Joval standing at the doorway.

"Come in Joval," invited the fair Elf.

Joval smiled to see Nayla sitting up in her bed, but his smile quickly faded as he turned to Arerys. "Perhaps another time. As we speak, Lord Dahlon Treeborn has returned to Nagana. He wishes to meet with you."

"What is this about?" asked Nayla, her eyes darkened with concern.

"He did not disclose the matter of business he wishes to discuss," replied Joval.

"I shall not keep him waiting," said Arerys, reaching for his cloak that hung from the back of a chair.

"Arerys, wait! I shall accompany you."

"Nayla, you shall remain here. I shall go see your father alone."

"No, Arerys, it is ill-advised for you to do so. You do not know Dahlon. I will not subject you to that man, not on your own!"

"He shall not be alone, Nayla. I shall be there with him," promised Joval.

Arerys stooped to kiss Nayla on her forehead as he turned to leave her in Nakoa's care.

"But, Arerys," she protested.

"Do not worry, Nayla. Joval will be there. I trust him," stated the fair Elf, following Joval.

As he led Arerys to the meeting hall, he was curious by the fair Elf's statement. "So were you being facetious when you told Nayla that you trusted me?"

"No, I was quite serious," stated Arerys. "In fact, an apology is long overdue."

"An apology? For what reason?" asked Joval.

"I was blinded by my own jealousy; I foolishly chose to abandon common sense and reason than to deal with the issue at hand," admitted Arerys. "I failed to listen to you and Nayla when you both were deserving of my ears. Nayla was able to forgive me. Now, I am asking for your forgiveness."

"You are forgiven, but I suppose I should apologize on behalf of Valtar's conduct. He acted in poor judgment. His loyalty was severely misguided."

"I shall have a few choice words to share with your man servant," said Arerys.

"I am afraid it will not be possible," replied Joval.

"And why not?"

"I have banished him from Nagana. He is no longer in my service," answered the dark Elf. "He had betrayed my trust; therefore I have dealt with him accordingly."

"Where did he go?"

"I do not know, nor do I care. The farther away he is from here the better it shall be for all. He has caused far too much grief in Nayla's life," replied Joval as he led Arerys up the stairs to the meeting hall. The dark Elf stopped in the vestibule, motioning Arerys to proceed no further.

"Has Nayla warned you about Lord Treeborn?" asked Joval.

"She has told me enough."

"He undoubtedly will be civil, possibly even ingratiating to you, but where Nayla is concerned..." the dark Elf's voice trailed as he searched for the words to describe Dahlon's treatment of the warrior maiden.

"Say no more," replied Arerys, noting Joval's concern. "I believe I have a fair understanding of what I shall be faced with."

"Very well," said Joval, pushing down on the heavy latch that secured the door. "Keep in mind I shall be close at hand if need be."

As the fair Elf entered the room, Joval stepped forward to make the introduction: "I present to you, the son of Lord Kal-lel Wingfield; Prince Arerys of Wyndwood."

The elders of Orien and Dahlon Treeborn rose from their chairs. They bowed in greeting. Arerys reciprocated, bowing before he stepped forward with Joval. Dahlon waved for a servant to seat both men at the table.

"Welcome Prince Arerys, welcome to Orien," said Dahlon. "I must admit, I am surprised you made this long journey."

"To seek your blessing in order to take Nayla's hand in marriage was well worth the trek, my lord," Arerys responded respectfully. "I would travel to the ends of the earth to be with her."

"So, is it true what Joval tells me? Your father has given his blessing to this union?"

"Most definitely, Joval speaks the truth. My father welcomes Nayla into our home and as my betrothed."

"Joval stated your father has issued an edict that will allow our kind, the dark Elves, to return to Wyndwood. Is that so?"

"Indeed he has," replied Arerys. "There shall no longer be a distinction between *dark* and *fair* Elves. We are all of one race, no matter our appearance, no matter what our belief systems are, we are all Elves."

"How noble and enlightened of Lord Wingfield," sniffed Dahlon. "I wonder what brought about this change of heart."

"It was Nayla," replied Arerys quite simply. "He was captivated by her wit and charm."

"Do not mock me, Prince Arerys. Nayla can be as charming as a viper."

"With all due respect, Lord Treeborn, then I shall ask that you do not insult my betrothed for when you do so, you insult me," stated Arerys, his words were succinct.

Maiyo Sonkai raised his hands for silence as he reprimanded Dahlon, "Lord Treeborn, in all fairness, perhaps your daughter is the *viper* you claim she is due to the rigors of life we subject her to, so we may maintain peace in our lands."

"All I am saying is that the King of Wyndwood is motivated for reasons other than his fondness for the prince's intended," stated Dahlon in his own defense.

"My father is no fool. He knows for Nayla to gain acceptance from the citizens of Wyndwood, he must end this rivalry that has existed between our people. Our race can no longer be divided. In a sign of good faith, he knows to accept her, is to accept all those Elves that departed from Wyndwood. You included."

"He would truly do this? Open the doors to allow us to return?" asked Dahlon.

"Yes, my lord. My love for Nayla is as such my father would do whatever it shall take for us to be united," stated Arerys.

"Is he aware that Nayla is a half-caste? That she is not a full-blooded Elf?" asked Dahlon, still skeptical of the fair Elf's claims.

Rising abruptly from his chair, Joval interjected, "My lord! Do not speak of Nayla in - "

Arerys motioned to the dark Elf for calm. "Yes, my father knows, just as I do. That does not change his opinion of her. He regards Nayla in the highest esteem and with the greatest respect. He is honored to accept her as my wife and to embrace her as if she were his own daughter."

Dahlon took a moment to consider the fair Elf. "Tell me something, Prince Arerys. If I sanction this union, if I give my blessing, does this signify that we are part of the Alliance once more?"

"Of course, we shall be as one again. Why do you ask?"

"I am well aware that your journey to our country is two-fold. Not only are you here to seek my daughter's hand in marriage, you are here to bring Eldred Firestaff to justice. Joval claimed that you had arrived with Prince Markus of Carcross and the Wizard of the West in a bid to capture the Sorcerer."

"Yes, we are here to assist in this matter," admitted Arerys. "I know the gravity of the situation. It was revealed to me by the Watchers that if we cannot stand as a united front against the Sorcerer, our people shall fall to the wayside."

"It is true, the shadows of war loom on our horizon. Did the Watchers reveal the outcome?" asked Dahlon.

"No," responded Arerys, "Eliya, the Watcher of the Future would only say that if we failed in our bid to assist Lindras Weatherstone in the capture of Eldred Firestaff, then we shall be doomed; both Elves and mortal man."

"Do your warriors come? Do the soldiers of the Alliance follow you into Orien?" asked Dahlon, a spark of hope burned in his blue eyes.

"No, my lord," responded Arerys. "The men have returned to their respective countries after waging war on the Plains of Fire against the soldiers of the Dark Army. We are here with the intention of capturing the Sorcerer before there is a need to rally the forces. We intend to stem the tide of evil before it washes over us."

The elders stared at Dahlon, their disappointment was evident upon their faces.

"This is not good," groaned Dahlon. "You have not even the slightest inkling as to how dire our situation truly is."

"I beg to differ, my lord," contested the fair Elf. "We shall capture the Sorcerer before he can incite a war. If we are called to arms, then we shall muster the warriors of Orien to do battle."

"Prince Arerys, you have no idea how deep this pile of dung is that you and your friends have stepped into! You are wallowing up to your neck in trouble and you do not even know it!"

"Are you saying that your own warriors will refuse to stand up to the Sorcerer and his followers?"

"What Lord Treeborn means to say is; though our forces are more than willing to go to war, our numbers are such that we shall never survive a full confrontation. An all out war against the Imperial Army will mean our annihilation. It will be genocide," explained Joval.

"If it is a show of force you require, then I shall send forth word to my father and he shall muster the soldiers of the Alliance," offered Arerys.

"It is a good thought, but that is all it shall be – a thought," said Dahlon.

"I swear, they shall come," declared the fair Elf.

"That is all well and good, but we shall all be dead by the time they reach the gates of our city," stated the senior Elf.

Arerys was stunned by Dahlon's words; he looked to Joval for better understanding.

A profound silence filled the room as each man and Elf deliberated on the gravity of the situation. The silence was only broken by the pounding on the door as Markus and Lando entered the room.

"Elders of Orien, Lord Treeborn, forgive our intrusion, but we must speak," said Markus as he and Lando approached those in council.

"And who are you?" asked Dahlon, rising from the table.

Joval rose from his seat to introduce the stranger to those present: "This is Prince Markus of Carcross. He has ventured to our lands to assist us in our quest to capture the Sorcerer."

"Ah, so you are the mighty prince, the one that slew the Dark Lord on Mount Hope," said Dahlon as he nodded in recognition.

"That is I," admitted Markus. "Though we ensured that the Sorcerer's power would not eclipse those of Beyilzon's by delivering the Stone of Salvation to the Watchers, he shall now rely on his alliance with the regent to immerse the lands in darkness once again."

"That I already know, Prince Markus. I have only today returned from my travels to meet with Prince Tokusho, the Crown Prince of Orien, and even as we speak, he stokes the flames of war."

"Then we shall rally the kings and soldiers of the Alliance," offered Markus.

"Prince Markus, you know how long the journey is; the soldiers of the Alliance will not arrive in time," explained Joval. "It shall be too late."

"You speak as though we now stand on the brink of war," responded Markus.

"A crimson dawn is about to bathe this land in blood, indeed we stand poised on the eve of destruction, Prince Markus. The crown prince has made it clear of his intention to claim the throne by force if necessary; even if he should die trying. Already he has set into motion events that shall lead to either his doom or success and ultimately, our people's destiny," stated Maiyo, speaking on behalf of the other mortals seated next to him.

"Can you not request that he curtail his plans until we can unite our armies?" asked Arerys.

"No, his hand has been forced. If he does not claim his title as the rightful heir to the throne by his sixteenth birthday, then his failure shall be viewed as an abdication of the throne. His uncle, Tisai Darraku, shall ascend. He shall shed his unwanted title as the regent for he shall be crowned the new emperor," stated Dahlon.

"But the people, will they not rise up to protest his rule?" asked Markus.

"Chaos and civil unrest shall be the order of the day, but it shall only be a matter of time before the people shall be crushed for their insubordination by the regent's power and his alliance with the Sorcerer," said Maiyo with a heavy sigh.

"But these are the people! They must have a voice!" protested Lando.

"His subjects barely scrape by, they eke out a meager existence while they are forced to pay exorbitant taxes to support the regent's decadent lifestyle. As far as Darraku is concerned, he considers these people to be merely the dregs of society. He views the sick, the down-trodden and the impoverished as a burden that is better to be scraped off his feet. Even those who desperately cling to religion in hopes that their God, and the powers that be, come to their aid, must do so in secret for the regent is a heathen. Once he is in place, he shall appoint *himself* as their new god," added Dahlon, his shoulders drooping with the weighty burden of his words.

"Is the regent truly demented?" asked Lando. "There is only one God and I hardly believe the Maker of All shall stand for such absurdity."

"Why do you think he and the Sorcerer are in partnership? They are two of a kind. I swear they were cut from the same cloth! As for our God, where is He now? We have been abandoned and cast to the winds," retorted Dahlon. "We have but one hope left."

"What might that be?" asked Markus.

"Nayla, she is our last chance," advised Dahlon.

Arerys slowly rose from his chair, scrutinizing the senior Elf as he spoke, "What do you mean by this?"

"Our hope lies with causing turmoil within the regent's inner circle, to cause dissension and chaos within," suggested Dahlon. "There is none better for this task than Nayla."

"You would cast your own daughter into a den of wolves?" cried out Arerys, in disbelief.

"Those wolves have little chance against this warrior," assured Dahlon with a laugh.

"I shall not allow this!" protested the fair Elf.

"Prince Arerys, listen to the voice of reason," pleaded Maiyo.

"You call this reason?" asked the Elf, exasperated by the elder's words. "I would say her own father premeditates her murder!"

"Please, Prince Arerys," said Maiyo, wringing his hands in woe. "Lord Treeborn speaks the truth. Nayla is most suited for this task."

Joval turned to look upon the fair Elf, his eyes locking with Arerys' as he spoke, "Master Sonkai and Lord Treeborn are quite right about Nayla. If anyone can infiltrate the Imperial Palace, it would be she."

Arerys was momentarily stunned that Joval would turn against Nayla, offering her up for this service.

"It is obvious the woman you claim to love has not been forthright about her occupation," stated Dahlon with mild amusement.

"I know what she is. She is a warrior and the captain of her own battalion," remarked Arerys.

"Oh, she is so much more, Prince Arerys. Nayla Treeborn is also a highly skilled spy and a deadly assassin," responded the senior Elf. "How do think we have managed to survive in this country for as long as we have?"

Arerys turned to Joval, searching for the truth. "Tell me this is not so!"

"It is true," admitted Joval. "Nayla is these things and more. She does so in a bid to maintain peace in this land by extricating those who dare attempt to bring death and mayhem to our borders."

"If this were true, Nayla would have told me," snapped Arerys.

"To the contrary, Prince Arerys, none know of her activities beyond that of being a captain. Not even the men in her own battalion are aware of her true calling," insisted Joval. "What she does, she does in secret; for her own safety and the safety of others."

"Even if this is to be the case, Nayla is in no condition to under-take this mission," stated Arerys.

Dahlon gave him a knowing smile as he responded, "Believe me, Nayla shall rise to the occasion."

Maiyo Sonkai and the elders stood up from their chairs as the sen-ior of the mortals spoke, "Let us reconvene at a later time, perhaps tomorrow. We shall see what Lady Treeborn has to say about this mat-ter. It is pointless to continue this discussion without her presence."

"I believe we are all in agreement," said Joval, bowing to the eld-ers as they turned to leave the meeting hall.

"I shall deliver this news to Nayla," said Arerys.

"No, Prince Arerys, Joval shall send word," stated Dahlon. "I request a moment to speak to you in private."

Joval gazed at the fair Elf for some indication that he wished for his continued presence. Arerys merely motioned for him to leave with Markus and Lando.

As the hall emptied, Dahlon motioned for the servant to secure the door so he may meet with the Prince of Wyndwood without any dis-ruptions.

"Sit, Prince Arerys," said Dahlon, drawing a chair out for him. "If you are to wed my daughter, then there are some issues that require your immediate attention."

"This sounds rather ominous. I take it you do not give your con-sent for this union willingly," replied the fair Elf.

"Let me share some sound advice with you," said Dahlon. "I know what it is like to be trapped into wedlock. I too found myself in a similar situation, taking on the honorable, and onerous, task of marrying a woman because there is price to pay for such a dalliance."

"You speak as though my relationship with Nayla is nothing more than for physical pleasure,"

"I too was young once, I know how easy it is for a full-blooded Elf to get caught up in the throes of passion. You however have been blessed for word has it Nayla is no longer with child."

"Blessed you say? Am I mistaken to believe you find some gratification in our loss?" queried Arerys.

"No! What I am saying is that you are no longer obligated to wed Nayla. I do not hold you to this promise if it pleases you and your father."

"I find your words truly appalling. I am here because I love Nayla, whether she carried my child or not, it makes no difference to me. And let me assure you, I am not one to be forced into any type of situation I do not desire to be in," lashed out Arerys. "Alas, I am saddened to no end our child has been lost due to the Sorcerer's cruel hands, but I shall tell you this now, I still have every intention of wedding Nayla."

Dahlon sank back into his chair as he considered Arerys' words. He then leaned forward to face the fair Elf as he attempted to reason with him. "Listen to the voice of experience, Prince Arerys. Let me speak to you candidly; Nayla is like her mortal mother. She is headstrong, opinionated and dangerous! She is not worth the anguish she shall bring to your life. Ultimately, she will betray your love just as your mother betrayed me."

Arerys stared into Dahlon's cold, blue eyes. "My mother? What do you know of my mother?" growled the fair Elf, rising before Dahlon.

"Plenty, but it appears the beautiful Lady Katril Brookstone has chosen not to acknowledge my involvement in her life."

"You speak in riddles; I fail to understand this."

"Why do you not ask your mother?"

"My mother left for the Twilight over two hundred years ago," stated Arerys. "She tired of the turmoil and strife of this realm. She chose to join her family in the Haven."

Dahlon's eyes were clouded in unmistakable sorrow upon learning of his beloved's departure. "Are you sure that is why she left?" asked the dark Elf. "When the time came, did you even bother to ask her why she chose to leave."

"I told you why she left!" snapped Arerys.

"She told you only what you wanted to hear!" shouted Dahlon, rising up to meet Arerys' unyielding stare. "Your mother and I, we were once lovers. It was I who was to wed Lady Brookstone, not Kal-lel Wingfield."

"You lie!" cried out Arerys, a painful shockwave traveled up his arm into his shoulder as his fist slammed down upon the table. "You wish to tarnish my mother's good name!"

"I would never do that to Katril, I only wish for you to understand," responded Dahlon, regret and sadness filled his troubled eyes. "You should have been my son, Arerys! You would have been my child, not that half-caste woman that bears my name but not my likeness!"

"Say no more!" retorted the fair Elf as he desperately attempted to stifle his anger. "I wish not to hear any more of this... of this... demented tale!"

"Our history is not quite what it appears; it is merely a façade to allow Kal-lel to save face amongst our people. All these centuries, our race has been divided: all for the love of a woman. Where all believed this division was due to racial and religious intolerance, it was merely a ruse contrived by your father to conceal the real reason why I was banished from Wyndwood."

"You are telling me it had nothing to do with race or religion?" questioned Arerys.

"Absolutely not, it was a blatant lie to justify Kal-lel's actions. Your father stole Katril away from me. It was sanctioned by the elders that he would marry her. Though I too was born to a high house, I am not a Wingfield – one destined to be king. The elders arranged for Kal-lel and Lady Brookstone to wed. She protested, but eventually she chose to forsake me, binding to Kal-lel. Your father drove me out and all those like me followed. It was his insurance that Katril and I would never be together again."

Arerys slowly sank back into his chair as though Dahlon's words pierced his heart and wounded his very soul.

"My departure was never voluntary. I chose to abide by Kal-lel's lie so the *dark* Elves would leave Wyndwood with me, for if our people knew the truth, that this division was the result of one woman's love and betrayal, they would never have stood for it," claimed the senior Elf. "Your mother was one woman I would have surrendered my life for. I loved her dearly, and to have discovered that she chose to abide by the elders' wishes, binding herself to Kal-lel, drove me to despair."

"My mother never mentioned you, not even in passing," stated Arerys bluntly.

"It does not surprise me. She knew if the truth be revealed, not only would she fall from favor in Kal-lel's eyes and the eyes of the elders, but a nation would also rise up in anger over this division of our people," explained Dahlon.

"My father has never mentioned this to me."

"Of course, Kal-lel would never admit to this. He would never admit that Katril was in love with me; that I was forced to reside with the other dark Elves in Elmgrove, the southern reaches of Wyndwood only to be driven from our lands because he feared Katril and I would continue our affair. But it mattered not for in the end, she chose to wed your father, bending to his whims and the whims of the elders."

"If she was so in love with you as you claim, then why did she not choose to leave Wyndwood to be with you than to wed my father?"

"Only she can answer that question. I begged Katril to leave with me, to begin a new life elsewhere, away from Wyndwood. Alas, my words fell upon deaf ears," answered Dahlon with a heavy sigh. "I promised my heart and my soul to that woman, even pledging my undying love for her with a band of silver she accepted and wore; never on her finger for all to see, instead, she kept it close to her heart."

"On a fine chain of silver she wore about her neck," added Arerys.

"Yes, that is the one! You know of this ring?" asked Dahlon, his eyes sparkled with excitement.

"She never took it off until the day she departed for the Haven."

Another long, heavy breath escaped Dahlon. After all these many years, Katril had continued to wear his token of love, surrendering it only upon entering the Twilight. "Whatever became of the ring?"

"My mother told me it was a treasured family heirloom. She gave it to me, asking that I pass it on to my chosen bride."

"Nayla wears Katril's ring?" gasped Dahlon, astonished by this revelation.

"She wears the ring my mother cherished and handed down to me. You have no proof you had gifted this ring to my mother."

"If you still choose not to believe my words, then look upon the band of silver Nayla wears. If indeed it is *the ring*, you shall find three words engraved on the inside of the band."

"What are these words?" queried Arerys.

"It shall read: *For an Eternity*," stated Dahlon. "But tell me, Prince

Arerys, if my words prove to be true, will you take heed of my advice to leave Nayla be?"

"So she can continue to do your dirty work?" growled Arerys in contempt.

"Do not be a fool, Prince Arerys, take my advice, for there are other maidens more worthy of your hand."

"Lord Treeborn, I shall take heed of your wisdom by following my heart. I shall wed the woman I love. I shall not let this chance slip through my hands as you did," decided Arerys.

"But the future queen of Wyndwood should be one befitting of this title, not a half-caste such as Nayla," protested Dahlon.

"You amaze me, Lord Treeborn. She is your daughter, your own flesh and blood and even now, as my betrothed, indeed as the future queen of Wyndwood, you still deny her. She is more fit and worthy of this title than any woman I know. And it shames me to no end her own father speaks of her in this manner."

"It is clear to me that you are blinded by your love for her," responded the senior Elf, his fingers drumming impatiently on the tabletop as he listened, unscathed by the fair Elf's harsh tone.

"Just as it is obvious to me that your contempt for her lies in the fact that she was begat with a woman you did not love. Nayla is not the product of your love for my mother so you have spent all of Nayla's life punishing her because *you* made a mistake. You did not fight for my mother's hand as you should have if you claim to love her as you did."

"So Nayla has spoken to you of our relationship?"

"I know enough to say I only came by this way to seek your blessing because my father insisted that I consider your standing, that I respect you as her father: to follow protocol. Otherwise, I see no reason to seek your consent for this union."

"Do not be swayed by her words, Prince Arerys, she will lie to better her standing in life," advised Dahlon.

"I do not need to hear her words to judge for myself the kind of man you are," replied the fair Elf.

"I am sure she has tainted your opinion of me with lies, telling you that I am a despicable soul; cruel and unmerciful in my dealings with her. Perhaps, she even described me to be a monster of sorts."

"Truth be told, Nayla did not even use so many words. In fact, I believe she merely likened your personality and charm to that of a *viper*," responded Arerys, abruptly rising from the table to leave.

CHAPTER 17

THE ART OF DECEPTION

Markus waited patiently for Arerys in the courtyard as a brilliant, golden sun continued to climb high into a pale blue sky. He smiled pleasantly at the citizens of Nagana; mortals and Elves staring at this stranger from a far away land as they passed his way. The curious gazes cast in his direction were many, especially from the mortals of this country.

Markus felt he presented himself as a bit of an oddity. At slightly over five feet and ten inches tall, he was only as tall as the shortest Elf, yet he stood a good five inches taller than the average Taijin man. Though he appeared to be tall in stature like an Elf, he lacked some of their physical attributes, most notably the distinct, pointed ears. There were other differences too. Where Elves are practically devoid of body and facial hairs, save for the hair on their head, eyelashes and brows, comparatively speaking, Markus was rather hirsute. His beard and moustache that grew during his trip to Orien was becoming quite thick and unkempt.

"My lord, are you lost?" asked a familiar voice.

Markus turned around to find Taiko Saikyu standing before him. He gave her a friendly smile as he responded, "No, I am waiting for Prince Arerys, he is in counsel with Lord Treeborn at this moment."

"Well, he shall be there for quite some time I assume. Lord Treeborn can be quite long-winded if he chooses to be so," replied Taiko, placing her basket of freshly cut flowers upon the ground as she spoke.

Markus laughed lightly upon hearing her words and the directness with which she spoke. He smiled again as he admired the large, sunny yellow chrysanthemums she had with her.

"Those are lovely flowers; they are bright as the summer sun."

"Indeed they are," Taiko responded with a demure smile, her raven-black hair was highlighted with a halo of silvery-blue in the brilliant sun. "I believe Lady Treeborn shall appreciate these blooms, they should brighten her disposition."

Markus' expression suddenly saddened upon hearing Nayla's

name. "It is most unfortunate, the loss she suffered," said the prince in a hushed tone.

Taiko's head lowered in remorse as she responded in a solemn voice, "Yes, her anguish is great, my lord, but it was not meant to be. Fate had decreed it."

"Fate?" asked Markus, his voice tightened in anger. "Nayla's unborn child died at the hands of the Sorcerer. Neither fate, nor destiny had anything to do with it."

"Perhaps you are right, my lord," agreed Taiko, her dark brown eyes sparkled with life as she picked the basket up in her hand. "In the meantime, may I entice you with a meal? My intuition tells me Prince Arerys shall be preoccupied for quite some time to come."

Markus' eyes glanced to the door of the meeting hall. It was still securely closed.

"Why do you not follow me to the dining hall? I shall prepare a meal if it pleases you so."

There was no telling how long Arerys would be and the attention Markus garnered from the citizens of Nagana was beginning to wear thin on him. "I suppose it would do no harm," replied Markus.

"Very well then," smiled Taiko, taking Markus by his arm as she led him through the bustling courtyard.

The sunlight filled the great dining hall as Markus peered into the vast, empty room. "Is no one else to join me?"

"That is correct," answered Taiko. "Truth be told, I wish I could say it would be me joining you for a meal, but it is not fitting for a servant to be seen dining with such an esteemed guest to our city."

"I do not feel it is appropriate for me to partake in a meal in this splendid room alone. I shall forego this meal until later."

"If that be the case, I shall deliver a meal to your bed chamber," offered Taiko.

"No, I do not wish to trouble you,"

"It is no trouble, my lord," insisted the servant. "It would be my pleasure. I shall only be but a moment."

"Very well," replied Markus. "I shall wait in my chamber."

He watched Taiko disappear from the dining hall before he exited through the courtyard. As he passed the meeting hall, the door was still closed. Markus quickly made his way to his bed chamber. He closed the door behind him. As he walked across the room to place his cloak into the wardrobe, he glanced at his reflection in the mirror. He stopped for a moment to consider his scruffy beard.

The mirror does not lie; I have certainly seen better days, thought the prince as his fingers ran through the coarse, dark whiskers.

Taiko skillfully balanced the tray in one hand as the other rapped gently on the door. Markus greeted her with towel in hand as he wiped his face dry.

"You were right! You did not take long at all," admitted Markus as he turned away to replace the towel by the wash basin in the adjoining room.

As he returned to join Taiko, she was momentarily startled.

"What is it?" asked Markus.

"You look so different without your beard," stated Taiko as she moved closer to gaze upon his freshly shaven face.

Markus awkwardly rubbed his chin with his hand and said with a shrug, "I have never been partial to facial hair; it makes me look older than my years."

"Well, I do admit, the beard did hide your true appearance," smiled Taiko.

"And what is my true appearance?"

"Let me just say that you do not require a beard to look distinguished. I much prefer this look."

"Well, that is reassuring," smiled Markus, accepting the goblet of wine she handed to him.

"Drink," insisted Taiko, gently pushing the goblet to his lips.

Markus swallowed a small amount of the wine. He paused momentarily, savoring the unusual flavor and bouquet of the carmine liquid before him. "This is… unique," stated the prince, searching for the words to describe the wine as he sampled another sip. "It is most unusual. I do not believe I have ever tasted anything like it."

"Yes," agreed Taiko, offering to top up his goblet. "It is a very rare vintage."

"Please join me in a drink," insisted Markus, swallowing more of the wine as his palate tried to discern the distinct aftertaste.

Taiko smiled innocently as she answered, "I am not permitted to drink while I am performing my duties."

"Very well then, I do not wish to jeopardize your position here," replied Markus, savoring another sip of the robust wine. "So tell me, Taiko, have you been in service long?"

"Long enough to know that I shall be severely chastised if it be known that I was in your bed chamber,"

"I shall not breathe a word of this to a soul," promised Markus with a smile.

"That is kind of you, my lord," acknowledge Taiko. "It has always been in your nature to be kind."

The prince frowned upon her words, seating himself on the edge of his bed. It was as though his knees buckled, no longer able to support his weight. "You speak as though you know me, yet I do not recall ever meeting you before my arrival in Nagana."

"Can you truly say that, my lord?" asked Taiko in a gentle voice as she leaned in close to his face, taking his drink from his hand. "Can you look into my eyes, into my very soul and say in all honesty that you do not know me?"

Markus gazed into her deep brown eyes. He felt every fiber of his being unravel. He felt as though his body and mind were melting into a warm, calm pool. He felt his soul, lulled into a state of absolute bliss. His eyes slowly closed as Taiko's lips softly caressed his. Markus answered her kiss, their mouths met as he drew her closer, kissing her slowly and tenderly.

Taiko straddled his body as she gently pushed him onto his back. "Tell me that you remember me," she pleaded in barely a whisper, her mouth desperately seeking his.

Markus' heart raced as a familiar voice whispered into his ears. His face blanched and his eyes flew open in shock and surprise as sudden recognition set in.

"What devilry is this!" shouted Markus as he struggled to sit up, grabbing Taiko by her wrists. His eyes squeezed shut as he fought to dispel the ghost before him. "This cannot be; you are dead!"

Taiko began to sob upon hearing the harshness in his tone. "No, Markus, you are wrong, perhaps in body, but not in spirit. Look upon me. It is I, Elana."

"How can this be? I was there! You died in my arms," cried Markus, his eyes slowly opening to gaze upon this apparition come to life.

"My soul is trapped, trapped within this body by the Sorcerer's own doing. Your kiss - when our souls touched, allow you to see me for who I truly am."

"This is a cruel hoax!" denounced Markus. "Mine own eyes deceive me!"

"Markus look upon me. Look me in my eyes and tell that you do not know who I am," pleaded the woman before him. "If you truly loved me, if your love for me has endured, then you would know that it is I."

Markus reluctantly gazed into her eyes, searching her soul. In a blink of an eye their entire life together: their meeting, courtship and life together in marital bliss, even Elana's death flashed before him in an overwhelming tidal wave of memories and emotions. Tears welled and tumbled down his cheeks as his trembling hand touched her gently upon her face.

"Elana?" asked Markus, hoping against hope the woman before him was truly his long departed wife.

"I have waited an eternity for this moment," she whispered, pressing his hand to her cheek.

"How is this possible?"

"I only know that as I passed from this realm, Eldred Firestaff somehow laid claim to my soul. For what reason I do not know, but now, here I stand before you."

Markus' hand reached out to remove the ribbon securing her hair in place. It cascaded down around her shoulder like a waterfall of chestnut brown silken strands. His fingers ran through her tresses as he inhaled the soft perfume of spring flowers. Everything about her rang true: the hair, the hazel eyes, her soft, alabaster skin, even the delicate scent of her perfume was undeniably real. For a brief instant, he was absolutely mesmerized. The realization this woman was unmistakably his wife; that somehow Elana had returned to him, filled him with great elation. Markus felt his heart swelling in his chest as though all the love he ever felt, that had lay dormant upon her passing five years hence, was now resurfacing.

"I have missed you, my Markus."

The prince gently drew her into his arms, holding her close. For a lingering moment, he stared into her inviting, hazel eyes. It was as though he had stepped into a familiar dream. His lips tenderly caressed hers as he felt her body trembling in anticipation.

As their mouths met again, they kissed with forgotten passion as her fingers struggled to remove Markus' clothing.

Nakoa was startled by Arerys' silent approach as she opened the door to Nayla's bed chamber.

"Forgive me, my lord," gasped the lady-in-waiting. "You surprised me!"

"I am sorry, Nakoa. We Elves do tend to be light on our feet. It was not my intention to catch you by surprise," apologized the fair Elf, stepping past her. As he entered the room, he noticed Joval suddenly rise up from the edge of the bed where he sat, conversing with Nayla.

Arerys motioned him to remain seated as he said, "There is no need to leave Joval."

"I was just informing Nayla of our meeting with the elders and Lord Treeborn," stated the dark Elf, feeling a need to explain his presence.

Arerys stooped to gently kiss Nayla upon her forehead before speaking further.

"So Joval has disclosed the nature of our meeting? The course of action the council wishes to take in a bid to snuff out the embers of war before they ignite into great flames?"

"Yes," answered Nayla in a weary voice. "I have heard."

"So you willingly undertake this mission?" queried Arerys.

"If it shall bring lasting peace to our people, then yes, I shall," vowed the warrior maiden.

"This is suicide, Nayla! You shall be signing your own death warrant," protested the fair Elf.

"You speak in haste, Arerys. Have some confidence in Nayla; do not underestimate her. She may surprise you," averred Joval in her defense.

"Your father made claim before us that you are an assassin. Are his words true?" asked Arerys.

Nayla glanced over at Joval, only to have him avert his eyes from her gaze. She then looked upon her betrothed.

"It is so," she answered in a small voice.

"Why did you not disclose this to me before?"

"There are some things better left unsaid, Arerys. For the sake of security, only Joval and a select few know of my true calling," explained the warrior maiden. "If it appears that I was being deceptive, I am sorry."

"Valtar had warned me that you were trained by the Kagai Warriors; that you were exceedingly dangerous, but to what extent, I had no idea until now."

"Knowing that it was I who killed those soldiers you had discovered as you ventured through Talibarr, the ones unmarred by sword or arrow, I assumed you would understand. The very fact that I had even breached the Iron Mountains where my brother warriors failed, I believed would speak for itself," said Nayla with a heavy sigh as the memories of facing the perils of western Imago alone replayed in her mind.

"You are willing to immerse yourself into a pit of snakes for the likes of Dahlon Treeborn? I fail to understand your logic in light of how that man treats you!"

"Arerys, you pride yourself on integrity, on doing what is right and honorable. You willingly go to war to protect the weak and the innocent because it is within your character to do so," stated Nayla.

"What you do is suicidal," said Arerys in protest.

"What I do is no different. And I do not do this for my father; I do this to keep peace in our land and to uphold justice for all. I do this to remove the shackles that bind the weak and downtrodden. I do this for the dignity of my people," she answered. The fires of war burned in her eyes as she summoned her courage to face the inevitable.

"But Nayla, how do you intend to enter the Imperial Palace?" queried Arerys. "It shall be impossible!"

"It shall be difficult, yes, but impossible? No," answered the warrior maiden.

"I have no doubt as the dread of war looms ever closer, the grounds and the battlements of the palace shall be well secured. And if you do enter, you shall never leave alive!"

Nayla glanced over at Joval for support, to allay Arerys' growing fears.

"She has done it before, Prince Arerys," stated the dark Elf.

"You dare not say!" gasped Arerys, unable to believe his ears.

"Joval speaks the truth. I have infiltrated the Imperial Palace before in a bid to save one of my brothers," confirmed the warrior maiden.

"And she did so successfully," added Joval with unmistakable pride, as he recalled her harrowing escape. "Not only did she get in and out, she returned with the warrior that was held captive deep in the dungeons of that wretched place."

"And you are willing to do this again?"

"Think on it, Arerys, if I do not, what shall befall the fate of the people of Orien, both man and Elf?"

Arerys drew in a deep breath as he agonized over her words and Eliya's warning of impending death and destruction if they failed to bring the Sorcerer to justice and to end the regent's reign of tyranny.

"If it is of any comfort to you, Arerys, I place my faith in what I believe in. I believe I can do this otherwise I would place this responsibility onto the shoulders of one more capable for there is much at stake here," stated Nayla.

"Truth be told, I do not relish the idea of subjecting you to such a deadly task. The mere thought of deliberately placing you in such danger after almost losing you is more than I can bear," declared the fair Elf.

"Arerys, this is not the first time I have undertaken such clandestine missions. I have infiltrated the enemy camp on a number of occasions. Each time I have returned. It shall be no different this time," promised Nayla.

"I fail to understand how," replied Arerys, clearly ambivalent to the situation he was now forced to accept.

Joval gave the fair Elf an encouraging smile as he answered, "My lord, Nayla is a Kagai Warrior, trained by Master Hunta Saibon and his forefathers. She is skilled in the art of war, and the art of deception. She is skilled enough to have survived such dangerous missions in the past."

"But this is the Imperial Palace we speak of," protested Arerys.

Nayla offered him a comforting smile as she responded, "There are places far more treacherous than that palace, my love."

"Where may that be?" asked the fair Elf.

"One place does immediately come to mind: Joval revealed to me that you were sequestered in a private meeting with Dahlon," said Nayla.

"Indeed I was," responded Arerys.

"You look none the worse for wear," said Nayla as she searched his blue eyes for signs of what had transpired.

"Yes, your father wanted to know of my intentions where you are concerned," replied Arerys.

"What did he say?"

"Nothing that would alter my decision to wed my beloved," said Arerys with a gentle smile.

"Seriously, Arerys, what did he say?" asked Nayla, brimming with curiosity.

Arerys considered her words before answering, "What he said was of little relevance to me. Let us just say that he knows exactly where I stand, just as I know his position."

Markus lay upon his bed, his heart still racing as he fought to catch his breath. He was utterly exhausted but emotionally exhilarated by this unexpected encounter. "Must you leave now, Elana?" he asked as his hand caressed her cheek.

"I must," she answered in a whisper, "but before I do, Markus, you must promise never to use this name before others."

"Why?" asked Markus, made curious by this strange request.

"Only you can see me for who I truly am. Your undying love has returned me to your arms, but as I said before, the Sorcerer still holds control of my soul. Until I am free of his hold, I shall remain trapped within this body. Where you see Elana, the others see Taiko."

"What can I do to break the Sorcerer's hold over you?" asked Markus. "What must I do to break this enchantment?"

"What you ask is much too dangerous a task to undertake."

"So it can be done?" queried the prince.

"Yes, but at great risk. I prefer to remain trapped in a prison of the Sorcerer's making than to endanger your life."

"Tell me, Elana, what is it? What must I do to free you?" pleaded Markus.

Her hazel eyes sparkled with light and hope upon hearing his words. She gently kissed him upon his chest as she answered, "The Wizard's staff. I shall need Lindras Weatherstone's staff."

"That shall not be difficult. You know Lindras shall help us. If he can break this spell, he will."

"No, Markus. You do not understand. *I need the staff!* I must use the power of the Wizard's crystal orb to render the Sorcerer temporarily powerless so my soul may escape his clutches. All I ask is for just one night, just one chance," said Elana, her eyes pleading to him.

"You are asking me to steal away with Lindras' power? His staff?" asked Markus, baffled by her appeal.

"It is only stealing if it is not returned. He shall have it back when I am done," promised Elana.

Suddenly, an expected knock on the door startled both she and Markus. Elana scrambled to dress.

"Markus! It is I, Lando!" said the voice on the other side of the door. "Are you in there, Markus?"

"Give me a moment!" shouted the prince as he hastened to dress.

As Elana twisted her long hair up into a knot, she turned to Markus to make a final plea, "Remember, you must call me Taiko when all others are near. Only you can see me for who I truly am. If you reveal this secret, your friends shall accuse you of being demented, you shall lose their trust. Promise me, Markus," begged Elana.

"Very well," agreed the prince.

Elana stole away with one final kiss before departing. As she opened the door, Lando was startled to see Taiko as she quickly bowed in acknowledgment of his presence. She slipped past the knight, her hands smoothing out her clothes as she hastily made her way down the corridor.

Lando entered the room, his eyebrows raised in astonishment. He looked upon Markus as the prince forced his feet back into his boots.

"Evidently, my appearance is ill-timed," said Lando, embarrassed by his unexpected arrival.

"To the contrary, my friend, Ela-" Markus bit his tongue as he corrected himself. "Taiko was just leaving." There was a moment of awkward silence as Lando watched Markus attempt to work out the wrinkles of his shirt with the flat of his hands. Tossed to the ground in a crumpled heap in the heat of passion, his efforts to smooth out his apparel was somewhat futile.

"It is not my intention to offend you, Markus, but I am curious," said Lando.

"How so?" asked the prince, struggling to button the cuffs on his sleeves.

"For five years I have seen women practically throw themselves at you, yet you remained true to your wife, even in her death. Though you never swore to a life of celibacy, neither have you pursued other romantic interests in the five years hence. What is the meaning of this?" asked the knight.

Markus looked up at Lando, his hand brushing back his dark brown hair from his eyes.

"I wish I knew the words to explain it, Lando. I suppose there are many qualities I see in Taiko that I once saw in Elana," answered the prince.

Lando frowned as he considered Markus' words. "That is strange. I see nothing even remotely similar; Taiko is as different from Elana as I am from Arerys."

"Perhaps in physical terms, but inside – in her heart, I see so much more to Taiko than what meets the eyes," explained Markus.

"I suppose I should not be so hasty to judge, after all I really do not know the woman," responded Lando.

"It would serve you well to reserve judgment. In time, you shall see for yourself what I speak of," assured Markus.

"So you are infatuated?" asked the knight.

"I would not describe my feelings for Taiko as being a mere case of infatuation," responded Markus. "But enough about me; what brings you to my door?"

"Ah, yes! I bring word from Lord Treeborn: He wishes for the men of the Order to reconvene for a meeting tomorrow morn. In the meantime, he has requested your presence, to join him and the elders for a special feast befitting such esteemed and royal guests," replied Lando. "In fact, I must deliver word to the others."

"You best be on your way, my friend," suggested Markus, securing the clasp of his cloak. "I shall see you in the dining hall. I hope this is not a long event for my intuition tells me that tomorrow shall be exceedingly trying."

As the men of the Order gathered in the dining hall, the many candles set upon the table cast a warm, inviting glow beckoning all into the great room. Its flickering light danced off the fine silver cutlery, crystal goblets and porcelain dinnerware.

Lord Treeborn welcomed his distinguished guests, motioning them into the dining hall. Servants quickly seated the men before hurrying off to deliver the epicurean delights created by the kitchen staff for this special dinner.

"Tonight, there shall be no talk of war or strategies, regents or Sorcerers. We shall use this time to enjoy the company of our most honored guests!" announced Dahlon, as he raised a goblet of wine before his company.

"I speak on behalf of Prince Arerys, Lindras Weatherstone and Lando Bayliss; we are honored to be graced with your presence and the presence of the elders," stated Markus, bowing his head in respect.

Dahlon smiled upon hearing Markus' kind words as he gazed at all those in attendance. "I see the Wizard is not present. We shall wait for him."

"That shall not be necessary, my lord" stated Lando.

"Of course it is. Lindras is an honored guest at this table," responded Dahlon.

"I must apologize on behalf of Lindras Weatherstone, my lord," replied the knight. "He shall not be joining us on this eve."

"What has become of the Wizard?" asked Dahlon, baffled by Lando's words.

"He is on an errand," stated the knight.

Dahlon frowned as he thought upon the Wizard's mysterious

absence before he answered, "Well, we shall not speak of this for I am certain it shall only lead to discussions of matters I prefer to waylay until tomorrow."

"Very well, my lord," acknowledged Lando.

"Yes, instead, let us make a toast to wish Lindras success in completing his so-called errand," said Dahlon, raising his wine goblet on high.

The men raised their goblets in honor of their absent comrade.

Joval turned to Dahlon. "I know it is on your mind, my lord, but Lady Treeborn shall not be joining us this evening."

"Oh yes, of course," said Dahlon, as though Nayla's absence was the next subject he had intended to broach. "It is better for her to rest, to regain her strength for the task that awaits her."

"Yes, it is not everyday one is called upon to undertake such a deadly mission," answered Arerys, his blue eyes turning cold as he glared at Nayla's father. "And in case you were curious, your daughter is incredibly resilient. She shall be fine in a day or two."

"Yes, I was about to ask of her," said Dahlon.

"I am sure you were," replied Arerys, fighting to control the bitterness in his voice.

Maiyo Sonkai tapped on his goblet to gain everyone's attention as he spoke: "Prince Markus, regale us with your bold tales of adventure! Tell us how you defeated the Dark Lord."

His fellow elders nodded in agreement, wishing to hear of his incredible tale.

Markus raised his hands in resignation, "I am afraid I am not a teller of grand tales, this is Lindras Weatherstone's passion."

"Do not be modest, Prince Markus. Please, we wish to hear. It shall give us hope that perhaps we too may defeat our adversaries," persuaded Dahlon.

"If you insist," conceded the prince. "And if this be the case, then I shall have to tell you of one of the bravest, most cunning warriors I have ever chanced to meet. A courageous warrior who helped us to survive the perils of our quest, I shall tell you of our alliance with Nayla Treeborn."

As the cock crowed upon the coming of the morning sun, servants hustled in and out of the meeting hall. Preparations were made for the members of the Order to reconvene with the elders of Orien and Lord Treeborn.

The men took their places at the table as servants delivered a morning meal while Taiko filled drinking vessels. Her eyes peered up discreetly at Markus as she gave him a gentle smile. His heart raced silently within his chest as he looked upon her hazel eyes and chestnut hair. He longed to touch Elana's face, but Markus merely responded with a small nod in acknowledgement of her presence as she went about her task. She retreated from the room as Dahlon Treeborn shooed her from their presence with a wave of his hand. Taiko immediately picked up her tray. She bowed as she left, closing the door behind her.

Dahlon Treeborn took his place next to Master Sonkai, "Men, today we meet to discuss the course of action we shall take to defeat the Sorcerer and to install Prince Tokusho as the rightful heir to the throne of Orien. His eyes flashed as they took stock of those in his company as he spoke: "I see Lindras Weatherstone is still not amongst us. When is he due to return? Shall we wait?"

"Waiting will not be an option," stated Lando. "We do not have the luxury of time, especially since we do not know when he shall be returning."

Suddenly, a tremendous clatter from just outside the door reverberated through to the meeting hall causing all to rise up onto their feet in alarm. Joval leapt up from his chair and raced to the door. He quickly threw it open to find Taiko, kneeling down as she collected the empty urn and silver goblets that slid from the silver tray she carried.

"I am sorry Master Stonecroft," said Taiko as she apologized for her carelessness, her dark brown eyes were moist with tears of embarrassment. "I was attempting to secure the door when I lost hold of my tray."

"Accidents happen, you best be on your way for we have important matters to discuss," said the Elf as he helped Taiko stack the items back onto her tray. As he glanced up, to his surprise Nayla was advancing up the stairs.

"What happened here?" asked Nayla.

"It is nothing, my lady – an accident, that is all," said Taiko as she bowed hastily, turning to leave with her tray.

Joval smiled at Nayla as he asked, "Are you well enough to join us, warrior maiden?"

"I have just come from the sanctuary where I lit a candle and a stick of incense for the child I lost. I feel some sense of closure now and I am feeling fit enough to attend this session. Besides, if Dahlon is intent on plotting out the strategy that might lead to my ultimate demise, at least I would like a hand in how this shall play out," answered Nayla in a whisper. She followed Joval into the meeting room as her eyes watched Taiko disappear in the busy courtyard.

"Nayla, I am pleased you are able to join us," stated Maiyo Sonkai, bowing to her as she took her place next to Arerys. "It is most difficult to speak of strategy without your expertise."

"I would never think of missing out on such an opportunity, Master Sonkai," said Nayla with a confident smile. "Besides, no one knows better the layout of the Imperial Palace than I."

"That is true indeed," said Maiyo, genuinely appreciative of the warrior maiden's knowledge and skills.

"Yes, Nayla, how good of you to join us," added Dahlon. "We were in the midst of discussing Lindras Weatherstone."

"What of the Wizard?" queried Nayla.

"Quite simply, he has disappeared," stated Markus.

"Disappeared? I was told he was on an errand of sorts!" Dahlon sat up in his chair, alarmed by the prince's words. "Do not tell me he has forsaken us. Do not tell me he runs in fear of the Sorcerer."

"To the contrary, Lord Treeborn," responded Markus. "He did not disclose where he was going, nor did he state when he would return. He would only say that he has gone for much-needed assistance."

Dahlon leaned forward on the table, his head braced in his hands as the tide of despair lapped at his heels. "I pray you are right, Prince Markus. With the soldiers of the Alliance unable to assist in our cause, only a greater power can aid us now as we approach our darkest hour."

"I assure you, Lord Treeborn, Lindras Weatherstone shall not forsake us. We have not been abandoned," declared Markus. "But we are in no position to waste time; we must devise a plan, one that shall guarantee our success; with or without the Wizard's help."

"First and foremost, we must secure the passage on Borai Mountain. We must ensure that another incursion does not happen," said Joval.

"Consider it done," said Maiyo with a bow. "We have already sent forth warriors with falcons to deliver word if the Imperial hordes cannot be held at bay."

"I have already sent word to Master Saibon of the impending peril, that his warriors must ready themselves for war," said Nayla. "Unfortunately my own falcon, Tori, the swiftest and most competent flier, is missing."

"Lord Treeborn, you had disclosed that Prince Tokusho already works to claim his title and he must do so before his sixteenth birthday," recalled Joval. "Exactly how much time do we have?"

"We have eighteen days," said Dahlon. "Perhaps less as word has been received early this morn from those loyal to the prince that the regent, Tisai Darraku plans to storm Prince Tokusho's residence in Shesake."

"He plans to murder the prince?" asked Nayla.

"As much as he would like to be rid of his nephew, he dare not attempt it. Those faithful to the prince have learned that the regent plans to take him captive, long enough to prevent his ascension to the throne," responded Maiyo.

"Do we know when?" asked Joval.

"That, we are not certain of," responded Maiyo, "but it is obvious he must do so before the prince approaches his sixteenth year and as you already know, this date is fast approaching."

"Forgive my ignorance, Master Sonkai, is it fair to assume that in order for the prince to claim his title, though it be his birthright, he must do so at the Imperial Palace?" asked Markus.

"Not only must he be at the palace to be crowned upon the throne, he must unlock the vault where the crown has been secured since his father's death," replied the elder.

"Does Prince Tokusho possess the key to the vault?" inquired Markus.

Maiyo turned to his fellow elders as they conversed in Taijina. Finally, he responded, "We assume he does,"

"You are not certain?" asked Arerys

"It is said, only the prince can access this vault, this being the case, I can only assume he has the only key," stated Maiyo.

"So it is my understanding we must protect the crown prince, overthrow the regent, capture the Sorcerer, guard the pass on Borai Mountain and do this all before an all-out war can ravage eastern Imago? In less than three weeks?" groaned Lando, overwhelmed by the weightiness of this exercise.

"Eighteen days to be exact," reminded Joval, watching the knight shake his head in dismay.

"Come now, Lando, you who braved the quest to see the Dark Lord taken down in defeat, are you implying that this is a much more daunting task?" asked Arerys, with raised eyebrows.

"It is my age, good Elf," responded the knight. "Unlike your kind, unfettered and untouched by the cruel hands of time, I do feel my age. Perhaps, I am growing too old to take on such a perilous quest."

Nayla smiled at the knight's words, even as Dahlon reprimanded her, "What is this? You smile in the face of adversity, Nayla? Obviously you already scheme the regent's demise."

"If I know my master, Hunta Saibon shall send warriors to guard the northern passage while others shall devise a multitude of snares and traps for those foolish enough to enter our lands. The remaining Kagai Warriors will undoubtedly head south, to Borai Mountain to join forces with the warriors of Orien. Together, they shall guard the pass," stated Nayla.

"But what of the prince?" asked Lando. "If there are plans to abduct him, how do we circumvent this? Do we even have enough time to arrive at his residence to protect him from the Imperial Soldiers?"

"Time is of the essence," answered Nayla. "We shall send word immediately to evacuate Prince Tokusho; we shall have warriors meet them on route to deliver the prince to the Imperial Palace. That is what Joval shall do, he shall take a battalion through the passage on Borai Mountain and deliver Prince Tokusho safely for his own coronation," instructed Nayla.

"And while Joval is preoccupied with this, what shall you be doing?" asked Dahlon.

"I shall do what you had intended; I shall infiltrate the Imperial Palace to deliver chaos and mayhem. There are powerful warlords aligning themselves with the regent. They trade their armies for the right to sit on his council; for the privilege to be a member of his higher echelon of society. To *remove* them would be the equivalent of amputating the regent's arms and legs; he shall be rendered powerless!" averred the warrior maiden, the fire in her eyes ignited at the prospect of executing this operation.

"And what of the Sorcerer? How do you plan to put his reign of terror to an end?" posed Dahlon.

"It shall not be my doing, I shall merely clear the path so Lindras Weatherstone can deal with him accordingly if indeed Eldred Firestaff should show his face," countered the warrior maiden.

Suddenly, Nayla rose from her chair. To everyone's surprise, they watched as she glided silently across the floor, drawing her short sword as she neared the door.

The men in attendance stood up from the table, mystified by the warrior maiden's actions. She motioned with her hand for them to resume their conversation.

In one swift, smooth movement, Nayla forced the door open. She momentarily disappeared from sight as a frightened scream rang through the meeting hall.

"So what do we have here?" asked Nayla as the fingers and thumb of her left hand tightened around her victim's windpipe.

"I bring water," Taiko gasped, forcing her words through the warrior maiden's choking grip. It was as though Nayla was about to rip her windpipe away from her throat. Taiko's dark brown eyes were wide open in sheer terror as she stared down at the tip of a sword poised dangerously close beneath her chin.

"How long have you been here? How much have you heard?" asked Nayla as her grip thrust Taiko against the door frame.

"I swear, my lady, I heard nothing!" cried out the frightened woman, attempting to hold forth the urn of water to prove to the warrior maiden of her intention.

"Nayla! What is the meaning of this?" asked Markus, coming to Taiko's assistance as he guided the deadly blade away from its intended victim.

"There is a spy amongst us, one who is skilled in the art of deception!" declared Nayla.

"I assure you, Taiko is no spy!" Markus responded, his left hand defiantly squeezing the warrior maiden's wrist in an attempt to loosen her suffocating grip.

"How do you know, Markus? How do you know for sure?" countered Nayla, reluctantly releasing her hold.

"I just do," stated Markus, embracing the trembling woman in his arms, attempting to quiet her fears.

"That is hardly an adequate answer! Do not tell me you have been deceived by your heart; beguiled by this woman's beauty!" hissed Nayla in anger.

"Enough!" shouted Dahlon, "Let us not waste anymore precious time. Your paranoia gets the best of you, Nayla. You should be ashamed of yourself. Taiko is nothing more than domestic help: a harmless woman of all things!"

"A harmless woman you say? I laugh at your sentiment! Am I too a harmless woman?" retorted Nayla, as she gingerly pointed her sword towards her father. "I think not!"

Once again Joval placed himself between father and daughter as he signaled for two warriors stationed in the courtyard to guard the meeting room from the base of the stairway, instructing them to allow none access to the door. Taking the urn of water from Taiko, he ordered her not to return until she was called upon. She quickly bowed as she hastily retreated down the stairs past the guards, her black hair now in a muss after her confrontation with the warrior maiden. One hand wiped away her tears as the other soothed the ravages of Nayla's attack on her throat.

Joval directed all to re-enter the meeting hall as he secured the door. Those in attendance quickly took their place back at the table.

"Nayla is correct, Lord Treeborn," admitted Joval as he reclaimed his chair. "I had already warned you there has been a breach in security, that the secret passage on Borai Mountain was secret no more."

The warrior maiden sheathed her short sword, thrusting the scabbard through the knot of her belt before sitting down. Her eyes glared at Dahlon as she spoke: "When I encountered the Sorcerer, he admitted that he had planted a spy here."

"Why would he admit to this to you?" asked Dahlon, with a doubtful scowl. "If that be the case, he is a bigger fool than we ever suspected for he knows we would flush his accomplice out. It would only be a matter of time before we capture him."

"He willingly admitted this only because he thought he was going to dispose of me; that I would not live to divulge this information to you. And *you* are the fool to assume that Eldred would use a man for this purpose," Nayla snapped in defiance.

"I was the one to bring Taiko Saikyu into our service. Are you implying that I failed to take appropriate measures to ensure she is not a spy," challenged the senior Elf.

"Do you really know her? Did you know who recommended her for the posting? Did you check her background before inviting that woman into the palace?" queried the warrior maiden.

"I am *not* accountable to you!" growled Dahlon, slamming his fist on the table. He rose up to confront his daughter.

"No, you are not, but you are accountable for the security of Nagana and the safety of all the people within the walls of our city," retorted Nayla, leaning across the table to meet his unyielding stare. She was not moved or intimidated by his stance or demeanor. "And if you are so sure Taiko Saikyu is not a spy, then why on two occasions has she been found standing outside the meeting room? Our grounds may be secure, but need I remind you, these walls are thin."

"Come now, Nayla, be reasonable! Taiko is not here to defend herself," cautioned Markus, attempting to pacify the warrior maiden while removing suspicion from Taiko.

"So you shall defend her, Markus?" asked Nayla, stunned that he would come to this stranger's defense.

"It is merely a coincidence that she was at the door. You heard her. The first time she was having difficulty securing the door. Her hands were full. The second time, she was delivering fresh water to us. It was a coincidence, a matter of bad timing; that is all," responded Markus.

"Let common sense prevail. It is better we side with caution," recommended Maiyo, raising his hands for calm. "I shall provide Master Stonecroft with a record of our staff. We do have several new hires; in times of uncertainty it would serve us well to delve into their history. It is possible that there are those unscrupulous enough to lie to gain entry into the palace if it would serve their evil purposes."

"Very well," conceded Dahlon, reclining in his chair. "This brings us back to the subject of Lindras Weatherstone. Before Nayla took it upon herself to accost palace staff, she mentioned about 'clearing a path' for the Wizard. That is all well and good, but how do you know he shall be returning; that he means to even come to our aid?"

"I trust Lindras. The men of the Order trust Lindras. Perhaps you should place your trust in the Wizard too," recommended Nayla.

"But Lindras Weatherstone is nowhere to be found! How can we be sure he shall be coming to our aid?" asked the senior Elf, his dark blue eyes were clouded with concern.

"Have some faith, my lord, he shall be here in our time of need," swore Lando.

"Let us hope the Wizard does indeed arrive in time," groaned Dahlon with a weary sigh.

"And as we have so little time to spare, I shall take my leave tomorrow at first light," stated Nayla.

"And what of the rest of us?" asked Arerys. "We did not come all this way to idly sit by."

Nayla smiled at the fair Elf as she offered, "Gentlemen, by all means, you are welcome to join me if you are up for a little adventure."

"Only you can make such a dangerous mission sound like nothing more than an afternoon outing," said Markus, his eyes rolling in dismay.

"We shall be by your side, Nayla," promised Arerys, giving her hand a gentle squeeze. "We shall penetrate the walls of the palace with you."

"No, you shall not," advised the warrior maiden. "I shall be going inside. You, Markus and Lando shall wait for me on the outside. I shall call upon you if I should fail to accomplish my task."

"You shall not fail, Nayla," stated Joval with confidence.

"But how do you intend to enter this time?" asked Dahlon.

"The last time I infiltrated the Imperial Palace, I did so as a domestic; a cook to be exact. Many of the soldiers died that day and a good number of the royal guests fell ill," recalled the warrior maiden as she pondered this dilemma.

"Take note, Arerys, *do not* let this woman cook for you. It is obvious now your betrothed is not well versed in food preparation," said Markus with a laugh as he winked at the fair Elf.

The men, even Nayla, laughed at Markus' good-natured teasing. For a brief moment, the gravity of their situation was lifted, although be it temporary.

"Pay no attention to Markus," urged Nayla. "It was merely a *secret* ingredient that did not agree with their palates. No doubt the regent, as did his descendants, has his staff sampling his food lest he be poisoned. Though it was long ago, Darraku shall not be deceived by the same ruse twice. I shall have to come up with another guise," answered Nayla. "When the time is right, I shall disclose only to those who shall be in my company, what my plan shall be."

"And we shall be leaving tomorrow morn?" asked Arerys.

"Most definitely," replied Nayla. "If we all leave tomorrow, it shall take several days for Joval to rendezvous with Prince Tokusho, if the prince departs from his residence in Shesake immediately. During this time, I shall lead the rest of you into the heart of enemy territory; into Keso. There, we shall watch and wait for the most opportune moment to strike. Even before Joval can deliver Prince Tokusho to the palace, I shall be dismantling Darraku's regime from the inside out."

"So, Lord Treeborn, as we go off to avert a war, I assume you shall take an army to Borai Mountain to fend off an incursion should we fail," said Arerys.

The senior Elf cogitated on Arerys' words before he answered, "My place is to protect the walls of this city and those inside. I shall remain here to coordinate our efforts."

"Of course; how foolish of me. I should have known," replied the fair Elf, agitated by the mere fact that this high Elf was willing to endanger the lives of all others, including his own daughter's, on the front line of battle. All the while, he planned to remain behind the relative safety of the great stone walls of the fortress city.

"In the meantime, my staff shall ready the horses and provisions for this journey. I shall have the warriors prepare to leave tomorrow, only those on horseback shall accompany Joval east of the Furai Mountains," said Dahlon. "Joval, send word to Prince Tokusho, tell him of the impending plot to abduct him and our plans to facilitate his reclamation of the throne."

"It shall be done, my lord," replied Joval with a bow.

"As it is apparent the kings of the Alliance shall not be coming to our assistance and as we have no guarantee that we shall succeed in aiding Prince Tokusho with his ascent to the throne, a war of unparalleled magnitude may still ensue. I have no doubt the Sorcerer shall be riding high on the wake of this destruction," stated Dahlon.

"Nayla had mentioned the warriors of Orien, including the Kagai Warriors, only number four or five hundred. How do we stem this tide of evil if the regent's soldiers outnumber us so greatly?" asked Lando.

"It shall take some ingenuity," stated Joval, turning to the warrior maiden. "Nayla, as a Kagai Warrior, what do you recommend? What would Master Saibon do in this situation?"

"Just because we lack the men, it does not mean we have to be lacking in power – in weaponry," said Nayla, reaching for a piece of parchment and the inkwell. As she carefully dabbed the nib of the writing quill into the indigo blue ink, she quickly sketched the schematics for a weapon used by her fellow warriors.

The men gathered around Nayla as she drew.

"Is that a catapult of some kind?" asked Lando.

"Yes."

"Nayla, we have catapults, but their range is very limited; only good if we wage war outside the walls of the city," stated Joval.

"Our numbers shall be as such that we must engage in war from the battlements to protect Nagana," added Dahlon.

"Yes, a conventional catapult would do no good," agreed Nayla, dipping the nib of the quill into the inkwell. "What I have in mind is slightly modified."

When the warrior maiden was done, the men studied her diagram in profound awe.

"Do you understand what I have drawn here?" asked Nayla, looking at the stunned expression on their faces.

"Yes!" said Joval excitedly. "This is designed to launch fifty or more arrows at a time!"

"Exactly," confirmed Nayla.

"But what do we use to hold the arrows in place? Do we build individual compartments for each projectile?" asked Lando.

"You may, or you may do what we have done. We merely take stalks of bamboo of uniform size, cutting them down just below the joints so arrows can be dropped in without fear of falling out the other side. Lashed together, you can make this device capable of launching a dozen to over fifty arrows at a time," said the little warrior. "Plus, hidden behind the walls of the city, an assault of this kind shall lead the enemy to believe that a vast army of undisclosed numbers awaits them inside."

"You are brilliant, Nayla!" stated Markus as he admired her handiwork.

Arerys smiled proudly at his betrothed as he responded, "Intelligence and beauty; that is why I wish to marry this woman."

Maiyo and the elders beamed in pride at the warrior maiden. "We shall have our weapons-makers modify the catapults based on your design, Nayla," said Maiyo gratefully.

"Do so with haste, Master Sonkai," agreed Nayla. "Time shall be a rare commodity; it is better spent making the arrows to arm the catapults than to build these mechanisms of war from nothing."

Maiyo hastily rolled up the parchment to deliver it to those responsible for its construction. He bowed in gratitude as he turned to leave.

"Master Sonkai," called Nayla.

"Yes, Lady Treeborn?" responded the elder.

"I strongly recommend you make the section holding the arrows moveable so you may adjust the trajectory. If it is designed correctly it shall easily launch a multitude of arrows high over the walls of our fortress city and well beyond."

"Of course," agreed the elder. "Is there anything else we should consider?"

"Yes, there is one more thing," said Nayla. "Test it. Do not wait until the day of war arrives to use it. Test it first."

Maiyo Sonkai and the elders bowed in understanding and gratitude as they departed the meeting hall with the diagram in hand.

"Let us hope this contraption works, Nayla," said Dahlon in a huff as he watched the elders hurry down the stairway.

"Of course it shall work, my lord," stated Joval tersely.

"I assume this meeting is over now?" asked Arerys as he watched the three men disappear through the courtyard.

"There is one more matter that must be addressed," replied the senior Elf, his gaze turned once more to his daughter. "There is a very likely chance that if war is not averted, it shall be Eldred Firestaff leading the charge into battle. If the Wizard of the West fails to come to our aid, what do you recommend we use to battle the Sorcerer, one endowed with the power to control the element of fire?"

Nayla took a moment to consider Dahlon's question. As she rose from the table to leave the meeting room, her suggestion was droll and simple: "Water. And plenty of it."

CHAPTER 18

A BETRAYAL OF THE HEART

As the warrior maiden made her way through the bustling courtyard, Arerys rushed up to her side, stopping her in her path. He turned her about to face him as he kissed her upon her lips.

"Now what was that for, my lord?" asked Nayla as she peered into his eyes that sparkled like stones of sapphire.

"You are absolutely incredible," marveled Arerys, smiling down at the warrior maiden.

"How so?"

"It is as though you have learned to ride in the eye of the storm. You are calm while all else may be raging about you. You are focused and confident even as the possibility of war looms on the horizon," said the fair Elf in great admiration.

Nayla gave him a gentle smile as her hand touched his face. "You are no different, my love."

"But the manner in which you are able to stand up to your father… He can be most difficult indeed, yet you do not let his words or actions beat you down," said Arerys.

"It was not always this way," admitted Nayla. "Let us say that things have changed since I first returned to Nagana."

Arerys gently kissed her upon her hand. "And now where do you go, my lady?"

"Well, if you feel a need to know, I was about to return to my bed chamber," answered Nayla.

"Perhaps I should escort you," suggested the fair Elf.

"Well, if you thought my etching was interesting, perhaps you would like to join me. I can show you the tools of my trade," whispered the warrior maiden as she tempted him with a most seductive smile.

Arerys was very intrigued by this invitation as Nayla led him away by his hand.

In the corridor leading to the guests' quarters, Lando caught up to Markus as he headed back to his bed chamber.

"I wish to speak to you if you have a moment to spare, Markus," requested the knight.

"Of course, Lando," said the prince, inviting him into his room. "Come in."

"Thank you," responded Lando, grateful that Markus would make time for him.

"I get the distinct impression there is much tension between Lord Treeborn and Nayla," observed Markus as he closed the door to his bed chamber.

"Now that is an understatement, Markus," replied Lando, a distinct expression of displeasure was cast over his face. "My time spent with Joval has revealed much about the warrior maiden and her life as the daughter of a high Elf. Unfortunately, my own opinion of Dahlon Treeborn where Nayla is concerned leaves much to be desired. I must admit, it makes me truly appreciate and admire Nayla's tenacity and courage in dealing with her father."

"So you are telling me he is always this abrupt and harsh in his dealings with her?"

"You do not know the half of it, Markus. How she puts up with that pompous, arrogant Elf is beyond me," stated Lando. "He is insufferable and leans towards prolixity; deliberately becoming long-winded when he feels Nayla should be subjected to ridicule, especially when it is before Joval Stonecroft or the elders. When it comes to his daughter, Dahlon Treeborn is completely lacking in compassion."

"Perhaps it is a daughter's love and loyalty for her father that allows her to overlook his callous treatment," offered Markus.

"I think not. Believe me, with what little I do know, he has given her no reason to feel love or even family loyalty for him. And if she does, it is sadly misplaced," said Lando, his tone ringing with a bitter sting. "As much as I know Arerys loves her, I do not envy his choice of father-in-law. I fear Lord Treeborn shall be as hard on Arerys as he is on Nayla simply because he will be guilty by association."

"I am hoping that Dahlon Treeborn will be more civil to Nayla because of her new standing as the princess to the Prince of Wyndwood," stated Markus as he picked up the bottle of wine Taiko had delivered to his room the previous day. He uncorked the bottle, sniffing the aromatic bouquet. "Would you care to join me?" asked the prince as he poured some of the red wine into a goblet.

"No, but thank you, go ahead," answered Lando as he sat upon a chair.

Markus examined the contents of the bottle and with a shrug, poured the remainder of the wine into his goblet. He sat on the edge of the bed as he sampled the dark, carmine liquid; it now seemed rather insipid, having lost a bit of its edge. Even its bouquet was not quite as heady and intoxicating as before. Markus accounted these things to the delicate nature of the rare vintage Taiko had selected. As he swallowed the wine, he noticed that the unusual after-taste was nowhere near as noticeable as the first time he had indulged in the dark liquid. *Perhaps the wine needed more opportunity to breathe,* thought the Prince, swallowing down another sip.

"Tell me, Markus, have you given any more thought to Nayla's remark that there is a spy here in this palace?"

"It is a very real possibility," admitted Markus. "However, I did not appreciate Nayla's supposition that it was Taiko."

"Markus, please tell me you have good reason to believe Nayla is wrong."

"Of course she is wrong, my friend."

"How do you know?" asked the knight. "Do you have proof or do you say this because you have bedded her and now you feel obligated to defend this woman?"

"I am truly insulted by your words, Lando! You know me better than that," said Markus, stunned by his comment.

"You know it is not my intention to insult you, Markus," stated the knight, his hand raised, gesturing in apology. "I am merely saying that perhaps it would serve you well to be objective; to base your opinions on facts, not on what you desire to be true."

"I understand your concern," said Markus, setting his goblet down. "At this moment in time, I cannot disclose to you what I know of Taiko Saikyu. I can only say she is not what Nayla accuses her of being."

"So be it," answered Lando, rising from his chair. "I suppose I shall have to trust you where Taiko is concerned."

"Thank you, my friend," said the prince in relief. "In time, the truth shall be revealed and the real spy shall be exposed."

"I pray it shall happen before it is too late," replied Lando with a heavy sigh as he made his way to the door. "If we fail to install the rightful heir to the throne, if we do not put an end to the regent and the Sorcerer's tyranny, this is one war that shall guarantee a lopsided victory for the enemy."

"Where is your faith, Lando?" asked Markus, as he escorted the knight to the door.

"It left by way of the Wizard," he answered as he departed the room.

Although he knew it was Lando's feeble attempt to be facetious, he also could sense his deepening worry, for indeed, the task they now faced was daunting, if not impossible. He closed the door behind Lando, his footsteps diminishing as he strolled down the corridor.

As he turned, Markus let out a sudden gasp of surprise only to have it stifled by Taiko's hand. He clutched his chest, in an attempt to calm his pounding heart as the other removed her dainty hand from over his mouth.

She stood upon her toes to kiss him fully on his mouth. Markus' surprise and anger slowly melted away with the soft caress of her lips upon his. She peered up at him ever so innocently.

"You gave me quite the fright! Do not ever do that again, lest you accidentally meet with my sword!" He admonished her, releasing his grip from her wrist.

"I am sorry, my lord," said Taiko apologetically.

"How did you get in here?" asked Markus.

"How soon you forget! I work here. Remember?"

"Yes, I know that, but I did not see you enter."

"I concealed myself when I heard the knight's voice. There is a tendency for suspicion and false accusations to run rampant during times of civil unrest. He, like Lady Treeborn, seems to be of like mind where I am concerned," said Taiko in despair. "Your friends do not trust me."

"They do not even know you, they do not see you for who you truly are," replied Markus as he held her in his arms. "Unfortunately, it shall remain so until Lindras Weatherstone returns."

"It is true then. He is gone."

Markus could see the undeniable disappointment in her doleful, hazel eyes as tears began to well. "There, there, Elana. Lindras *shall* return, and when he does, I shall see to it that I secure his staff for you."

"It shall be too late," she cried in a whisper, as though his confirmation crushed her imprisoned soul.

"Whatever do you mean?"

"If my soul is not released by the time the Sorcerer returns, I shall be cursed for all eternity. I shall be forced to live in the body of others for all time."

"Is there any other way? Can the Sorcerer's spell be broken by other means?" asked Markus, detecting the palpable sense of urgency in her voice.

"There is, but I cannot ask this of you," she sobbed.

"Tell me, Elana! You are my wife, I shall do whatever it takes to break the Sorcerer's hold over you!" declared Markus, embracing her trembling body close as he stroked her chestnut hair. "I cannot bear to see you suffer in this manner."

"You must truly love me, even after all this time," she cooed in pleasure as she gazed into Markus' dark brown eyes. She gently touched his face with her hand.

"My love for you never diminished, Elana," said Markus, kissing her upon her forehead. "Tell me what I must do to release the Sorcerer's hold on you."

Her eyes darkened with sadness as she turned away from him. "Do not ask of this, Markus. Even for you the price shall be too great," answered Elana.

"I beg of you, Elana, tell me and I shall make it so," pleaded Markus, taking her by her hand.

She sat upon the edge of the bed, her downcast eyes no longer able to look upon Markus. He knelt before her, stooping to look upon her sad face. His fingertip followed the sad trail of tears on her cheek, wiping them away. Lifting her chin so their eyes could meet, he slowly kissed her. She answered his kiss, pressing hard against his mouth, stealing away his breath as she pulled him down upon her body.

His heart pounded wildly against his chest as she kissed him with unbridled passion, rolling over him so that now, she straddled his body.

"You are the love of my life, Elana," Markus whispered. "I had pledged my eternal love to you and it never died, even when you were taken from me."

"Markus, you know that once my soul is set free, I shall no longer exist in Taiko's body. She will be herself once again, while my soul will finally be with the Maker of All," answered Elana, her voice barely audible. "Our time together, this time we share shall be fleeting."

"It matters not," protested Markus. "I shall willingly die just to have this moment with you. I have been so lonely without you, Elana. My life has not been the same. Not even the passing of time has eased the pain of heartache and sorrow I have endured for so long."

"I too have felt the depth of your sorrow for my love for you is boundless, not knowing the passage of time," replied Elana in a gentle whisper.

"Then tell me, my love, what must I do?" asked Markus, his fingertip tenderly tracing the soft curves of her lips.

She leaned close to his ear and with a whisper, she answered, "I need the blood of an Elf - a fair Elf."

"Par... pardon me?" stammered Markus.

"You heard me, Markus."

"Arerys' blood? A drop? A cup? How much blood do you speak of?" asked the prince.

"His life," answered Elana.

Markus seized her wrists, pushing her off his body. His mind reeled as if her words hit him as surely as he was struck by a powerful fist. His stomach tightened in a knot, repulsed by this disturbing request.

Elana's bitter tears flowed once more upon witnessing Markus' reaction. "I knew it would be too much to ask; to have you choose between your friend's life and that of your wife's," she sobbed.

Markus gasped, his heart was cast into a sea of guilt upon hearing her claim. "But Arerys... he is my closest friend. He is a brother to me!"

"Is your love for him greater than your own love for me? For if it is, then you never really loved me as you claimed," cried Elana.

"Of course I love you, you are my wife."

"If you are true to your words, then you shall prove it," she stated, an unfamiliar hardness came over her face. "You would prove your love for me."

Markus watched in stunned silence as Elana crossed the room towards the door. As she stepped out, she whispered, "If you love me Markus, you shall meet with me before the midnight hour. We shall see then how strong your love is and where your devotion lies."

With that said, she abruptly closed the door. Markus slumped down upon his bed as he agonized over her terms. His head was now braced in both his hands as the suffocating weight of her words bore down unmercifully upon him.

Nayla glanced down the length of the corridor before shutting the door, her fingers worked quickly to secure the latch. She smiled as she felt Arerys come up behind her, enfolding her body in the warm embrace of his arms. He kissed her upon her neck causing a soft sigh to escape as she reveled in his gentle touch.

She turned to face the Elf as she asked, "I thought you were here to see my weapons?"

He smiled as he answered, "Am I not holding the most dangerous of weapons in my arms as we speak?"

"Indeed you are," she replied, her hands casually slid up along his arms and with the slightest of movement, she pinched the smallest amount of skin and flesh on Arerys' triceps.

The Elf emitted a sudden yelp of pain, releasing his embrace as his hands vigorously rubbed the object of her assault. Her movement was so subtle; he didn't even know what she had done.

"What did you use on me?" he asked.

"Would you care for me to demonstrate again?" she offered with a smile.

"No! I would rather not!"

Nayla giggled upon hearing Arerys' ardent protest. She strolled over to her dresser, sitting down on the chair to face the mirror. She watched his reflection as the Elf approached her with caution. "Now, would you care to see my *toys*?" she asked coyly.

"Not if I get hurt in the process," stated Arerys, still rubbing the two tender spots on his triceps.

"I promise you will not get hurt, not even a little," she said with a smile. Nayla reached beneath the drawer with both hands; pushing up and then back slightly. The false bottom of the drawer came away. The warrior maiden laid the tray on top of the dresser. She watched Arerys' reflection in the mirror as he stared down at the contents of the tray.

His brows furrowed in curiosity as he studied the benign objects Nayla proudly displayed before him.

"So this is your deadly array of weapons? A lovely fan, a beautiful hair ornament, a silk ribbon, dusting powder... I do not understand," stated the Elf in bewilderment. "How can these be weapons?"

She gingerly picked up the wooden hair ornament, winding it into her hair until only the silk blossoms protruded from her dark tresses. Her hand released her hair and as it cascaded down around her shoulders, in a flash she pulled the wooden ornament apart. Sheathed inside was a thin, razor-sharp blade. Though only six inches in length, Arerys could see immediately that even a small blade such as this could inflict a deadly wound if used correctly.

Nayla sheathed the blade, and then picked up the ornate fan. The Elf could see the ribs were constructed of solid, thin strips of metal. The silk that bound and perfectly spaced each rib was beautifully hand-painted with an exquisite image of a swallow-tailed butterfly hovering over a cluster of sunny, yellow chrysanthemums. Her deep brown eyes peered up innocently at Arerys from behind the painstakingly crafted fan.

"In case you get hot?" he queried.

She contemplated his words for a moment, cooling herself with the light breeze of the fan as she casually sauntered over to a fruit bowl. Her left hand picked up a ripe, red apple as her right hand deftly folded the fan closed. Nayla tossed the apple into the air and as it fell downwards; her right hand suddenly flicked the fan open. Snapping loudly, it exploded into life, sweeping upwards diagonally from her left to her right. The white flesh of the fruit flashed in the air as the apple tumbled to the floor in two perfect halves. Arerys was totally dumbfounded as Nayla stood before him, nonchalantly fanning herself with the offending weapon.

She smiled in obvious pleasure as she approached him. "See these ribs?" asked Nayla, her finger pointing carefully to the very edge of the fan. "Each is made of forged steel; the tip of each rib is sharpened, as deadly as the blade of a knife. Closed, it is an effective striking tool, especially on pressure points."

"Pressure points?" asked Arerys, unfamiliar with this term.

"Yes, like right over here," she answered as her right thumb pressed down on his left forearm. Compressing the muscle sheathing the radius bone just below the crease of his elbow, his knees buckled under the excruciating pain she ever so briefly inflicted on him.

As he straightened himself, rubbing his arm as though to erase the sharp, phantom pain, he asked, "Do you enjoy hurting me?"

"No, Arerys, I just want you to understand. I want you to know that even though I may walk amongst the enemy once I enter the Imperial Palace, you need not worry about me," said Nayla confidently as she gently kissed his arm much like a mother would lovingly kiss away the aches and pains of a child.

"I have no doubt you shall hold your own, Nayla, but how do you suppose you shall enter?" asked the Elf.

"As domestic help, as a cook, it was easy to access the palace, even to bring my weapons in with me if I desired. They shall not be fooled in the same manner twice," responded Nayla, placing the folded fan back onto the tray. "If the regent stays true to his nature, once a month he wines and dines his loyal cronies. Part of his strategy to keep them on side is to entertain the warlords with courtesans."

"Are you telling me you plan to become a courtesan?" gasped Arerys, alarmed by what Nayla proposed.

"Why should I not? I have used this ruse successfully before in other situations," stated Nayla.

"You did what?" asked the Elf, stunned by the complacency of her words.

"Let me assure you, Arerys, I am skilled in the art of deception. It is nothing more than a high-stakes game. I have always been the victor and in this case, the men die before they even get very far with me," stated the warrior maiden.

"I trust you know what you are doing, Nayla."

"Look at these weapons and tell me that they are not perfect for such a disguise," declared Nayla, pointing to the tray on the dresser.

Arerys' blue eyes gazed upon the strange array of weaponry. "I suppose you are going to tell me this cord of silk ribbon is a deadly weapon too."

"Yes, it is. There is a thin string of wire worked into the fabric. It is designed for garroting."

The Elf's hand subconsciously touched his throat as he contemplated the possibility of strangling a person with the silk ribbon. His attention then turned to glass jar of fine, white powder. "I take it, this is no ordinary face powder," said Arerys, pointing to the small jar.

"It is blinding powder."

"And this is not perfume in this ornate, little vial either, am I correct?" queried the Elf.

"It is perfume if you choose to wear it," said Nayla as she uncorked the vial for Arerys to smell the delicate floral scent. "However, if you consume it, even a small quantity, you shall perish. Though it smells sweetly of wild blossoms, this plant; its rose-colored, thimble-shaped flowers, its tall, spike-like stem and velvety green leaves produces a deadly substance that wreaks havoc with the heart."

The Elf recoiled from the vial Nayla held before him. He then picked up a small jar filled with a vermillion-colored cream. "I know! This is no ordinary lip paint. It, too is laced with some deadly poison," supposed the Elf, cautiously examining the content of the tiny jar. "Yes, the *kiss of death*."

She laughed as she snatched the jar from his hand, placing it back onto the tray. "You are so silly! This is ordinary lip color. For occasions such as this, I like to look my best," confided Nayla with a knowing smile. "After all, a girl should look the part. If my job is to kill, then I should be appropriately dressed to do just that. I shall be dressed to kill."

"So it is true then? You are an assassin."

"Such a harsh title, however it will do. Suffice it to say, I am one of the best, and I am not boasting. I merely speak the truth," acknowledged the warrior maiden.

Arerys could not help but smile at her response as he gazed down at his little warrior maiden. Embracing her in his arms he asked, "You truly believe you can do this?"

She raised herself up onto her toes to kiss his lips as she answered confidently, "I *know* I can."

With the coming of dusk, the men of the Order gathered in the dining hall to partake in a dinner hosted by the elders. Joval and Lando were the last to arrive as they worked together all day to ready the warriors for the trek to the Borai Mountain and beyond.

Nayla deliberately chose to sit as far as possible from Dahlon. Arerys took his place by her side after seating her, not even questioning her motives.

Markus sat between Arerys and Lando. The knight looked upon the prince; Markus appeared pallid and seemed withdrawn.

"What troubles you, Markus? Why so morose?" asked Lando in a whisper.

"There is no need for concern, my friend," answered Markus in a soft voice, not wishing to draw unwanted attention. "I fear the wine I had consumed earlier was not fit to drink. I shall be fine once I get some food into my stomach."

As though his wish was answered, servants paraded into the dining hall with tray after tray laden with a delectable selection of food. Taiko moved with ease from guest to guest, pouring wine into each goblet. As she served wine to Maiyo Sonkai, seated directly across from Markus, she discreetly smiled at the prince. Markus quickly averted his eyes from her, shifting in his chair uneasily as Elana's hazel eyes sparkled in the candlelight as she winked at him.

From where she sat, Nayla casually observed this social intercourse between Markus and Taiko. She frowned inwardly as she watched with dismay as Taiko's dark brown eyes flirtatiously gazed at the Prince of Carcross. Even Markus' own response was curious as she noticed how his eyes quickly dropped away from Taiko's gaze. The woman's pleasant smile abruptly dissolved in response.

Though the evening meal was impeccably prepared and was flawless in presentation and taste, the food was consumed in relative silence. Each member of the Order mentally orchestrated his part in this mission as Nayla continued to ponder the identity of the spy. Her dark brown eyes were discreetly watching the servants as they went about their business, ascertaining those new to the staff from those in long-time service.

Maiyo conferred in Taijina to his fellow elders before rising up from his chair, hoisting his goblet of wine high. He cleared his throat to garner everyone's attention as he announced, "I would like to make a toast: I wish each of you success in this mission; that we deliver a quick end to this strife that shall see Orien restored to its former glory."

"Here! Here!" cheered Dahlon, "To the success of this mission! The next time we gather, there will be cause for celebration." The senior Elf held his goblet towards Arerys, his head bowing in recognition of his future son-in-law.

"Yes, of course!" stated Maiyo. "When the regent has been brought down in defeat and Prince Tokusho restored as the rightful heir to the throne, we shall make immediate plans for Nayla's union to Prince Arerys. It shall be a wedding of the grandest proportions!"

"That is kind of you, Master Sonkai, but let us deal with one matter at a time. Do not be so eager to plan such a spectacle, for though I shall do everything in my powers to bring down the regent, there are no guarantees in life. If I be captured, I shall do what is expected of any honorable Kagai Warrior."

Arerys' eyes darkened upon hearing Nayla's words. His face blanched as he thought of the unthinkable. "Are you saying – "

"I am saying that I shall not be returning," stated the warrior maiden, her voice unaffected by the gravity of her own words. "I shall be forced to take my own life, lest I be tortured to reveal the whereabouts of my clan and of the strategy we have set into place to overthrow the regent."

Arerys' heart sank for he knew there was no turning back. His betrothed had already determined her path, willingly facing her destiny, whether it leads to success or to her own demise. He knew she could not be persuaded to change her mind.

Nayla could sense Arerys' mounting fear as she reached for his hand. "Fear not, my love, I have every intention of returning to you, but let it be known now, I shall not jeopardize your life and the lives of others should I fail in my bid."

"Arerys, need I remind you, Markus and I shall be close at hand. If Nayla's plan should go awry, we shall be there to aid her," promised Lando.

From his place across from Dahlon Treeborn, Joval gazed down the length of the table to the fair Elf. He stated with the greatest of confidence, "It shall not be long there after that I shall join you with Prince Tokusho by my side. I know we shall succeed, even if we fail to bring down the Sorcerer, should we defeat the regent, Eldred Firestaff shall no longer pose such a great threat. He shall no longer have the backing of the Imperial Army. That blood-thirsty scoundrel shall scurry off like a rabid rat to hide in fear and shame."

"I shall pray the spirits guide you with good wisdom; for our God to keep all of you safe," said Maiyo in a solemn voice.

As the night wore on, there was no more talk of the impending war. Instead, all spoke of better times and happier days and the return of these golden moments no longer overshadowed by the evil specter of war.

After the last of the wine was served, the men finally parted company. They dispersed to their separate quarters with the exception of Arerys. With great stealth, he silently made his way through the dim-lit corridor to Nayla's bed chamber. He gently rapped on her door upon which it opened ever-so slightly. Nayla pulled the door open as she seized Arerys by his arm. She eagerly yanked him into the room, locking the door behind him. Nayla thrust the Elf against the door as she proceeded to kiss him with great passion.

"I say! Do you intend to ravage me?" asked Arerys, answering her kiss.

"If that is what you desire," purred Nayla as her arms wrapped around his waist. "Tomorrow brings uncertainty for all; perhaps it would be wise to take advantage of this moment."

"You speak as though we may never have this time together again."

"I am a firm believer in the Kagai credo that one should treat every day as if it were the last."

Arerys smiled down at the little warrior maiden as his hands caressed the satiny smoothness of her silk robe against her bare skin. His fingers worked to loosen the sash as he slowly peeled the robe off her shoulders.

He brushed her dark tresses back as he stooped to ply gentle kisses along the nape of her neck. Nayla sighed in surrender under his tender touch. In the flickering light of the many candles, Arerys' eyes could make out the dark tattoo on her right shoulder blade as well as the many long, silvery scars of long forgotten wounds that once lacerated her small back.

"What does this mean?" asked Arerys, his fingertip gently tracing the indigo blue ink that permeated deep into her skin.

"It is the sign of a Kagai Warrior, we all bear this mark," said Nayla in a whisper. "It is the means by which we are identified should we be cut down in the field of battle."

"Yes, I have seen it before on your brother warriors, but what does it mean?"

"In Taijina, the upper symbols spell the words *for justice*. The lower symbols mean *for peace*," the warrior maiden answered. "It is what we are trained to fight for and shall willingly die to uphold," explained Nayla as she pulled the silk robe over her shoulders to conceal the tattoo and the many linear scars surrounding it.

Arerys' hands stopped hers. He gently whispered into her ear as he leaned over to kiss her, "Do not be ashamed, Nayla. This is an honorable mark to bear; to be worn with dignity and pride. There are few who have the strength to do what you have done, or possess the courage to face the enemy alone as you intend to do."

"It is not the mark of the Kagai Warrior I mean to conceal, Arerys. I know you have seen my scars," replied Nayla in a soft voice. "I am not like you. The scar you bear from the sword of the Dark Lord's making shall eventually fade. For me, I shall be made to bear my scars until the day I die."

"Do I appear to be that shallow?" he asked, wounded by her insinuation. "Believe me, Nayla, I am not bothered by these scars," insisted Arerys.

"How can you not be bothered? You are an Elf; you are flawless. My scars are permanent. I have been pierced by arrows, bloodied by the blade of swords, and broken by halberds," said Nayla, shuddering involuntarily as she recalled the many times Joval had come to her aid; mending her broken bones, healing her bloody wounds. "My body tells the tales of the many battles I have narrowly survived."

"I do not care, Nayla, for though you feel your body is damaged, I can see how resilient you truly are. Inside, your soul is intact. It is still whole and good. It takes incredible fortitude of both body and mind to survive as you have."

Arerys planted a kiss upon her forehead, embracing her small body against his. Her eyes closed as she rested her head against his chest, the steady beating of his heart in her ears calmed her soul. For now, Nayla had found temporary respite from her day to day existence. Her arms tightened around Arerys as she released a contented sigh.

Arerys' fingertips gently traced her soft cheeks, lifting her chin so their mouths met. His lips lightly pressed against her full, sensuous lips, teasing her into wanting more. Nayla melted into his arms as he kissed her lovingly. Suddenly, their moment of intimacy was broken by an abrupt knock.

Nayla shouted through the door, "I am busy, Nakoa. Come back in the morning!"

"I am sorry to disturb you, my lady; it is I, Taiko Saikyu. I seek the Prince of Wyndwood."

Nayla's eyebrows arched in curiosity as she asked, "What is your business with Prince Arerys?"

"Prince Markus of Carcross requests his presence immediately."

Nayla wrapped her robe around her body, tightening the sash as she nodded for Arerys to open the door.

The Elf peered through the door at the woman as he asked, "What is so urgent that Prince Markus cannot wait until the morn?"

"I apologize, my lord, what business he has with you, I do not know. He did not reveal the nature of the matter he wishes to discuss. I am here to deliver this message, nothing more," stated Taiko, her head bowed in submission.

"Very well, tell Prince Markus I shall be there momentarily," responded the Elf. Taiko bowed once again before turning down the corridor.

Arerys turned to Nayla, looking to her for some understanding as he stated, "I shall not be long, my love. I know Markus would not seek me out at such an ungodly hour unless it was truly of great urgency."

"I shall wait for you," replied Nayla as she craned her neck to give Arerys a quick peck on his cheek before sending him off to Markus.

Through the dark courtyard, the Elf made his way. He glanced up to the diminishing light of a waning crescent moon as a thin veil of cloud-cover drifted over its face. The night air was balmy and still, devoid of the usual sounds made by the creatures of the night. Arerys' acute hearing could only make out the sounds of leathery bat wings fluttering high overhead. The small, winged creatures eagerly hunted nocturnal insects, pursuing their prey in frenetic flight.

Bats, they are nothing more than bats. They are not the portent of evil, thought Arerys as he rushed up the stairs and silently made his way through the dim-lit corridor. Knocking on the door as he entered, the Elf was stunned to find Taiko embraced in the prince's arms.

"What is going on, Markus?" asked Arerys, his curiosity piqued as he watched him release the woman from an embrace. He could immediately see that Markus was troubled, his face was flushed and his eyes were dark and brooding.

"I do not know where to begin," the prince answered reluctantly.

"At the beginning would be wise."

Markus exhaled a heavy breath, his shoulders seemed to slump under the sheer burden of his worried mind. "Very well," he said. "I have a dilemma for which I do not know the answer."

"Go on, I am listening," prompted the Elf.

"Elana… my wife…"

"What of her?"

"She is here."

"What do you speak of Markus? Elana is dead."

"Let me explain," said Markus, motioning the Elf to sit.

"There is nothing to explain! I was there when you buried Elana. I was there to share in your grief!" stated Arerys, his concern for Markus escalating.

"You do not understand."

"You are correct, Markus. What in hell's name is going on?"

Markus took Taiko by her hand as he presented her to the Elf, "This is Elana."

"No, this is madness," stated Arerys tersely, looking upon the Taijin woman. "You jest, right?"

"No, Arerys, I speak the truth," insisted Markus. "You just cannot see her as I do, this is Elana."

"Have you taken leave of your senses? This is Taiko Saikyu, hired on by Dahlon Treeborn to keep house," corrected the Elf. "Perhaps you have indulged in a little too much wine tonight, my friend."

"Arerys, listen to me, this is Elana. Though you cannot see her as I do, I promise you, it is she. This is my wife, Elana."

"Do not make of mockery of Elana's life and death," reprimanded the Elf as he shook his head in disappointment. "I too wish for her to be alive, Markus. I wished Elana did not die for I stood by and watched as a part of you died on her passing. Alas, one cannot change history."

"I suppose it is better to say that Elana did pass on, but her spirit lives on in the body of Taiko Saikyu," explained Markus. "You just cannot see it, for it is my love for Elana that allows me to see Taiko for whom she really is."

"I see her for whom she is, Markus. Let me assure you, this is not

Elana. Your desire to have her back is so great, your mind and your heart deceives you," reasoned Arerys. "As much as I love and miss Elana too, I know with all certainty she is gone."

"Listen to me!" pleaded the prince.

"No, Markus, you shall listen to me. I can understand you lusting for this woman, perhaps, even being in love with her, but this does not make her Elana," scolded Arerys with great consternation.

Taiko gently squeezed Markus' hand as she pleaded with him, "It is no use, though Arerys be your friend, he does not believe you."

"I believe he wishes you were Elana," countered the Elf with an angry scowl, pointing an accusing finger towards her. "Tell him, woman! Tell him who you are!"

"I know this woman's heart. She is Elana," stated the prince.

"You may think you know her heart, but it is your own heart that deceives you, Markus!" insisted Arerys. "Perhaps she is the spy Joval and Nayla warned us about. Are you the one, Taiko?"

Her chin dropped to her chest and she began to sob, felled by the Elf's stinging accusation.

Markus pulled Elana away, standing between her and Arerys, his hand motioning the Elf for calm.

"You must believe me, Arerys. The Sorcerer somehow trapped Elana's soul. Unable to pass from this realm, she is forced to live in the body of Taiko Saikyu. The woman you see may indeed be Taiko, but the soul within is that of Elana's."

"What enchantment have you been put under? What spell has this woman cast upon you to make you believe the impossible?"

"Arerys, were you not the one to tell me the old adage of 'seeing is believing' does not always hold true in all cases, that sometimes, 'to believe is to see'?" asked Markus in desperation. "Have some faith. Please choose to believe this one time."

"I have known you almost all your life, Markus. I believe you are weary; perhaps you have partaken in too much wine. If you continue to insist that this woman is Elana, then I shall be forced to believe that common sense and logic eludes you, my friend," responded Arerys as he turned to leave. "We best speak in the morning when your head is no longer lost in this fog."

The Elf opened the door to exit only to have it come slamming to a close as Markus rammed the door shut with his shoulder. Arerys was startled by his aggressive behavior, but as he faced the prince to reason with him, Markus suddenly thrust the Elf against the door, holding his dagger close to his throat.

"Do not force me to do this, Arerys," pleaded Markus, his hand was trembling as he attempted to steady the blade.

Nayla sat before her mirror, staring through her own reflection. She absentmindedly ran the wooden comb through her long tresses, biding her time until Arerys' return. She placed the comb back down on the dresser as her hands reached beneath the drawer to remove the false bottom. Placing the tray upon the dresser, she gazed upon the deadly assortment of weapons before her. Nayla picked up the throwing darts, studying the thin, narrow blades as she contemplated whether she should dip them in the small, ceramic vial of poison. Her thoughts abruptly dissipated as a loud pounding jarred the door to her bed chamber.

"Nayla! It is I, Joval! Lando and I need to speak to you! Are you in there?" called the dark Elf. "It is of the utmost importance we speak to you *now*!"

Nayla leapt up from the chair and ran to the door. Immediately, she could see both Lando and Joval were distressed.

"Nayla, Lando and I have been studying the records of the staff given to us by Master Sonkai. There seems to be a discrepancy in the records of one of the staff members," stated Joval.

"Let me guess: Taiko Saikyu?"

"Yes, after speaking to long-time staff, we have discovered that her claims of coming into service to replace a staff member who fell ill and died are false," said Lando.

"Are you saying this staff member is not dead?"

"Indeed she is quite dead, but it is the manner of her death that concerns us!" exclaimed Joval. "According to her neighbors, Taiko Saikyu was boarding with the woman when she died in a mysterious fire; not of an illness."

"Think on it, Nayla! It is all too convenient. She claimed to the head of household that she was the niece of this dead woman when in fact the deceased had no family apart from her long departed husband. And the fire; that is a sure sign she is in alliance with Eldred Firestaff," explained Joval.

Nayla gasped, "She *is* the spy. That is how she knew Arerys was here!"

"Where is he now?" asked Lando.

"He departed with her, she claimed Markus was in need of his presence," stated the warrior maiden, her heart was racing with the realization that Arerys and perhaps, Markus too, was in great peril.

"We have no time to lose!" declared Joval. "We must find them!"

Nayla grabbed her sword from the stand, unsheathing it as she ran after Lando and Joval. The three dashed through the palace grounds, retracing Arerys' footsteps. Upon reaching Markus' bed chamber, Joval burst through the door with such force, the impact sent both Markus and Arerys tumbling to the floor. Taiko scrambled across the rug, seizing Markus' dagger in her hand. Lunging for Arerys, she grabbed a fistful of his blonde locks as she yanked him onto his feet. Guiding him up by the point of the deadly blade, she held the others at bay, using the Elf as a shield.

Lando pulled a dazed Markus back onto his feet, only to have the prince push him away.

"What is this, Markus? What are you doing?" asked the knight, startled by the prince's action.

"It is not what it appears to be!" shouted Markus. "I just want Arerys to understand! I need him to help me! To help Elana!"

"Elana? Who is Elana?" asked Nayla, her sword drawn and pointed towards Taiko.

"His dead wife," answered Arerys, only to have Taiko yank back on his hair, exposing his throat so the cords of his neck were taut.

"Markus, what has become of you? Elana is long dead," said Lando, confused and startled by his words.

"You do not understand!" protested Markus.

"Markus, listen to what you are saying! You have always been the voice of reason, what you say now makes no sense whatsoever!" declared the knight.

"Lando, please, I swear to you, this is Elana. Though you cannot see, Elana is here!" pleaded Markus.

"Markus, you have been deceived by this woman," stated Nayla. "She is a spy! She conspires with the Sorcerer!"

"You lie! Can you not see? Can none of you see? This is Elana!"

"Markus; listen to me!" pleaded Joval. "Nayla speaks the truth! This woman is not who she claims to be!"

The prince began to tremble as he looked upon the woman holding Arerys at knifepoint.

"I know what I see, and I see my wife!" cried Markus in anguish.

"Markus, Taiko has somehow tricked you. This is not your wife. In your heart, you want to believe this so much so that somehow your eyes now deceive you!" stated Nayla.

"Do not listen to her, my love," hissed Taiko, pressing the dagger closer to Arerys' throat.

"Markus, do you truly believe Elana would hold your best friend at knifepoint?" asked Lando. "Elana would never do such a thing to Arerys. He was a friend to her! Remember?"

Beads of perspiration broke out on Markus' forehead as he silently considered Lando's claim.

"Ask her Markus! If she truly is Elana, she would know how she died. Ask her how Elana died!" shouted the knight.

"What a foolish question!" spat the woman. "*I* died in childbirth. Our daughter was stillborn!"

In a daze, the prince's eyes were filled with confusion as he blinked hard, focusing on her words.

"Markus, if you do not believe us, if you insist on believing what your eyes see, then please, look to the mirror," pleaded Nayla, pointing to the dresser. "The mirror does not lie!"

He slowly turned his gaze to the silvery sheen of the mirror mounted to the dresser. He shuddered as his eyes took in the reflection of a raven-haired, brown-eyed Taijin woman.

"No! It was my son that died, not a daughter!" he gasped as the horrifying realization set in that she held Arerys by the blade of his own dagger. "And Elana would never do this! She would never ask me to murder a friend!"

"Well, if you do not, my dear prince, then I am more than willing to take this Elf's life!" snarled Taiko, backing away from Markus as she continued to press the blade to Arerys' throat. "Lay your weapons down and show your hands or I shall spill his blood."

Lando and Joval instantly dropped their swords, but Nayla continued to veer forward with her weapon still poised at Taiko.

"Did you not hear me? Unhand your weapon or I shall slit your prince's throat."

Nayla shrugged her shoulders in indifference as she stepped a little closer. "It matters not to me; there are other Elves to be had," she said with a cruel laugh.

Arerys' eyes grew wide in shock upon hearing the warrior maiden's cruel words.

"I mean it! I shall kill him!" declared Taiko, pressing the blade to Arerys' throat. A thin red line of blood rose to the surface of his pale skin.

"Nayla! I do believe she is quite serious!" added the Elf in obvious distress.

"And so am I," hissed Nayla, her words now as deliberate as her actions. "I have not forgotten how easily you had discarded me when you thought I had betrayed you with Joval!"

"Damn it, Nayla!" cursed the dark Elf. "Whether you are angry with him or not, he is still the Prince of Wyndwood! Drop your weapon! Do it now!"

The warrior maiden considered her sword for a lingering moment. As she tossed it to the floor, her eyes locked with Arerys, and then quickly glanced up towards her right hand as she raised it in surrender.

Suddenly, Arerys' right hand darted up to catch Taiko's knife-wielding hand as his left elbow slammed into her chest. As he dropped to the floor, the throwing dart Nayla had discreetly palmed in her hand flew out with a vengeance, striking Taiko on the left side of her neck as she reeled backwards from the impact of Arerys' blow.

With a resounding crash, Taiko stumbled back, smashing through the window. She plummeted to the gravel and rocks below. Joval and Lando wasted no time; they raced out the door leaving behind Nayla and Arerys to tend to a visibly shaken Markus.

Nayla helped Arerys to his feet as she apologized, "You know I did not mean the things I said."

"I was a wee bit concerned for a moment," admitted the Elf as his left hand concealed the wound left by Taiko as he began the process of healing himself. "You sounded very convincing."

Both he and Nayla turned to see Markus fall to his knees, looking shocked and bewildered. "What have I done? Please forgive me Arerys. I do not know what had come over me!"

"You have done nothing, my friend," answered the Elf in a gentle voice. "You merely followed your heart."

"I cannot believe I could be so gullible," lamented the prince.

"You were under that woman's spell, Markus. There was nothing you could do once she began to weave her evil magic," said Arerys.

"Arerys, if you are both well, I shall join Joval and Lando. I wish to speak to this woman if she has survived the fall," stated Nayla.

"Be on your way, Nayla, make haste. I am fine. I shall join you shortly," said Arerys with a nod as he helped Markus to his feet.

Nayla took up her sword as she dashed out to find Joval. As she raced down the stairs, she could see torch after torch lining the battlement high on the city walls come to life, peeling back the darkness of night.

She could hear Joval shouting orders to drop the portcullis on both the west and east gates. His orders were soon followed by the echoing clamor of the heavy iron grates descending to bar the gateway to the fortress city.

As she rounded the corner of the building, the shards of broken glass that had rained down from above glowed. The sharp fragments reflected the light from the dancing flames of the many torches licking high into the ebony sky. Nayla's eyes could make out the crimson blood staining the ground in a random splatter of drying droplets in the dim light. Amongst the blood and shattered glass lay her throwing dart. She carefully picked up the thin blade, examining the still-wet blood sheathing the weapon.

"Joval!" she called out as lights throughout the palace and the surrounding buildings flickered on as the people woke to the sound of the commotion outside.

In the distance, she could make out Joval's form heading towards the west gate. "Joval!" she called out once again. "Does Lando detain the woman?"

The dark Elf turned to respond, "She is nowhere to be found!"

"What do you speak of? Are you telling me she fell from the window and was still able to walk away?" asked Nayla.

"Walk away? Yes. Is she unscathed? No. There is blood, presumably her own," answered Joval, turning away to speak to the warriors guarding the gateway.

"Damn it all!" cursed Joval, striking at the bars of the portcullis with his hands. He ordered the guards to keep the gateways secured until they had scoured the city for the woman.

"Do you believe she escaped?" asked Nayla.

"She either escaped before we could bar the gateways or she is still amongst us," stated Joval, making his way to meet Lando at the east gate.

Nayla was forced to run to keep up with the dark Elf's long, deliberate strides. He stopped long enough to instruct warriors to sweep the grounds in search of the spy before continuing on. Before long, Lando rushed up to him with news.

"There is no sign of the woman," panted Lando, his chest heaving from his sprint. "The warriors guarding the east gate and those in the watchtowers saw nothing."

As the trio turned back to the center courtyard, they were met by

Dahlon Treeborn and the elders.

"What is the meaning of this? What is the need for all this commotion?" asked Dahlon with an indignant huff.

"We have discovered the identity of the spy," answered Joval.

"Have you now? Who may that be?" asked Master Sonkai, his weathered hands anxiously rubbing together in worry.

"It was Taiko Saikyu," replied Nayla. "She was in the midst of attempting to murder Prince Arerys."

"Is the prince safe?" asked Dahlon, genuinely concerned for Arerys' well-being.

"Yes, he is safe," answered Joval as a weary sigh escaped him. "And now it is imperative we find that woman before she can relay information to the Sorcerer."

"My intuition tells me Taiko is long gone; spirited away by the powers of the dark arts. If this be the case, Eldred Firestaff has not been working alone here; he has forged a new ally by taking on an apprentice."

CHAPTER 19

THE ELEVENTH HOUR

Taiko's eyes slowly adjusted to the erratic light given off by the torches lining the gloomy tunnel. Her bloodied hands reached out as she felt her way along the subterranean labyrinth meandering deep into the bowels of the earth. Following the network of tunnels, she entered a catacomb that fed into a series of caverns, each becoming larger the further she journeyed on.

As she entered a huge chamber, her nose wrinkled and burned, assaulted by the noxious odor of brimstone. Orange-red cauldrons of molten lava churned and belched around her, filling the great cavern with an eerie glow and suffocating heat. Taiko slumped down wearily against a pillar of stone. In the red glow of the chamber, her drying blood appeared black against her pallid skin. She moaned in pain as she tugged at a large shard of glass embedded deep in the top of her shoulder.

"So my dear, you have come home," cackled a familiar voice echoing through the cavern.

Taiko struggled back onto her feet as her eyes nervously darted about the chamber, searching for the Sorcerer. As she advanced forward, Eldred suddenly materialized from behind the massive column of a broken stalagmite.

"I hate it when you do that!" said Taiko with a startled gasp, recoiling from his abrupt appearance.

"So where is the Wizard's staff? Give it to me now!" demanded the Sorcerer.

"Do you not even care enough to ask me how I am?" snapped Taiko.

Eldred's head hung down in a mock gesture of shame as he responded, "Of course, how rude of me. So how do you fare, my dear?"

"How do you think I fare? Look at me!" raged Taiko, holding forth her bloodied arms for the Sorcerer to see. "Look at what Nayla Treeborn did to me!" she continued as she lifted her black hair off her neck to show the wound left by the warrior maiden's dart.

"Consider yourself lucky, woman," grumbled the Sorcerer, turning away from Taiko.

"Lucky? What does luck have to do with this?"

"Normally, her darts are poisoned. Had it been, you would be dead," answered Eldred.

Taiko's hand touched the small but deep wound, wincing in pain as she thought upon his words. Eldred took up his staff, pointing the crystal orb towards the woman as his eyes closed. She could hear him mumbling an incantation under his breath as a dazzling white light pulsated, and then bathed her in its brilliant glow.

When he was done, Eldred lowered his staff. He momentarily considered the woman before taking his place on his high, stony throne.

All the lacerations and scrapes Taiko had received from her earlier mishap miraculously vanished. She stood in silent awe as she assessed his handiwork. "This is amazing. I would never have thought you were capable of doing good with your craft."

"There are many things I am capable of, both good and evil. I however, prefer evil. It is much more gratifying," responded the Sorcerer with a self-satisfied laugh. "But enough of this banter. Give me the Wizard's staff! I want it now!"

"I do not have it," admitted Taiko, slowly stepping back, away from Eldred.

"You incompetent mortal!" growled the Sorcerer, his staff poised towards her. "Where is it?"

"It is gone, along with the Wizard."

"Why did you not follow him?"

"His departure was unannounced, it was abrupt," replied Taiko. "Dahlon Treeborn knew not of his absence until he was gone."

"Are you telling me that Lindras has disappeared?"

"Yes, and not even the Prince of Carcross is aware of his whereabouts. Lindras Weatherstone is gone. Vanished," insisted Taiko, snapping her fingers. "Like a puff of smoke."

"Damn it, woman! You are a worthless apprentice!" snarled Eldred. His fist slammed down on an ancient book of runes used to summon the forces of evil. An eon of dust, accumulated between the tattered sheets of parchment, burst forth in a great cloud. "I told you she was of no use to us!" His words shot over his left shoulder to his invisible partner, hidden somewhere in the dark recesses of the cave.

"My worth has little to do with the Wizard's disappearance. Had you been a better mentor, had you only given me greater powers," retorted Taiko as she pointed to his collection of spells and incantations, "perhaps the outcome would have been different."

"You were not ready for more," grunted the Sorcerer. His gnarled fingers drummed impatiently on his precious, leather-bound book as he eyed the woman. "Did you not gain any knowledge that might serve my purpose?"

"What I do know is Lord Treeborn and his few allies shall be concentrating all their efforts on Prince Tokusho's return to the Imperial Palace, and to uproot the regent. As for the kings of the Alliance, not even Kal-lel Wingfield or his people shall be coming to Treeborn's aid," replied Taiko.

"Are you certain of that?" quizzed Eldred; his soot-tainted fingers twirled his dirty, gray moustache as he listened with great interest.

"Oh, I know it. Both the princes of Carcross and Wyndwood delivered this news to Lord Treeborn. They had no idea how dire the situation was when they embarked on their trek. Needless to say, my lordship was not pleased," said Taiko, noticing the Sorcerer's eyes glow with delight upon hearing her words. "Plus, you should know they are so overwrought with worry where Regent Darraku and Prince Tokusho are concerned, they have made no plans of how they intend to extricate you."

"How intriguing," said Eldred, his bony fingers thoughtfully rubbing his gaunt face as he considered Taiko's words. "This is much too easy! What with the Wizard of the West abandoning them like the coward that he is, this shall be an easy victory."

"How so?" asked Taiko.

"If they choose to ignore my might, if they prefer to treat me as nothing more than a mere carbuncle on the back-side of humanity, they shall be caught totally unaware. They shall pay dearly for their ignorance when I show up at the fortress city with the entire Imperial Army," stated Eldred, his gnarled hands rubbing together in gleeful anticipation of the impending war. "We shall be no match for them; they shall be crushed by the power of my wrath."

"And what shall my part be in all of this?" queried Taiko.

"You? You have proven yourself to be a worthless apprentice!" snarled Eldred. "*We* do not need you!"

"You promised to teach me more!" declared the woman, the color draining from her face.

"You do not deserve to learn from me," retorted the Sorcerer, twisting his moustache with the tips of his fingers as he plotted his next course of action. "I have healed your wounds; that is more than you deserve. Be gone from my sight before I decide to reduce your mortal form into a pile of ashes!"

A gray dawn was ushered in with the trumpeting of horns as the warriors gathered in the courtyard. From a high balcony, Dahlon Treeborn and the elders watched as the men fell in line, waiting for their orders. Their quiet observance was disturbed only by a messenger sent forth by Joval Stonecroft. He delivered word that, after searching the palace grounds and the city, the warriors could find no trace of the spy. Taiko Saikyu had vanished.

In the great courtyard, Joval gave instructions for the battalion leaders to select only twelve of their best Elven warriors for the trek to Shesake, Prince Tokusho's residence in exile. Three hundred warriors were to secure the pass on Borai Mountain while the remaining one hundred and fifty-four were to protect the fortress city in case the enemy penetrated the mountain pass.

Three men worked feverishly to crank the massive winch, lifting the heavy iron grate that secured the gateway. As the portcullis on the west gate was raised, the army proceeded to march out of the city in a long procession. Joval instructed the twelve warriors to ready their horses as he made final plans for their departure.

The Elf moved swiftly, his light strides sweeping him up the stairways towards Nayla's bed chamber. Just as he was about to knock, Arerys opened the door motioning him to enter. Markus and Lando were already there.

"Are you ready to depart?" asked the dark Elf, watching Nayla as she secured the false bottom of the dresser back into place.

"We are as ready as we will ever be," announced the warrior maiden.

"And you, Markus? How do you fare this morn?" asked Joval.

"I am fine now, thank you for asking," answered Markus, his eyes falling away in shame after last night's near disaster.

Nayla secured the weapons in her pack as she said to Joval, "We are prepared to leave now. We shall travel with you and your men to Borai Mountain. From there, we shall go our separate ways."

"Time grows short, let us leave now," said the dark Elf, leading the party out to the courtyard.

Joval led the way to Borai Mountain. Their steeds galloped past the infantry as they marched in a steady procession, leaving the warriors behind in a cloud of dust. Detouring off the main road, the dark Elf escorted the Order and the twelve warriors northeast. The unmarked trail they followed would lead them directly to the once-secret mountain passage and onward to eastern Orien.

By late afternoon, Nayla and the men crested the mountain. For a moment, all gazed across the infinite horizon line to the east. Angry thunder clouds gathered and brewed on the distant mountains far to the northeast, growing ever darker with the sun's waning light. The group pressed on, proceeding down the slope along a path hidden by a large ridge. This ridge projected from the mountainside like the exposed and twisted spine of an ancient dragon long laid to rest. It effectively concealed this path, keeping it secret until Taiko Saikyu had delivered word to Eldred Firestaff, revealing its whereabouts.

As they journeyed downwards, the Elves listened and watched for signs of enemy advancement. With nothing more than the persistent 'caws' of a few hungry ravens circling high overhead and the trill songs of finches as they fluttered from the seeding crown of one thistle plant to the next, the group continued their descent.

At the base of the mountain, a small herd of white-spotted deer silently retreated into the bamboo forest as the loud snorting of horses spooked them away. Arerys felt more at ease as he watched the fleet-footed creatures disappear into the grove. Such shy, retiring animals would never remain in the area if they sensed any kind of danger.

Joval brought his horse to a stop as he dismounted. Nayla and the others did the same.

"This is where we shall part company," said the dark Elf. "It shall be a seven-day ride to Prince Tokusho's estate in Shesake. And then it shall be another eight days to the Imperial Palace in Keso. We shall meet sooner if Prince Tokusho already heads in our direction."

"That shall only give us two days to place the crown prince on the throne! What shall happen if you are somehow delayed?" asked Markus.

"I am sorry, my friend, but time conspires against us," apologized the Elf. "We must travel long and hard if we even hope to make good of what little time we do have."

"Then let us waste no more time with talk," said Lando. "Let us get on with this task."

"Yes, Lando is right. We shall have to make haste if we are to dispose of the regent and his cronies," advised Nayla, approaching the dark Elf.

"I shall meet you in Keso. I shall have Prince Tokusho by my side," promised Joval as he embraced Nayla in a farewell hug. "Stay safe, little warrior."

"You too, my friend," whispered Nayla, as she reciprocated with an embrace of her own.

Joval turned to the others, clasping each by their wrists in a final gesture of parting and good luck.

"Do not worry, Joval," said Arerys. "We shall keep Nayla safe."

"I know," said the dark Elf as he smiled in approval. "We shall be off now."

As he turned away to mount his steed, Markus caught him by his shoulder, stopping the Elf.

"You are one of us now," announced Markus, raising his right hand. "For the Alliance!"

All present, Joval included, raised their right hand high and proud as they echoed the prince's declaration.

Nayla watched with a heavy heart as Joval and the twelve warriors charged away on their steeds towards the distant storm clouds looming on the horizon. She felt a weary sigh escape her as she coaxed her mare towards the east.

For twelve long days, the warrior maiden rode her mare at a relentless pace, leading the men of the Order along invisible trails cutting through the many valleys. As the thirteenth day of travel came to an end, from the top of a hill, hidden within the shadows of the forest, Nayla's finger directed the men's attention to the east. Silhouetted against the impending darkness, the tall spires of the watchtowers pierced the cobalt blue sky. The impenetrable walls of the Imperial Palace loomed before them.

Dawn crept in as the weary travelers slept fitfully beneath the cover of a tree. Arerys woke to the sound of RainDance snorting loudly as she grazed next to Arrow. The Elf stretched and rolled over to where Nayla slept only to find her bedroll empty. He bolted up in alarm. His abrupt movements caused Markus and Lando to stir from their slumber.

Markus propped himself up on his elbow as he gazed with half-closed eyes towards Arerys.

"Nayla is gone!" exclaimed the Elf, feeling the bedroll to see if it was still warm from her body.

"What do you mean, she is gone? Gone where?" asked Markus, rubbing the sleep from his eyes.

A small piece of parchment secured by a throwing dart on a tree trunk rattled in an invisible breeze, as though trying to catch the Elf's attention. Arerys removed the dart, examining the message.

Remain here.
I shall return.
NT

"What does it say, Arerys?" asked Lando through a great yawn, stretching as he sat up.

"Nothing really, only to remain here and that Nayla shall return," answered the Elf, his eyes turning a deeper shade of blue with his growing concern.

"Then that is what we shall do," recommended Markus, flopping back down upon his bedroll. "We shall wait for Nayla."

"But what if she is in trouble?" asked the Elf, standing to seek out a better vantage point.

"Have some faith in your woman, Arerys," suggested Lando as he struggled to stand upright. "Nayla is probably very close by. Knowing her, she watches the comings and goings at the palace. That is all."

"Yes, Arerys, you really should have more faith in your woman," a gentle voice agreed in a whisper.

Arerys turned to see Nayla as she appeared before him. The Elf breathed an audible sigh of relief as he embraced her.

"Do not disappear like that again, Nayla," admonished Arerys. "You had all of us worried."

"I apologize. I did not mean to cause any of you concern," responded the warrior maiden.

"Where did you go?" asked the Elf.

"I paid a visit to an acquaintance of mine," confided Nayla. "And I have returned with some useful information."

"Can your friend be trusted?" asked Markus, rising up from his bedroll.

"Most definitely! In fact, he works for us, gathering vital information and sending it off to Anshen, to Master Saibon."

"But how do you know he can be trusted? In times of civil unrest it is easy for people to switch allegiance," warned Lando.

"For one, unbeknownst to the regent, he is Master Saibon's kin. Plus, he is the direct descendant of the one who helped me enter and escape the palace when I came to rescue my Kagai Warrior brother."

"What is his name?" asked Arerys.

"I prefer to keep him safe. It is best I not utter his name lest one of you is captured. What you do not know, you cannot divulge."

"Very well then," responded the Elf in understanding. "So what is this information you have?"

"Darraku is in the midst of planning a grand celebration to mark his own coronation as the new emperor of Orien," replied Nayla. "The festivities are slated to begin on the eve of Prince Tokusho's impending birthday."

"His birthday?" asked Markus.

"Yes, as you recall, if Prince Tokusho is not installed as the emperor, if he fails to make his claim before his sixteenth birthday, it shall pass on to the next in line; his uncle, Tisai Darraku. The regent shall ascend to the throne at the stroke of midnight."

"So his guests do not arrive until that evening?" inquired Lando, bundling his bedroll to secure to his saddle. "That does not give us much time at all."

"We have no choice, Lando. To make matters worse, fourteen days ago, the regent sent forth an army, seven thousand strong to an undisclosed destination."

"Where do you think they go?" asked Arerys. "There were rumors of plans to abduct the crown prince."

"Those loyal to the prince shall guard him with their lives. They will die to keep him safe, but even so, to send seven thousand soldiers? Even one hundred soldiers are more than enough to overpower the prince's guards," answered Nayla, her eyes scanning the walls of the distant palace. "Something is not right."

"Do you suppose they lie in wait to ambush Joval and his men?" asked Markus.

"If they have not already succeeded in capturing the prince, then I have no doubt they shall be waiting for Joval as he delivers Prince Tokusho to Keso."

"There shall be no time to warn him," said Lando with a gasp.

"I know," responded Nayla. "If my intuition serves me well, the army's movement coincides with Taiko Saikyu's escape from the fortress city. I have no doubt she is aware of some, if not all of our plans. If this be the case, the Sorcerer is planning to mount an attack on Nagana."

"What do we do, Nayla?" asked Arerys. "Do we turn back? Do we warn your father of the impending danger?"

"It shall be too late. I know the road the army has taken if indeed they are heading east. It shall only be a matter of days before they breach the Furai Mountain range to enter western Orien," replied Nayla.

Lando shook his head in despair as he groaned, "Where is Lindras Weatherstone when he is needed the most?"

"Lando, I fight this war on behalf of my people. The rest of you have been inadvertently drawn into this. If you choose to leave I shall understand. For myself, I have no choice in this matter. If my people are to die, then I wish to die with them and I shall do so fighting," declared the warrior maiden. "I shall not wait until the enemy comes to my door."

"I shall not abandon you, Nayla. I, too am willing to face this evil by your side," responded Arerys.

"And I shall be made all the stronger knowing you are here for me," said Nayla with a confident smile.

"I have no intention of turning back," promised Markus.

"Nor I," added Lando. "I have never been one to run from danger. So what if we are so greatly outnumbered? By the grace of God, we may still be the victor."

"Now that is the Lando I have come to know and love," said Nayla with a grateful smile. "Hold onto your faith, for that is all we have left now."

"So here we shall remain," said Markus stoically. "What do you have in mind, Nayla?"

"I have been advised that the kitchen staff prepare for a banquet to mark the regent's impending rise to the throne. Darraku's cronies, the four most powerful warlords that guard his domain and prosper from his reign shall be there," stated the warrior maiden. "I shall be there too."

"But how do you plan to enter?" wondered Markus. "I am sure your reputation precedes you."

Nayla laughed gently at the prince's words as she responded, "The regent knows of me, but none of his soldiers have survived an encounter with me to return with an accurate description. As I understand, the grander my exploits, the larger I become. Apparently, by all accounts, I am some type of she-devil, as tall as the tallest Elf and more deadly than the Kagai Warriors!"

The men looked upon the diminutive woman before them, laughing as they visualized this tiny warrior as a hulking brute capable of dispatching men with her bare hands.

"Getting in shall be easy," said Nayla. "Getting out shall be another story."

"So how do you plan to gain entry?" asked Lando, perplexed by her statement.

Nayla thought for a moment before she answered, "His friends seem to be impressed by his lavish events; Darraku always hires courtesans for such affairs to keep these men entertained and in his pocket. Word has it, the local brothels have closed. Those farther away are reluctant to send girls as rumor abound that these girls never return home from such affairs."

"Are you telling me you intend to infiltrate the palace as one of these women? As a courtesan?" asked Markus in dismay.

"Why yes, Markus. That is my intention."

"Arerys, perhaps you should talk some sense into Nayla," suggested the prince. "This is downright foolhardy, suicidal even!"

The Elf studied Nayla's deep brown eyes for a lingering moment. His hand gently touched her cheek as he responded with a knowing smile, "I do believe Nayla shall make a lovely courtesan."

"Have you lost your mind, Elf?" asked Lando. "They shall kill her if they find out who she really is!"

"That is, *if* they find out," stated Arerys. "Nayla knows what she is doing."

"For now, we must play the waiting game; the social event of the century shall begin in three days. We shall wait for the most opportune moment to strike," said Nayla.

The hours passed slowly as day dissolved into night and back into day again. All took turns keeping watch as the others slept. When they were not asleep, they kept their eyes busy surveying the battlements high along the palace walls.

As the large full moon climbed high into the night sky, bathing the land in its cold light, Arerys' acute sense of hearing detected the hoof beats of fast approaching horses. His far-seeing eyes skimmed the horizon to the north. Braced in the darkness with nothing more than the pale moonlight to guide them, the Elf could make out the forms of fifteen Imperial Soldiers on horseback. They were charging towards the palace with great urgency.

Nayla stood up as she noticed Arerys suddenly rise very straight and tall, like a wild animal alerted to danger.

"What is it, Arerys? What do you see?" she asked in a whisper, moving silently so as not to wake Markus and Lando.

"There are riders in the distance, I had hoped it to be Joval and his men, but alas, they are not," answered the Elf. "Imperial Soldiers are heading to the palace, and they move with great speed."

Nayla leapt up onto a rock, standing upon her toes for a better vantage point as she craned her neck to see over the dense vegetation covering the hillside. "What is it that they have?"

Arerys leapt up by her side, his blue eyes piercing the darkness. "Either they have captured an exceedingly large wild boar for their feast or they hold something of far greater value," assessed the Elf as he watched a soldier wrestling with the struggling form concealed within a large burlap sack."

Nayla's heart sank and her shoulders slumped upon hearing Arerys' observation. She said with a heavy sigh, "If the Imperial Soldiers do indeed hold Prince Tokusho, then that would mean Joval has failed. He is dead."

Arerys could sense her anguish, holding her close in his arms, he whispered, "Do not think the worst, Nayla. Joval is a great warrior, one of the best I have ever seen. If indeed they hold the prince, it does not mean that Joval is dead."

"Come what may, Arerys, as the eleventh hour draws ever closer, we have no choice in the matter. Tomorrow, I shall enter the palace gates. If we are all doomed, I shall wreak unspeakable havoc in the regent's life and those loyal to him before I, too go down in defeat," stated Nayla with the greatest conviction.

Under a bleak morning sky, Markus and Lando woke to the sound of Arerys readying their steeds. Nayla tossed their packs to them, "Rise and eat quickly for we must be on our way."

"Where are we going?" asked Markus, rising up from his bedroll.

"Last night as you slept, Imperial Soldiers returned from the north," explained Arerys as he positioned the bit into RainDance's mouth. "It would appear they have the prince."

"What?" asked Lando, leaping up onto his feet. "What of Joval? Where is he?"

"That we do not know," answered Arerys.

"Nor do we have the luxury of time to find out," added Nayla, cinching the saddle on her mare. "There are a number of villages along the roadway south of Keso. Somewhere along this route we shall come across those attending the event, including a courtesan or two."

After a quick bite, the four set off, keeping to the shadows of the surrounding forest lining the road to the palace. Finding a secluded spot from which to watch the traffic, Nayla and the men waited.

As the morning gradually became afternoon, the travelers using this road increased. It became quickly obvious which ones were merely travelers using this route and which ones were destined for the Imperial Palace. The ornate carriages driven by well-dressed coachmen entered the palace gates.

"Nayla, how will we know if the carriage contains a courtesan?" asked Markus. "I hardly think we shall be able to stop and inspect each one as they pass."

"A courtesan can never afford the use of such a fancy carriage but aside from that, it shall bear a small red flag so the carriage can be directed to the servants' entrance," answered Nayla.

"Why through the servants' entrance, I thought you said she would be the entertainment?" queried Lando.

"That she is, but she is not regarded with the same esteem as one of his guests. She is unable to mix and mingle with the celebrants. Instead, she shall be whisked away in secret for the regent wishes not to offend the wives of his special guests. The courtesans are discreetly delivered to private rooms to service the men."

"Nayla, look!" said Arerys as he pointed to a simple carriage moving northward, a small red flag was mounted to the door.

"Our time has come, men," announced the warrior maiden. "Mount your horses!"

As the carriage neared, Nayla led the others through the forest, coming to a stop directly in front. The horses drawing the carriage reared up in fear as the coachman attempted to control his panicking steeds. Markus seized the reins to hamper their movement as Arerys and Nayla drew their swords as they boarded the carriage, trapping the driver between them. The coachman, a Taijin mortal of short stature cowered. He stared in disbelief at the towering, fair-haired Elf, having never seen an Elf, fair or otherwise in his life.

"Please! Do not rob me!" pleaded the coachman, speaking in Taijina. "I barely scrape by with all the taxes I am made to pay. I have nothing of value!"

"I do not wish to rob you, good sir," replied Nayla in fluent Taijina, holding forth a small, silk bag. "I wish to reward you."

She dropped the bag onto the lap of the frightened man. Its contents jingled as he picked it up in his hand. He anxiously tugged at the draw-string, his eyes widening in surprise as he looked upon the gold pieces.

"There is more to be had," promised Nayla; "if you cooperate."

Lando pulled his horse up to Nayla's side as he disclosed, "There is a young lady inside. She looks none too happy to be part of the regent's celebration."

Nayla instructed the coachman to follow Markus off the road. Concealed within a thick grove of trees, the warrior maiden removed her pack from her horse's saddle before climbing into the carriage.

Inside, a girl of perhaps no more than fifteen years of age wept bit-terly. Nayla looked upon her with compassion, stroking her head to calm her fears as she spoke in the language of her people. "Do not weep, child. It is time for you to return home."

"I cannot go home. I have been sold into prostitution by my own mother. We have no other means to survive; if I do not do this, my fam-ily shall starve," sobbed the girl. The black eye liner she wore smudged and ran as her tears stained her powdered face.

"You need not do this, nor shall your family starve," responded Nayla in a calm voice.

"The regent has paid handsomely for my presence for there are no women to be had," whimpered the girl through her tears.

Nayla opened her hand, placing a small, silk bag into it. "I believe this is far more than your mother received from the regent. It is yours in exchange for your pass to enter the Imperial Palace.

The girl immediately ceased crying as she eyed the gold pieces, stunned by her unexpected turn of good fortune. Without a word, she fished out the pass she had tucked into the wide sash of her dress, gratefully pressing it into Nayla's hand.

"When I have been delivered into the palace, the carriage shall return to take you home. Do you understand?"

The girl nodded, feeling the weight of the gold in her hand.

Nayla removed her swords and then her cloak, concealing her war-rior raiment beneath a beautiful, red silk gown exquisitely embroi-dered with gold and silver threads. The girl watched in silence as Nayla transformed her appearance before her very eyes. The warrior maiden unbraided her dark tresses, sweeping it up onto her head. It was at this moment the girl noticed the ever so slight point tipping each of her small ears. She gasped in awe, "You are the warrior maiden of Orien!"

Nayla did not respond, drawing her hair lower, and then tightly pulling it back to conceal the Elven points of her ears.

"Please tell me that you are her, tell me you have come to liberate us from the regent's tyranny," pleaded the girl.

"No, I am not the warrior maiden that you speak of," disclosed Nayla. "I understand she is much taller than I."

The girl's smile quickly faded. "I was so hoping for salvation."

"There is nothing wrong with having hope," said Nayla with a smile, securing the wooden hair ornament into her upswept hair so only the silk flowers were exposed. Her little fingers worked deftly to tie the silk ribbon into a perfect bow that served to hold her hair in place.

She then dusted her face with a fine white powder, and then using the reflection of the blade of her sword, she used a stick of black kohl liner to accentuate her large, almond-shaped eyes. Carefully dabbing her fingertip into a ceramic jar of vermillion cream, she spread the color onto her lips so they looked like the velvety petals of an exquisite, red rosebud.

Nayla finished her transformation with a few drops of her deadly *perfume* dabbed behind her ears and along her neck. She placed all of her jars and vials into a silk purse along with her newly acquired pass. Picking up her iron fan, Nayla flicked it open. The young girl stared, mesmerized by the dramatic change.

As Nayla stepped out from the carriage, Lando, Markus and Arerys gasped, stunned by her transformation.

The Elf smiled as he complimented her, "You look like a fine porcelain doll."

"This is truly amazing!" marveled Lando, circling around her in disbelief.

"I would never have guessed it was you, Nayla!" exclaimed Markus.

"That is a good thing then," replied Nayla, her dark brown eyes peering coyly at the men from over top of her beautiful fan.

Nayla motioned for the girl to remove herself from the carriage. As she did so, she handed to Nayla her cloak and her long and short swords. The warrior maiden laid her cloak upon the ground. She placed the swords side by side on the cloak, carefully wrapping them inside.

She turned to Arerys handing to him her weapons for safe keeping.

"Nayla, are you not taking your weapons with you?" asked Markus, his eyes grew dark with worry.

"There is no need for concern, my friend. I shall be fine," replied Nayla.

"Believe me, Markus, she is very well equipped for the task at hand," assured Arerys with a knowing smile.

Nayla then removed the silver ring from her finger as she placed it into the Elf's open hand.

"I shall keep it safe for you, my love," promised Arerys, planting a kiss gently upon her hand.

"I know you will," said Nayla with a gentle smile.

"How will we know if you have succeeded in doing away with the regent and his cronies?" asked Lando.

"Once it is time for you to enter the palace, I shall send you a signal," said the warrior maiden. "We shall have to work quickly for I shall have to rescue the prince from the dungeon first before I can deliver him to the throne room."

"The signal, Nayla, what is the signal?" asked Markus.

"When the time comes, you shall know what it is," answered Nayla, turning back to the carriage. "I must be on my way now."

Arerys embraced her in a final hug, holding her close as he whispered, "I love you, Nayla. Please be careful."

"I love you too," replied the warrior maiden, her arms tightening around the Elf, feeling his heart beating against hers.

As the carriage made its way onto the road, traveling northward to the palace, Arerys watched in silence as the coachman urged the steeds on to make up for lost time. The Elf's hand slowly opened to reveal the circlet of silver Nayla had placed into his palm. He considered the ring for a moment, picking it up between his thumb and finger. His heart began to race in horror when his keen eyes detected the three dreaded words he did not want to see. Inside the band he had gifted to his betrothed was inscribed *For an Eternity.*

CHAPTER 20

CHAOS WITHIN

The coachman followed the procession of carriages through the gated walls of the palace. A soldier glanced inside, giving Nayla a lewd smile as he gazed upon her. She batted her long, dark lashes at him from over top of her fan. He closed the door and Nayla could hear him giving instructions to the driver to deliver his passenger to the servants' entrance.

Bringing the carriage to a stop on the north side of the palace, the coachman leapt down to open the door for his passenger. Taking Nayla by one hand, he assisted her as she stepped out.

"Thank you," she said with a polite smile.

"The pleasure is all mine," responded the coachman as he bowed. "I hope you have a pleasant stay."

"Oh, I certainly will make the best of my time here," promised Nayla.

As the coachman steered his carriage away to exit the palace grounds, Nayla found herself surrounded by three Imperial Soldiers.

"What do we have here?" asked one.

Nayla produced the pass, presenting it to the soldier. By her elaborate gown and her painted face, he knew immediately what she was there for.

The captain thrust the pass back into her silk bag, snatching it from her hand. He tossed it to another soldier, instructing him to search it for weapons.

"I assure you, there is nothing more than items of a personal nature required by a woman of my status," said Nayla, watching as the soldier rifled through her possessions.

"These are dangerous times, my dear," said the captain as his lips curled with a lecherous smile. "I must take every precaution to ensure the safety of the regent and his guests. Raise your arms."

"Very well," replied the warrior maiden. She folded her fan as she raised her arms up.

The other two soldiers began to chuckle as their captain zealously tended to the business of patting her down for weapons. His hands skimmed over the luxuriant silk fabric, feeling her down her waist, over the curves of her hips, and along the length of her thighs and legs. As he stood up, his hands felt her shoulders then moved swiftly down to her breasts where they remained for a lingering moment.

Nayla smiled coyly at the soldier, bringing her fan down to strike him sharply on the back of his hand. "Regent Darraku would not be pleased to know that I have been pawed by one of his soldiers," she scolded. "However, once I am done, I am sure I can make some time for you and your men."

She watched as the lust in the soldiers' eyes burned as she smiled seductively at them.

"Well, let us not keep your host waiting!" said the captain, pushing his comrades aside to make way for Nayla. "Perhaps we shall meet up later, my dear."

He wasted no time to deliver Nayla to one of the many bed chambers. "You shall be called upon after the banquet. Remain here. Do not wander the palace grounds," warned the captain, closing the door behind the courtesan.

Nayla's eyes gazed up at the fine brocade tapestries adorning the walls. Beneath her feet, a soft rug made of the finest wool cushioned her against the hard, wooden floor. *So this is how the regent spends the people's money,* thought Nayla. Her fingers fondled the ornate, gold leaf worked into the finials of the beautifully crafted chairs. From the window of this room Nayla could see the soldiers standing high on the battlement. There could have been no more than two dozen pacing the high walls. Below, at least another two dozen guarded the entrance to the palace and its grounds. Nayla assessed their minimal presence to the fact that Darraku had sent forth such a huge contingent of soldiers to make war in western Orien, all who remained were just enough to protect the palace against civil unrest until the other soldiers returned.

No doubt the regent believes a civil uprising would never occur. Well, I shall sow the seeds of rebellion that shall create pandemonium within these walls, thought Nayla as she listened to the noise and commotion of the merry-makers in the courtyard below. She watched as the crowd funneled into the grand dining hall for a sumptuous banquet. The festivities were about to begin.

Nayla waited patiently, seated upon the soft down and feather mattress of a great canopy bed. She sat with her legs crossed, her back straight. Her fingers were entwined in the configuration to summon the energy of the earth. Here her soul lingered in this calming twilight, lulled by the energy flowing deep down inside of her. When her eyes slowly opened Nayla felt refreshed, as though she had awoken from a deep sleep. She gazed out the window to the west. The burning orb of a fiery red sun barely peeked over the Furai Mountains, its diminishing light cast the darkening horizon in a deep shade of mauve.

As she stood up, the door opened. A servant escorted one of the regent's most esteemed guests into the room. As the servant turned to leave, he discreetly instructed Nayla to proceed to the other awaiting guests immediately after she was done. Nayla merely nodded in understanding as a large man, large as far as Taijin men went, stepped through the doorway towards her.

"The regent never ceases to amaze me," grunted the warlord with an approving smile. "I was sure there were no more courtesans left in these parts."

Nayla patted the bed, inviting the man to join her. As he sat down, she knelt behind him, her small hands reaching in front to remove the clasps from his cloak. Her fingers gingerly ran through his straight, black hair, and then gently caressed the skin of his neck.

"So, do you possess the skills to take a man such as myself to heaven?" asked the large Taijin, his eyes closing as he enjoyed the sensation of her gentle touch.

"To heaven and beyond, my lord" promised Nayla in a whisper. "In fact, I shall deliver your soul to realms you have only ever imagined possible." Her arms wrapped around his neck as she leaned in close to kiss his cheek.

"Now where can you take me that is better than heaven?"

Nayla's hand drew back the warlord's long hair, exposing the back of his neck. She lightly kissed him causing him to shudder in pleasure, and then she playfully bit him on his neck.

"What better place is there for the likes of you than Hell," hissed Nayla into his ear. The man suddenly gasped in shock as the sensation of pleasure took an abrupt turn to pain.

She had unsheathed the long, thin blade hidden in her hair ornament, ramming it deep into the back of his neck between the cervical vertebrae, effectively severing his spine.

The warlord slowly sank to the floor, his eyes rolled back into his head as the dying nerves wracked his body with involuntary spasms. Nayla wiped the blade clean on the counterpane, sheathing it as she tucked the ornament back into her hair. She slowly opened the door, peering out into the corridor.

There stood the servant, delivering wine to her next intended victim. Nayla stepped out, closing the door quietly behind her.

"Done so soon?" queried the servant.

"Yes, my lord was a wee bit excited and I assure you, I am very good at what I do. I made short work of him as you said to be quick about it; that others were awaiting my company."

She gestured the servant to be quiet as she whispered, "Do not disturb him. He was already made weary by his long journey; he wishes to be left to sleep."

The servant nodded in understanding. "You better make haste. Three others await their turn with you."

"Goodness! I am busy this evening," said Nayla with a smile as she disappeared into the next room.

"Ah, it is about time," a man admonished her as she ducked into his chamber. Short in stature, his dark eyes gleamed with a cruelty that seemed to compensate for his lack of height. His balding head and ring of graying hair made him look much older than his actual years.

Nayla smiled pleasantly at the man, taking the bottle of wine from his hands. "Allow me," offered Nayla, taking up a silver goblet. "Make yourself comfortable while I pour your wine."

The man wasted no time. He proceeded to strip his clothes off in frenzied anticipation. As he struggled with the mother-of-pearl buttons of his shirt, Nayla secretly reached into her silk bag for her vial of *perfume*. Removing the cork seal, she quickly poured some of the clear poison into the warlord's drinking vessel. She swirled the carmine liquid in the bowl of the goblet. As she turned to the man, he continued to fumble with his buttons. Nayla continued to smile at the flustered man as she inhaled the delicate bouquet of the red wine.

"This is delightful," said Nayla as she breathed in the aromatic scent emanating from the goblet; "fruity with a hint of flower."

She raised the silver goblet to her lips, tipping it back so as to taste the wine. She turned the goblet around so the red stain from her lip paint was facing away from him as she offered it to the man. He snatched it greedily away from her grasp and proceeded to gulp it down, throwing the empty goblet to the floor.

"Quickly, woman, time is wasting away here!" he ordered as he motioned for Nayla to finish unbuttoning his shirt as he stood before her. He proudly thrust his small, inflated chest out, his hands placed authoritatively on his hips. Her small fingers made easy work of the iridescent buttons, forcing them back through the holes that kept the man's shirt closed.

"The sleeves! Unbutton the sleeves!" he demanded, shaking his arms before her.

As Nayla worked to unfasten his cuffs, her heart began to pound loudly in her chest. *Why is the poison not working? He should have fallen over dead by now,* her thoughts raced as she toiled with the last button. The man tossed his silk shirt off, letting it fall to the floor in a heap.

"Get down on your knees before me," he barked his orders. "My trousers! Remove them!"

Nayla complied, her hands dropping down to unfasten his belt. As her fingers pretended to struggle with the buttons lining the front of his trousers in an attempt to buy more time, the man savagely seized her by the crown of her raven hair, thrusting her face to his groin.

"Not with your hands, use your teeth! Undo the buttons with your teeth," demanded the crazed man. His eyes looked wild with excitement as beads of perspiration collected on his forehead.

Why are you not dead yet? Nayla wondered as she was forced into submission before the warlord. As his trousers dropped down about his knees, Nayla proceeded to stand up. Again the warlord seized her by her hair, forcing her back down.

"Do not kneel before me like a fool. Get to work," muttered the man, wiping the sweat from his brow with the back of his hands.

Nayla cringed in disgust as he forced her face down to his groin. For the longest second she considered the flaccid, wrinkled member dangling before her like a ghastly, flesh-colored maggot. The overpowering, musky odor of urine and sweat emanating from the matted clump of pubic hair assaulted her senses. The mere thought of this wizened organ in her mouth made her want to retch.

Suddenly, the warlord's whole body began to quake. His hands clutched his chest as he stumbled backwards onto the bed. His eyes seemed to glaze over as the poison finally took hold, causing his heart to burst. He convulsed wildly, and then he was very still.

Satisfied that he was dead, Nayla made her way to the next chamber. She breathed in a slow, deep breath, composing herself before knocking lightly on the door as she entered. Inside another warlord awaited her much anticipated arrival.

As she stepped in, the man, already devoid of shirt, rose up from the bed. He beckoned her to approach.

Nayla placed her silk bag on the night stand. His hand patted the bed, motioning for her to sit down next to him. His black hair was peppered with gray and he seemed almost fatherly, until he placed his hand on her inner thigh, sliding it up along the silk fabric of her gown.

"So what is your pleasure, my lord?" asked Nayla, as she knelt on the bed behind him, massaging his shoulders to escape his groping hand.

The warlord groaned with pleasure as her fingers worked on the knotted muscles at the base of his neck. Suddenly, he dropped to his knees, clasping her small hands into his as he begged, "You must help me. I have done wrong. I must atone for my sins."

"What... whatever do you mean? I do not understand," replied Nayla, pulling away from his grasp.

"I have been bad. Very bad," he whispered, like an errant boy admitting to sinful thoughts. "I must be punished."

"Pardon me, my lord," responded Nayla, bewildered by his request.

"You heard me; I have been bad, most wicked. I must be punished for my actions," insisted the man, trembling in anticipation. He stood up, reaching for a bag next to the night stand. He quickly dumped its contents onto the bed. Inside were lengths of rope, a large, silk kerchief and a riding crop.

Nayla looked at the items scattered before her. She began to giggle at his absurdity as she responded, "Surely you jest!"

The warlord seized her by shoulders, shaking her as he declared; "I have been very bad! I *must* be punished!"

"Let me understand this, you want *me* to punish *you*? You wish for me to inflict pain onto your body?" asked Nayla in stunned disbelief.

"Yes! Yes! Tie me to the bed post! Gag me with this!" ordered the warlord excitedly, holding forth the silk kerchief.

Nayla reluctantly took the large square of silk from his hand.

"And then use this!" prompted the man, presenting her with the riding crop.

"Well, if you insist," responded Nayla, her shoulders arched in indifference.

She proceeded to bind his wrists high on the posts of the canopy bed as he knelt on the mattress.

"Tighter! Tie them tighter," he insisted as he strained at the silken cords.

"Whatever pleases you, my lord," answered Nayla, giving the rope a firm yank as she continued to play out his bizarre fantasy.

She dangled the silk kerchief before the warlord as she ascertained his instructions, "Are you sure you wished to be gagged?"

"Indeed, do it now!"

Without a word, Nayla complied with his wish, securing the silk kerchief around his mouth, and then tying a knot around to the back.

The little warrior leapt down from the bed, standing before the man with the riding crop in her hands. "Do you really wish for me to dole out this punishment?"

The man stared down at Nayla, his eyes wide and dark in anticipation and excitement. He enthusiastically nodded his head in response. She could see by his erection straining against the seams of his trousers that he was strangely aroused by all of this.

Nayla hopped back onto the bed. Standing behind her intended victim, her hand held the riding crop ready to whip his bare back. As she raised it up high, her hand began to tremble as haunting memories from long ago came flooding back of her own caning that left the multitude of scars upon her back. She could not find it in her heart to whip the warlord, even under his persistent urgings.

She lowered the riding crop. Leaning in close to the man's ear, using the leather-bound strip of bamboo to raise his chin, she whispered, "Tell me, just how bad have you been? Have you stolen from the people?"

The man nodded, his eyes gleaming in the candle light.

"Have you murdered innocent men? Perhaps you have raped helpless women?"

Again, he nodded. Through his gagged mouth she made out a muffled: *Yes!*

Nayla's blood began to boil as she listened to his muted confession. "Do you really wish for me to punish you?" asked Nayla, the tip of the riding crop lightly tracing the lines of his broad shoulders.

The man's eyes became wild with excitement as he pulled at his tethers, feigning his fear of her wrath. Nayla whispered softly into his ear, "If this is your desire, then so be it."

As her red lips lightly brushed by his cheek; the warlord's eyes closed in anticipation.

Nayla's hand swiftly unfastened the silk ribbon causing her dark hair to tumble down upon his bare shoulders as she drew the garrote around his neck, twisting it tighter and tighter.

"For all the innocent people that have died by your hands," grunted the warrior maiden, "now you shall die by mine!"

The man attempted to struggle to his feet only to have the warrior maiden tighten the wire embedded into the silk ribbon deeper around his neck as she forced him down onto his knees. His eyes seemed to bulge from his head and his face turned blue as Nayla braced one knee against his back as she continued to unmercifully strangle the man. When she was done, his head flopped forward, lolling on his chest.

"You were right. You did deserve to be punished," whispered Nayla into his now deaf ears.

Releasing an audible sigh of satisfaction for a job well done, she gathered her silk bag, heading out the door. For a brief moment, she stood alone in the corridor, regaining her composure. Her eyes gazed down to the window at the end of the large hallway; the sky was now a deep cobalt blue as stars began to dot the night sky. She was quickly running out of time.

She gently knocked on the last door in the corridor, smoothing out the creases of her gown before entering. The door opened and before her stood a very handsome Taijin man with smoldering brown eyes and ebony hair. He welcomed her, inviting Nayla into the bed chamber. For a moment she was stunned, somehow she had pictured all of Darraku's cronies as vile, ugly monsters, with lecherous smiles and that wanting, hateful look in their eyes.

"Well, are you not a pretty one," he said, his fingers casually stroking back the stray wisps of her long, dark tresses from her cheeks.

"Thank you, my lord," replied Nayla as she bowed, lowering her guard as he drew closer.

"Did I say you can speak?" the man reprimanded her as he circled around her. He eyed her defenseless form much like a hungry wolf would study its helpless prey before attacking.

Nayla shook her head in response.

The man smiled at her as his hand softly caressed her face. The fleeting thought of having to kill this man actually bothered Nayla for he was unlike the others. He was very pleasing to the eyes and gentle with his touch.

Without warning, the man forced Nayla against the wall; pinning her wrists with his hands. His large frame pressed up against her body as he kissed her roughly, thrusting his tongue into her mouth. His hands began to grope her body as his fingers fought to untie the long sash around her waist.

Nayla was caught off guard by his brutish assault. Immediately, she understood that his handsome, good looks did not change the fact he was a monster like the other warlords. He was just as cruel and calculating, perhaps even more murderous than the others.

The warrior maiden pushed him off of her small body, her right hand flicked her fan open to create a small, unimposing barrier between them. She stood before him, gently fanning herself as she considered the warlord. His large hand swept his black hair away from his brows.

"Oh, so you like it rough. You want to play, do you?" snarled the man as a lewd smile curled his lips.

The warlord seized her by her left hand, dragging her towards the bed. Nayla resisted, digging in her heels.

"Do not play coy with me! I was promised a woman and I shall have one!" insisted the man, tugging at the warrior maiden. "Do not waste any more of my time!"

"You stand corrected, sir. You are wasting my time!" Nayla's right wrist snapped up, closing the fan tightly into the palm of her awaiting hand. With jarring impact, she struck the warlord's hand, breaking his hold.

"Why you little witch!" he shouted as he rubbed the red welt swelling across the back of his hand. He turned to slap Nayla only to have her duck beneath his arm. As he turned in an attempt to backhand her with his fist, the fan she continued to wield in her right hand blocked his blow. With his right arm still extended, Nayla struck down hard with the end of the fan. The folded ribs drove deep into his biceps, separating the muscles until it made contact with bone.

As he screamed out in agony, Nayla's hand snapped the fan open once more. The man lunged at her upon which she pivoted out of the way. With a single broad, sweeping motion, the blade-like edge of the steel ribs sliced cleanly through the man's throat. His muted scream gurgled out from the fresh wound. His hands struggled in a futile bid to hold this gaping cut closed as blood pulsated from his carotid arteries. Dropping to his knees, he fell dead to the floor, his passion and anger now spilling out around him in a growing pool of crimson.

Nayla casually stepped over his body as she headed to the window. As she gazed out, a bright full moon shone down from an ebony sky. She quickly assessed she had one, perhaps one and one half hours before the first stroke of midnight. Her dark eyes quickly scanned the upper perimeter of the palace walls. Somewhere out there, the men of the Order waited for a sign.

She forced open the window. Grabbing hold of the rich velvet drapes hanging down almost to the floor, she tossed them outside.

"Here is your sign, men," whispered Nayla under her breath as she picked up a burning candle from the nightstand, holding it forth to ignite the fabric.

Soon, bright orange flames licked up high into the night sky as the burgundy velvet was quickly consumed by fire.

"Look, Markus! Over there!" exclaimed Arerys, pointing to the flames illuminating the palace wall.

"Could that be the sign Nayla spoke of?" asked Lando.

Arerys' far-seeing eyes focused on the figure at the window, he watched as Nayla shed her gown to reveal her warrior garb concealed beneath.

"Indeed it is," stated the Elf, taking his bow into his hand, "I pray the soldiers are few when we enter."

Crouched low in the undergrowth, watching the activity along the palace walls, the three men were so engrossed that even Arerys failed to notice the light footfalls approaching from behind. They froze as the glint of steel flashed in the moonlight by their throats. Lando and Markus gasped in surprise as Arerys turned swiftly, drawing his bow.

"You really should take greater care," said a familiar voice.

As the swords withdrew, the men turned to find Joval and his warriors silhouetted against the darkness.

"Thank goodness, Joval!" gasped Markus in relief. "We thought you had been killed."

"What happened?" asked Arerys. "Were you attacked?"

"No," answered the dark Elf. "The Imperial Soldiers reached Shesake a good half day before we arrived. They mounted an attack on Prince Tokusho's estate, killing his guards and making off with him in the process. We came in time to witness the carnage they left behind."

"Well, your arrival here is timely," stated the fair Elf. "Nayla is inside the palace. We only now received the signal to enter."

"Judging from the commotion, the palace guards have been alerted to Nayla's presence," noted Lando. Even he could hear the shouts as instructions were given to secure the gateway. The loud rattle and clamor of the portcullis as the large iron grate was dropped into place boomed in the night air.

"Already there are more soldiers guarding the entrance to the grounds," added Markus, noticing the men that gathered just inside the entrance of the gateway.

"We shall never enter from there," observed Arerys, turning to the dark Elf. "Any suggestions, Joval?"

"Follow me," said the Elf, leading Arerys and the others to the east wall of the palace. "We shall have to move quickly."

"Do you know of a secret passage?" asked Lando.

"No, we are climbing over the palace wall," stated Joval as he and his warriors armed their bows. They worked quickly to secure small, light grappling hooks of steel to their arrows. Joval gave the orders to launch their modified projectiles. The metal hooks clanged as they hit their mark, rattling loudly against the granite floor of the battlement as the Elves retrieved their slack lines until, with a loud '*clank*', the hooks latched onto a solid piece of masonry.

A guard posted to sentry duty watched in alarm as the hooks skidded across the stonework. He carelessly leaned over the wall to assess the danger below. Before he could withdraw, Joval took deadly accurate aim; his arrow mounted with a grappling hook struck the guard square on his chest with such force the soldier was send hurling off the battlement into the courtyard below.

Joval quickly worked the line until it was no longer slack; giving it a hard yank to ensure it was properly anchored. "Make haste men, we shall not keep Nayla waiting."

The warrior maiden hastily wiped the make-up off her face with her silk gown before disposing of it. She dashed to the wardrobe, her hands grabbing articles of clothing, throwing them to the floor until she found what she was looking for. Nayla picked up the sword, removing it from an ornate, black lacquered scabbard.

This shall do quite nicely, thought Nayla, her right hand checking the weight and balance of the deceased warlord's finely crafted weapon.

Before she had a chance to escape, Nayla could hear the heavy footfalls of approaching soldiers. She could hear their cries of shock as they entered the bed chambers, each one containing a dead warlord, each killed in a different fashion.

"Who could have done such a thing? Who could get past my guards to do such damage," raged the regent, looking upon the dead warlord still gagged and bound to the bed posts.

"There was only one person up here, my liege," answered the captain. "I delivered a woman – a courtesan you had hired, here as you had instructed."

Darraku's body trembled in rage as he shoved the captain to the floor. "You fool! That was no courtesan. There is only one woman who is capable of wreaking havoc of this magnitude. That was Nayla Treeborn, the warrior maiden of Orien!"

The soldiers all gasped in disbelief.

"Do not stand there like a bunch of blithering idiots, find the she-devil! Find her, and kill her!"

"She is still here," whispered the captain. "I had posted a guard at the bottom of the stairs, unless she climbed out of the window, she is still in the bed chamber with Master Shesaiji. She may be doing away with him as we speak."

The regent motioned for the men to check the room. The three soldiers crept down the corridor, Darraku followed close behind. Suddenly, the captain kicked the door in as all four burst into the darkened bed chamber. Their nostrils were assaulted by the acrid smell of smoke and freshly spilled blood still mingling in the air as they stumbled into the darkness. As their eyes adjusted to the cold light filtering in from the moon, they could see they were too late; Shesaiji lay dead in a crimson pool of blood on the floor before them.

Darraku knelt down to pick up the offending weapon, snapping the fan open. He examined the still-wet blood that seeped through the silk, obliterating the once beautiful image of a butterfly and blossoms. Without uttering a single word, he motioned for the soldiers to check the room. Two soldiers looked beneath the bed while the captain searched the wardrobe for the warrior maiden. All they found were the tools of destruction disguised as the benign accessories of a courtesan.

"She must have left through the window," said one soldier.

Another leaned out over the sill. "But how?" he asked as he pulled down the smoldering remains of the curtains.

Suddenly, Nayla dropped down from the dark recesses of the ceiling where she clung to the rafters. The men jumped in surprise, scrambling over the bed to nab her. Her hand flashed out sending a blinding cloud of white powder into their faces. All four began coughing, falling to their knees in pain as their eyes watered and burned.

Slamming the door shut, Nayla looped one end of her long, silk sash to the doorknob. She then dashed across the corridor to the opposite room, lashing the other end of the sash to its doorknob. Satisfied that the soldiers would meet with resistance as both doors opened inward, she charged down the dim-lit corridor with sword in hand.

As she quickly peered out of the window at the top of the stairway, she could see Arerys, Markus, Lando, and much to her surprise, Joval with his warriors.

Joval is alive! Nayla's heart rejoiced with the happy news. She watched for a brief instance, as the flash of cold steel glistened in the celestial glow of the stars and the moon as swords were drawn and readied for battle. She could make out the warriors of Orien mounting an attack from above with their bows and arrows.

With little time left to spare, Nayla raced down the spiral stairway. The sound of more footsteps pounding up the stairs, echoed loudly with the rattle of armor and weapons. The warrior maiden lowered her sword, moving deliberately and swiftly towards the enemy. She was unseen and unheard, charging towards them. As they rounded the corner, Nayla emitted a bone-rattling call summoned from deep within the core of her body as she collided headlong with the two soldiers in the lead.

She dropped to her knee just as the unsuspecting soldiers came over top of her. Immediately rising up, she slammed one soldier with her shoulder as the other met with the pommel of her sword handle. The men cried out in pain and surprise as this unexpected assault caused them to fall backwards onto their comrades. With the resounding crash and din of swords, shields and armor tumbling down the spiral stairway, the soldiers landed in a tangled heap on the floor below. Nayla calmly stepped over them, picking her way through the bodies and weapons that lay scattered all about. She scooped up a shield as she sprinted to the courtyard.

Before her, a full battle against the Imperial Soldiers raged. Nayla did not hesitate, joining in the fray. She dashed to Arerys' side, striking down the soldier he was fighting.

He smiled upon seeing Nayla. "Joval is alive!" announced Arerys as he turned to face his next foe.

"Yes! I know!" she called back, her sword now bathed in blood as she swiped at another soldier.

"Nayla!" shouted Joval as the dark Elf struck down a soldier. "You must get to the dungeon. You must free the prince!"

"Do you know the way, Nayla?" asked Arerys, ramming his sword through a soldier's body, kicking him off to release his blade.

"Yes! If you and the others can hold these soldiers at bay, I shall do my best," shouted Nayla over the screams and crash of steel against steel.

Just then, a soldier armed with a halberd swung out at Arerys. The Elf easily pivoted away from the large axe, but he did not anticipate the soldier's next move. Instead of raising the halberd up high to swing down, the soldier yanked the blade that was embedded into the ground, twisting his wrists as he did so. The axe abruptly swung upwards striking Arerys' sword with such force it was sent flying from his hand. The unarmed Elf stood before the soldier, dodging another incoming blow.

"Arerys!" called Nayla, tossing her sword to him. "Catch!" Her throw deliberately thrust the handle forward, allowing the Elf to seize it safely by the pommel. Arerys snatched it from the air, bringing it down upon the soldier as he struggled to free the blade of the axe from the ground.

He turned to see Nayla dash by Lando and Markus as they fought the enemy. Her eyes were set on the prison garrison. With nothing more than the shield in her hand, she raised it high to deflect the mighty blow of a halberd. The angry soldier lifted the great axe up high again; Nayla stood her ground until the very last second, angling away as the axe came down. The powerful blade struck the large, wooden hitching post. Horses tethered to the heavy wooden beam whinnied in fear, rearing and straining at their reins to escape. The soldier grunted loudly as he struggled to remove his halberd that had bitten deep into the post. As he struggled, Nayla turned on him. Taking up the shield, she tilted it sideways. With all her might, she slammed the edge of the shield into the soldier's throat. Her adversary stumbled backwards from the impact, his windpipe crushed by the debilitating blow she delivered.

Nayla wasted no time to see if the soldier was indeed dead. She dodged and angled as deadly blades swung towards her as she made her way to the garrison. Arerys watched as she disappeared from his sight.

"What is she doing? She has no weapons!" called Arerys, alarmed by her actions.

"That shall hardly deter her," stated Joval, taking a glancing blow from his rival.

The entrance into the gloomy, stone structure appeared unguarded as Nayla crept through. As her eyes adjusted to the light from the flames of the torches mounted on the far wall, a dark figure leapt out from the shadows. He threw his arms around her body, seizing the warrior maiden in a powerful bear-hug.

"Got you!" exclaimed the captain in triumph, tightening his arms around Nayla's small body. He held her close, squeezing her in a constricting embrace.

With her arms pinned firmly to her side, she lacked the strength to break his hold. She ceased her futile struggle.

"Now that is more like it!" growled the captain. "I hardly think the regent will care now if I have my way with you."

As he pressed his nose against her head to inhale the sweet scent of her perfumed hair, Nayla slammed the side of her head into his face, cracking his cheekbone.

The captain screamed in pain, wrapping his arms around her so tightly she was now raised off the ground. With her arms still firmly pinned to her side, Nayla reached down with her right hand, seizing a small bit of skin and flesh on his inner thigh; grinding it between her finger and thumb as it ripped away from his muscle.

The man wailed in agony, cursing as he dropped Nayla so he may nurse the stinging pain. Driving her fist hard into his face, the captain stumbled back from the impact. The warrior maiden turned to run only to be tackled from behind. As she fell to the ground, the captain seized her by her ankles and with a violent twist, flipped Nayla onto her back. Crouching between her knees, he pinned her to the ground by her wrists.

She could feel the heat and smell the rancid odor of his foul breath as he leaned in close to her face, hissing into her ear, "So, do you still think you can make some time for me?"

Overpowered by the much larger man, he bore down with all his weight to subdue the warrior maiden. Nayla gave him a small smile, as though she now surrendered, but the captain was not to be fooled again. He pressed down unmercifully, trapping her against the cold, hard ground.

Suddenly, Nayla's legs flew up; wrapping around the captain's arms, slamming them against each other. She quickly locked her ankles together. He was now ensnared between her legs as she rolled to her side. With his arms securely trapped and unable to right himself, Nayla continued her movement, rolling forward. A distinct popping sound could be heard just as the man screamed in excruciating pain as she easily dislocated both his shoulders.

"This is all the time I can spare," said the little warrior, kneeling over the groaning figure. Her hands systematically searched his body until she found what she was looking for. Taking a large ring festooned with many keys, she ventured further into the garrison that now echoed with the loud groans of the captain as he lay writhing in agony.

Nayla ducked into the long hallway. She gagged. For a moment, she was almost overcome by the foul stench of decay and human waste hanging thick in the dank, musty air. Suddenly, the whole area echoed as prisoners pressed up against the iron bars, looking in awe at the tiny, raven-haired warrior as she darted from cell to cell, her dark eyes desperately searching for the prince.

"It is she! It is the warrior maiden of Orien!" called out one prisoner.

"At last! Salvation from this hell-hole!" shouted another, as filthy hands strained through the bars to touch Nayla.

"She has come to rescue us! She has come to set us free!" an ecstatic voice rang through the cell block.

Soon a chorus erupted into the night air as the prisoners began to chant: *"Freedom! Freedom! Freedom!"* They rattled defiantly against the iron bars, pounding their tin cups against the floor and the walls. Nayla's ears ached with the overwhelming racket that echoed and amplified through the corridor. She took stock of all the dirty, emaciated faces; their sunken, vacant eyes pleading to her. She did not have the heart to leave them, yet she did not have the time to try each key to set them free.

Nayla tossed the ring of keys to one of the prisoners. "Set yourselves free!" shouted the warrior maiden over the growing din. "Do any of you know where they hold Prince Tokusho?"

An elderly prisoner who had not seen the light of day for almost two decades nodded to her, his gnarled, filthy finger pointed to a passage way at the far end of the corridor.

The torches illuminating the passage flickered and danced. It was the only sign of Nayla's presence as she silently glided by, making her way through the long, gloomy tunnel.

The little warrior's eyes quickly adjusted to the dim-lit passage, her ears could discern the voices of three, perhaps four soldiers that stood between her and the young prince. As she hastened her pace, the soldiers assigned to guard this special prisoner glanced up. Nayla glared at them, indeed there were four guards, and each was armed with a sword. She assessed the passage to reach the prince was tall, but very narrow. If they choose to attack, they shall have to do so one soldier at a time.

Suddenly, Nayla charged towards the first guard. He stood his ground, waiting for her to come within his striking distance. As she neared, the soldier scoffed, "She bears no weapons! She is anxious to die!"

Raising his sword high over his head, he swung down at Nayla. She quickly pivoted to the soldier's right side; seizing the pommel of his sword handle she easily yanked it away, breaking the hold against his thumbs. In one smooth motion, the blade swung down and backwards toward the soldier, striking him in his groin. As he doubled over in pain, Nayla rammed the pommel straight up under the soldier's chin, cracking his unshaven jaw line in two. He was unconscious before he hit the ground.

Nayla seemed almost nonchalant as she stepped on the soldier's chest to pass over him. She glanced up to see the next soldier staring in disbelief that this diminutive, unarmed woman had taken down a man much larger than she. With no room in the narrow passage to slash out at her sideways, the soldier pointed the tip of his sword towards her heart. He lunged straight for her. To his surprise, she did not retreat. Instead, Nayla deliberately stepped towards him, angling away from the blade so she was positioned to his immediate left. She jammed his arms so he was unable to slash out at her. Seizing hold of the soldier's left wrist with her left hand, she punched out at his right bicep. She hit his arm with the extended knuckle of her middle finger, separating his muscles to strike down to his very bone.

The pain was instant, resounding through the soldier's body, effectively killing the nerves in his arm. His sword tumbled to the ground. As Nayla retracted her punch, her right arm folded, slamming her elbow up into the soldier's vulnerable throat, crushing his windpipe. The soldier collapsed onto his hands and knees, clutching his throat as he gasped and sputtered, struggling to breathe. Nayla unceremoniously stepped onto his back, flattening him to the ground as she sized up her next victim.

As her eyes locked onto the third soldier, he drew his sword high over his head, waiting for Nayla to approach. She veered closer and as she watched him, the slight movement of his shoulders telegraphed he was about to strike. The little warrior suddenly rushed the man, jamming his forearms over her head so he was not able to bring the blade down. The palm of Nayla's right hand abruptly struck upwards, popping up the end of the sword handle. The combination of the soldier's own grip on his sword and Nayla's upward strike on the sword pommel caused the blade to slam down onto the soldier's helmet. The shockwave of the impact was enough to be felt right through the man's skull. His eyes rolled up into his head as he crumpled onto his knees, falling forward.

Nayla calmly stepped over the body. Before her stood the last sol-dier; behind him, Prince Tokusho waited and watched in awe as his rescuer easily picked off one man after another. She sized up the last soldier standing. He trembled before this she-devil, his sword quaking in his hands as Nayla slowly advanced towards him. Again, she timed her movement, waiting for the exact moment he would strike.

As he brought his sword down, Nayla moved in, jamming his arms overhead. Seizing the sword handle by the gap between the soldier's own hands, she suddenly dropped straight down. As she lowered her-self, she placed her right foot against the soldier's left hip. Using his own energy as he fought to bring his sword down upon her, Nayla's foot hoisted the man up and over her body. He was sent crashing onto his back as she, using his momentum, rolled backwards over the man's body, landing squarely onto his chest. The last image to be seared into his memory was Nayla leaning down with all her body weight, forcing the blade through the soldier's throat to his cervical vertebrae, sever-ing his spinal cord thus ending his wild, thrashing spasms. With the tip of her sword buried into the ground under his neck, she pushed down on his head with one hand and pulled with the other to extract the sword.

Wiping off the mixture of blood and earth on the soldier's uniform, she advanced towards the bars of the prison. With no key to open the padlock, Nayla took the cumbersome sword, striking and hacking at the lock. Prince Tokusho stood back, shielding his eyes as sparks flew with each strike. Finally, the worn and rusted padlock broke, falling to the ground.

"Now I understand why you are a legend in Orien," said the prince. "Thank you for coming to my aid."

Nayla bowed before him. "With all due respect, my lord, legends usually apply to long-departed heroes from days gone by. I assure you, I am still very much alive... at least for the time being."

"Nonetheless, heroes make their mark by the blade of a sword. You do not even need a sword to leave your mark in this world."

"Well, my liege, you are about to make your mark, we must get you to the throne room immediately!"

She took him by the hand, guiding him through the dark, narrow underground corridor. As they emerged from the prison garrison, a riot was in full swing in the center courtyard as liberated prisoners joined Joval and the others in their fight against the Imperial Soldiers. Though unarmed, the taste of freedom mixed with revenge empowered the men, driving them on with sheer adrenaline.

Nayla and the prince crept along the stone wall, dashing up the stairs. She led the boy through the large archways, through a massive hall dripping in opulence. Everywhere beautiful, gold candelabras and chandeliers illuminated the high ceiling while the walls were ensconced with magnificent brocade tapestries and rich, velvet curtains.

"This is how your uncle spends the people's hard-earned money, my lord. Living high off of the blood and sweat of others so he may enjoy a decadent lifestyle," whispered Nayla. She escorted the prince into the throne room, pushing open the heavy double doors.

Prince Tokusho's eyes darted about the grand room with high vaulted ceilings and tall windows. A winding staircase led up to the row of balconies lining the walls of this spectacular room. Against the opposite end of the room, the gilded throne, its high back and seat cushioned in rich, burgundy velvet awaited the prince.

"The vault where your father has stored the crown is over there," said Nayla, pointing to the far corner of the room. "Did you bring the key?"

"What key do you speak of?" asked the young prince.

"Emperor Shekata left a key to access the vault. I was told only you can unlock it," stated Nayla.

"I have no such key!" cried out Tokusho as they rushed to the corner of the throne room. Concealed behind the heavy drapery was the great vault

Nayla studied the door. The hinges were on the inside of the locked vault. There were no pins to remove. She tugged at the lever, but it was securely sealed. Pry marks revealed Darraku's own failed attempts to access the vault. Her hands traced the panel of granite for any discrepancies or weak points.

"What is this?" asked Nayla, her fingertips touched the engraved impression on the cold, hard stone. There, carved into the granite, two hand prints became apparent; a small, slender one overlaid upon a larger imprint.

"These must be the hand prints of my father and my mother," said Tokusho. His hand lay over top as he fought to remember his long-departed parents.

"The elders of Orien said you are the only one who can unlock this vault. They swear you possess the key. Perhaps it is a riddle. Think, my lord! What do you have that the regent does not? What is the one thing you possess that he lacks – that prevents him from entering this vault?"

"I do not know! The only thing I have left of my parents is this legacy: a title, a palace and riches that are no longer mine."

"Titles, money, jewels… these items can be had by anyone!" stated Nayla. "Think! What is the one thing you possess that no one else does; the one thing that may give you the power to open this vault!"

"I am a mere mortal, the only child of Emperor Shekata's and Empress Metasu's flesh and blood! I do not possess the power to penetrate this slab of stone."

Nayla looked at the prince, "That is it! Nobody but Lindras Weatherstone can do this!" Her hand felt the perfect impressions, the every line and wrinkle bore on the palm of a hand.

"Lindras Weatherstone?"

"Yes, the Wizard of the West, his element is the earth. He helped to seal this vault and the only one who shall unlock it is the rightful heir to the throne. Place your hand over the impression," instructed the warrior maiden, her eyes sparkled with excitement in the candlelight.

The prince placed the palm of his right hand directly over the ones left by his departed parents.

"Push!" ordered Nayla as she pressed her shoulder against the great panel of granite. "Push with all your might!"

"This is useless. It will not budge," groaned the prince, his hand slapped against the cold, hard rock. "Oww!" The palm of his hand throbbed, turning an angry shade of red as the prince shook off the sharp pain.

"Are you hurt?" asked Nayla, taking his reddened palm, checking for shattered bones. Suddenly, it dawned on her. She reached into her vest pocket, pulling out a throwing dart. The long, thin blade came alive in the flickering light of the overhead candles.

"This is the key!" announced Nayla, holding forth the slim projectile.

"Your blade?"

"No, your blood!" said the warrior maiden as she seized the prince by his wrist.

"What?" asked the startled young prince, attempting to free himself from her grasp.

"It is the one thing Darraku does not possess; he is not of your father's and mother's blood! Forgive me for this, my liege," said Nayla as she lanced two thin lines across the palm of his hand.

Blood slowly seeped up through the superficial wound as Nayla positioned his palm over the impression on the stone. The ground rumbled and groaned while overhead, the light cast by the many candles flickered and danced as the palace shook to its very foundations. The great stone door slowly swung back. The prince reached up for a candle, holding it forth into the dark vault. Inside, a massive treasure trove of gold and silver bullion; precious gems of emeralds, sapphires and rubies glistened in the candle's unsteady light. The prince gasped at the unexpected wealth they had stumbled upon.

"There!" said Nayla, "On the pedestal!"

Perched on top was the emperor's golden crown, studded with emeralds and rubies and encrusted with diamonds. It sparkled in the candle's light. The prince reached for the crown with his trembling hands, his heart racing with the excitement of the moment.

"To the throne! Quickly!" shouted Nayla.

The prince snatched up the crown in his hand, momentarily surprised by its weight. Nayla grabbed him by his arm, dashing up the steps to the throne.

"Sit!" she ordered.

The prince threw himself onto the throne as Nayla raised the crown over his head as she announced: "As God is my witness I crown thee the new emperor of -"

Nayla's words fell short. The prince glanced up to see the silver blade of a dagger thrust against her throat as a dark figure appeared from behind the throne, grabbing the warrior by her hair.

"So you are the fearsome warrior maiden of Orien," growled an angry Darraku. "Somehow, I imagined a woman of much greater stature. You are a runt: a pip-squeak!"

"And you are much more corpulent than I thought, but I suppose living high off the taxes you collect from the people will do that to you," hissed Nayla.

He pressed the blade against Nayla throat, as he eyed the gleaming gold crown with its dazzling array of jewels.

Prince Tokusho rose up from the throne as he pleaded, "Do not harm her, if it is me you want, then I am yours."

"Dear nephew, I may not be able to kill you, but I can certainly kill this woman," mocked Darraku, yanking back on Nayla's hair. "All I need is to keep you off the throne for another three minutes. When the clock strikes midnight, my time shall come and yours has passed."

As the prince raised his arms in surrender, again he pleaded, "Let the warrior go."

"Just a little more time and the crown shall be mine!" gloated the regent.

The young prince glared at his uncle as he declared, "What you do is tantamount to high treason!"

"Treason you say?" asked Darraku, mocking his words with a sinister laugh. "How can this be treason? The only witness to your failure to secure your title shall be dead. As far as the people shall be concerned, the boy prince was too cowardly to ascend to the throne, to face the responsibilities that come with power!"

"You have more eyes watching you than you can count," shouted Joval, throwing open the double doors as he marched into the throne room. He was followed by Markus, Lando and Arerys, the warriors of Orien, along with the multitude of freed prisoners that poured through the doors into the great room. Their advance was short-lived when it soon became apparent Darraku now held Nayla by the edge of his dagger.

"Ah, it is the Stewart of Nagana! How kind of you to show for my coronation!" said Darraku with a laugh. "Or perhaps, you and your friends have come to see me put this little warrior out of her misery?"

Arerys looked over to Joval. Both began to edge closer to the throne as those behind them followed, pressing in on their quarry.

"I shall kill her!" warned the regent, pulling back on Nayla's head to fully expose her throat. The Elves froze, raising their hands to motion for all to cease their advance.

"I am but one! The lives of many are counting on you, Prince Tokusho, do it now! Take your place!" demanded Nayla.

"No..." gasped the prince, shocked that this woman would willingly give her life for him.

"Take the crown," ordered Nayla, tossing it to the prince.

Tokusho caught the crown in his trembling hands, raising it over his head. He faltered as he watched crimson droplets of blood begin to trickle from Nayla's neck.

As the great clock in the palace tower sounded the first stroke of midnight, Tokusho froze. His frightened eyes searched Nayla's for reassurance.

"Do it! Stake your claim! There shall be no second chance for you or your people!" shouted the warrior maiden. Her eyes scanned the anxious crowd standing before her. Seeking out the fair Elf, she called out, "I am sorry, Arerys!"

"Nayla!" screamed Arerys in anguish.

"You dare defy me!" snarled Darraku as he yanked back sharply on Nayla's hair. He raised the dagger high to plunge into her throat as the warrior maiden closed her eyes, preparing to meet her fate.

"Darraku!" a voice echoed from high above.

The regent glanced up to the balcony just in time to see an arrow fly towards him, striking him directly in his forehead. For a moment, Darraku reeled from the impact; his dark, lifeless eyes stared up in disbelief at the shaft of the arrow protruding from his head. Suddenly, he keeled over backwards, very dead.

Nayla knew full well anarchy and chaos shall follow if the monarchy was sought by the powerful warlords or wealthy landholders vying for control. She fell to her knees by the throne, "Now, my lord, before it is too late!" she pleaded.

Prince Tokusho's trembling hands struggled to position the crown upon his head as the distant chime of the clock announced the midnight hour.

For a moment, a prolonged hush filled the grand room as the last chime tolled, echoing through the night air. Its sound reverberated in the hearts of all present. As the echo dissolved into the darkness, the realization that it heralded the beginning of a new era for the people of Orien finally began to sink in. Suddenly, the room erupted with the cheers of the prisoners and the palace servants that had joined in the uprising. The new emperor rose up confidently from his throne, offering his hand to the warrior maiden to lift her to her feet.

"You did it," said Nayla, releasing a great sigh of relief as she used her forearm to wipe away the thin line of blood from her throat.

"No, you did it," smiled Tokusho. "If it were not for you, I would not be here now. How can I ever thank you enough?"

Paying homage to the young emperor, Nayla knelt before him to kiss the ring bearing the royal family's insignia worn on the index finger of his right hand. "All I ask is that you govern the lands as your father would see fit. Emperor Shekata ruled with kindness and compassion, with a reverence for all life. He had the foresight and the humanity to allow his people, no matter what their race or religion, to live without fear of oppression or persecution."

"I shall honor your wish, warrior maiden. I know it would please my father."

As Nayla rose to her feet, the men of the Order raced up to the throne to embrace her in a great hug. She smiled as Arerys stood before her. He gave her a generous smile as he pulled her close to kiss her lovingly upon her lips.

The new emperor stared up in awe at Arerys as he exclaimed, "You are a fair Elf!"

Arerys bowed before the boy as he responded, "No, I am just an Elf."

Joval introduced Tokusho to the men of the Order, "This is Prince Arerys of Wyndwood, Prince Markus of Carcross and Sir Lando Bayliss of Cedona." Each bowed in respect to the newly crowned emperor. "And of course, you know Lady Nayla Treeborn."

Tokusho expressed his gratitude when the sea of people before him suddenly parted as an Elf, with bow still in hand, advanced to the throne.

Nayla's eyes narrowed as she scrutinized the Elf kneeling before her, his head bowed in humility.

"Valtar Briarwood," announced the warrior maiden as she stared down at him. "It was your arrow that downed the regent."

"Yes, my lady," acknowledged Valtar.

Joval looked on in stunned disbelief, his lifelong friend that had betrayed both he and Nayla had returned. Despite their harsh exchange of words, Valtar appeared in time to save the life of the one he despised so.

"You spared me from certain death, Valtar Briarwood," said Nayla. "A life for a life; is that what you seek from me?"

The Elf's head remained bowed as he answered contritely, "I seek your forgiveness, my lady. I pray you can find it in your heart to forgive this worthless soul. Though I spared your life, now I am asking for you to take pity upon mine."

"Do not grovel before me, it is unbecoming of my warriors to behave in this manner," replied Nayla.

"So you forgive me?" Valtar asked hopefully as he rose up before her.

Nayla looked to Joval.

"It would take a very big person to find the strength to forgive, Nayla," stated Joval. She could see in the Elf's eyes that he was hoping for some sign of compassion.

She turned to Valtar, looking up at the Elf. For a long moment, she considered him as the others waited in silence for her decision. Suddenly, the crowd gasped in surprise as they watched her fist fly out punching Valtar square in his face. The Elf fell backwards, dumbfounded by her assault.

Nayla knelt down by his side as she whispered, "That was for my loss. I believe I *may* begin to consider forgiving you."

As he lay sprawled on the floor rubbing his aching jaw, she extended her hand to assist Valtar up onto his feet.

"I promise, I shall make up for my foolish ways," vowed the Elf, taking her hand. "In the meantime, my captain, war looms on the horizon for those in western Orien. The Imperial Soldiers have breached the Furai Mountains via the Borai passage. It shall only be a matter of time before they surround the fortress city."

"The Sorcerer, does he lead them into battle?" asked Joval.

"Indeed he does," confirmed the Elf, slinging his bow back over his shoulder.

"And the Wizard of the West, where is Lindras?" asked Markus.

"At this point, I do not know. I met up with him when I was banished from Nagana. We sent word to your father, King Bromwell that we were in dire need of his help and all those he can muster from the Alliance."

"But how?" asked Markus.

"I *borrowed* Nayla's falcon, it was the only bird that knows the way to your father's castle," answered Valtar. "Lindras sent word to meet in the Emerald Forest."

"Are you daft? There is no passage through the Iron Mountains from the Emerald Forest," stated Lando.

"Perhaps the Wizard is aware of a passage the rest of us do not know of," suggested Arerys.

"Or perhaps he shall create a new passage using his mighty powers," said Valtar.

Nayla and the men of the Order looked upon Valtar, and then simultaneously burst out laughing.

"Obviously, you do not know Lindras as we do," said Markus with a chuckle.

"Yes, his powers leave much to be desired," added Lando. "The potential is there, but he has no desire to perfect his craft."

"Even so," said Markus; "we all know there is a vast river, deep and treacherous coursing the length of the Iron Mountains. None can cross into Orien except from Talibarr via Deception Pass."

"Say what you will," replied Valtar tersely. "Lindras promised to return with help. I believe his words to be true."

Suddenly, a cold wind howled through the corridors, causing the many candle flames to flicker or extinguish in response. It whipped through the throne room, embracing all in a great chill. Lightning flashed across the sky as dark gray clouds materialized from nowhere to release a torrent of rain. The palace shook to its very foundations as thunder rumbled and lightning crackled directly overhead. All ducked to the floor as the high windows imploded, showering them with a multitude of sparkling shards of glass.

The huge double doors into the throne room blew open with a mighty gust of wind. Before them stood Lindras Weatherstone, to his left was Tylon Riverdon, the Wizard of the South; to his right stood Tor Airshorn, the Wizard of the North.

"Well, I am glad someone still has faith in me," said Lindras as he and his brother Wizards entered the throne room. The citizens of Orien dropped down to their knees. Bowing in reverence, they recognized the Wizards as the spirits of the elements, the ones they believe worked with their God to guide and protect them.

Nayla raced through the crowd, embracing the Wizard in a hug. "Thank goodness you are here, Lindras! I knew you would come, I just did not know when or where you would appear!" she exclaimed as Arerys and the others stepped forward to greet the Wizard.

Lindras drew back his great hood; his blue-gray eyes twinkled as he introduced Tor and Tylon to his friends. "Unfortunately, time is of the essence, there shall be more time for pleasantries should we survive this war," said Lindras apologetically.

"We must leave now if we are to put a stop to Eldred Firestaff's treachery!" urged Tylon. The long, silver whiskers of his moustache and beard held neatly together by a band of gold glistened as the crystal orb on his staff pulsated. Suddenly, a steady glow of light was projected onto the high, vaulted ceiling for all to see. Images of an immense army laying siege to the fortress city played out before them. Soldiers employed great battering rams to hammer on the portcullis and the wooden gates that now secured both the east and west entrances to Nagana.

"It shall take us almost two weeks to return," stated Joval with a gasp. "Even if we ride like the wind – pushed our steeds to exhaustion, we shall never arrive in time. Our people are doomed to perish!"

Tor stepped forward, his weathered and lined face creased with a kind smile as he asked, "Why ride like the wind when one can ride on the wind?"

"What do you speak of Wizard? What are you suggesting?" asked

Arerys, his brows twisted into a frown.

"Of course, my brother!" said Lindras excitedly. "They can travel by way of our powers!"

"Lindras, these are mortals and Elves you speak of, I hardly think they are suitable to travel as we do," warned Tylon, shaking his head in disapproval.

"We have no choice! We must leave now!" stated Nayla. "By whatever means, Lindras! Make it so!"

"Nayla, be careful what you ask for," whispered Lando, leaning in close so only she may hear.

"I admit to transport mortals and Elves is not without risk, especially since we now lack the combined powers of Eldred's staff, but it can still be done," assured Lindras.

"So be it," responded Tylon, turning to guide Nayla and the men to the courtyard. "But be forewarned, it shall not be a pleasant ride."

As the warriors of Orien turned to follow the men of the Order, Emperor Tokusho shouted, "Lady Treeborn, warrior maiden of Orien, a new dawn rises over our country! I shall hold true to my words by honoring your wish. I pray we shall meet again!"

Nayla turned to look upon the young ruler. She bowed as she exited the room: "Do your father proud, my lord! If the fates conspire and luck smiles down upon us, perhaps we shall meet again."

In the courtyard, the men of the Order and the warriors gathered. Lando returned to Nayla her swords, whereupon she secured them to her belt and refastened her cloak. She then stood next to Arerys, anxiously clutching his hand. As the group stood in a tight circle, the three Wizards raised their staff on high. The crystal orbs began to glow, driving back the darkness of night with a spectacular show of white light. A cold wind howled down from the north, swirling around them faster and faster. Suddenly, a bolt of lightning split the angry sky. In a blink of an eye, they were gone.

CHAPTER 21

THE WAR OF THE WIZARDS

It was as though the air was sucked from their lungs and their bodies shredded by invisible hands as the combined powers of the three Wizards delivered them back to western Orien. Nayla, the men of the Order and the Elven warriors materialized from thin air as angry storm clouds rumbled through the black sky, shaking the earth as the sound of thunder crashed overhead. The Wizards' reluctant passengers were dumped unceremoniously into the center of the courtyard before the palace, landing hard into a dazed heap.

From the tangle of arms and legs, Lando groaned in pain as he grunted at Nayla, "Did I not warn you to be careful of what you ask for?"

"I shall never ask to be moved in such a manner again, that was not my idea of riding the wind. It was more like being pummeled, thrashed and whipped by the elements," complained Nayla as she struggled for her breath.

"I told you it would not be pleasant," said Tylon wryly, extending a hand to help the warrior maiden up.

Arerys and Joval helped Markus and Lando up onto their feet as the resonating boom of the battering rams slammed against the gates.

"Quickly men, head up to the battlements! My brothers and I shall deal with Eldred!" yelled Lindras as he and the Wizards of the North and South touched the crystal orbs of their staff together. In a brilliant flash of white light, the three instantly vanished.

Joval raced up the stone stairway, leading Nayla and the others to the west wall overlooking the thousands of Imperial Soldiers massing below. They joined the other warriors, battling back the soldiers that breached the high wall. The loud whine of hundreds of arrows skimming over their heads launched by the modified catapults filled the air. Nayla watched as the soldiers below merely raised their shields to deflect the hail of arrows.

"Do not launch the catapults simultaneously. The attack must be random, not timed or the enemy shall anticipate when to raise their shields!" shouted Nayla to the captain below who was orchestrating the assault in her absence.

The next catapult attack was random, catching the soldiers below by surprise as arrow after arrow rained down upon them with deadly results.

Valtar and the men of the Order joined Joval and the other warriors in beating down the soldiers that breached the wall while dodging the enemy arrows that skimmed by.

Each time the warriors threw the ladders down, the ladders were repeatedly erected. And each time, more soldiers took the place of those tossed to the wayside.

"Ropes! I need ropes and horses!" Nayla shouted to the warriors below. "Tie them to the horses and throw the other end to us!"

The men grabbed hold of the ropes as they were tossed up.

"Secure them to the ladders," ordered the warrior maiden. "When I give the order, we shall remove them all at once!"

As the warriors held the enemy at bay, tossing soldiers down upon those waiting below, the ropes were tied onto the ladders. Giving the signal to Nayla that the task was done, she ordered the captain below to ready the horses.

"Stand clear men," shouted Nayla as she motioned to the captain below. Whipping the steeds into action, the animals bolted. The ropes immediately grew taut as the horses panicked, galloping across the courtyard. Suddenly, ladders were hoisted up and over the walls as frightened soldiers in the midst of climbing were abruptly hauled up, some with such force they were catapulted into the center courtyard.

"Good thinking!" Joval shouted to Nayla as he and the other warriors pitched the ladders over the wall and into the courtyard. Now the warriors of Orien were able to aim their arrows without the constant threat of soldiers breaching the walls of the fortress city.

An ear-splitting cry suddenly drowned out the sound of battle, piercing the night sky: "*Wraarggh!*"

"What in hell's name is that?" asked Markus, his eyes straining in the darkness to make out the massive black shadow silhouetted against the still dark horizon.

As Arerys released another arrow, he glanced up. "I do believe it is… a dragon!"

"Oh no, you jest! That is not a dragon!" protested Markus.

"Oh yes it is, Markus. And guess who is riding high on the back of the beast."

Eldred's dark, recessed eyes glowed as he basked in the carnage from the back of the ancient reptile. Its massive head shook in rage as it attempted to shed the metal restraints that clamped its jaws firmly shut. Its large, plate-like scales rattled loudly in protest against the chains that effectively hobbled its large, leathery wings, preventing the great dragon from taking flight.

"Keep steady you stupid beast!" shouted Eldred, striking the dragon on its head with his staff. He watched as a black sea of soldiers pounded relentlessly on the walls of the fortress city like the waves crashing down to wear away the walls of a sea cliff.

The Sorcerer squealed with delight. He lowered his staff to the surrounding forests, discharging a red ball of fire. The flames spread rapidly, consuming the dry forest litter and igniting the shrubs, groves of bamboo and stands of trees with a rampant hunger.

"This ends now, Eldred!" demanded Lindras, standing before the Sorcerer.

Eldred cackled like a demented soul as he looked down at the Wizard. "You pathetic fool! You are no match for me! Do not even think that your powers alone can take me down!"

"He is not alone!" declared Tylon Riverdon, appearing before him. He stood defiantly by Lindras' side.

"Ha! What is this, the Wizard of the South comes out of hiding? This is too funny! Where did you dig him up from Lindras? The sands of the Painted Desert?" snorted the Sorcerer with amusement.

"This ends now, Eldred! Do not force us to use our powers!" shouted Lindras.

"Let me see, your element is *earth*. Tylon's element is *water*. Hmm, I believe together, you make *mud*!" said the Sorcerer, throwing back his head to release a diabolical laugh.

With that said, both Lindras and Tylon lowered their staff, discharging a bolt of blue energy to send Eldred hurling to the ground.

The Sorcerer scrambled to his feet, immediately drawing close to the dragon's body, using its massive form as a shield from which to prepare his assault on the Wizards. As he lay in wait for Tylon and Lindras to seek him out, unbeknownst to the Sorcerer, Tor Airshorn was close at hand.

The Wizard of the North silently approached the dragon, his open hand raised to the great beast as a gesture for calm. The ancient reptile stared down at the Wizard, managing a stifled snort through its suffocating muzzle. "You poor creature," lamented Tor with sincere empathy, recalling his many years trapped in the body of a dragon due to Eldred's vengeful nature. "I know all too well what it is like to be enslaved – to be trapped in a like manner."

Tor gave the dragon a gentle pat on its snout as he gazed into the black, slit-like pupils of its fiery, red eyes. He could sense how its state of enslavement had broken the magnificent creature's spirit. Taking pity upon the beast, Tor struggled to remove the heavy iron pin that clamped its muzzle painfully closed. The dragon gave its massive head a shake, sending the metal restraint flying. It bounced and careened across the field of battle, striking down all those in its path. Those near to the ones wounded by the flying metal screamed in horror as the dragon suddenly raised its head, belching a steady stream of fire in their direction.

The beast lowered its head, scooping Tor onto its snout. The dragon swung its head around, depositing the Wizard onto his back.

The Wizard of the North moved down the dragon's expansive back. He worked to unshackle the tangle of iron chains holding the beast's wings down. From his high vantage point, Tor glanced down to see Eldred preparing to launch a ball of fire at Lindras and Tylon as they rounded the dragon's hindquarters.

As the Sorcerer lowered his staff, releasing a flaming ball of energy, Tor summoned the power of his element, the wind, to blow the projectile of flames from the Wizards' path.

Lindras and Tylon immediately retreated in response.

Eldred's eyes shot up to Tor. "You again!" hissed the Sorcerer, as he scowled at the Wizard of the North. "You cannot leave well enough alone. Was it not enough I had turned you into one of these creatures!"

"That is why I am setting this one free!" shouted Tor, pulling the last of the chains away from the dragon's scaly back.

The great beast bowled the Sorcerer over as it abruptly unfolded its massive wings, stretching them out for the first time in centuries. It bellowed as its head recoiled, its huge plate-like belly scales reverberating with its mighty call.

As its head tipped back, Tor uttered some words into the beast's ear before sliding off its back to join Lindras and Tylon.

Another great roar emanated from the dragon. Its large wings began to beat as it raised its massive form off the ground. Lifting itself over the tree line, the dragon flew towards the fortress city, swooping low over the horrified soldiers. The frightened men scattered as the beast blasted its fiery breath across the battlefield. The wind churning beneath its large, leathery wings was enough to knock the soldiers off their feet. Now the enemy was forced to divert their attack from the walls of the fortress city to the dragon as it skimmed low over their heads.

Without the body of the great reptile to shield him, Eldred stood before Tor, Lindras and Tylon. Lowering his staff, he took aim.

"Enough, Eldred! You have a long overdue appointment with the Maker of All! Come with us now, it is ill-advised to put up a fight!" ordered Lindras.

"I shall not be the one to fight you," snarled the Sorcerer, bringing his staff down with a mighty *'craaack'*! The earth began to quake as the tortured ground buckled and heaved before the Wizards. They watched as the earth ripped apart before them.

"Oh no, my brothers, I shall call upon Beyilzon. The Dark Lord shall do my bidding now!" screeched Eldred as he lowered the crystal orb of his staff into the gaping wound in the earth.

"Are you mad? Beyilzon is dead! His evil destroyed!" shouted Lindras.

"Oh, he is indeed dead in body, but not in spirit. Thanks to the black hearts of mankind, he lives on!" stated Eldred, his crystal orb growing brighter in intensity.

"You shall not get away with this, Eldred. The earth is my element! It is mine to command!" the Wizard of the West yelled in defiance over the deafening clamor. Raising his staff before him, a great show of dazzling white light emanated from the crystal. The earth groaned as Lindras' powers worked on healing the gaping wound.

Eldred's vile magic tugged at the earth, fighting to keep it open. Finally, he yielded to Lindras as Tor and Tylon lowered their staff, striking the Sorcerer with a blue bolt of energy to send him flying through the air, landing hard against a tree trunk.

"Do not kill him!" shouted Lindras, using his staff to heal the great tear in the earth. "We must not kill Eldred!"

The Sorcerer raised himself up from the ground, shaken by the great surge of energy coursing through him. His hunched body, stooped from centuries of dwelling in caves and traveling through low, subterranean tunnels, struggled to upright himself.

"You are so pathetic, Lindras. Even now, I am willing to crush you like an insignificant gnat, yet you do not even have the courage, the fortitude to do what others would. You do not have the nerve to kill the likes of me!"

"Believe me, it would be so very easy to kill you, but you are the pathetic one if you cannot see it takes more courage, more compassion to steady one's hand than to use it to snuff out a life," retorted Lindras as he and the other Wizards veered closer to Eldred.

"Do not show me pity!" the Sorcerer snarled at Lindras. "Pity is for the weak!"

"What I show is not pity, more so mercy," answered the Wizard.

"Well, where I go, I shall show no mercy to the Elves," shouted Eldred, his crystal orb glowed, bathing the Sorcerer in an eerie blue light.

"He is leaving for the Twilight!" exclaimed Tylon, watching as Eldred's body became a translucent shadow, dissipating into the night sky, his staff dropping from his hand.

"He must not get away!" shouted Tor, raising his staff to summon the strength of all his powers. An invisible wind howled from the north, forming a wind funnel that swirled around Eldred's black soul, pulling it down. "I do not know how long I can hold him!"

Tylon hoisted his staff to the sky calling upon the powers of his element. The sky became unnaturally dark as storm clouds materialized, blotting out the cold light of the moon and the stars. Thunder rolled as a flash of lightning crackled across the sky. Suddenly, the heavens opened up as a torrential downpour of cold rain cascaded from the heavy, gray clouds.

The swirling funnel of wind created by Tor sucked the rain into its core, pummeling Eldred's soul downwards.

"Freeze him, Tor," ordered Lindras, "Freeze him so his soul cannot leave this realm!"

The Wizard of the North's breath passed over his crystal orb. The condensation forming on the surface of the globe instantly crystallized into sparkling, white frost. The wind he controlled emitted a deafening roar as it turned icy cold.

Suddenly, the wind vanished as a massive block of ice came crashing to the ground. Encased in the center was Eldred's form. A look of absolute dread and unadulterated hate was etched across his frozen face.

"This shall hold him quite nicely, until he can be delivered to Mount Isa," stated Lindras, admiring Tor's handiwork.

"Let us get this over with," suggested Tylon. "Let us do so now before he finds a way to escape again."

With staffs held aloft, the three Wizards summoned the powers of their elements. With a brilliant flash of light, they and the large ice mass imprisoning the Sorcerer vanished against a predawn sky.

As the land was enveloped in darkness once more, a cloaked figure silently emerged from the forest, staying within the shadows of the trees.

"What is this?" asked the voice in a whisper, stooping to pick up the crystal orb of the Sorcerer's shattered staff.

Joval and Arerys watched in excitement as the Wizards made off with their quarry.

"It is done, the Wizards have contained the Sorcerer!" announced Joval to the cheers of the warriors protecting the wall.

"Duck!" shouted Markus as the great dragon swooped down low over the Imperial Soldiers before flying up and over the west wall of the fortress city. "I hate dragons!"

"Hate is a strong word, considering that the beast did away with a good number of soldiers for us," stated Arerys.

"Too bad it did not take more out before it departed," said Markus, watching the ancient reptile disappear to the east, following the impending light of the morning sun.

"You would think the soldiers would cease: retreat knowing that the Sorcerer has been defeated," called Lando.

"They now act on behalf of the regent, they do not yet know that he is dead," shouted Nayla as she narrowly dodged several arrows whizzing by her head.

"Captain Treeborn!" a warrior shouted from the courtyard. "We have no more arrows!"

Dahlon Treeborn raced down from the palace stairs, barking orders at the warriors: "Raise the portcullis! Open the gate! We shall finish this in the battlefield!"

"Lord Treeborn, we are still greatly outnumbered!" shouted Joval. "We shall never survive!"

"We have no choice in this matter! Nayla, get your warriors prepared for battle, do so now!" ordered Dahlon.

"Either we wait until we are trapped and cornered like animals within these walls or we face the enemy and we fight them now," stated the warrior maiden. "You know what my choice shall be, Joval. What you and the others do, is up to you."

"Then let us go to war," Joval answered in a calm voice. He was prepared to meet his destiny as he followed Nayla down the stairs.

Arerys, Lando, Markus and Valtar proceeded behind them along with the remaining warriors guarding the battlements. As they mounted their steeds, Joval turned to Dahlon: "You shall ride by your daughter's side for the first and last time."

"Joval, you know I must remain here to strategize, to direct the warriors if you and the others should fail," stated the senior Elf.

"Not this time, my lord," responded Joval, unceremoniously seizing Dahlon by the scruff of his neck as he turned to walk away. "You are coming with us!"

Joval gave Dahlon a shove, directing him to a waiting steed. Already Nayla and the others were sitting high on their mounts, waiting for the heavy iron grate to be raised.

Nayla turned her horse about to face her warriors, "Ready men?"

The warriors raised their right hand high in salute to their captain.

"Let us face the enemy!" shouted Nayla, leading her men through the gateway. As Arerys, Valtar, Markus and Lando followed closely behind Nayla, Joval glanced back to see Dahlon sitting on his steed, watching his daughter lead the charge.

"You coward," muttered Joval as he turned away; coaxing his stallion to catch up with the warrior maiden.

As Nayla and an army of fewer than three hundred warriors emerged from the fortress city, the Imperial Soldiers were in the midst of regrouping. With the departure of the dragon Tor had set free, the remaining four thousand or so soldiers prepared to engage in combat once more to take Nagana down in final defeat.

Beads of perspiration formed on Lando's forehead as he gazed at the vast army assembling before them.

"The odds are not good, Markus. I pray to God that if He does not see fit to aid us in our time of need, at least the Maker of All shall show us mercy by ending this confrontation quickly," stated the knight.

"This is one quest that does seem insurmountable now," admitted Markus, shifting uneasily on his steed as he eyed the enemy soldiers. "Nonetheless, if we are to die, if this be our destiny, then let us not go down in defeat without a fight."

Raising his right hand up high, Markus bellowed above the din of the approaching army, "For the Alliance!"

In a final gesture of defiance, Nayla's entire army echoed the prince's sentiment, drawing their swords and raising it high against a crimson dawn.

As Nayla drew her sword to signal her warriors into battle, the distant trumpeting of horns caused the Imperial Soldiers to halt their advance. The startled soldiers turned westward to face the resonating sounds echoing across the battlefield.

Joval sat high on his steed, craning his neck to see the shadows emerging from the forest.

Far across the field, the banners of Carcross, Wyndwood, Darross and Cedona unfurled. They were carried high and proud, fluttering and snapping in the brisk morning breeze.

"They have come!" shouted Arerys, "The soldiers of the Alliance have come!"

Markus and Lando stared in surprise and disbelief as an army of more than six thousand strong marched onto the battlefield. Kal-lel Wingfield and his son, Artel led the way.

"Look!" said Nayla, pointing northward. "My brothers, the Kagai Warriors, they have arrived!"

Thirty-one warriors charged towards Nayla's battalion, ready to offer their brand of justice in a bid to defeat the Imperial Soldiers. Leading the way was Hunta Saibon, riding proudly on a dark steed; his walking stick was replaced by a staff from which a long, curved blade came alive, glistening in the early morning sun.

"Thank you, God!" said Lando, his eyes turning to the heavens as he whispered these three words under his breath. He drew his sword as he waited for Nayla to give her orders.

For a long moment, the silence was deafening as the soldiers of the Alliance and Nayla's army braced for war. They looked upon the Imperial Soldiers. Now they were the ones so badly outnumbered: sandwiched between their adversaries with no hope of escape.

Nayla urged her steed forward, motioning for the others to stand down. Charging towards the enemy, she hollered, "The regent is dead! Prince Tokusho is now the emperor! Do you wish to die with the regent, or do you serve the emperor?"

An oppressive silence hung in the air.

The soldiers of the Alliance pressed in as Nayla's warriors began their advance. With no chance of escape and no direction from the Sorcerer, to everyone's surprise, like falling dominoes, the Imperial Soldiers cast down their weapons, dropping down onto their battle-weary knees with their hands held behind their heads in surrender.

The commander of the Imperial Army cautiously advanced towards Nayla, his hands held high, devoid of weaponry.

"Do you speak the truth, warrior maiden?" asked the man, his eyes filled with suspicion. "If your words are tainted, if Tisai Darraku continues to reign, then we shall be forced to do battle even if it shall mean our demise."

"You blindly follow a madman? You willingly sacrifice your life and the lives of your men for that tyrant?"

"Though he may well be a tyrant, he is also the regent. We have no choice in this matter for we are Imperial Soldiers sworn to duty: to wield our swords for whoever sits in power on the throne."

"If that be the case, Prince Tokusho has ascended to the throne," stated Nayla, dismounting from her steed. "He is now *your* new emperor and you shall do his bidding."

"How do we know that? What proof do you have?" queried the commander, his brows were clenched in thought as he gravely considered her words. His eyes nervously scanned the Kagai Warriors as they fell into line with the warriors of Orien, preparing to do battle by their side.

"If it were not so, do you truly believe I would allow you to return alive to Darraku, only to return once more with greater forces when you now know our plight? Our numbers were thinned by our dealings with the Dark Army. My warriors are few. I am no fool. If that were to be the case, if the regent were still alive, I would be forced to use my people's alliance with those to the west to end this war now," stated Nayla, glancing over the commander's shoulder at the great show of force from western Imago.

Standing before her, he nodded in agreement as he released a weary sigh. His shoulders drooped, relaxing as the military burden he was forced to bear eased. "Your reputation precedes you, warrior maiden. I have heard tales; whisperings of your great skills and bravery on the field of battle. And though you wield a mighty sword, it said that you are a warrior of great compassion and humanity," said the commander, dropping to his left knee as his head bowed in respect. "I now understand the people's words to be true where you are concerned."

"Rise up my brother, I understand your loyalty to the throne, but do not be misguided by blind loyalty. Your emperor awaits you in Keso. Leave in peace."

Without another arrow spent or another drop of blood shed, the Imperial Army returned eastward. The war was over.

The fortress city played host to the kings of the Alliance. Upon the great stairway leading into the palace, Dahlon Treeborn received his honored guests amidst a cheering throng consisting of warriors and the men, women and children of Nagana and the surrounding villages.

Dahlon and the elders of Orien received the kings from the distant countries first before honoring the heroes of the war. As Dahlon introduced Markus and then Lando, the men took their place at the top of the stairs. As he proceeded to announce the others names, Nayla turned to retreat into the crowd. Joval and Arerys caught up with her before she could disappear, becoming one with the people.

"Unhand me, both of you," whispered Nayla. "Joval, you know I am not partial to pomp and ceremony."

"The people needed a hero, someone to champion their cause; that hero would be you, Nayla," stated Joval as both he and Arerys escorted the little warrior to her place next to Markus. "You are most deserving of a hero's welcome."

Nayla turned to face the growing crowd. Her heart soared to see Hunta Saibon amongst the throng, smiling at her with great pride as row upon row of warriors and citizens dropped to their knees, bowing their heads in respect to the warrior maiden. With his introduction complete, Dahlon and the elders extolled their praises. Their words were soon drowned out by the thunderous applause and cheers of the grateful people as they honored the mortals, Elves and even the half-caste woman who was instrumental in defeating the regent, ending his reign of tyranny. Now peace and the promise of prosperity were restored to the lands of Orien with their rightful heir to the throne in place.

Dahlon seemed to revel in the adulation, raising his hands for silence as he prepared to make another speech.

"It is with great pleasure that I announce the betrothal of my daughter, Nayla Treeborn to Arerys Wingfield, the Prince of Wyndwood!" said Dahlon with obvious pride.

Arerys smiled down at Nayla, embracing her in his arms as she breathed a sigh of relief her father had finally given his blessing.

"Is that the best you can do, Arerys?" asked Markus, prompting him with a playful shove. "For goodness sake, give the woman a kiss!"

Before an ecstatic, cheering crowd, Arerys held Nayla in his arms, kissing her lovingly upon her lips.

"I do love you, Nayla," whispered Arerys, gazing upon the warrior maiden with great adoration and genuine pride.

She looked into the Elf's deep blue eyes, smiling sweetly at her betrothed. Suddenly, screams from the crowd pierced the air. Nayla gasped as she was slammed hard against Arerys' chest. Her eyes flew wide open in shock, as she stared up at the Elf's face. As though time moved in slow motion she watched as pandemonium ensued. She could see Markus, Lando and Valtar race down the stairs towards the panicking crowd. Her ears rang as Arerys cried out in anguish. Joval caught her as she slipped from his embrace.

Nayla's breathing became sharp and jagged as Arerys knelt by her side, propping her up in his arms. Joval held her steady with one hand on her shoulder as the other took hold of the arrow that pierced straight through her vest of chain mail. As he pulled on the shaft of the arrow, Nayla cried out in pain, clutching desperately at Arerys. She watched as the fair Elf's face blanched, contorting in horror. He groaned as he came to realize the arrow had traveled straight through her body to protrude almost an inch outside her chest, shattering her breastbone. Staring in shock, he watched it disappear as Joval tugged the lethal projectile from her back.

Arerys looked to Joval for reassurance, but he could see the tears streaming down his face as the dark Elf cried out in anguish, "She is dying, Arerys! The arrow has struck too close to her heart!"

"No! Nooo!" wailed Arerys, holding her close to his chest. "Not now! Not to Nayla!"

The Elf glanced up at the faces gathering around them. He noticed Dahlon as he passively looked on.

"Please, my lord, for pity's sake, she is your daughter! Save her!" begged Arerys as he watched Nayla's eyes slowly close. A cloudy haze was cast over them as everything around her blurred into a mass of colors before swirling in an abyss of absolute blackness.

"She is dying, Prince Arerys," stated Dahlon, unmoved by his pleas. "It is her time."

Again, the Elf pleaded with Dahlon. "Where is your heart? Where is your compassion? My god, she did this for you! She went to war for you and your people! Swallow your damn pride! Heal her! Or bless her with the eternal life of our people so she may enter the Twilight. Do it now!"

"Even if I tried, this wound is well beyond my capacity to heal, it shall take more than my powers alone to assist her," stated Dahlon.

In desperation, Arerys seized him by his arm, yanking the high Elf in close as he whispered, "Do it, or so help me, the world shall know about you. Then I shall do what Nayla never had the heart to do; I shall kill you myself and prevent you from entering the Twilight as she never will."

Kal-lel stepped forward, "Stand aside, my son, Dahlon and I shall do what we can."

Kal-lel glared into Dahlon's unfeeling eyes, "Well, my old friend, I strongly suggest you assist. When we are done, perhaps you should consider entering the Twilight. There is someone waiting there for you."

Dahlon was taken aback by his words as he whispered, "Katril? Do you speak of Katril Brookstone?"

Kal-lel nodded once in affirmation.

As Joval ordered the anxious crowd to move back, the high Elves set to work, racing against time as Nayla's pulse fell rapidly and her breathing became shallow and labored.

Arerys watched as her wound disappeared, even her tattoo and the old scars she bore from battles of bygone days faded under the combined powers of the two high Elves. As they continued to work their magic, Nayla's body suddenly shuddered as her last breath slowly escaped her.

Kal-lel stared up at his son as he sadly whispered, "We have failed. She is gone, Arerys. I am sorry."

"NO!" wailed Arerys, sobbing as he collapsed to his knees by Nayla's side, scooping her lifeless form into his arms.

"We healed her body, but her soul eludes us. Her heart is whole, yet we could not make it beat," said Kal-lel; his own tears fell as he felt the crushing weight of his son's anguish.

CHAPTER 22

A NEW BEGINNING

Pushing his way through the growing mob, Hunta Saibon knelt down next to the grieving Elf. "Perhaps I can help, Prince Arerys."

"But you are not vested with the powers to heal as an Elf would be," sobbed Arerys through his great tears.

"But neither is she a full Elf, Nayla is half mortal," reminded Master Saibon.

Arerys reluctantly lay Nayla down as the warrior priest raised his hands over his head, clapping his hands together once. He briskly rubbed his palms together as he focused on gathering his energy.

As he opened his eyes, his right hand hovered over Nayla's chest; just at the arch of her breastbone. His hand came down swiftly, striking her with the heel of his palm, compressing her heart and diaphragm.

As his hand moved away, suddenly, Nayla bolted upright. She was gasping like a drowning person surfacing for a breath of life-giving air. Her breathing was fast and deep, her pulse raced as she struggled to sit up. Her eyes were wild with fear and confusion as she stared up at the people gathered around her.

"Welcome back," said Saibon with a kind smile, as he gently patted her face.

Arerys tears fell fresh as he embraced Nayla in his arms. He whispered, "Do not ever do that again."

"Do what?" asked Nayla in a confused daze as she held Arerys' trembling body close to hers.

"Die – do not ever die on me," sobbed the Elf.

The crowd parted as the three Wizards made their way up the stairs to where Nayla lay, embraced in Arerys' loving arms.

"What is all this commotion about?" asked Lindras, as he and his brothers smiled down on the couple.

"It is nothing, I am quite fine, Lindras," replied Nayla, struggling to her feet.

Arerys scooped her up into his arms, "You are not walking, Nayla."

"I assure you, I am fine," protested the warrior maiden.

"I suggest you get used to this, Arerys," said Lando with a smile as he gave Joval a knowing wink.

With Nayla safely in his arms, Arerys and all those in attendance followed Dahlon Treeborn into the palace. Outside in the courtyard, a bright morning sun heralded the beginning of a new day. The crowd soon forgot the mayhem that had ensued during the assassination attempt on Nayla's life. Instead, all reveled in great celebration.

Under the cold light of a full moon, veined and shining brightly like a perfect stone of opal, an exhuberant crowd gathered in the courtyard to witness the nuptials of Arerys Wingfield to his beloved, Nayla Treeborn. Having almost lost Nayla twice that day, Arerys was unwilling to wait until they returned to Wyndwood. He asked that they be wed on this very eve. It seemed to be the most opportune time for the kings of the Alliance and those of importance in Orien were all present.

Decked out in Elven finery, the Prince of Wyndwood was dashing in his formal attire, albeit in sylvan colors of silvery-white with green and brown accents. Nayla was lavishly dressed in a shimmering silk gown of white with silver and gold threads embroidered throughout. Her long, raven tresses tumbled loosely about her shoulder; her head crowned with a halo of fragrant, white night-blooming jasmine.

There was something ethereal about the couple as they stood beneath the moonlight and the flickering orange flames of the many lanterns illuminating the great courtyard.

With Markus by Arerys' side and Nakoa by Nayla's as their witnesses, they were blessed in union by the King of Wyndwood. As the couple turned to face each other, they were joined by the palms of their left hands as Arerys' brother draped a silken cord around their wrists, passing the loose ends to his father. Kal-lel's voice carried gently through the night air as he recited an ancient prayer in Elvish, blessing this union. As Arerys and Nayla both repeated their vows, Kal-lel knotted the silken cord as he explained, "This represents your lives, now bound together as one by the knot of this cord. This circle it forms has no beginning and no end; it shall symbolize your eternal pledge of love, forsaking all others."

Arerys kissed the circlet of silver his mother once cherished that Nayla now wore on the finger of her left hand. He then sealed their pledge of undying love with a passionate kiss on Nayla's lips as the night sky exploded with sound and light. A breath-taking shower of sparkling white light cascaded down over those gathered for the celebration. The splendid show of fireworks signaled to citizens far and wide of the day's triumphant end.

A great banquet followed the ceremony. Lindras, in all his wit and wisdom was asked to preside over the festivities that not only marked the union of Arerys to Nayla, but celebrated the dawn of a new era for the citizens of Imago. Not only for the people of Orien, but for the race of Elves too, for they were now united as one. As guests wined and dined on a cornucopia of gastronomic delights, the Wizard of the West enthralled all as he regaled them with his great tale of adventure.

Lindras, with his usual flare and animated style, began his tale with his departure from Nagana to seek out the help of Tor Airshorn and Tylon Riverdon, his collaboration with Valtar, and his bid to gather the soldiers of the Alliance.

"But how did you get word so quickly to King Kal-lel and the others?" asked Dahlon.

"That was the easy part. I had asked Valtar to *borrow* Nayla's little falcon for Tori was the only bird that knew the way to King Bromwell's castle in Carcross."

"Yes, once I received the message from Lindras, I in turn, dispatched falcons to Wyndwood, Darross and Cedona," added Bromwell. "I must say though, I had grave doubts about the note when Lindras gave instructions for all to gather in the Emerald Forest."

"By which way did you come?" asked Joval, intrigued by Bromwell's words.

"To all our surprise, Lindras led us from these forests through a pass that delivered us straight through the Iron Mountains," answered King Augustyn.

"But, my liege, how can that be?" wondered Lando, turning to his king for answers "There is no mountain passage leading into Orien from the Emerald Forest. We all know that."

"Indeed," agreed Augustyn. "Thanks to Lindras Weatherstone, there is a passage now! He used his awesome powers to literally level a pass straight through into this country. We were able to make good time as we were no longer forced to enter via Talibarr and the northern reaches of the Iron Mountains."

Lando smiled at the benevolent Wizard whose blue-gray eyes sparkled with light as the King of Cedona shared this tale. "So Lindras, it would appear you have been honing your craft in our absence," said the knight, offering the Wizard a generous smile.

"It is amazing what one can do when one sets his mind to the task at hand," marveled Lindras.

"Still, that does not explain how you crossed the mighty Reyuzan River," stated Joval. "That has always posed an insurmountable barrier of which none could enter into our lands from the west."

"Ah! This is where the tale becomes even more fantastic," said King Sebastian. "Upon crossing the Iron Mountains, we were met with the treacherous waters of the mighty river. It was greatly swollen with the summer run-off from the snow melting on the many mountains feeding into the Reyuzan River."

"So tell us!" called out Arerys from the head of the great table, "how did you cross?"

"It was absolutely amazing, Arerys!" stated Artel with much excitement. "Just when we thought all hope was lost, the Wizard of the South, Tylon Riverdon, used his powers to stem the tide. He drove the mighty river back! A miraculous feat made all the more incredible when Tor Airshorn, the Wizard of the North used his powers to freeze the waters into a massive wall of shimmering ice so we may all pass safely."

"Amazing indeed!" marveled Arerys as he recalled Eliya's words of wisdom during their meeting on Mount Isa. "So the words of the Watcher of the Future proved true: together you did move heaven and earth to accomplish the impossible!"

"Indeed, we did," said Lindras as he nodded in acknowledgement to Tylon and Tor.

"From this point eastward, it was a relatively easy trek to Nagana," stated the King of Darross.

"But who led the way?" asked Nayla. "None from the west of the Iron Mountains had ever made the journey from this point."

Lindras smiled proudly as his steady gaze turned to Valtar, seated at the far end of the table. "While Tylon, Tor and I deliberated on the best method to capture the Sorcerer and worked to set our plans into motion, Valtar was busy. It was he who ventured westward to mark the trail that would set King Kal-lel and the soldiers of the Alliance on a direct course to Nagana. After he was done with this task, I loaned him Tempest so he may ride hard and fast. I instructed my steed to deliver Valtar to eastern Orien. I asked that he seek you out for I knew that you and the men of the Order would be greatly outnumbered as you attempted to overthrow Regent Darraku in a bid to install Prince Tokusho as the emperor."

Nayla's dark brown eyes scrutinized the dark Elf that had been the bane of her grief. "So you seek redemption; to atone for what you had done?"

"As I said before, Princess of Wyndwood, I only seek your forgiveness," said Valtar, his head bowed low before her.

Nayla sat up tall against her chair, her back was straight and rigid as she listened to his words. It was the first time she had been addressed by her new title.

Hunta Saibon leaned close to Nayla as he whispered, "My child, a single deed done bears far more weight than all the words that can ever be spoken. And remember, the first step to healing is to forgive."

She smiled kindly at her master as she addressed the Elf, "Valtar, though I willingly dispense punishment to those deserving; let it not be said I have a cold heart. You are forgiven."

"Thank you, your grace," said Valtar, he sat upright as though an immense burden had been lifted from his weary shoulders. "Your show of kindness shall be repaid many times over, I promise you."

Joval smiled at Nayla, pleased that she found the strength and compassion to forgive his friend.

"Lindras Weatherstone! What has become of the Sorcerer of Orien? Where is Eldred Firestaff now?" queried Maiyo Sonkai. The other elders nodded; eager to learn of the Sorcerer's fate.

"As we speak now, the Maker of All has dealt with him accordingly," replied Lindras. "He is a non-entity now, stripped of his powers, devoid of greatness. He has been humbled."

"Yes, he now wanders this realm as a mortal, forced to live the remains of his days amongst the ones he despises the most," added Tor. "It is hoped he shall learn compassion and humility towards mankind in doing so."

"Pray tell he was not deposited with the upstarts, Beyilzon's followers north in the Shadow Mountains," said Arerys with a gasp.

"Heavens, no!" responded Tylon. "In fact, he wanders alone in the Painted Desert far to the south where I shall keep a watchful eye on him."

"I say, it shall be a most humbling experience for the great Sorcerer of Orien to live as one of us," said Lando with a satisfied laugh.

"Humbling indeed," agreed Lindras. "This brings to mind, you gave everyone a terrible fright today, Nayla."

"Yes, life can be so very fragile," said Arerys as he gave Nayla's hand a gentle squeeze.

"Was the culprit seized?" asked the Wizard.

"Unfortunately, the one who dispatched the arrow somehow disappeared into the panicking crowd," answered Markus.

"Yes! When we rushed down to seize that murderous fiend, he seemed to have vanished!" replied Lando. "Gone without a trace."

"Even securing the gates and searching the crowds produced no results," added Valtar. "Whoever it was, he was gone."

"At least did you see who it was that aimed the arrow at Nayla," asked Arerys.

"I am afraid not, my friend," responded Lando. "Other than being clad in a dark, hooded cloak, the murderous culprit made good his escape with none in the crowd able to identify him."

Nayla looked to Arerys' lucid blue eyes. It was clear that she drew great concern from this.

"Fear not my lady, I assure you, both you and Prince Arerys shall be safe for as long as you remain here on our lands," promised Maiyo Sonkai, his gaze turning to the warriors posted at all the doorways leading into the banquet room. "There is no need to begin your new life living in fear of retaliation for now we are aware of the potential for danger. We shall be vigilant; watchful of this danger."

"Speaking of a new life, I would like to be the first to wish the couple well," said Markus, attempting to change the somber mood into a reason to rejoice and celebrate. He rose up with a silver goblet of wine in his hand, turning to gaze upon the happy couple. "I wish to make a toast to my dear friend, Arerys and his lovely bride, Nayla. Though this world be filled with uncertainty, and peace is often short-lived, I pray you both find a world of happiness and an eternity of love and peace in each others arms! Here is to the Prince and Princess of Wyndwood."

All in attendance rose, raising their goblets high to honor Arerys and his bride. During the height of the celebration, none had noticed that Kal-lel Wingfield and Dahlon Treeborn were absent, silently slipping away from the table.

In the vestibule outside the great banquet hall, the two high Elves met for the first time in over seven centuries. They quietly considered each other.

"This has been a great day – a triumphant day, Dahlon Treeborn. One would never believe that within such a small measure of time, really a mere speck of sand in the hourglass of an Elf's life, that we ended a war in the morning and celebrated a magnificent wedding by day's end," marveled Kal-lel, as he broke the awkward silence between them.

"I never thought I would live to see the day you would allow my people back to Wyndwood; that our race would one day be united again," said Dahlon.

"It is ironic that our love for one woman tore our nation apart, and now, many centuries later it would be the love our two children share that would bring our people together," said Kal-lel.

"It is true, the old adage: love can make you, or be the death of you," Dahlon replied with a knowing smile.

"It is amazing what love can do to two normally clear-thinking, pragmatic men," said Kal-lel with a weary sigh, shaking his head in regret. "This situation has gone too far and our people have suffered greatly because of our pride. If Arerys had not already told you, his mother, Katril had left for the Twilight long ago. Though I loved her with all my heart, her love was never returned in the same manner. She was a dutiful wife and a loving mother, but it crushed her heart to be separated from her true love."

Dahlon's gaze fell to the floor; his heart was moved to no end as he listened to Kal-lel's confession.

"At times, it drove me to despair that she did not love me as I loved her, just as surely as it consumed you with despair that she was not with you. She loved you, Dahlon, this I cannot deny. Katril had always loved you. If you choose to enter the Twilight, she will be awaiting you in the Haven," said Kal-lel.

"You would surrender her to me?" asked Dahlon, stunned by his words.

"She had surrendered her heart to you long ago," answered the Elf king.

"If that be the case, then I wish to enter the Twilight now," stated Dahlon, confident of his decision.

"And what of your guests?" asked Kal-lel.

"Tell them I am long overdue for a prior engagement," he answered with a smile.

"And what of Nayla? Do you not wish to bid farewell to your daughter?" queried Kal-lel.

"If I leave now, she will understand," said Dahlon. "Just tell her that I am sorry."

"Sorry? Sorry for what?" asked Kal-lel, perplexed by Dahlon's words.

"There is no need for explanation. Nayla will understand," stated the Elf. For a lingering moment, he listened to the cheerful sounds of celebration and joy drifting from the banquet hall. He watched in silence as Hunta Saibon hugged his daughter as he never could while Kal-lel's son looked on, gazing lovingly at his bride,

"Yes, Nayla will understand," said Dahlon in a whisper as he disappeared down a long corridor.

Through the secured gateway to the city, a lone, dark figure pressed up against the portcullis, listening to the merry sounds of celebration as it meandered through the courtyard and on through the heavy iron grate.

"Be happy now, for your happiness shall be short-lived. Your suffering is only about to begin, Nayla," snarled a voice filled with contempt as it withdrew into the darkness.

Pronunciation of Places and Names

In the language of the mortals of Orien, the following vowels are pronounced as follows:

Symbol:	Keyword:
a	f**a**t
â	**a**pe
ä	f**a**ther
ê	m**ee**t
i	b**i**te
ô	g**o**
yoo	**u**nited

Anshen:	än-shên
Anzan:	än-zän
Arashe:	a-rä-shê
Baikasai:	bâ-kä-sâ
Borai:	bô-râ
Ekare:	ê-ka-rê
Ero:	ê-rô
Esan:	ê-sän
Esshu:	ês-shyoo
Furai:	fyoo-râ
Fureko:	fyoo-rê-kô
Hanmai:	hän-mâ
Hebeku:	hê-bê-kyoo
Hegashe:	hê-ga-shê
Henan:	hê-nän
Hetai:	hê-tâ
Hunta Saibon:	hyoon-ta sâ-bôn
Kagai:	kä-gâ
Kaisheke:	kâ-shê-kê
Kansai:	kän-sâ
Kareda:	kä-rê-da
Kekai:	kê-kâ
Keso:	kê-sô
Keyofu:	kê-yô-fyoo
Kohai	kô-hâ
Magare:	ma-gä-rê

Maiyo Sonkai:	mâ-yô sôn-kâ
Maiyu:	mâ-yoo
Medara:	mê-dä-rä
Medore:	mê-dô-rê
Megoto:	mê-gô-tô
Metasu:	mê-tä-syoo
Nagana:	nä-gä-nä
Nakoa:	na-kô-a
Orien:	ô-ri-ên
Reyu:	rê-yoo
Reyuzan:	rê-yoo-zän
Safiya:	sa-fi-ya
Saijun:	sâ-jyoon
Saiyo:	sâ-yô
Shekata:	shê-kä-tä
Shesaiji:	shê-sâ-jê
Shesake:	shê-sä-kê
Shenyu Menai:	shên-yoo mê-nâ
Sheya:	shê-ya
Taija:	tâ-jä
Taijin:	tâ-jên
Taijina:	tâ-jên-a
Taiko Saikyu:	tâ-kô sâ-kyoo
Takai:	ta-kâ
Takaro:	tä-kä-rô
Takesha:	ta-kê-shä
Tisai Darraku:	ti-sâ där-rä-kyoo
Tokusho:	tô-kyoo-shô
Usage:	yoo-sa-gê
Yasai:	ya-sâ

368

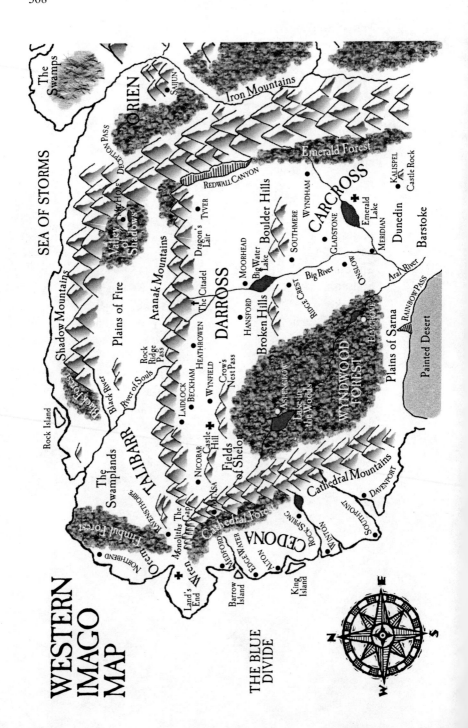

About the Author

*L.T. Suzuki is a practitioner and
instructor of the martial arts system,
Bujinkan Budo Taijutsu;
a system incorporating six traditional
samurai schools and three
schools of ninjutsu.*

Other books written
by the Author

Imago Book I, Tales from the West

Imago Book II, Tales from the East

*Imago Book III, A Warrior's Tale
(available fall of 2003)*

ISBN 155395619-2

9 781553 956198